Behind These Doors

Radical Proposals Book 1

Jude Lucens

Greenwose Books

Scotland

Behind These Doors: Radical Proposals Book 1
©2018 by Jude Lucens

Print Edition ISBN: 978-1-912734-01-6
Ebook Edition ISBN: 978-1-912734-00-9

Development Editor: KJ Charles
Line Editor: May Peterson
Cover art and design: Lennan Adams at Lexiconic Design

This is a work of fiction. All characters, events, and places in this book are
products of the author's imagination, or are used fictitiously. Any
resemblance to actual persons, living or dead, is entirely coincidental.

http://judelucens.com

For all who don't belong:
may you find your people.

— Acknowledgements —

Many thanks to KJ Charles, as terrific an editor as she is a writer, and to May Peterson for additional insightful development advice and meticulous line editing.

Many thanks also to Anne, Liv, Emma T, and RL Mosswood, who generously beta-read and helped improve this novel with their encouragement and thoughtful criticism, and to all in Group whose enthusiasm kept me writing over the last couple of years.

Thanks to Lennan Adams for the stunning cover art and design and for endless patience, and to Kris Ripper for a timely and very kindly metaphorical smack on the wrist, and for early encouragement to write this at all.

And thanks, always, to Chris: brainstormer and world-builder, patient alpha and omega reader, supportive critic and critical support, without whom I'd never have time or capacity to write.

Any remaining errors, offences and infelicities are, of course, my own. In all likelihood, one of the kind people above suggested they were a bad idea, but I thought I knew better.

— Contents —

Behind These Doors   7

Gutter Roses   373
(A Radical Proposals Short Story)

— Chapter One —

FRIDAY, 12TH JANUARY 1906

The actors below stepped back from their final curtain call, and Aubrey slid his palm from Rupert's thigh, where it had lain for half the last act.

Rupert, whose warm hand had rested absently over his, pressed his fingers and let him go, then leaned forward, looking past him at Henrietta, the only other person in the box. "Enjoyable, beloved?"

"Ridiculous." She grinned. "I liked it."

Two Naughty Boys had been amusing in parts, but mostly so absurd as to be dull: without his lovers' company, Aubrey'd have left after the first act. But now that it was over, so was their time together, and he wished he could turn back the hours, like the pages of a book, to the moment the heavy asbestos curtain rose on the opening scene. Instead, as the electric lights brightened, he stood and offered Henrietta his arm.

"It's the energy," she explained, taking his sleeve to rise from her chair. "The liveliness."

"The pranks even you wouldn't have dared as a child," Aubrey suggested.

Her eyes gleamed. "That, too."

Aubrey picked up his top hat and ebony cane and followed Rupert and Henrietta out of the box, through the private retiring room, and into the corridor beyond.

A party of young fellows tumbled out of a box ahead of them and hurtled towards the stairs, voices loud, footsteps muffled by the thick, moss-green carpet.

"Good evening, Henrietta."

Aubrey startled at the grim voice behind him, and Henrietta's back stiffened.

"Hernedale. Fanshawe," Lowdon added.

Aubrey tipped his hat with the silver knob of his cane, since there was no escaping it. "Evening, Lowdon."

"Edgar." Henrietta turned with a chilly smile for her older brother. "We didn't expect to see you here."

Rupert turned last, reluctance in every move. "Evening." He glanced up the corridor beyond Lowdon. "Might we hope to see Mrs Lowdon?"

"Sadly, no. She intended to accompany me but was indisposed."

"How… unfortunate."

Aubrey heard what Rupert didn't say: that Lowdon should've stayed at home to keep her company. He disagreed. Lowdon's absence would be compensation enough for missing any play.

Lowdon kept pace with them down the staircase, towards a roar of voices.

Halfway down, Rupert paused. "My dear. Do you think…"

Aubrey looked past them, into the huge crush-room heaving with patrons—chatting, discreetly flirting, edging apologetically towards the doors.

"Better go back till it clears a bit," Henrietta decided.

Aubrey's spirits lifted at the prospect of a few more minutes together: he'd missed Rupert and Henrietta dreadfully over the week they'd been away from London.

Rupert sighed. "Care to join us, Edgar?"

"Delighted, Hernedale." Thus Lowdon, as might have been expected, poisoned their companionable interlude before it began.

A mahogany table dominated the far end of the retiring room, and upright chairs, upholstered in cerulean blue silk, stood along the walls. An attendant, carrying the remains of refreshments they'd shared earlier, slid out, leaving behind only a neatly folded copy of The Times.

Henrietta stood at the entrance to the box, staring into the theatre, while Rupert laid his top hat on the table, then settled behind it and unfolded the newspaper.

Aubrey closed the door to the corridor. "Something happening?" he asked Henrietta.

"Not a blessed thing."

Lowdon, seating himself beside Rupert—as though Rupert hadn't made it perfectly plain he wanted to be left alone—harrumphed and glared at her, as though 'blessed' counted as swearing.

Rupert's lips tightened, but Henrietta ignored her brother. "Just restless," she told Aubrey.

In solidarity, he set two chairs beside her. He sat and had barely removed his hat when there was a quiet tap at the door. Henrietta strode towards it.

"Attendant," Rupert said, without looking up from the paper. "He'll open it himself."

Henrietta opened the door anyway.

It wasn't an attendant.

A well-made fellow in his mid to late twenties—clad in a black dinner jacket rather than proper evening dress—removed his top hat and bestowed an unnecessarily charming smile on Henrietta. "Sincere apologies for the interruption," he said, "but I thought I saw something fall, and indeed…" He opened his hand. A small, golden mass lay on his gloved palm.

"Oh!" Henrietta glanced at her wrist. "The catch must be faulty. Thank you very much."

The stranger poured the fine chain bracelet into her hand without touching her. "Be a shame to lose part of a matched set." He must've noted her necklace. "Fabergé?"

"Well spotted." Henrietta brightened, and they launched into a conversation Aubrey couldn't follow, because his lack of knowledge of the subject was exceeded only by his lack of interest in it.

Having delivered the bracelet, the stranger really should have left, and taken his improbable charm and light golden tan with him. Instead, he lounged in the doorway of their retiring room, frankly flirting with Henrietta, regardless of the fact that he'd been neither introduced nor properly invited to join them.

But Aubrey couldn't regret it. Henrietta was happy. And he, sitting unobserved on the other side of the room, was quietly indulging a warm, giddy hum of attraction.

The fellow's unbuttoned jacket revealed a black waistcoat drawn smooth and tight across a muscular chest and drew the eye down the lean lines of his body. He stood a respectable distance from Henrietta, but his smile, the humour in his tone, the confidential angle of his body, suggested a friendly intimacy which didn't exist between them.

"Dash it, Hernedale!" Lowdon's voice ripped Aubrey's attention from muscular shoulders. "Look to your wife!"

Henrietta froze, transformed in a heartbeat from languid Aphrodite to outraged Artemis, and the stranger lost his smile.

Damnation! Why shouldn't Henrietta flirt, if she chose to? But Aubrey had no right to defend her with her husband there. Would never, in any case, have the right to challenge her brother's humiliating reprimands.

Rupert raised an admonitory finger. "One moment, Edgar." He skimmed his page to the end, then sighed and looked up. "There. You're quite comfortable, I believe, Hettie?"

"Perfectly, thank you." Henrietta glared at her brother, who glared back, his moustache bristling like an irate blond hedgehog.

"As I thought." Rupert folded the newspaper with care and exquisite regret. "I'm sure I'd have noticed, had you required assistance."

"Of course you would." Henrietta glided across the room and laid a delicate, gloved hand on his sleeve. "My dear..." She glanced at the stranger.

"I beg your pardon." Rupert met the stranger's gaze. "Do come in. Hernedale. Pleased to meet you."

Rupert wasn't averse to turning the social screws when annoyed. Besides, it was the perfect response. Turning the fellow away would have licensed Lowdon's assumption of authority over Henrietta and condoned his insolence towards Rupert.

"Lucien Saxby." The stranger stepped in, offering Rupert a dazzling smile. "Delighted to meet you." Tucked beneath Saxby's arm, half-hidden by the hat in his hand, was a riding cane.

The fellow wasn't dressed for riding. Why the devil must he carry a—

"By my word, Hernedale!" Lowdon rose from his chair.

"Lady Hernedale, may I present Lucien Saxby," Rupert said, unperturbed. "Mr Saxby: Mr Lowdon, my wife's brother. Rising in your honour, I believe."

Flushing, Lowdon swelled to his full, majestic height. "I *beg* your pardon!"

Lowdon absolutely deserved the mockery. But it put Saxby in a damned awkward position, and while the fellow really ought to have kept to the strict bounds of propriety...

Saxby's smile faltered, but he gamely nodded a greeting. "Pleased to—"

"I *find*—" Lowdon jammed his top hat onto his sleek, pomaded head. "I must take my leave."

"Goodness!" Henrietta murmured. "So soon?"

Lowdon fixed her with an icy blue stare. "I regret, madam. Something in the air here... disagrees with me."

"I expect you'll feel much better outside," Rupert agreed.

Lowdon strode towards the doorway.

"Please convey my regards to Mrs Lowdon," Rupert added, "and wishes for her swift recovery."

Lowdon cast him a glare of withering scorn, and stamped ineffectually into the corridor, his tread muffled by the carpet.

Saxby stared after him. "Perhaps I'd best—" He settled his hat on his head.

"Aubrey Fanshawe!" Desperate to retrieve the situation, Aubrey leapt to his feet. His chair teetered. He snatched at it and dropped his hat and cane.

When he turned back from putting everything to rights, Saxby was watching him.

"Er." Aubrey clutched his cane in front of himself. "Delighted to meet you."

Interest kindled in Saxby's eyes and a slow smile dawned. "And I..." The riding cane drifted upward and nudged the brim of his hat. "...to meet..." He glanced down and back up Aubrey's body. "...you." He held his gaze, as warm and intimate as though they were the only two people in the room, and Aubrey the only focus he could ever want.

Aubrey's throat closed. His face burned. A rapid throb in his neck warned him his pulse was hammering.

"Care to join us, Mr Saxby?" Rupert asked.

Aubrey wrenched his attention from Saxby's smile.

"Very kind of you—" Saxby faced Rupert "—but I regret, I'm not at liberty to accept, this evening."

Rupert's gaze strayed to the newspaper. "Another time, perhaps."

"I look forward to it. Good evening, Lady Hernedale. Lord Hernedale." An enchanting smile for Aubrey. "Mr Fanshawe."

Aubrey clutched the smooth, narrow length of his cane and watched Saxby stroll out.

"For heaven's sake, Aubrey," Henrietta murmured. "Go after him."

After all, Rupert and Henrietta would leave soon, anyway.

Rupert's attention refocussed. "Fellow said he was busy this evening."

Aubrey stared between them, aware that his judgement was currently... somewhat compromised.

"He might change his mind," Henrietta urged.

Aubrey looked at Rupert, who shrugged. "Worst he can do is say is no."

"*Worst* he can do—" Damnation! Aubrey lowered his voice. "—is *blackmail* me! Or have me arrested for importuning, if I've misread him."

"Aubrey," Rupert said, "you definitely haven't misread him."

Henrietta shook her head. "Couldn't have been clearer."

Restless, Aubrey strode across the room and looked out. Saxby's shapely, inappropriately clad form was disappearing down the stairs.

"Damnation!" He cast a desperate glance back at Rupert and Henrietta.

Rupert sighed. "Just go if you're going."

"Don't forget dinner tomorrow!" Henrietta blew him a kiss.

He raised his cane in acknowledgement, then raced along the corridor and down the stairs, searching the crowd below for a black dinner jacket.

THE GAIETY'S VAST circular crush-room—panelled in hardwood and supported by bronze-capped marble columns—still heaved with theatre-patrons. Standing two steps up for a better view, Aubrey stared towards the main doors and to either side of them. Then hopelessly began a more systematic scan of the crowd.

"That was quick."

The voice was quiet, but Aubrey almost swallowed his tongue. Saxby stood on the step beside him, hat tipped back at a jaunty angle, riding cane tucked under his arm. He was almost a full head shorter than Aubrey.

"I assume you have a suitable private place?" Saxby murmured.

A private place? *Private*?

"You—" Aubrey coughed and tried again. "You said you had another engagement tonight?"

"Naturally." Saxby gazed into the crowd with placid interest, as though casually conversing with an acquaintance. "I was unable to accept Lord Hernedale's kind invitation, since I'd already accepted yours."

Aubrey stared at him.

"Shall we?" Saxby tilted his head towards the main doors.

Should he? Oh, Lord.

He'd assumed the offer in Saxby's eyes was for desire briskly sated in a quiet alley—a place men of his class wouldn't stumble across them, unless they had business of their own to hide.

A suitable private place…

Now that Saxby'd asked, it seemed churlish to suggest anything less. Rooms could be hired for the purpose, but Aubrey wasn't familiar with Uranian spaces: they'd always seemed to him more vulnerable to discovery by police than a random dark alley. And hotel staff were suspicious of pairs of men since the Wilde trials.

"Don't feel obliged, if you've changed your mind." The back of Saxby's gloved hand brushed his. "It's quite all right."

Aubrey looked down into gentle hazel eyes. "Oh. No, it's—" He should bow out. Instead, he was ashamed he'd ever distrusted the man with those eyes. Besides, while he *could* walk away, it'd be terribly rude, and—

Damn it all, he wanted Saxby more now than ever.

"It's this way."

Saxby searched his eyes. "You're sure?"

Aubrey produced a confident smile. "Of course."

He was sure this was the stupidest, most risky thing he'd ever done.

BY THE TIME they passed the doorman guarding the entrance to Albany's Ropewalk, Aubrey was distinctly uncomfortable in the trouser area. Saxby had said not a single untoward word, and his deportment was everything that was proper, and yet the tone of his voice, the curve of his lips, the shadow of his eyelashes upon his cheek, all ached with dark promise.

The Albany rule that nobody speak in the walkway and hallways didn't help. They paced the covered Ropewalk, past side paths to others' buildings, in perfect, unplanned synchrony, bound by a conspiracy of enforced silence and mutual purpose.

Bringing men home was a risk Aubrey never took, and yet here he damned well was. It was too late to rescind the invitation, and a traitorous part of him delighted in that. This moment didn't belong to the mind, but to the body, and to core-deep, unfettered impulse.

Anxiety pounced as he unlocked his front door. He turned on the electric light in his entrance hall and stood back to let Saxby in, glancing down the stairs to the basement, across to his neighbour's door opposite, then up towards the upper chambers; reminding himself that fellows did bring friends home from time to time, especially if it grew late and the friend lived outside the City. Locking the door firmly behind them brought a measure of calm.

"Please, avail yourself." He indicated the coat-stand as he put his cane in the base, then shrugged off his overcoat.

"You're Lord Letchworth's son?" Saxby removed his hat to reveal light brown hair, pomaded and smoothed to perfection, hairline describing a tempting curve behind his ear and across the back of his neck.

Averting his eyes, Aubrey dropped his gloves on the shelf under the hall mirror and turned to the drawing room. "Younger son."

At the sideboard, he picked up a decanter. "Brandy, Mr Saxby?"

"Thank you." Saxby stepped into the drawing room, looking around. "Though you might drop the 'mister'. Under the circumstances."

"As... might you."

"Your bedroom?" Saxby indicated the double doors opposite the fireplace.

"Indeed. We might—" His face warmed, and he turned back to the decanter "—adjourn there. Later."

Silence.

Had he been too forward? He turned. And flinched. Saxby was close beside him.

"Apologies. Did I startle you?"

"Perhaps a little." Heart hammering, he pressed a glass into Saxby's muscular bare hand, then picked up his own.

"One learns to be discreet, in my line of work," Saxby said.

"Of... work?"

Saxby raised an amused eyebrow. "Some of us must work for a living."

Aubrey's neck heated. He wasn't a *complete* fool. "What *is* your line of work?"

Saxby sipped his brandy, holding Aubrey's gaze. Well-shaped lips tilted in a half-smile. "I'm a journalist."

Aubrey froze.

"With the Daily Mail." Saxby cradled his glass in one hand.

A cool, crawling sensation under Aubrey's skin suggested blood was draining from his face. It wasn't clear quite where it was going, though, since his trousers now fitted perfectly. "Politics?" Hoping he sounded nonchalant, he fumbled his glass onto the sideboard before it fell from numb fingers. "Sports?"

Saxby turned the glass in his hand, watching the amber liquid sway. "Society."

It all became plain. The charm. The approachability. The deceptive, gentle gaze which had seduced him into inviting the fellow home, and explicitly into his bed.

He clung to the sideboard as the room swayed and his world crumbled. "Do you mean to—to expose me?"

"Certainly." The gossip journalist looked up with a mischievous smile. "But not in the papers, and only if you wish it."

Dear God. Aubrey closed his eyes.

"Are you well?" Saxby's glass clicked down on the sideboard.

"Perfectly." His lips were numb.

"Do sit down."

The weight of Saxby's hand on his sleeve shot a shiver of desire through his abdomen: suggestive flesh defeating judgement.

"I shall do quite well here." Forcing his eyes open, Aubrey groped for his glass and drained it.

"I expect you needed that, but do sit, now. You're dreadfully pale." Saxby slid an arm around his back, and despite himself, Aubrey leaned into him. Really, it was very pleasant to be looked after, even by a Judas.

Saxby steered him to the sofa then disappeared behind him while Aubrey sat with his feet on the hearthrug and stared into the fire.

"There you go." The damned fellow settled beside Aubrey like an old friend and folded his nerveless fingers around a brandy glass.

Aubrey's attention wavered from the glass to Saxby.

"Journalists aren't demons, you know. Not all of us, at any rate. And I'll personally vouch for the quality of the brandy."

This was a farce. An inappropriately dressed gossip journalist who'd entrapped him was recommending him his own brandy, trying to set him at his ease in his own home. But he couldn't undo what was already done. So he closed his eyes, sipped his excellent brandy, and sank back into the sofa.

Warm fingers nudged his chin. His eyelids shot open. Saxby was tugging on his bow tie.

"What are you *doing*?"

"Loosening your collar." Deft fingers plucked the stud from the front of his collar. Saxby rubbed his knee as though it were an obedient dog, then walked away again. "Stud's on the tray for now, all right? Beside the decanters. It'd just roll off the table." He returned with his own glass of brandy, sat down, and bestowed a charming smile upon Aubrey. "You'll soon feel quite the thing."

Aubrey stared back with a creeping awareness that he must look utterly debauched: lounging on the sofa, brandy glass in hand, bow tie hanging loose, and collar spread wide to bare his throat. Worse yet, that awareness, combined with Saxby's smile, provoked a dismaying degree of interest within his own mind.

"Do relax." Saxby rubbed Aubrey's knee again. "I don't write about Uranians at all. Only consider: quite aside from any natural scruples, I'd find myself rather short of willing companionship, don't you think?"

"I—imagine so."

"Quite. So you needn't worry."

He needn't—! Aubrey stared at him. As though a spell in prison were nothing to worry about! Aside from the disgrace to himself and his family, hard labour might as well be a death sentence.

Saxby's smile held firm.

Aubrey closed his eyes and let his head sag back. He might as well do as he pleased. The devil take good manners and poise alike: nothing could be retrieved from this situation.

Silence filled the room, but for the regular tick of the mahogany clock on the mantelpiece, and the sigh of fabric against fabric as Saxby drank, or crossed his legs, or whatever the devil he was doing. It was almost peaceful, the turmoil inside balanced by the undemanding quiet.

Fingers whispered across his temple. "Don't worry, beautiful," Saxby murmured, "I won't betray you."

And then he couldn't open his eyes, because they'd let the tears out, and that was a humiliation too far. Instead, he swallowed hard: swallowed the tears and unmanly fear and locked them deep in his aching chest.

"It's the loneliness, isn't it?" Fingertips stroked his hair.

But he wasn't lonely: he had Rupert and Henrietta, and he was sure to meet the right woman eventually.

"I feel it, too." Saxby's fingers brushed the tip of his ear. "At times I become—so very tired of being alone."

An aching lump swelled in Aubrey's throat. His eyes and the bridge of his nose burned. Because there were times—there *were*—when he felt terribly, terribly alone.

"Hush. It's all right." Saxby took the empty glass from Aubrey's hand and guided his head onto his jacket shoulder.

"We're both here." Warm breath in his hair. "For now, at least, we needn't be lonely."

Aubrey left his head there, leaking slow tears into woollen cloth. Because it *was* enough, for now. Or at least, it was better than nothing, which was very nearly the same thing. And it was pathetic—despicable—that it was enough; that he wanted a man who might deliver him to the gossips and the law.

"I'm sorry I teased. Truly. Didn't mean to frighten you."

Aubrey was supposed to say he wasn't frightened: it was what men did. But the words wouldn't come.

Saxby sighed. "I need to move, beautiful." He lifted Aubrey's head and shoulders and leaned him back on the sofa. "Just a sec."

Aubrey cracked damp eyelids as Saxby leaned forward and took off his boots, and then warm hands eased the pumps from his own feet.

Sitting back in the corner of the sofa, Saxby stretched out his legs and drew Aubrey closer, between his thighs. "That's better." He urged Aubrey's head onto his chest and folded his arms around him. "Much more comfortable."

Aubrey relaxed, breathing in thyme and wool and leather. His belly rested alongside a warm ridge—evidence of Saxby's arousal, of their likeness—but Saxby only held him. His own cock twitched and swelled, but he ignored it, drifting, instead, in a tranquil haze.

Sometime in the endless now, lips brushed Aubrey's temple, and he lifted his face to Saxby and parted his lips as naturally as a daisy opening to the sun. Saxby brought his warmth nearer, offering the strength of his arms and the heat of his dancing tongue. Gentle fingers mapped the curves of his face and naked throat, sparking whole-body shudders. A muscular arm cradled him closer. A firm hand stroked downward and unbuttoned his trousers to release his throbbing cock.

And then... Saxby pressed his whole hand, palm to fingertip, along the length of Aubrey's cock, and held it, warm and safe, against his belly. And kissed him. And kissed him.

19

Until Aubrey rocked into his warmth, desperate for more.

Saxby's hand wrapped around him. Aubrey thrust into his strong, sure hold, fumbling over Saxby's trouser buttons, reaching into his drawers. His fingers discovered a broad cock, gnarled with need and weeping with want, and Saxby moaned into his open mouth.

He slid down, forgoing the delights of Saxby's mouth and hand for the grounding of his solid cock. Closing his lips over the crown, he nursed slow, salt tears from him, swallowing his loss, one hand coaxing more from Saxby's body, the other appeasing his own.

Restless hands cupped Aubrey's face, raked his hair, but never pressed him. A thumb stroked the junction of his mouth with Saxby's cock, and he moaned, working faster.

"Fanshawe!" Saxby gasped. "I'm going to—!"

Aubrey locked his lips around Saxby's crown, sucking and swallowing, tugging both their cocks with awkward, aching arms. Saxby's hips jerked forward and strong hands clamped Aubrey's shoulders, setting him awhirl in a haze of bliss. He moaned, and Saxby gasped and groaned, and the bitter salt of his release flooded Aubrey's mouth. Sobbing, half-drowning, but still latched on to Saxby's warm, pulsing cock, Aubrey thrust his way to giddy, muscle-knotting satisfaction in his own familiar hand.

When he came back to himself, he'd collapsed over Saxby, cheek against his damp, softening cock, and he was weeping. Again. Or perhaps, still.

"Fanshawe," Saxby whispered, stroking Aubrey's hair.

He sighed and squeezed Saxby's thigh, then wiped his sticky hands and face on his shirt-tail.

Saxby urged him upward and settled his head on his shoulder. Aubrey lay, quiet and still, staring into the burning heart of the fire.

"Let me know when you're ready to retire," Saxby murmured at last. "With or without me."

He pressed his face into Saxby's shoulder, inhaling warmed wool and the sharp ozone of their mutual release. "I assume— you need to go."

"If you want me to." Saxby cradled the back of Aubrey's head. "Or I'll stay if you want me to."

Aubrey shut his eyes. One wasn't supposed to want. Want was childish, demanding. Like tears.

Broad fingers moved lower, massaging his neck where it met his shoulder.

Aubrey tilted his head, unfolding beneath the cosseting. Muscles resigned their tension each by each, until he sagged over Saxby, draped along the solid contours of his body like a cloak of heavy silk, like a cape of airy feathers.

"Stay," he whispered.

— Chapter Two —

Dear *God*!

Aubrey jolted awake in bluish pre-dawn light, his mind horribly clear. He stared at Saxby, asleep beside him. At the gossip journalist who knew his name, his family, his home address. At the most spectacular error of judgement of his life.

He needed him out. Immediately. But he needed to be covered before he faced him; needed to be himself, not this vulnerable, inadequate dupe.

Heart hammering, he eased out of bed and into the adjoining dressing room. And paused at the washstand. One ewer of water. One basin. But he couldn't expect Saxby to leave without washing. The sink in the WC was too small for the ewer, so he couldn't refill the basin. But he couldn't expect Saxby to wash in his used water, and he certainly wouldn't wash in Saxby's. Ringing for another basin and more water would raise impossible questions. Unless—

No. He couldn't pretend Saxby was a friend who'd stayed overnight: he'd never stayed before and never would again.

Damnation!

Aubrey used the water closet, then pulled on the nightshirt Grieve had left on the valet stand beside the wardrobe. Then he took a deep breath, turned on the light, strode back into the bedroom, and turned on that light, too.

"Saxby." Firm tone: that was good.

"Mmm?" Saxby opened bleary eyes. "Morning."

"My valet. He'll be here soon. You have to get up."

Saxby stretched, his compact, muscular body drawing Aubrey's unwilling gaze. Smiling, he propped himself on an elbow. "Front door's locked, and the key's still in it. You might ask him to come back later."

"What reason could I possibly give for that?"

"Late night?" He swung to his feet, still smiling. "Entertaining a friend?" He reached for Aubrey's hand.

"Wash basin's in here." Aubrey turned away and strode into the dressing room.

A long moment later, Saxby walked past him to the WC, and closed the door silently behind him. The hard jet of his morning stream meeting water made Aubrey flinch. There was something grossly intrusive about the sound. About a stranger releasing body wastes in his private rooms.

The chain rattled and clanked, was followed by the flush, and Saxby stepped out.

Aubrey indicated the marble-topped washstand, and Saxby picked up the ewer and poured water into the basin. Without meeting his gaze, Aubrey handed him a face cloth, then took another into the WC and shut the door behind him.

It smelled of warm, fresh urine: Saxby's or his own, he wasn't sure. Either way it was particularly revolting this morning. He stripped off his nightshirt and wet the cloth at the tap. And discovered the room was too small for a chap his size to wash in. He might've tolerated barking his elbows and spine on the walls, and his shins on the lavatory, but knowing Saxby would hear him thumping around like a landed conger eel was—

Damnation.

He put the nightshirt back on and let himself out of the WC. Keeping to the opposite end of the dressing room from Saxby, he wiped the residue of the night from his face and neck.

Saxby turned to watch. "We… could share the basin."

"Oh no! I shall do perfectly well here. Perfectly." The cloth was already drier than he liked, but it'd be embarrassing to go back to wet it at the sink. He'd have a bath later.

Saxby, unaffectedly naked, and as dismayingly attractive in the morning as he'd seemed the previous night, continued to watch him.

Heat crawled up his face. "Please. Do help yourself to the basin. Grieve won't be long."

Saxby washed and dressed, casting Aubrey wary glances he pretended not to notice, while Aubrey did his discreet best inside his nightshirt with a drying and increasingly dirty cloth, feeling foolish, but determined not to undress in front of the fellow.

Aubrey finished at last and stared at the cloth in his hand. Would two cloths in the basin look suspicious? What if... he'd dropped his cloth on the floor, say? He'd have needed anoth—

"Are you all right?" Saxby sat on the dressing-stool beside the valet stand to pull on his boots.

"Perfectly." Aubrey strode the length of the room, dropped his cloth into the basin, and turned to the wardrobe.

Saxby's head bowed as he laced his boots. Below the curve of his hairline, the smooth nape of his neck rose from his collar, paler than his face. Aubrey swallowed, staring.

Yesterday's dinner jacket was rather limp. Sobriety and unforgiving electric light revealed thinning sleeve edges, and lapel and shoulder stained with oil from... from...

Dear Lord, probably from Aubrey's pomade.

Heat flooded his entire body. He snatched the wardrobe doors open, hiding from the awful sight.

He'd given his address to an impoverished man, who'd have every reason to blackmail him. To a fellow who could destroy his reputation without a shred of personal risk. He couldn't counter an accusation of importuning by describing Saxby's enthusiasm for what followed, not without admitting to the graver crime of gross indecency himself. And yet, knowing that, he'd succumbed to a pretence of kindness. He'd wept on Saxby's shoulder. He'd voluntarily taken his cock into his mouth. Worst of all, he'd begged him to stay the night. He was weak, weak, weak. He hid his burning face in the wardrobe.

"Might we... shake hands, before I leave?"

"Certainly!" Aubrey turned, trying to achieve dignity in a nightshirt.

Saxby's naked hand gripped his own, and for a horrible moment, Aubrey feared he meant to thank him for his hospitality, which really would've been too much to bear.

"Don't worry so," Saxby said instead. A second hand joined the first, cradling Aubrey in warmth, sapping his hard-won poise. He lifted Aubrey's hand, turned it, and pressed a light, stubbly kiss to the inside of his wrist. "Not about me, at any rate." He patted Aubrey's knuckles and released him. "I'll see myself out."

Aubrey stared after him, a lump rising in his throat.

No. He swallowed hard.

No. He would not be upset.

Turning to the wardrobe, he fumbled for a dressing gown, hyper-aware of the soft tread receding across his drawing room, of the pause in the entrance hall. He shrugged into quilted silk. A key ground in a lock. A door quietly opened. Closed.

Aubrey squeezed his eyes shut and took a deep breath. He smoothed his collar and tied the dressing gown cord with care, focussing on each detail. Going over his plans for the day: breakfast, shave and bath, tailor, lunch at his club. Oh, and the bank. Mustn't forget that.

He was quite calm.

The wash basin caught his attention as he walked past. With a single finger, he fished one of the cloths from the soapy water, then squeezed it, wrung it into a tight, hard knot. Then he opened the dressing room window and hurled it as far from himself as he could.

LUCIEN CLOSED FANSHAWE'S door and walked to the building entrance with quick, light steps, keeping a wary eye on the basement stairs for the valet. He shouldn't have stayed. It'd been warm and comfortable, and Fanshawe'd seemed to need someone, which was always hard to resist, but— While the Albany doorman who'd seen him last night had probably been spelled, Lucien would still have to walk past someone observant, and it wasn't even eight o'clock.

But it was absurd to be anxious. He stepped firmly into the Ropewalk. Gentlemen occasionally had friends spend the night. They wouldn't usually leave so early, but only his own consciousness could betray him.

He strode along the walkway towards Vigo Street, towards the bulky, uniformed back of the doorman.

"Morning." He summoned a disinterested, aristocratic tone.

The doorman turned, astonished recognition on his moustached, middle-aged face. Lucien faltered, then tightened his expression, which had slackened with surprise.

The fellow was Uranian, though he hadn't seen him for a year or so, since he'd taken up with a permanent—

Noel. That was it.

"Morning." Noel's face blanked, saying as clearly as words that he was at work and couldn't talk, and certainly wouldn't acknowledge a fellow Uranian.

That was a bit of luck. Lucien strode past him without a backward glance.

A morning breeze, crisp and icy, nipped ears and nose and chin as he turned into Regent Street. He closed the top button of his overcoat, wishing he'd worn a scarf. He'd have liked to turn up his coat collar, but—

A gentleman never appears to be uncomfortable. He does not turn up his collar like a farmhand.

A small and shivering Lucien had pointed out to his father that he wasn't a gentleman, and that, anyway, he'd often seen gentlemen turn their collars up against the cold.

A gentleman may bend the rules: that's his privilege. A gentleman's gentleman may not. Forget that, and you'll spend your life as a footman.

A white, over-bright sun struggled to climb magnificent, soot-blackened buildings. Blinking against the glare, Lucien looked up into a cloudless, eggshell-blue sky. Possibly, he shouldn't have told Fanshawe he was a working man, but it'd seemed dishonest not to, when the chap clearly hadn't worked it out for himself.

Lucien's upbringing had left him with a swankier than average dialect, and he reflexively slipped into aristocratic diction among nobs. His clothes were relics from a time he'd had to accept patronage, and as well-made as any aristocrat's. Seven years on, they looked rather tired, but could still pass a casual inspection thanks to his expert care. He cultivated the upper-class illusion for work, lulling the nobility with familiar social cues, but he wouldn't pretend in his private life, not even for a casual encounter.

A sign chalked on the pavement demanded **Votes for Women!**

Watching for traffic, he crossed Piccadilly Circus into Coventry Street. A delivery cart rumbled past, drawn by blinkered horses, driven by a huddled shape in a vast cloak. Further down the road, men unloaded supplies from a cart outside a music hall.

He hadn't meant to frighten Fanshawe; hadn't known quite how to break it to him, and nerves had made him grin. And then... he'd hoped flirting would lighten the atmosphere. Poor chap. He'd read of people going grey with shock: turned out to be bloody alarming in the flesh.

The pavement announced a **Votes for Women Procession**. *Procession?*

Lucien paused to read the rest of the chalked notice.

Votes for Women Procession
February 19th 1906
You **ASSEMBLE** at St James Park District Railway Station
at 10:00
You **MARCH** to the Caxton Hall at **10:30**

He stared. London wasn't bloody Manchester! No respectable woman would march here. At best, a few daring souls would walk a block or two before losing their nerve.

But the signs persisted at intervals along his route: outside a music hall on Coventry Street, at Leicester Square, outside the Theatre Royal. Someone, or someones, had been very busy.

Busy as Fanshawe, trying to avoid his eyes this morning.

Lucien irritably swatted a clump of grass in a pavement crack with his cane. He'd *tried* to reassure the chap, damn it! The fact was Fanshawe'd been comfortable as long as he felt looked after: it was what nobs were used to. And Lucien'd looked after him because it was what *he* was used to. He didn't entirely like the person he became around the nobility: it was too easy to for habit to take over.

Well. No need to distress the fellow again. He'd stick to his own class in future: to men who wouldn't stare in sober horror if they woke beside him.

He let himself into his boarding-house off Drury Lane, and checked his pocket watch as he climbed the stairs. Quarter past eight. He was in good time for breakfast. Once in his living room, he hung his outdoor things on the coat-stand beside the doorway, then dropped onto the threadbare sofa at the cold hearth, his breath steaming.

Waste of money to light a fire when he was leaving for work in an hour. Maybe he could get away with just changing his jacket. Glancing down, he sighed. His clothes had rather wilted under the pressure of a big aristocrat lying on them.

Poor bloody Fanshawe. The set at Albany clearly wasn't a pied-à-terre, kept for late nights on the town or casual bedding. Everything about it suggested a permanent home, from the quantity and variety of clothes in the wardrobe, to the slight depression in the sofa marking a favourite seat. Lucien had expected a room rented by the hour—the fellow could afford it, and it'd be more comfortable than outdoors. Instead, Fanshawe'd taken him home, taken him into his own bed, and slept beside him. Like a lover.

Lucien dwelled on Fanshawe's long eyelashes, on dark brows vivid against pale skin, and haunted brown eyes. Poor bugger must be terribly lonely, to bring strangers home. Obviously needed someone to care—

No. Time to get moving, if he was becoming sentimental. Fanshawe had friends and good health. He had wealth, for God's sake! And birth, too: a kind of material security Lucien would never have. You couldn't afford to feel sorry for a chap like that. You couldn't delude yourself that he needed anything from you, or wanted you for anything more than a quick fuck. Might as well try to befriend a bloody mink.

As the morning had proved.

His bedroom door opened outward, to maximise what little space there was. Lucien edged between the foot of his bed and the washstand, then along the narrow gap between bed and wall to the curtain that masked the back corner of the room. The rail behind it—standing in for the wardrobe that would never fit in this room—held lounge suits, an outmoded frock coat, and another dinner jacket. No evening dress, since he'd never accompanied William to social events. A quilted dark green damask dressing gown gleamed amid the black: William's particular gift to him, like his overcoat and winter boots, because William imagined everyone felt the cold as he did, and because Lucien couldn't bring himself to refuse them as he did everything else. Shelves behind the rail held the rest of his clothes.

He stripped to wash and shave—despite the chill, despite the water being much colder than the water in Fanshawe's lavishly heated rooms—because his wash there had left him feeling not quite clean. Shivering, then, he dressed, tied a cravat around his neck, and wrapped himself in the dressing gown, wounded by William's easy generosity even as he appreciated it.

Yesterday's rumpled clothes drooped over the foot of his narrow bed. He made a quick paste of French chalk and applied it to the pomade stains, then laid them flat, ready to brush, sponge, and iron when he got home.

The heel of a palm thumped the door to his rooms, and he stepped back into the living room as his landlady, carrying his breakfast tray and the first post, nudged the door open with a bony hip.

"Morning."

"Good morning, Mrs Emmott." Lucien swallowed reflexive annoyance as she clattered the tray onto the table in the corner of his living room. His irritation was as much a product of his training as his unobtrusive presence, and that annoyed him too: he was more than his bloody training.

Mrs Emmott tramped out, slamming the door behind her.

Door handles exist to facilitate the closing *of doors, Lucien, not merely their opening.*

God knew he didn't pay her enough to expect the level of service he'd been trained to provide—and accustomed to receiving—nor did he want anyone to have to provide it for him. It was just… comfortable.

Lucien unfolded his napkin and polished the water-marked cutlery till it shone, then ate his porridge and bread and butter while leafing through his post. Despite the dressing gown and food, he was chilled. He abandoned a letter from his cousin to wrap his hands around the teacup while he drank, but felt no warmer. Fanshawe's rooms had been—

No.

It was early for work, but the office would be warm, and the fuel wouldn't cost him a penny. He hung up his cravat and dressing gown, put on a collar and tie, and pulled on his jacket and boots. His portable writing desk—a plain oak box—stood on the end of the table. He tucked his correspondence under one side of the writing slope, filled his fountain pen, and locked the desk.

The walk itself would help warm him up, and at least if he was working, he wouldn't be brooding over Fanshawe.

WHITEFRIARS AND CARMELITE Streets were heaving. Flat-bed carts ferried massive cylinders of paper to the basement presses while shop assistants carried bundles of the day's newspapers back to newsagents' shops. Behind it all: the muted thump and clatter of the presses.

It wasn't much quieter on the ground floor of New Carmelite House. Vendors elbowed their way to the cage at the far end of the space, shouting numbers through the bars at men who calmly recorded the names of their shops, counted out newspapers, and handed them through a narrow hatch. Lucien climbed the stairs, into relative quiet.

"Who's that?" Jameson bellowed from his office.

Unusual for the editor to be here so early. He'd have worked late into the night, preparing copy for the morning paper.

"Only me." He peered round the door.

Dark pouches hung under Jameson's eyes, and the room smelled of whisky and cold coffee, of stale cigarettes and ashes, but his thin blond hair was neatly combed. "Saxby!" He beckoned. "Good man. What d'you think of this?" The chair creaked as he grabbed a handbill from a pile of papers and slid it across his ink-stained desk.

Votes for Women Procession

"I think I've seen it chalked all over the pavements this morning." Lucien slid the bill back.

"Have you, though?" Jameson travelled everywhere by cab. "Young woman handed this to m'wife yesterday."

"Yes?"

"There's a story here." Jameson tapped the handbill with a broad finger. "And you're just the fellow to get it."

"I'm…" Lucien stared at the upside-down bill.

BE EARLY. BE LOYAL. BE CHEERFUL.

"This—is politics, Mr Jameson."

"Indeed."

"And—I write for the *Society* pages."

"Indeed." Jameson bared long, yellowed teeth in a grin.

"Might be more in Huggins' and Dawlish's line?"

"You think young women will confide in Huggins or Dawlish?"

Put like that, it did seem unlikely.

"Huggins and Dawlish are very well for speaking to men. You do well on the Society pages because you charm women.

31

And here we have… Women." He flourished an open hand at the handbill.

"But not a Society event," Lucien suggested.

"Don't be a snob, Saxby."

Lucien bristled. "I only meant it's not my—"

"A lot of middle class women buy our paper. This is news about middle class women, and we *will* get this story." Jameson glared at him.

Buggery. "Understood, Mr Jameson."

"Good fellow." Jameson nudged the handbill towards him. "Young woman said she was from the Women's Social and Political Union."

Lucien paused, fingers on the bill. "The WSPU's in Manchester."

"Also, obviously, in London. *Again*, Saxby. Recall: they lobbied Parliament only last year. Look it up in the archives."

Lucien's face heated. "Will do."

Jameson nodded at the bill. "State Opening of Parliament. Should be interesting, don't you think? Considering the trouble they caused Churchill in Lancashire."

Trouble? "I expect so." Clearly, he had a lot to catch up on.

Lucien trudged upstairs to his office with the handbill. Damn it, if he'd wanted to be a political journalist, he'd have signed up for it.

No one else had arrived yet. The long table down the centre of the room held neat stacks of paper in front of wooden chairs. Floor to ceiling cubbyholes, crammed with folders of press-clippings, stood along three walls. Lucien put the handbill at his spot on the long, sloping table that ran the length of the room beneath wide sash-windows, then hung his outdoor things on the coat-stand beside the door.

By the time his colleagues started trickling in, he'd made the detailed notes on *Two Naughty Boys* that he should've made the previous night instead of going home with Fanshawe, jotted a few evocative phrases, and produced a strong opening paragraph.

Madeleine Enfield—Rubenesque curves confined in a black, tailored skirt and jacket that washed out her pale olive skin; dark hair smoothed back in an elegant chignon—paused beside him and tapped the handbill. "What's this, then, Saxby? Never've guessed you'd support the WSPU."

"I don't." Lucien wiped and capped his pen, and stretched his fingers. "Not particularly against them either. Jameson wants me to cover the event."

"*You?*" Miss Enfield snatched her hand back.

"I did suggest it wasn't my field, but he thought I'd do better with ladies than Huggins or Dawlish."

"And you didn't suggest *I* might be best positioned of all?"

Lucien stared at her. "Can't honestly say it occurred to me."

Miss Enfield swept to her seat two chairs along and settled herself with ostentatious grace.

"Might be too dangerous for a lady," Lucien offered. "Stewards and police have physically removed these militants from political meetings."

"I am *well* aware of that, thank you." Miss Enfield dug a pen and an embroidered case from a black and gold tapestry bag, drew spectacles from the case, and slid them onto her face.

A chortle from the table behind them. "Oh, you're in hot water now, Saxby!"

"*Do* be quiet, Chiddicks," Lucien and Miss Enfield said, almost in chorus.

Lucien grinned at Miss Enfield.

She grinned back reluctantly. "Damn it all, Saxby. How will I get out of this frocks and bonnets department if he never gives me a chance?"

"I rather like the frocks and bonnets department," Lucien said mildly.

"You mightn't if it was your only option. Besides, you've already had your share of adventure."

Adventure. Squashing memories of gnawing hunger, of the choking stink of desperation and sewage rotting under a merciless sun, he mustered a smile. "I'll suggest you cover the story: not as though I want it."

"Too late." She slid a sheet of paper towards herself. "He'll think you're ducking out because you aren't up to the job."

Good point. Lucien fidgeted thoughtfully, twisting and sliding his pen lid off and on again with his thumb.

"Good night last night, Saxby?"

"What?" Lucien half-turned, looking into Chiddicks' pale, grinning face.

"Your mind's obviously not on your job. More… on the job, as it were."

"For God's *sake,* Chiddicks!"

"Ignore him." Miss Enfield slid a folder from her stack of research. "He's clearly deprived."

The office stilled, breathless. Then erupted in hoots of laughter.

Old Tomlinson—who was only middle-aged, but was older than Young Tomlinson in Advertising—patted her shoulder, his Victorian whiskers quivering. "I think you meant 'depraved', my dear."

"I know what I meant," Miss Enfield said irritably, "and I *meant* what I said."

The hoots turned to roars.

Lucien leaned towards her. "Look. What if we work on this together and share the credit? All interviews you conduct specifically attributed to you."

Brown eyes searched his own.

The comments around them grew bawdier: all directed at Chiddicks, but thoroughly unsuitable for the ears of the only woman in the office.

"Shall we go and make a start?"

She laughed. "I'm not a delicate flower of womanhood, you know." Casting a quick glance around, she added, "Nor ignorant. But all right."

He closed the office door behind them.

"Thanks, Saxby," she said gruffly. "Assuming you come through on your offer."

"I will."

"Well. Thanks. I may go mad if I have to cover garden parties and coming out balls for the rest of my life. Nine years is quite long enough to devote to that nonsense."

"Nine years?" Lucien stared at her.

"If you're about to say I look as youthful as a debutante, you can save it."

He wasn't, because she didn't. But she didn't look much past her mid-twenties, either.

"I feel every one of my thirty-four years and if I'm still doing this at forty, I may have to find a pistol and a nice, deserted spot in the park, because this, quite frankly, is a waste of my life. I don't like self-involved society girls or their ambitious mamas, and I have no desire in the world to charm them into conversation."

"It's a game, isn't it?" Lucien suggested. "Getting past snobbery and reserve to make a connection and get the story. A sort of test of skill."

"A game suggests fun. I can do it, Saxby, but it's not fun. You're good at it, and you like it, and I'm delighted for you. But I'm not here because I like it. I'm here because it's the only section of the paper they'd let me work on."

"Maybe this'll help." The comment felt inadequate. It'd never occurred to him that Miss Enfield—or any woman—might want different work.

The politics office was over-crowded. Lucien dug out the file on the WSPU while Miss Enfield cleared a corner at the end of a table.

"Right." He flipped open the file. "So the WSPU presumably belongs to the National Union of Women's Suffrage Societies—"

"Split from."

"Pardon?"

"The WSPU split from the NUWSS because it wasn't militant enough for them."

Oh God.

Gritting his teeth, Lucien made endless notes on names, dates, and events.

"D'you really need all that?" Miss Enfield asked at last.

He crushed down annoyance at the sheer waste of time and energy. "Frocks and bonnets man, remember? If you want analysis of the latest Parisian fashions, I'm your fellow. Or military: I could do that, too, if I had to. Jameson should've put you onto this story in the first place, not me."

"True enough." She watched him carefully. "I can write the background, if you like: save you the bother."

"Please do; save me making a fool of myself in print. We'll put your name first in the by-line: you clearly deserve it. But I have to learn this anyway, so I'm not a complete ignoramus on the day." He bent over clippings and notebook.

Pankhurst: Mrs Emmeline. Daughters: Christabel, Sylvia, Adela. And there was at least one son who might—

"Know what, Saxby?"

He looked up, stifling a sigh.

"You're all right, for a fellow."

A laugh escaped him. "Blokes can be a bloody nuisance, can't they?"

Miss Enfield gave him an odd look. "Certainly can."

For the next hour, Lucien struggled to memorise the dynamics of the various women's suffrage groups, while Miss Enfield explained interconnections between people and events. By the time she suggested they tackle more urgent stories, his head felt over-stuffed with the quarrels and political differences which had hived what seemed dozens of groups, and he felt obliged to apologise for wasting her time.

"Don't worry about it." She patted his arm. "Nice to see a fellow taking an interest, even if it's under duress. And I've less work than usual lined up today."

Back in their own office, he ignored his colleagues' chatter and worked over lunchtime, hoping to make up for lost time. Throughout the day, Miss Enfield picked up his completed work along with her own, dictated it to a typist, and took the finished copy to Jameson. Even so, most journalists had left by the time he dictated his final story and carried it to the editor's office.

Jameson raised blood-shot eyes from his page as Lucien put the copy on his desk. "Ah. Saxby." The patronising bonhomie of the morning had frozen into disgust.

Lucien stilled. "Can I help you, Mr Jameson?"

Jameson set down his page and reached for another, tucked between two stacks of paper. "I've had a letter about you, Saxby."

— Chapter Three —

A DIFFIDENT TAP at his front door.

Aubrey capped his pen without a shred of irritation. This story wasn't working anyway: like the others, it'd be late. He stretched in his chair, waiting for Grieve to come in after a courtesy pause, but the door continued not to open.

Shutting his work in the secrétaire, he glanced at the clock— half-past six: who the devil would call at this time of evening?— and answered the door.

It was Saxby, complete with riding cane, in a bowler hat.

Why was he back? Dear Lord! Did he imagine Aubrey was a convenience? Not that—Aubrey's spirit shrank to a painful knot—not that he hadn't given him reason to think so.

"Awfully sorry," he managed, clutching the doorknob. "Splendid to see you and all that, but I'm afraid I have an engagement this evening."

"I quite understand." Saxby's face was tight and pale in the light spilling over Aubrey's shoulder. "I shouldn't have troubled you at all, except that— I find myself in a spot of bother and wondered whether you might help."

Oh.

Oh. "You— You mean to—" Recalling himself, Aubrey glanced at his neighbour's door across the entryway, at the stairs to the upper chambers, then out at the Ropewalk. Quite aside from breaking Albany's rule of silence, his situation wouldn't be improved by his neighbours overhearing Saxby's blackmail terms. Nor Grieve, for that matter, downstairs in the basement. "I suppose—you'd better come in."

Saxby removed his bowler and trod past him into the drawing room with quick, tense steps.

Aubrey locked the front door, so they wouldn't be interrupted, then went to confront the predator.

"I really am most awfully sorry." Saxby was standing in the middle of the drawing room. "But I can't unwind this coil myself, and have nowhere else to turn."

"I see." Aubrey folded his arms. He had no intention of making this comfortable.

"I've just had an unexpected interview with my editor."

Of course. He'd claim his editor was demanding a scoop, but payment would make it easier to withstand the pressure.

"He informs me that a—a complaint has been lodged against me, by Mr Edgar Lowdon."

"*What?*" Aubrey's arms dropped to his sides.

"Alleging that I—" Saxby swallowed "—that I harassed Lady Hernedale at the theatre last night."

"Good God! You'd better sit down."

Saxby perched on the edge of the sofa, half-twisting to keep Aubrey in view. "I really didn't mean to—" His bowler trembled as he set it beside him. "Look here, Fanshawe, did I distress the lady?"

"Not at all!"

Saxby rubbed his face. "That helps, though only she herself could confirm it."

Aubrey poured a glass of brandy: a fellow'd need it after a shock like that.

"I'll write to her. Apologise." Saxby reached for the glass.

"You'd better— Look." Aubrey put the glass on the occasional table beside the sofa. "Better take your gloves off. You're likely to drop this otherwise."

Saxby flushed. "I apologise for presenting myself in such a condition."

"Quite all right."

It wasn't, and they both knew it: it was damned embarrassing all round. Aubrey took Saxby's bowler and riding cane out to the coat-stand while Saxby unbuttoned his gloves.

"Nothing else you could've done," Aubrey said, as he came back in. That, at least, was true. "I know Lady Hernedale… tolerably well. I saw nothing to suggest she was offended."

Saxby crammed his gloves into his overcoat pocket.

"Better give me your coat, as well."

Saxby stood, shrugging it off. "I can—"

"Quite all right." It'd give him a moment to think, and Saxby a chance to recover himself.

The woollen overcoat was warm from Saxby's body. He hung it, surrounded by the thyme that scented Saxby's pomade.

"I was over-familiar, wasn't I?" he heard from the drawing room.

Aubrey paused, his hands still on the dense, soft coat, his face embarrassingly close. "Perhaps… a trifle forward."

A whispered oath.

"But she wouldn't have answered you if she was offended." He walked back into the drawing room. "And if you'd gone too far, Hernedale would've dealt with you. As would I."

"Lord Hernedale seemed… preoccupied."

"But far from oblivious, I assure you." Aubrey further delayed by pouring himself a glass of brandy.

Saxby's colour was better, thank goodness. He'd been half-afraid the fellow would faint on him. Aubrey plucked the empty glass from his hand, re-filled and returned it.

"As it happens…" He settled on the opposite end of the sofa with his own glass. "I'm dining with Lord and Lady Hernedale this evening. I'll mention the matter to them."

"That would—" Saxby took a deep breath. "That is, on the one hand, I'd be very grateful if you would, but on the other, I wish you wouldn't distress the lady."

Aubrey stared at him in blank incomprehension.

"I'd better write a letter of apology, without mentioning her brother's complaint."

Understanding dawned, and a huff of laughter escaped Aubrey. "Your delicacy does you credit. But you should reconsider the advisability of concealing anything from Lady Hernedale which concerns her. Whether or not you'd asked for help, I'd have had to tell her, once I knew it myself."

Saxby's face was bleak. "You must do as you think best."

"Cheer up. I'm quite sure you haven't offended."

"I suspect you—" Saxby fumbled his glass onto the occasional table and sank his face in his hands. "Quite aside from a—a natural mortification and concern that I might've discomforted a lady, I suspect you underestimate the gravity of my situation."

"I doubt it. Nothing casual about losing one's reputation."

"My job is at risk." Saxby met his gaze. The whites of his eyes were pink. "Worse, my *career*'s at risk. If I lose my reputation, no periodical will hire me, nor even print my work on a free lance basis."

"That *is*..." Aubrey glanced away, uncomfortable. "Yes, I quite see."

"Even if my editor comes to believe me innocent, this could still ruin my career. I'm a social events journalist. How will I gain access to such events if Mr Lowdon maligns me to sponsors and organisers?"

"I'll talk to Lord and Lady Hernedale. I'm sure we'll come up with something between us."

Saxby flushed. "That's—"

Aubrey felt Saxby's profound humiliation at being the subject of such a conversation. At being disgraced, and needing help to uphold his good name.

"If—you would. I should be greatly indebted to you."

"Certainly not, old chap! Good heavens!" Heat swamped Aubrey's face. "It's not as though— I mean, you didn't—" Seeing Saxby so defeated was dreadful. "It's Lowdon's damned debt, not yours! And I dare say Lady Hernedale will collect in full."

FANSHAWE'S VALET, GRIEVE—tall, thin and impeccably groomed; perhaps in his forties—inclined his head in greeting as he walked through the drawing room. Lucien smiled back, then tensed. A valet expected to be ignored by his gentleman's visitors: he might've thrown him off his stride.

Fanshawe and Grieve disappeared into the bedroom, and Lucien dropped his head in his hands. When would he learn? This was precisely why he was in his current bind. He managed when he was prepared, but surprise and ease were his downfall. Still shaken from a pair of painful interviews, Grieve's greeting had reminded him so of Dad that— He pressed his fingertips into his temples. Then, following Fanshawe's suggestion, he stood to peruse the bookcases flanking the chimney breast: he'd look less mopish with a book in his hands.

Reading should've distracted him, but the room was over-warm, and his mind leapt again and again to his dilemma, pressing the bruise he most wanted to ignore. He'd read only two pages when he heard movement behind him.

Fanshawe emerged from his bedroom, a vision of elegance in a dinner jacket. "You've found something."

Lucien swallowed and produced a smile. "*Reginald*." He foolishly held the book up in evidence.

Fanshawe's lips were narrow, with a slight droop at the corners that suggested gentleness. Or uncertainty. "Jolly good. Playing cards in that drawer." He tipped a satin-smooth chin towards a bookcase, easing his manicured fingers into form-fitting kidskin gloves.

"Right. Thanks."

Grieve appeared, and Fanshawe wordlessly held out a wrist. The valet bent to button his gloves, then fetched his overcoat.

Lucien watched Fanshawe slide his arms into the sleeves. Watched Grieve lift and smooth the coat across bony shoulders, then enfold Fanshawe's tall, barely-muscled body in soft, brushed wool.

He'd have liked to help Fanshawe.

Grieve vanished into the hall, returning to hand Fanshawe his cane and to settle a black silk top hat on dark, otter-sleek hair.

"Well. So long."

Lucien blinked and raised *Reginald* again. "Enjoy your evening."

The front door opened and closed, and Grieve flowed past into the bedroom.

Lucien returned to the book, but concentration eluded him. Damn it, Fanshawe was a much better bet for soothing the savage breast than Saki.

The soft, familiar noises of tidying in the bedroom ceased. Grieve padded through the drawing room and out of the set.

Fanshawe wearing an informal dinner jacket rather than evening dress gave Lucien hope: evidently, he was a close friend of the Hernedales. But—he put *Reginald* down and paced the opulent drawing room—how would he live independently, if Fanshawe failed?

In a drawer under the bookcase, he found a silver playing card box with 'AF' engraved at the top right corner. Settling at the mahogany dining table between the bedroom doorway and the vast, curtained window overlooking the Ropewalk, he laid out a hand of Patience.

Red nine onto a black ten.

He could always re-enlist: he had an excellent reputation with the Hussars. Black five onto red six, uncovering a black eight. Onto the red nine.

Buggery. He rubbed his face hard. The Battle of Ladysmith had sucked every romantic ideal of war from him—and he hadn't many to start with—and the siege afterwards had crushed him entirely. You couldn't protect men from stupid orders, or enteric fever, or starvation. He hadn't saved Peter Ormerod, or George Butcher, or Emrys—

No. No sinking into those memories.

Black jack on red queen; no further moves. He flipped the first three cards from the deck. Nothing helpful on top.

Voting rights for British settlers in the Transvaal had seemed a worthy cause. But the photographs he'd seen after the war, of skeletal Boer and African children in British concentration camps...

There were things... things it was never right to support, even unwittingly, in any cause.

Next three cards: nothing useful.

A discreet tap at the front door. A calculated moment later, Grieve entered the drawing room, white-gloved, carrying a large tray.

"Dinner, Mr Saxby."

"Oh." Lucien swept the cards into their box. "Thank you. I didn't expect that. Didn't mean to put you to any bother."

"No trouble, Mr Saxby. It's only a meat pie from the bakery." Grieve set the table and lifted dishes onto padded mats.

It was a huge pie, served with creamy potato matchsticks and peas. He poured Lucien a glass of claret and set the decanter beside him. "I might produce a gooseberry fool for dessert, if you wish?"

His palate did. But Grieve would've had the evening off if Lucien hadn't intruded. "No, thank you. This is more than sufficient."

Grieve picked up the empty tray and left the room.

The food was delicious, but without companionship, it didn't distract him from his thoughts.

Not the army. What might he be supporting if he re-enlisted? But he wouldn't work for the sort of careless or lawless employer who'd hire a fellow with a bad reputation either. That left living and working in Mum and Dad's hotel, or going back to William.

Another discreet tap. A pause, and Grieve carried in another covered tray.

"Tea, Mr Saxby—" He settled the tray silently at the end of the table "—should you care for it." At the sideboard, he set another decanter and a glass on a small silver tray, then brought them to the table. "And port. Might I assist you with anything else?"

"No. Thank you."

"Mr Fanshawe said I might retire after serving tea early, but should you require anything, please don't hesitate to ring." He inclined his head towards the bell-pull near the fireplace.

"Thank you. I'm certain I have all I need."

"Very good. Good evening, Mr Saxby."

Grieve glided from the room, no doubt to put his feet up, but not to relax, since he'd be half-waiting for Lucien to demand service.

He shouldn't have come. He'd panicked. A simple letter of apology would've alerted Lady Hernedale to the complaint: if he'd offended her, she could have ignored or accepted his apology; and if he hadn't, she might have written to say so, and he could've shown the letter to Jameson.

As it was, he'd disturbed Fanshawe, who'd probably never expected nor wanted to see him again. He'd obliged him to inconvenience himself and spoil his dinner party on his behalf. And he'd made Grieve work on a precious evening off.

Lucien drained his glass. Losing his reputation would be horrifying—humiliating—but it wouldn't destroy him. Unlike many, he had alternatives. He didn't like them, but at least they existed.

Swallowing the last bite of potato, he patted his lips with the napkin. He loved his parents, but he didn't want to live with them, and he loathed working in service.

William would welcome him back: he'd never wanted him to leave. But to return in disgrace... His face boiled. No. Not unless he was homeless and starving. He didn't want to live with William, anyway, had only joined the army because he'd needed a graceful reason to leave him.

He poured a cup of tea.

If worse came to worst, he'd admit his fault to his parents before they heard it elsewhere. He'd endure their appalled disappointment, then try to make up for the shame he'd brought them. They lived only a little more comfortably than he did—most of their wealth was invested in the hotel—but he'd save them an employee's wage. He'd become their perfect assistant and be grateful for it. At least it'd be service in his family's establishment, in what would one day be his own business.

It was more—so much more—than Mum or Dad had started out with.

— Chapter Four —

AUBREY WAITED UNTIL the servants left the dining room to raise the subject.

"I *beg* your pardon?" Henrietta—who never retired while the gentlemen drank port unless they had formal guests—fixed cold blue eyes on him.

"Edgar—" Rupert laced his fingers behind his head and gazed up at the ceiling "—is a despotic dodo. A mendacious moraliser. A hectoring—"

"He's an officious bully!" Henrietta thumped her glass down. "What right has he to police my social life?"

"None at all," Rupert agreed. "One more, and then I'll stop. He's a sanctimonious swill-spewer. There."

"Beautifully euphonious, my dear." Henrietta patted his arm. "You'll have to write to Mr Saxby's editor. If I do, it'll only provoke speculation that the fellow's my lover."

"I'm not sure that'll be enough." Aubrey rolled the stem of the glass between his fingers. "Lowdon may malign Saxby to sponsors and event organisers, too."

Henrietta's face tightened. "I'm getting a little weary of my blasted brother trying to control my every move." She leaned back in her chair. "Let me think."

The room settled into comfortable silence. Rupert took a book from his pocket and found his page, while Aubrey watched Henrietta sip port and twist her long gold and pearl necklace through porcelain-pale, manicured fingers. Her light brown hair had been coaxed into an elegant high roll framing her heart-shaped face. A few tendrils escaped, drawing attention to the perfect curve of her eyebrows, and to her long, slender neck.

"You look beautiful," Aubrey murmured.

Rupert glanced up from his book. "Exquisite."

"Thank you." Henrietta dimpled. "I work jolly hard at it. But do be quiet now. I almost had an idea, and if you'd interrupted me for anything else I'd have been quite annoyed."

"Lovely." Aubrey blew her a kiss. He'd watched her practice the dimple when they were younger, and advised on its effect.

Henrietta laughed. "Let me *think*, darling."

Obediently, and nothing loath, he transferred his attention to Rupert. To his dark hair and firm jaw and wide shoulders; to his broad, bare hand with a narrow scar along the side, legacy of an ill-conceived game of knife-catching in their youth. Rupert continued to read, but his lips curved, and he flexed his fingers.

"Hush!" Henrietta said. "I can hear you flirting."

Rupert laid his book on the table, folded his hands in his lap and gazed at the ceiling, prim as a choirboy.

"Dash it, Rupert!" But Henrietta was laughing. "Just as well I'd already come up with something."

"We have every faith in your wisdom," Aubrey assured her.

"Our Lady of Lucidity," Rupert agreed. "Our modish Minerva."

"Do you mean to keep that up all night?" Aubrey asked.

"Quite possibly, now I'm permitted to speak."

"Plan first, play later." Henrietta put her glass down with a decisive tap, and Aubrey re-filled it. "Rupert, this will require an escalation in social engagement for an extended period. Can you bear it?"

"Rather think I'll have to. Edgar might not have nailed this poor fellow to a cross if I hadn't needled him. Besides, anything that thwarts Edgar is its own sweet reward."

"You're the very soul of generosity." Henrietta kissed his hand. "Aubrey, your participation isn't essential, but would be helpful."

"Might I have details before committing myself?" Aubrey was as familiar with Henrietta's plans as with their comfortable silences.

"O ye of little faith! Rupert will adopt Mr Saxby. Socially, that is. He'll be seen regularly in Rupert's company; and we'll arrange to encounter him at events and include him in our group. Meanwhile, we'll afford Edgar the barest courtesy due to family. Thus we counteract any rumour that Mr Saxby offended me, or that Rupert disapproves of him, and simultaneously show why Edgar might be bitter enough to tell that lie."

"But that could go on for years." Aubrey refilled his glass and set the decanter in front of Rupert. "You can't just drop the fellow once you've lionized him. People'd wonder why."

"Which is why I said 'for an extended period'. Once he's established, we can gradually withdraw, provided we're always pleased to see him in public. Unless he does something beyond the pale, in which case we'd drop him as we would anyone else."

"It's an excellent plan." Rupert sipped his port. "Assuming he doesn't turn out to be tiresome. Only... You took the fellow home last night, Aubrey. Will it be awkward for you?"

"Er." It might be, but they could hardly ditch the chap to deal with this alone. "Not particularly."

"So that's all right." Rupert locked his fingers behind his head and stretched long legs out under the table. "You have taken into account, Hettie, that this might ruin your brother? Socially, at any rate."

Aubrey went to refill Henrietta's glass, but she touched the rim. "Thank you: I've had enough. Thing is, my dear, Edgar's trying to ruin Mr Saxby. Eye for an eye, you know. Anyway, even if we ruin him socially, Edgar has property and investments, whereas he's trying to take Mr Saxby's only source of income, too."

"True."

"Besides, we only know about Mr Saxby because he knew Aubrey's address and came to tell him. How many other poor blighters has Edgar destroyed just because I flirted with them? It can't go on: I won't have it."

"Well I, for one, will be delighted to give the pompous, poisonous piss-pot the cold shoulder." Rupert drained his glass. "You in, Aubrey?"

"One for all, and all for one." Aubrey raised his glass to them and drank the last of his port. When he lowered it, Henrietta was smiling at him in the way that always constricted his heart and shortened his breath.

"Are you staying tonight?" she asked.

"Can't." He put the glass down regretfully. "Saxby's in my set. Can't leave the fellow panicking all night."

"You— Aubrey, you just *left* him there?"

"He was in rather a state. Couldn't send him away."

"You might've brought him to dinner," Rupert suggested.

"Except he was in a state," Aubrey repeated patiently. "Anyway, we couldn't have discussed this with him here."

"He must've been alone for at least—" Henrietta turned to look at the mantel clock "—three *hours*!"

"I sent Grieve out for a meat pie for him."

"It'd have to be a monumental meat pie, to hold his attention for three hours." Closing his eyes, Rupert tilted his head back with a lazy smile. "A prodigy among pies." He rolled the words with sensuous satisfaction. "A prodigious pinnacle of pastry perfection."

Aubrey stood, grinning. "There are books in my set."

"Ah, well." Rupert opened dark eyes. "That's a horse of a wholly different hue."

"Mr Saxby should be seen with us tomorrow," Henrietta said. "Before Edgar's rumours can take hold. We might go to Richmond, I suppose. Meet him at, say, three o'clock? Wimbledon entrance?"

Aubrey cast his mind over his diary. "I can be there. But can you, Rupert?"

"I'm engaged." Rupert stretched and stood. "But it's nothing a man with a skilled tongue can't wriggle out of."

"Right-ho. I'll let you know tomorrow morning if he can't make it."

"I'll send for the carriage." Rupert closed the door behind him.

Aubrey bent to kiss Henrietta. She rested a warm palm on his cheek and parted her lips, so he slid a hand to the back of her neck, careful not to disarrange her hair, and let his tongue waltz with hers, his thumb stroking her soft skin from hairline to collar.

"Mmm." She drew away, enticingly flushed. "Tomorrow night instead?"

"Definitely." A week apart was too damned long. "You smell of bergamot."

"New hair treatment. D'you like it?"

"I do, actually. Smells very fresh."

The door opened behind him, and closed again. He dropped a kiss on Henrietta's forehead and turned to Rupert. "How's your lobby coming along?"

Rupert snorted. "General election. No one gives a toss for women and children during an election campaign."

"Why would they, when we can't vote?" Henrietta said bitterly.

Aubrey glanced back at her. "I'm sorry."

"Well." Rupert held out his arms and Aubrey stepped into them. "Should be easier once the Liberals are in power."

"Pfft." Henrietta's opinion.

It was a long-standing disagreement, and unlikely to be resolved in the next few minutes.

"It's always possible," Rupert told her over Aubrey's shoulder. "Anti-violence legislation, anyway. Probably not suffrage."

"Anything but suffrage," Henrietta muttered.

But she wouldn't interrupt their moment with politics once Rupert shut up. Aubrey kissed his cheek, offering a gentle embrace because one moved slowly with Rupert. But Rupert pressed a hand to the nape of Aubrey's neck and a thigh to his groin, and wrapped an arm tightly around his waist.

Aubrey melted into him, leaning his cheek against Rupert's as his body heated. After a moment's indulgence, he kissed his smooth jaw. "You're not in the least interested." This close, it was obvious.

"Not tonight." Rupert's hand slid over Aubrey's buttocks, pressed him closer. "But thrilling you is its own sweet delight." He brushed dry lips over Aubrey's. "And since Saxby's at your set, you shan't suffer for it."

Aubrey huffed a laugh into Rupert's shoulder. Rupert was unique. Henrietta, too. Nobody could substitute for either. But since he didn't want Rupert to have an attack of conscience and only touch him when he meant to carry through, he just said, "He mightn't care to stay. Don't suppose he meant to see me again after last night."

Rupert drew his head back and stared into Aubrey's face. "Really?"

Aubrey laughed and kissed his jaw. "Flatterer. I assure you, it happens."

Rupert sighed. "I will never fathom the mysteries of the higher libido."

"Doesn't matter: your attentions are always welcome. Anyway, it's just as well you're not interested, since I have to leave. If I have needs later, well, I'm blessed with two good hands and a vivid imagination."

Rupert's lips tilted deliciously, with just a hint of uncertainty. "An obsessive onanist."

"When provoked." Aubrey touched the tip of his tongue to the corner of Rupert's tempting lips, barely brushing his skin. "And now I really must go."

Henrietta blew him a kiss. "See you at three tomorrow, darling."

AUBREY STOOD IN his drawing room doorway, staring from the half-empty dishes on the table to the journalist peacefully sleeping on the sofa.

All evening, he'd imagined Saxby gnawing his fingernails, too anxious to eat. As it was, he might've stayed with Rupert and Henrietta after all: the fellow would never have damned well noticed.

He took a slow, deep breath. Then walked into the entrance hall, hung up his top hat and overcoat, and unbuttoned his gloves.

"You're back." The words were slurred with sleep.

A deep breath as he peeled off his gloves. Another as he laid them on the shelf under the hall mirror. "As you observe." He prepared a tolerant smile and returned to the drawing room.

Saxby was sitting up, blinking. His pomaded hair hung in untidy hanks, and glints at jaw and chin suggested pale stubble.

Deuce take him! Aubrey felt his careful smile sag. It was horribly unfair that Saxby should look endearing when he was annoyed with him. Horribly unfair that even Saxby's sleep-rumpled lounge suit rang a dulcet carillon of 'morning after and ready to go another round' rather than the dull clang of slovenliness.

He strode to the sideboard and grabbed a decanter. "Brandy?"

"Er... thank you. Are you well?"

"A little tired." Aubrey handed Saxby a drink, then dropped into the opposite corner of the sofa.

"And I'm keeping you awake."

"Not really." Aubrey sighed, rubbing his forehead. "It's not you. I'm irritated with myself."

Saxby sipped his brandy, watching Aubrey over the rim of his glass. He seemed wide awake, and tolerably recovered from his earlier distress. "I often find..." Lowering his eyelids, he sipped again. "...the best cure for irritation..." He caught a drip on the glass with the tip of his tongue. "...is... a good, hard shag."

Startled, Aubrey laughed. "Don't suggest it unless you're offering."

"I'm game if you are." Saxby put his glass down. "I've a fair few frustrations of my own to excise." He brought Aubrey's hand to his lips and drew the warm tip of his tongue over the pad of one finger. "Would you care to receive?"

Aubrey's cock twitched as he stared into Saxby's hazel eyes. This was unwise. Extremely unwise. It... wasn't a thing he did anymore, except with Rupert. Saxby seemed kind, but maybe he was the sort to flatter and cajole till he'd got all he wanted, then scald one with contempt and betrayal. And only this morning he'd regretted the night before. This *morning*, for God's sake! And this...

There was so much more to regret if he permitted this.

"Don't worry so." Saxby cradled Aubrey's hand in both his own. "I can receive."

Oh Lord, those gentle eyes.

Anyway, the chap already had everything he needed, if he meant to betray him: this wouldn't make any difference. And a fellow who offered to receive was less likely to humiliate him afterwards.

A reassuring thumb stroked his knuckles. "We can just talk, if you like. Or I can leave."

"No. Don't." Aubrey took a deep breath. "Your original suggestion was—that is to say, er—I believe it would suit us both."

Saxby eased closer.

"But before we begin, I might perhaps relieve a few of your concerns."

Saxby breathed warmth into Aubrey's palm, and kissed it. "Speak, then, lovely creature." A rasp of stubble, pressure of soft lips, and then that tongue tip, tracing his palm to the base of his thumb.

"You're making it awfully difficult even to think."

Saxby's lips curled into a sultry smile. "You say—" he kissed Aubrey's inner wrist "—the most delightful things." He nipped.

Aubrey gasped and shuddered. Swaying forward, he leaned his forehead on Saxby's shoulder.

"That's the way, beautiful." Saxby plucked the glass from Aubrey's lax hand, then stroked the back of his head. "You can tell me about it from there."

Aubrey slid his hand between Saxby's jacket and waistcoat, inhaling warm wool and dense thyme pomade. "Hernedale will write to your editor."

Saxby sighed, pressing his lips to Aubrey's hair. "I didn't offend the lady, then."

"Not a bit. And they mean to squire you around social events for a while: shore up your reputation."

Saxby's hand stilled. "That's... remarkably generous."

Aubrey rolled his head, impatient. Saxby smiled against his ear and resumed stroking.

"Not really. Mmm!" Aubrey arched his neck as Saxby kissed the flesh beneath his ear. "Oh, that's— Mmm. Ru—Hernedale says—it's his fault for needling Lowdon. Lady Hernedale's fed up with her—brother—interfering in—her social life. Look, may I tell you the—details tomorrow?"

A tug on his bow tie. "Certainly."

Aubrey lifted his chin. Deft fingers stripped the tie from his neck, plucked the studs from his collar, and removed it. He fumbled at Saxby's waistcoat buttons. The shirt beneath—made in the new style, soft and unstarched—lay against the man like a second skin. His face heated as he laid a palm on Saxby's warm, firm belly, as Saxby's hands framed his thighs, as Saxby nuzzled the side of his neck.

He eased jacket and waistcoat from Saxby's strong shoulders, tracing muscled arms beneath thin, smooth cotton as he freed them from the sleeves.

As the jacket pooled behind him, Saxby seized Aubrey's naked hands in a grip that made him shudder and melt.

"Saxby," he whispered into the soft shirt front, breathing an intoxicating hint of fresh sweat. "It's been... a while."

"I prefer to take it slowly anyway, beautiful," Saxby murmured into his hair.

Stubble grazed and prickled the side of his neck, was relieved by soft lips and smooth, subtle teeth.

"At least," he added, "to start with."

— Chapter Five —

SUNDAY, 14TH JANUARY 1906

"Fanshawe," Saxby murmured.

Aubrey startled awake in his dim bedroom. He stared at the broad, curtained window opposite, anxiety curdling his stomach and closing his throat.

"Does Grieve wake you early on a Sunday?"

"Later." Aubrey licked dry lips. Had he been drinking more than usual? "An hour later."

"Oh. Then I apologise for disturbing you."

"Quite all right." Two nights. He'd spent two nights with this gossip journalist, in a bed he'd only ever shared with Rupert.

Closing his eyes, he gathered his resolve and persuaded sleep-weighted muscles to roll him over.

Saxby lay at the far edge of the bed, watching him with wary eyes. His pale shoulders were bare above the Prussian blue counterpane, and a strong, lightly tanned hand curled on the pillow beside his face.

And—it wasn't so bad, him being there. Saxby could still destroy his reputation; be the catalyst for his arrest and disgrace. But he needed Aubrey now, so things were more evenly matched than they had been.

Aubrey rested his gaze on the angular jaw; let it drift to well-defined lips which had mapped his skin last night. After all, there was something pleasing in being Saxby's saviour. It set things

57

right between them, even though he'd wept on him. Even though he'd actually *asked* the damned fellow to fuck him.

Saxby watched him. "Should I leave?"

And because he'd asked—because he hadn't presumed he had the upper hand just because he'd fucked him—Aubrey said, "Not yet, unless you want to. But before Grieve arrives, since he knows you were here last night."

He was rewarded with a charming smile. A very charming smile, which drew the warmth from his body to his cheeks. A hand reached across the blue brocade desert between them, and broad fingers brushed his hair back from his face.

"I don't think—" Aubrey swallowed. "I mean there isn't—"

Saxby's face tightened. "Apologies. That wasn't an advance, though I understand it might seem that way." He shuffled onto his back and folded his arms behind his head, staring up at the cerulean silk tester.

Aubrey tensed and his cheeks cooled. "Quite all right." He understood the fellow's disappointment, but there was no need to sulk, for God's sake. "Are you free at three o'clock?"

Saxby faced Aubrey, and almost smiled. "I can be."

"Lady Hernedale suggested meeting at Richmond Park."

Saxby's face closed again.

"Robin Hood Gate."

"That's very kind of her."

Aubrey shrugged, awkward in his own bed. "She said you'd better be seen with them before you go back to—" Gossip journalism "—work."

Saxby's eyes softened. "That's really very generous of her. To consider that. And to act on it. I'll be there."

"Right-ho."

"Actually…" Frowning, Saxby rose onto an elbow. "If—it's not an intrusive question… How do Lord and Lady Hernedale believe you discovered the complaint?"

"I told them you came back to tell me."

"And… how did you explain me knowing your address?"

Aubrey stared at him. "Naturally, they assumed we'd met after I left them at the Gaiety. I told them I'd brought you home."

Saxby closed his eyes. "Naturally?"

Aubrey heaved up onto an elbow too, to bring himself to Saxby's level. "Well, in the first place, there was the way you looked at me. And then I dashed out after you, so..."

"I see." Saxby's voice was gritty. "I'd always supposed only another Uranian would notice that. It seems I must... revisit my assumptions."

"After all," Aubrey said, "it hardly matters."

Saxby's eyelids sprang open. "Just the night before last you were—were *concerned* I might expose you, and now you say it doesn't matter that they know this about you? That people I don't know hold this information about *me*?"

"It doesn't matter," Aubrey explained patiently, "that *these* people know."

"Surely you see the problem!" Saxby sat up, counterpane pooling around his hips.

Aubrey sat as well: too tense to stay still, not wanting Saxby to loom over him.

"You and I have *reason* to hold our peace, even if we come to dislike one another." Saxby's colour was rising unattractively. "If I expose you, I expose myself, and vice versa. But Lord and Lady Hernedale have no reason to avoid exposing me."

"Except then you'd have nothing to lose in exposing *me*," Aubrey said. "Which they wouldn't want. And anyway, they... wouldn't."

Saxby stared at him, openly incredulous.

Aubrey glared back. Was the fellow purposely insulting him, or was it simple ignorance? "I have given you my *word*!"

Saxby sighed and dropped back into the pillows, staring up at the tester.

It was unacceptable. Insupportable.

But at least it removed all temptation to ever again entertain him in private.

LUCIEN CLOSED THE front door to the set, still seething. Fanshawe hadn't given his bloody word: he'd given his opinion. He'd certainly question a similar assertion from Lucien, but then, nobs weren't expected to suspend their intellectual faculties on someone else's say-so.

He'd also refused to share the basin again, which… well, admittedly they'd parted on bad terms, but that might've improved things.

That's the nobility for you, Dad would say. *They're all a bit odd. Never mind it.*

Not that he could ever explain Fanshawe to Dad—or to William, for that matter.

Noel was guarding the entrance to the Ropewalk again—a stroke of luck—but he eyed Lucien with anxious suspicion.

Buggery. Fortunately, there was nobody in sight so early on a Sunday. "Buy you a drink sometime?" Lucien suggested. Noel's face tightened, so he added, "You and your friend."

Noel's face eased. "That'd be nice."

"Ale at the Lamb and Flag?"

"Yeah, all right. Eight o'clock Friday? I work Saturday to Thursday."

At least he'd be able to reassure Noel he wouldn't cause any trouble, for him or the residents of Albany.

Lucien walked home wondering why he'd stayed the night. Twice. With a man who wanted his body for sex but thought it too dirty or common to share a basin of water with afterwards.

But he knew why. Because Fanshawe'd seemed unhappy and tense. Because Fanshawe'd looked after him when he was distressed, and helped when he hadn't had to. Because Fanshawe was beautiful, and irresistibly responsive, and sweetly giving… if only at night.

At his boarding house, Lucien bathed in the shared bathroom and washed his underwear, shirts, and socks while French chalk drew the pomade stains from his suit. He sponged and ironed it and hung everything near the fire to dry, and then, since it was

Sunday, he took the forty-minute walk to Park Lane, and trod up familiar stone steps to a glossy black front door.

Almost before his hand left the door-knocker, Dawson, the butler, answered.

"Good morning, Mr Saxby." He let him in. "Lord Camberhithe is in the library."

"Reading?" Lucien asked, hopeful.

Dawson paused, then eased the door closed, while a footman took Lucien's outdoor things. "No, Mr Saxby."

Buggery.

Lucien strode across the high-ceilinged, marble-floored entrance hall, through an empty drawing room, and into the library beyond.

Half-covered by a blanket, William lay on a chaise longue near the blazing fire, his eyes closed. A glass of water stood on an occasional table beside him, together with his well-read copy of *Don Quixote*.

Lucien paused beside the long mahogany table in the centre of the room.

"I'm not asleep." William didn't open his eyes.

Lucien pulled up an armchair and sat down. "How've you been?"

He looked worse than he had a week ago: his face chalk-pale and gaunt; grey-brown shadows under his eyes. Older than his twenty-nine years.

"Tired. You?"

"Busy."

"Rather you than me." A corner of William's mouth lifted, then slumped. "Pass the glass, would you?"

"Get you a biscuit?"

"Too tired to chew."

Lucien held the glass to William's lips till he swallowed, then lifted it.

"Can hold it myself."

"I know." Lucien smoothed William's hair back from his face. "More?"

"No thanks."

Lucien put the glass down. "Anyone visit this week?"

"My father. Still wants me to move back home."

"Oh." Familiar tension settled behind Lucien's eyes. William's parents imagined 'home' would be more nurturing, even though he'd be no better cared for there, and a lot more frustrated. He'd spend almost as much time alone, too, since he wasn't well enough to travel with them. But they wouldn't badger him about it if Lucien moved back in.

Eyes still closed, William smiled wryly. "And Marjorie brought the kiddies to visit Uncle."

"Oh Lord."

William huffed a laugh. "Noisy little buggers. Only stayed half an hour. I didn't mind."

"Speaking of which, I'll have to leave earlier than usual today."

"Oh?" Anyone who didn't know William well would've missed the hint of disappointment.

"Got an engagement at three. Hernedale."

"Hernedale." William's eyes opened to weary slits. "I'm sure I heard something about him, years ago."

"He got married?"

"Doesn't everyone, except me."

Lucien hadn't, but he wasn't about to draw William's attention to it.

"Mind you, there *was* something about the wife…" William closed his eyes, frowning.

"Don't worry about it."

"No, wait: I remember that bit now. Charlie said she was a dreadful social climber, and a shameless flirt, and swore like a navvy."

William's youngest brother Charles had grown from a sly little snitch into a vicious, unprincipled gossip.

William cracked his eyelids. "Course, that was after she refused his third marriage proposal."

Sensible woman. "I've only met her briefly, but she seemed perfectly respectable."

"Damn it, there was something else... On the tip of my tongue."

Lucien's heart hurt for him. "Don't worry: it really doesn't matter."

"Got to know about a chap before you become associated."

Lucien waited, since he obviously wanted to think, but at last William blew out a sharp sigh.

"Bugger it all anyway. Tell you what, I could bear the rest a lot more easily if it didn't turn my damned brain to wool."

Dawson glided across the Turkish carpet to place a silver tray on the table. Tea for one, alongside a cup of clear broth. William's stomach must be very uneasy. And gooseflesh was rising on his thin wrists despite the oppressive heat of the room.

"Back in a sec." Lucien walked into the hall, then ran up the stairs and along the landing. He dodged a housemaid with an armful of sheets, passed the luxurious rooms that had once been his, and turned into William's bedroom.

William's portly, middle-aged valet, straight red-brown hair streaked with grey, was putting collars away in the dressing room beyond.

"Morning, McHenry."

The valet startled. "Damme! Where'd you spring from?"

"Sorry. Cardigan, please."

McHenry reached into the wardrobe. "You learned your Dad's lessons well."

So well that he wasn't sure who he'd be, without them. "Just habit, being quiet." Lucien managed a grin. "Thanks." He took the folded cardigan and ran back down to the library.

"Still awake, old chap?" he murmured.

"Mmm."

"Brought you a cardigan."

"Oh. Good idea. I am cold, actually."

Lucien sat on the edge of the chaise longue and lifted him forward.

"Damn it," William muttered. "I can do this."

"But you don't have to, for now." Lucien eased the jacket from his shoulders.

"Dear Lord." William leaned his forehead on Lucien's shoulder. "I'm so damned tired, Lucien."

"I know." He slid the cardigan onto him, and then the jacket, before leaning him back to do up the buttons. "Better?" He swept thinning, fine brown hair away from William's eyes.

"Will be." William's face was white.

"Pain?"

"Gut and back," William admitted. "Hips. Knees." He'd never been well for long. Had been too ill to send away to school, which was why his father had made Lucien—his valet's son— William's companion, to live and learn alongside him. It was surprising they'd got along as well as they had: the sedentary, often listless son of a marquis, and the active, horse-mad son of a valet and an ex-lady's-maid.

"It'll ease," Lucien murmured, holding his frail, cold hand.

William huffed. "Always does."

Until the day it didn't. He grew weaker year by year.

"Be better in a few weeks." A corner of William's mouth lifted. "If not, I've remembered you in my will."

Lucien squeezed his hand. "I want all your cravats."

"Be wasted on you. Anyway, I'd damned well buy you cravats if you'd let me."

"Leave a man some pride, William. I'll have your cravats from your grave or not at all."

"Won't be that easy." A little colour had returned to William's face. "You'll have to play McHenry for them. Backgammon. May the best man win."

"That'll be me, then." Lucien sat in the armchair to pour his tea.

"Might be surprised. Subtle man, McHenry."

Lucien helped William with the few sips of broth he wanted, then drank his tea while William dozed off. Once he'd settled, Lucien went to find McHenry, who'd been William's valet since he left the nursery. He'd half-raised them both with meticulous care edged with a resentful resignation William'd never seemed to notice.

"He's passing blood again." McHenry, grim-faced, picked a flatiron from the ironing stove in the basement kitchen and pressed it onto a shirt cuff. William had had an electric iron installed, but McHenry'd used it once, sworn at it, and never touched it again.

"Has he eaten?" Lucien leaned back against the wall.

"Not since breakfast yesterday." Mrs Spence, the small, wiry cook, hoisted a mountain of bread dough from an earthenware basin. "And that was only stewed apple." She slammed the dough onto the floury table, casting clouds into the air. White speckles settled on her warm brown skin and the cap that covered her springy hair. "Nothing but broth since then; not even boiled chicken, and he can usually manage that all right. Mabel! Whip that gelatine!"

Lucien mustered a sympathetic smile for the washed-out looking maid as she redoubled her efforts with the whisk. Dawson might be the butler, but it was McHenry and Mrs Spence, who'd known William since childhood, who ruled the roost between them.

"Probably for the best." McHenry slid the iron into a slot in the stove. "Might give him a chance to heal. The cramps after he eats are something awful." He eased the shirt round on the board.

"Laudanum?" Lucien asked.

"Won't take it anymore." McHenry dipped blunt fingertips into the bowl on top of the stove and flicked water over the shirt. "Gives him nightmares."

Lucien watched him pick up a second iron and smooth it over the shirt tail. "And you? Are you coping?"

"I'll do." McHenry grimaced. "Not as though he's off to balls every night."

"Here." Mrs Spence paused, wrist-deep in dough. "What d'you fancy for lunch, pet? I'm about to put together a bit of something for us all." She liked feeding him: had always had a morsel of left-over pudding for him when he was a child, and an injunction to 'just be a kiddie for a minute, all right?'

"Thanks, but I can't eat in front of him when he can't."

"Well, eat in here, for goodness' sake!" Mrs Spence started kneading again.

"I would, only…" He should just do without: it wouldn't kill him. "I need to be there when he wakes: I'm only here to keep him company."

"What? You wouldn't bother visiting the rest of us?" Her voice soared with false outrage. "Well, I am offended. McHenry, ain't you offended?"

Lucien grinned. "Course I'd visit *you*, Mrs Spence. Anything for you."

"Go on with your sweet-talk! I pity the woman you marry, truly I do."

Lucien ignored the anxious pang in his chest. "She's not even the hint of a dot on the horizon yet."

"That's her good luck, ain't it? She'd need eyes in the back of her head to keep up with your flirting."

"Save your sympathy, Mrs. Spence." McHenry slid the iron back into the ironing stove and flipped the shirt. "Can't see our Lucien ever marrying."

Lucien stared at him, chilled.

"Twenty-eight years old and I've yet to see him walk out with a single girl." McHenry picked up another iron and tapped it to check the temperature. "So you can save those doe-eyes for someone else, Mabel."

"I wasn't!" The whisk stilled.

"That's 'Mr McHenry' to you!" Mrs Spence lifted the dough and slammed it back onto the table. "And tuck that hair back: we don't need to be pulling it out of our teeth when we eat."

"*Mr* McHenry." Mabel dropped the whisk into the bowl, glaring, and shoved a tendril of white-blonde hair into her cap. "I never did, Mr McHenry."

"Just as well." McHenry smoothed the iron over starched white cotton. "Mark my words, he won't settle for less than a duke's daughter."

Lucien's breath escaped in a rush. "That's absurd."

"Oh is it?" McHenry's lips tightened in a one-sided smile. "Absurd. Heh."

"Daft, then." Lucien folded his arms.

"If you were going to marry a working woman, it'd have been 'daft' the first time round."

"Let the boy alone, McHenry."

"Never said there was anything wrong with it." McHenry slid the iron into the stove and peeled the shirt from the board. "Long as a man knows himself. And doesn't forget where he come from."

"No chance of that, around my dad."

"Course not." Mrs Spence dusted the flour from her hands. "Off with you, then, pet. Go see his lordship. I'll make a cold collation: if he wakes, it can wait till he dozes off again."

Lucien escaped gratefully and sank into the armchair beside William, who was still asleep.

He might as well let McHenry believe he was a snob: it was safer than the alternative. Damn it. He probably *should've* asked women to walk out with him from time to time, but it seemed cruel to raise hopes he'd never fulfil.

William was still asleep when Dawson brought his lunch, so Lucien ate at the long table, alone with his thoughts and the tick of the grandfather clock, marking off the seconds of William's life. The thought closed his throat, so he abandoned his meal to check the periodicals shelf: might as well do some research while he was here.

Nothing more recent than 1899: four years before the founding of the WSPU. William must've cancelled the subscriptions after Lucien left. Sighing, he sat in the armchair and flicked through *Don Quixote*.

A duke's daughter indeed! McHenry must think him a fool.

William roused several times to chat, and to ask—as always—if there was anything Lucien needed, but he dozed more than he spoke. In the still, silent room, McHenry's words drowned out Cervantes'.

Of course Lucien wasn't a snob.

But… Fanshawe was an earl's son.

No. He'd never consider himself too good for his own class. Besides, he had encounters with other working men. Frequent encounters. He was no less careful of their pleasure than he'd been of Fanshawe's.

He could never stay the night with them, though. Married men couldn't invite a fellow home, for obvious reasons; and, like most single working men, Lucien couldn't have visitors in his rooms at all, let alone overnight. The lodging houses that allowed that sort of thing had poor reputations: in a single visit, you could catch both syphilis and cholera, and lose not only your purse but the clothes off your back. Otherwise he—

Memory supplied the solid warmth of Fanshawe behind him, cradling him to sleep in a soft, clean bed; the soul-deep bliss of skin on skin.

Shit.

"William? I have to go." It was a bit early, but Lucien laid *Don Quixote* on the table. "I'll visit again tomorrow, instead."

"A'right." William half-roused.

"Don't wait up if you're sleepy: I'll come by the next night, as well."

"Lucien."

Lucien turned back.

"Thank you."

"Don't be absurd." Lucien squeezed William's cold, dry hand. "Where else could I scrounge a decent glass of brandy?"

IT WAS AN awkward, stilted outing.

To begin with, Fanshawe was in the gleaming black barouche too. And then Hernedale, of course, sat beside his wife, which left Lucien the seat beside Fanshawe. And that was…

Well. They hadn't parted on the friendliest of terms, and Lucien wondered why the devil the fellow had come, knowing he'd be there.

As the barouche rocked along the broad lanes of the park, Fanshawe's arm and thigh intermittently pressed his, then swayed away. An unnerving intimacy from a man he barely knew, and yet whose body—the scent and weight of it, the textures of its skin and hair, its involuntary gasps and sighs—was utterly familiar. The pressure of limbs which had slid along his naked flesh—had clamped around him and clung—kept his body alert to the possibilities, even as common sense left him wary of the unpredictable personality beside him.

Hernedale, without reading material in his hands, was disconcertingly shrewd. A glance flicked between Fanshawe and himself reminded Lucien that this man—Oh Lord! And Lady Hernedale, too!—had a fair idea of what had passed between them. That knowledge pressed on his chest like a boulder, even though they seemed friendly enough with Fanshawe that Lucien might, provisionally, accept the fellow's word that they were safe.

Lady Hernedale flirted with him, which was worrying, but Hernedale watched indulgently, even when Lucien cautiously followed her lead. So far, so good.

But Lucien had never in his life felt more like a lower-class intruder, which, considering his extensive experience in the role, was saying a lot. Hernedale and Fanshawe chatted with him, but it felt forced, and Fanshawe avoided meeting his gaze. It couldn't have been clearer that the nobs were only tolerating him out of charity.

They left Lucien at his boarding house with an invitation to the Victoria and Albert Museum the following Sunday.

"We'll work out further arrangements as we go along." Hernedale offered him his card and a gloved hand to shake.

Pride demanded that Lucien decline politely, save himself and them further discomfort. Pride also demanded that he redeem his reputation and maintain his independence. Mustering a smile and a humiliating murmur of gratitude, he submitted his own card and hand to Hernedale.

They drove away without a backward glance: tall, straight-backed, and unnaturally pale, like a matched set of well-maintained china figurines. Back to their real interests, now they were rid of the imposition of his company.

Lucien stared at his front door, then turned away. It was a cold afternoon, and the sun would soon set, but he was restless.

Tucking his riding cane under his arm, he let his feet carry him where they would, through the endless racket of horses' hooves, rumbling cart wheels, cries of street vendors, and the occasional stuttering growl of a motor car.

Apparently, his feet wanted St James' Park. Having arrived, he didn't quite fancy it, but it was quieter than the streets, and peace was what he needed.

It wasn't empty, of course. As Lucien trod deserted paths in the gathering dark, the odd whisper or chuckle reached him from shadowed trees; the regular beat of flesh on flesh; the occasional moan or muted cry. It was comfortable: he was among his people, even if he didn't know them all personally.

A footfall behind and to his right. He turned as a light brown hand brushed his sleeve, and Ben, small and powerfully built, fell into step beside him. "Wotcher, your lordship. What you doing here, all by yourself?"

Lucien's heart lightened despite the tease. "Waiting for you to brighten my dark evening." It was reflex, really.

"That right?" Ben's face softened. "Want to go somewhere, Luce?"

He was a good friend, and stunning besides; usually, Lucien wanted Ben as often as Ben wanted him back. But today he was wounded, shrivelled with uncertainty and mortification, and desperately self-protective.

"Thanks, Ben: not today."

Ben tugged his cap further over his tight curls. "Looking for someone else? Cause I can take off if you are."

"No. Just out for a walk." And in need of a friend.

Ben seemed to hear what he didn't say. He kept pace with Lucien, coat collar up and shoulders hunched against the cold. "New lad at the club last night," he offered.

Lucien followed the topic change gratefully. "Any good?"

"Needs more muscle and a tighter fist for boxing. S'like being swatted with your granny's shawl."

Lucien laughed. He didn't particularly enjoy instructing beginners, but the routine of practice was soothing, and the intense focus of sparring distracted him from the jangle of everyday concerns.

"Footwork ain't up to much either," Ben added.

"We can work on that," Lucien said. "And muscle will come."

"Said he'd be along Tuesday night."

Lucien sighed. "Got to visit a sick friend, Tuesday." He didn't speak about William outside William's household, or even about his own childhood: it was difficult to do without seeming above himself. "Might pop in towards the end, if he settles early."

Ben glanced at him, then away. "Ain't catching, is it?"

"No. Or I'd have caught it years ago."

"Only I can't afford to miss work. Besides—there's Jem and his chest." An edge of desperation in Ben's tone.

"How is he?"

"Made it to eight months old." Ben crammed his fists deeper into his coat pockets. "That's more'n we expected last month."

Lucien stared at him. "What does the doctor say?"

"What doctor?" Ben's shoulders tensed. "Where'd *I* get the money for a bloody doctor?"

Lucien winced at his own thoughtlessness. "From me, now I know it's a problem."

"Right. Well. I don't know." Ben took several deep breaths, staring up at the sky, though only the Evening Star was out. "Cath's auntie's brought him this far. Maybe her camphor and what-not will pull him through. If…" He blinked and blew out a long breath. It ghosted into the freezing air, fragile but corporeal, then dissipated. "Shit. I might come back to you on that, Luce. If he gets worse. I wouldn't for anything else, but—"

"I can afford it. Don't worry."

"Right. Well." Ben flashed Lucien a quick, hard smile, then looked up again, blinking. "Ain't as if I can pay you back, or give you anything in return. Cath could make you a nice coat or something, but you'd have to buy the materials yourself, so where's the point?"

"I could do with a nice coat."

"Could you?"

He needed almost a whole new wardrobe. But he couldn't afford that, and anyway, Ben spoke of Cath enough that Lucien knew she wouldn't have time to sew anything free of charge between caring for three children—one very sick—and the sewing piece-work that consumed her every waking moment and brought in only a few desperately needed pennies.

"But can you afford a doctor *and* good cloth?" Ben asked.

Lucien paused.

"There you go. Bad enough you paying for a doctor, let alone paying again just to soothe my pride."

"All right." Relieved, Lucien let it go. "Look. Better take my card." He slid the silver case from his pocket and offered Ben a visiting card. "Between my sick friend and a bit of bother at work, I won't be at the club as often. If I'm not home, my landlady'll take a message."

Ben took the card slowly. "Ain't serious is it? Your bit of bother?"

Anxiety buzzed in Lucien's belly. "Might have to change jobs." He snapped the case shut and put it away.

Ben held his gaze, wordless.

Lucien mustered a smile, trying to reassure himself as much as Ben. "I won't be out of work in any case, but I'd rather stay where I am, and being seen with a couple of nobs will help."

"These nobs." Ben tucked the card carefully into an inside pocket of his thin coat. "They all right with that, then? Keeping company with you?"

"So far."

Ben whistled, conjuring another briefly materialised ghost, and shoved his bare hands back into his pockets. "You really know how to land with your bum in the butter, don't you?"

"Seems like," Lucien agreed. He would never quite fit with his own class, but it'd be churlish to resent that not-belonging, considering the advantages it brought.

Ben sighed. When Lucien caught his eye, he forced a quick grin and glanced away.

Lucien paused, gazing at dark eyes framed by fine creases of worry, at full lips tight with stress that kisses could ease, at least for now. At shoulders hunched with tension that might be roared into the night, or gasped into a muscular arm or shoulder. At Ben, who hid his emotions behind a brusque mask, but who entrusted them, sometimes, to Lucien. Ben, who was strong and self-reliant, but whose immediate need Lucien could meet, in this, at least. Ben. Whose need looked for a twin in Lucien's body, and found one.

"Still want to go somewhere?" Lucien murmured. "Strictly for therapeutic reasons," he added, trying to lighten the mood.

"Whatever that means, your wordy lordship." Ben clapped him on the arm. "You know I'll make it good for you."

He did.

— Chapter Six —

AUBREY RETIRED TO his room in Hernedale House at the end of the evening. 'His' because he stayed so often that he kept toilet necessities and day and evening clothes here. 'His' because nobody else was ever allocated this room, across the hall from Rupert's.

Grieve had dressed him here for dinner before returning to Albany for the night. Other valets, Aubrey imagined, might produce a flow of polite chat as they dressed their gentlemen: "Pleasant weather we're having." "These cuff links look particularly well by firelight." Not Grieve. He worked in efficient silence, speaking only when necessary. Despite a decade as his employer, Aubrey had no idea of the man's real personality.

Now Aubrey changed into a nightshirt in front of a blazing fire. He picked up his book, climbed into the warmed bed, and relaxed into the pile of pillows.

Perhaps an hour later, the house was quiet. He pulled on dressing gown and slippers, crept into the darkened hallway, and slid into Rupert's bedroom.

Rupert was in bed. Reading, of course. Debonair above the neck, thanks to his precise, angular features and modish hair-cut; homey beneath, due to the white silk nightshirt and the counterpane tucked around his waist. Aubrey closed the door, opening to the tenderness of the moment.

Rupert glanced up from the calf-bound book, smiled, and returned to it.

Aubrey toed off his slippers and laid his dressing gown on the upholstered dressing stool. Then remembered the condom in the pocket, dug it out and laid the silver case on the bedside table—because one never knew, and it broke the mood to get up and hunt for it—and then, at last, climbed into bed.

Rupert absently raised an arm.

He settled his head on Rupert's collarbone, squinting at the book. *Lysistrata.* The Greek text was at an awkward angle, and he wasn't in the mood for it anyway, so he curled an arm around Rupert's waist, closed his eyes, and relaxed as long fingers combed his hair. Rupert turned the page, and Aubrey opened an eye. The scene ended in a page and a half. Good. He closed it again, waiting till Rupert shut the book.

"There." Lips pressed the top of his head.

Rupert had been unusually quiet all evening. It was on Henrietta's account that he'd met Saxby today, but somehow Aubrey felt responsible. "Tired from this afternoon, sweetheart?" He hadn't even had a book to retreat behind in the carriage.

"A bit." Rupert kissed the tip of Aubrey's nose. "As strangers go, though, he's relatively undemanding."

Undemanding but dismayingly alluring, even clothed and in the open air. The outing had been a horrifying exercise in avoiding hazel eyes and bracing against the occasional soft pressure of limbs; in reminding himself that he'd absolutely sworn off the fellow.

Henrietta strode in from the dressing room that separated her bedroom from Rupert's. Brown hair hung in a long plait down her lace-trimmed, ivory silk nightdress. "Are we talking about your Mr Saxby?"

"Not mine," Aubrey said quickly.

"He's quite charming." She slid into bed beside Aubrey and nestled close. "Seems to know more about our friends than I do," she added mischievously.

"Oh, well, you know." He wrapped an arm around her as she reached for Rupert's hand across his chest. "Society pages." Poor bugger'd have to face his editor tomorrow.

"Let's hope we don't end up in those pages," Rupert said.

"Well, I mean—" Aubrey craned to look up at him. "He knows nothing discreditable about you, so how could he?"

Henrietta's hand tightened on Rupert's. "He struck me as a decent sort anyway."

"Mmm." Aubrey didn't want to think about Saxby; he especially didn't want to think about Saxby betraying him. He tugged the sage green ribbon from the end of Henrietta's plait and began to unravel her hair one-handed.

"You'll be plaiting it later," she warned him.

"Mmhm."

"Right-ho then. No need to give yourself cramp." She laid her head on his belly, allowing better access.

He and Rupert unwound it, section by slow section, till it spread in bergamot-scented, gold-glinting glory over their chests. Then Aubrey slid his fingers into her hair and massaged her scalp.

"Ohhh." She grew heavier. "It never feels this good when Molly does it."

"Should hope not." Rupert eased his fingers into her hair, too. "It's inappropriate to tup the maid."

The fleeting brush and nudge of Rupert's warm fingers against his own in the cool silk of Henrietta's hair set Aubrey's heart racing.

Henrietta laughed. "You've an entire percussion section playing under my head, Aubrey." She slid a hand over the counterpane covering his hip, then stroked lower, along his thigh. Rupert's fingers tangled with Aubrey's in Henrietta's hair, and squeezed, and Aubrey gasped and tensed.

Henrietta's hand pressed upward. "Oh *Grandma!*" she breathed, "What a big—"

"—*hard* cock you have," Rupert murmured into his hair, stroking his fingertips.

"Oh, it *is*," Henrietta said, breathy and teasing. "So very, *very* hard." Her fingernails mapped his dimensions through the counterpane.

Aubrey clutched Rupert's fingers as his hips strained upward. "All—the better to fuck you with."

"What an eager wolf you are." Fingernails over fabric caught under the head of his cock, then slowly scratched up towards the tip. Aubrey groaned, pressing his lips to Rupert's collarbone.

Henrietta laughed, low and throaty. "You're very susceptible tonight, Aubrey."

"Are—are you?" he managed.

"Oh my dear." She grazed her knuckles down the length of his cock. "I'm positively desperate."

Rupert kissed Aubrey's head and gently untangled their fingers, and Aubrey's ardour cooled.

"Not susceptible tonight, darling?" Henrietta asked.

"Sadly, no." Leaning forward, he kissed her forehead, then Aubrey's. "But the dalliance was a delight."

"Shall we go to Henrietta's room?"

"Only if you'd rather. I'm enjoying your company." He picked up his book, and Aubrey met Henrietta's gaze.

There was as much to be said for loving in pairs as for conversation in pairs, but it was more comfortable when someone said in advance that they weren't inclined. One was perfectly entitled to change one's mind, of course, but— Well. The mood had been shattered.

Neither of them wanted Rupert to feel responsible for that, though.

Henrietta growled and gently worried the sides of Aubrey's counterpane-covered cock between her teeth: at the base, the middle, the tip. And the mood was restored.

"Like that, do you?" Aubrey seized her and tumbled her onto her back beside him.

"Oh I do!" She grinned.

Her thighs parted for his knee, and he gazed down at her heart-shaped face framed by bright hair. Undoing her top button, he bent and brushed his lips over her collar-bone. He undid the next, folded back the open edge and drew the tip of his tongue alongside the fold, from the swell of her breast to her throat. She tilted her head in invitation. He nuzzled and kissed and nipped her slender neck, and she gasped and clung to him as he opened the last two buttons.

Setting careful teeth at the junction of her throat and collarbone, he slid a hand up her thigh, under her nightdress, and she moaned, clutching his shoulders and curling towards his teeth. Impatient, then, he tugged at the nightdress, and something ripped.

"Damnation!" He sat up to assess the damage.

"Don't worry about it." Henrietta tugged at him.

"Don't know why either of you bothers with clothes in the bedroom." Rupert turned a page. "Can't improve on perfection."

"True enough." Henrietta sat up and pulled the nightdress over her head. "Take it off, Aubrey."

Aubrey stripped off his nightshirt. Henrietta folded her arms around him and sank back into the pillows, dragging him over her, sliding her limbs against his.

Awareness shrank to the glide of warm, living skin on skin; to lips and tongue and the soft press of small breasts in his hand, in his mouth; to fingernails gliding up his spine and into his hair.

Some uncounted time later, when she was moaning, pressing her soft, inviting quim into his mouth, while his thumb, slick from her vagina, rubbed over and around her ring, the mattress dipped, and a warm hand smoothed down his spine. He glanced up without pausing to see Rupert sitting naked beside him, one hand on his back and the other on Henrietta's thigh.

"Changed my mind," he murmured.

Aubrey wound the fingers of his free hand into Rupert's, still on Henrietta's thigh. Rupert kissed Aubrey's fingers, and Henrietta's knee. His other hand stroked lower, to cup and squeeze Aubrey's buttock.

Henrietta gasped as Rupert's teeth grazed her knee, as Aubrey circled her clitoris with his tongue. Aubrey closed his eyes and immersed himself in sensation: in the smooth, slick flesh between his lips; in firm muscle easing under his thumb; in the delicious warmth and pressure of a knowing hand on his balls and the base of his cock.

"Oh!" Henrietta clutched his hair and clamped her thighs to his head. "Oh God! Wait. Stop."

Aubrey stilled, pulse throbbing in his throat and ears. Henrietta pressed, soft and tense on the sides of his face, wet and silken on his tongue.

Rupert laid his head on Aubrey's back—a tickle of hair and a shallow scrape of stubble—then brushed his lips along Aubrey's spine.

Henrietta blew out a long breath, her body relaxing. "Just... not yet: that's all."

Aubrey flattened his tongue and licked her from vagina to clitoris in a single, firm sweep. "Right-ho."

Rupert moved, and Aubrey rolled to the side of the bed, reaching into the bedside table for a clean cloth. The mattress rocked behind him as he wiped his face and hands. When he turned, Rupert was lying on his back with Henrietta leaning over him, her hair shrouding their faces. She sat up, flinging back waist-length hair, and knelt astride Rupert's hips, facing him, then sank onto his cock. Rupert groaned and smoothed a palm over one small breast.

Tucking her legs close to Rupert, she held out a hand to Aubrey.

Aubrey straddled Rupert too, his back to Henrietta's front, thighs spread awkwardly wide to accommodate her knees. Henrietta tugged him closer. He leaned back as she leaned forward, each supporting the other's instability. Then she circled her hips, grinding onto Rupert, dropped her hand to Aubrey's cock, and rose.

Reaching back, Aubrey laid a hand, palm up, on Rupert's pubis, and she came down, wet and warm, on his fingers. As she rose again, he shifted his hand, and when she came down, her gasp told him he was in exactly the right spot.

Rupert slid his hands up Aubrey's thighs, over his hips, to his waist, as Henrietta stroked his cock and ground on his fingers. Aubrey wobbled, and Rupert's broad hand fanned across his ribs, holding him in position; holding his gaze, too, as he pinched Aubrey's nipple and held the pressure.

Aubrey groaned. Henrietta rested her soft face on his back, mouthing his skin till he shuddered helplessly.

Rupert released his nipple at last, but only to pinch the other one. Sensation needled through his body all the way to his balls.

"Oh God, Rupert!" He clutched the supporting arm.

Henrietta laughed breathlessly behind him.

"Is that good, Aubrey?" Rupert murmured.

"Yes!"

Rupert tightened his grip.

"Oh God, yes!"

Henrietta circled her hips, dragged her tongue and nipples across his shuddering back, drew her fingernails lightly up and down his cock.

Rupert released Aubrey's nipple and rubbed it with the ball of his thumb, soothing the sting. Then he folded his hand around Henrietta's, and squeezed.

And then there was only the burn in Aubrey's thighs and the breathless ache of Rupert's hard hand supporting him; Henrietta's soft, shifting weight, and her lips and tongue and hair on his back; the firm, regular tug on his cock, and Rupert's hungry dark eyes watching his heating face.

Then even the burn and Rupert's eyes receded, and primal rhythm was everything. He pounded into the warm cylinder of Henrietta's and Rupert's hands, panting and desperate, until climax seized him: wrenching a bellow from his gut, twisting every muscle almost to cramping, floating blobs of white light across his vision.

He came to with Rupert's semen-covered hand over Henrietta's, slowly, smoothly pumping his cock. "That's the way, beloved," he was crooning.

"Oh God," he panted. Pain seared the length of his quivering thighs.

Rupert twisted gently up, then down again. "Is that good?"

"Fuck." He leaned back against Henrietta, and she kissed his shoulder-blade, grinding onto his aching, almost numb fingers.

"Shit." Trembling, he fell forward over Rupert, bracing himself on his elbows, taking his weight from her. But it also meant his hand slid from under her. "I think… I'm done."

Rupert stretched up to kiss him, and the hands on his cock eased.

Henrietta laughed her low, throaty laugh. "Very, very *well-done*, I'd say." Her sticky hand slid to his hip as she nuzzled his back.

"Oh God, yes." Stiff and awkward, he rolled off Rupert and onto his back, then edged to the side of the bed on uncooperative thighs, reaching for the cloth.

"Don't worry," Rupert said. "I can wait."

No, he couldn't. Rupert abhorred mess on his skin, except at the height of climax. He must be twitching to be rid of it. Aubrey snatched at the cloth, head swimming.

"I'll do it." Henrietta took the cloth from his hand. "Enjoy the glow."

Closing his eyes, he floated, heart pounding, thighs burning, half-aware of movement beside him. A slightly sticky cloth wiped his groin and hip and fingers. The mattress sank beside him, and a familiar rhythm started.

He opened bleary eyes. Rupert arched over Henrietta, braced on his elbows, watching her stroke her clitoris.

She held out her free hand, and Aubrey hitched closer and took it. He lapsed into a warm haze, punctuated by the quick rock of the mattress, by the slap of flesh on flesh, by Rupert's moans and Henrietta's gasping cries, by her flexing grip on his hand.

Some time later, he roused. They were still labouring, hot and flushed and desperate with pleasure—desperate for more—but not quite there. He rolled Henrietta's nipple between finger and thumb. She gasped, and Rupert looked down, grinned, and delicately toothed the other.

Aubrey squeezed Henrietta's hand, then let it go and sat up to stroke Rupert's spine. Rupert arched his back and groaned, his lips clamping on Henrietta's nipple. Aubrey smoothed over Rupert's buttocks, then slid his fingers into the valley between them. Rupert gasped and pushed into his palm.

So Aubrey sucked a finger and pressed it to Rupert's ring. The effect was electric. Rupert sped up, moaning, and Henrietta groaned and twisted under him. Aubrey cupped her breast and rolled her nipple between finger and thumb as he eased into Rupert's warm, smooth flesh.

"Oh *God*!" Rupert's hips drove between Henrietta's body and Aubrey's finger, and Henrietta arched forward, yearning towards them both.

"Yes!" she moaned. "Rupert, fuck me! Aubrey, oh yes!"

Rupert wrapped an arm around Henrietta's thigh and lifted her leg, pounding into her.

"Oh! Oh yes!" Her eyes closed and her lips parted; her hair lay around her, a tangled glory of gold-flecked brown. Rupert stared down at her, wild-eyed, a light sheen of sweat over his face, hair hanging in untidy hanks.

Aubrey's satiated cock stirred and tried to rise.

"I'm close, Hettie," Rupert panted. "Are you—"

"Fuck me!" she gasped. So he did.

Aubrey pressed deeper, relishing the tight band of muscle sliding over his knuckle, the warm, smooth flesh beyond. Relishing Henrietta's soft breast in his palm; her firm nipple between finger and thumb. He kissed Rupert's shoulder—and Rupert groaned, long and deep. Muscle clamped around Aubrey's finger as he rammed close and tight into Henrietta and held still, panting.

"Oh, sweetheart. Sweetheart," Aubrey whispered into his skin, overcome by the warm, choking ache of love.

"Oh God!" Henrietta's hand worked between them. Aubrey stroked her breast and belly, resting his other hand on Rupert's smooth, round buttocks, letting it ride with him as Rupert managed a few more plunges. And Henrietta cried out. Her body arced and she clutched Rupert, shuddering and moaning, crushing her face into his shoulder. He kissed her head, crooning soft words of love, while her hand slowed, then stopped.

She gradually uncurled and fell back into the pillows. "Dear Lord!" she whispered.

Rupert bowed his head, resting his forehead in the crook of her neck.

Aubrey slid his almost-dry finger from Rupert's body by increments, allowing the muscle time to relax—he really should've fetched the oil. Then he collapsed beside Henrietta, and watched Rupert kiss the pulse leaping in her throat, and then her lips.

Turning, Rupert pressed warm lips to Aubrey's, his uneven breath rushing past Aubrey's ear. He laid his cheek along Aubrey's. "Love you," he whispered, resting his weight against him. "*Love* you." Then he rolled over beside Henrietta, fumbling for the cloth.

Aubrey closed his eyes, reached for Henrietta's smooth hand, and listened to Rupert's movements, soon over; to the thud of his own heartbeat, until it faded into inaudibility; and then to Rupert's and Henrietta's breath becoming slower, more regular, in the quiet room.

Beyond the foot of the bed, the un-banked fire popped and snapped, but uninvited January drafts crept in to pierce the comforting heat. He dragged the covers up over them all.

Henrietta snuggled backwards into his arms and drew Rupert closer, and Aubrey curled around her, nuzzling her tangled hair, dropping sleepy kisses on the back of her neck.

She wriggled. Stilled. Shifted again. And sighed. "Damn it all. I need the WC."

Yawning, Aubrey sat up and swung his legs off the bed to let her out.

She rolled over and half-fell onto her feet, her face in his lap. "Bloody nuisance," she muttered, groping on the floor for her nightdress. Standing at last, she dragged it on.

Rupert urged Aubrey back into bed and snuggled closer, an arm around his waist, as Henrietta closed the door carefully behind her.

They lay, loose-limbed and sated, until the door opened and closed again.

Henrietta handed Aubrey a wet facecloth and slid into bed beside Rupert. "I want a fireplace in the WC."

"That bad?" Rupert curled around her while Aubrey wiped himself.

"I'm frozen. And I have to get up again to plait my hair. We should install radiators."

Aubrey and Rupert stared at her.

She laughed. "You could still have your beloved open fires."

"Better get it over with." Aubrey passed the cloth to Rupert and dragged on his nightshirt and dressing gown. "We won't want to get up once we're comfortable." He twitched the counterpane from the bed.

"I don't want to get up *now*."

Aubrey swaddled her in the counterpane, settled her on the dressing stool, and brushed her hair as she yawned.

Rupert wiped himself, put his nightshirt on against the drafts, and took the used cloths to his dressing room. Then he brought Aubrey and Henrietta each a glass of water, banked the fire, and settled on the bed behind them to read. Fire crackled. Bristles hissed through smooth hair, stuttered over snarls. The atmosphere was soothing, almost hypnotic: it invited confidences.

Aubrey put the brush down to tease a stubborn tangle with his fingertips. "I let Saxby stay the night."

Henrietta half-turned, then paused and turned back. "Did you?"

"Er… Twice, in fact."

Silence.

Just as well he'd stopped seeing Saxby: the fellow fouled his judgement. He glanced behind him.

Rupert's book was open, but his attention was on Aubrey. "That's... unusual."

"Unprecedented," Aubrey admitted, picking up the hairbrush.

"He's charming," Henrietta mused. The brush hissed comfortably. "Good company, too."

Silence.

"Actually," Aubrey said at last, "he's— Well, I mean he *is* good company, but also rather uncomfortable. Sometimes."

"I hope you didn't feel obliged to come along today." A quiet tap as Rupert set his book aside. "Hettie and I are committed because we almost ruined the fellow, but you needn't be."

"No, I—" Aubrey paused the brush in smooth, glinting hair. "I wanted to." But why? Why did he let Saxby affect him this way?

"So." Henrietta snaked a slender arm out of the counterpane and reached back to pat his thigh. "You're not *that* uncomfortable with him."

"Evidently." Aubrey slid the brush to the ends of her hair. He was far too damned comfortable with Saxby, at times.

"S'pose you'd better just enjoy it while it lasts," Rupert said. Fabric sighed against fabric. "And end it when you've had enough."

Aubrey glanced round to see Rupert huddled under the blankets with his eyes closed. "D'you want some of this water?" There were only two glasses in the room. Of course.

"Had a drink before I brought yours."

"Right-ho." He put the brush on the dressing table. Gathering Henrietta's hair, he braided it, then pinched the end between finger and thumb. "Ribbon?"

"You had it last."

Damnation. "Hold this a minute." He handed Henrietta her braid, then looked on the bedside table, on the floor around it, and under the edge of the bed. He found it at last, in the bed, half under the pillow.

Taking the braid back from her, he tied off the end.

Henrietta stood and cupped his cheek. "Don't worry. He needs our help: he's not going to betray you."

Aubrey sighed.

"Seems a decent enough fellow in any case."

"Probably."

"Bit late if he isn't." Rupert hauled the blankets higher.

"Might as well enjoy it, regardless," Henrietta suggested. "Nothing to lose at this point."

"Oddly enough—" Aubrey climbed in beside Rupert "—that's not a particularly comforting thought."

"No." Rupert drew him closer. "'S true though."

Henrietta whisked the counterpane over the bed. "You'll only be perfectly safe when he drops off his perch."

Aubrey's heart clenched painfully.

She switched off the electric light, then climbed in beside him and tugged her nightdress straight. "Since you're not about to arrange that, you might as well stop worrying." In flickering, fire-lit darkness, she kissed his cheek, then reached for Rupert's hand and kissed his fingers. "Sleep well, my darlings."

MONDAY, 15TH JANUARY 1906

Aubrey woke to a dull red glow. The fire must've dwindled to embers. Time to go.

Rupert and Henrietta had both turned in their sleep, so he wasn't squeezed between them anymore, but he was overheated anyway: a drawback of sleeping in the middle. He eased up the bed, hoping not to disturb them.

Rupert stirred. "Going already?"

"It's that time," Aubrey murmured. He pressed a kiss to Rupert's forehead, then to his sleep-warmed lips.

"Mmm. Too soon." Rupert kissed him back.

"Always is. But since you're awake…" Aubrey nudged him.

Rupert groaned, but sat and leaned forward to let Aubrey out. Much more comfortable than sliding out of the top of the covers and shuffling down the middle of the bed on hands and heels and buttocks.

Aubrey kissed the nape of Rupert's neck an instant before he slumped back into the pillows.

"C'mere." Rupert reached for him.

"Another time." Aubrey squeezed his hand. "G'night, sweetheart." He picked up his dressing gown and slippers, eased the door open and slipped out.

Muted sounds downstairs told him servants were already at work. He dropped his slippers on his bedroom floor, his dressing gown on the chest of drawers, and climbed into bed, yawning. Might get a couple of hours' sleep before breakfast.

A thought struck him. "Shit!" He launched himself across the room and shoved a hand into each pocket of his dressing gown. "*Shit!*" He yanked it on, cramming his feet into slippers while knotting the cord: he'd pretend he was going to the WC, if a servant spotted him. Opening the door, he glanced along the hallway—empty—and slid into Rupert's bedroom, closing the door behind him.

"Mmm?" Rupert half-raised his head.

"Forgot my damned condom," Aubrey whispered. Reflected firelight glinted red from the edge of the case. He dropped it into his pocket, grateful it hadn't been knocked off the bedside table.

"Servants'd probably have—" Rupert yawned "—assumed it was mine, if they found it."

Aubrey stared at his dark shape in the bed. "No they damned well wouldn't."

Rupert paused. "Oh. No. You're right." As an only child, Rupert's title and property would be inherited by a cousin unless he produced an heir. Six years after his marriage, there was still no sign of one. "I might have one anyway. For—er—prostitutes or mistresses or what have you."

"In a case your valet has never seen. And you'd leave it in full view of your wife."

"I s'pose—"

"See you at breakfast." Aubrey opened the door, glanced both ways and slipped into his own room. He flung his dressing gown at the chest of drawers, kicked off his slippers, and dropped into bed.

It was unreasonable to be so annoyed—Rupert was half-asleep, after all—but Aubrey was buzzing with shock at how nearly he'd betrayed them all. For Rupert to brush it off was infuriating. This wasn't just an affair: those were common enough, and Henrietta's position would save her from complete ostracism. This was... was taking their *lives* in their hands—his and Rupert's, anyway—and even Henrietta mightn't ride out a scandal of them all in the same bed.

Aubrey shakily poured a glass of water from the decanter beside the bed. Sleep was impossible. And—he picked up last night's book—he wasn't in the mood for Tom bloody Jones.

He put the book down gently, out of habitual respect for Rupert's feelings. Then he lay back and glared at the ceiling, waiting for slow dawn to brighten the room.

RUPERT WAS QUIETER than usual at breakfast. Not *sullen*, of course—he was never sullen—just... quiet. Aubrey wished he could apologise for his earlier sharpness, but the breakfast room's door was, naturally, open to a house full of alert servants.

Henrietta looked fresh from her usual pre-breakfast horse ride, but she was quiet, too. Obviously she'd noticed the mood between Rupert and himself.

The butler brought in the morning post. He offered one side of the silver salver to Henrietta, waited while she took several envelopes, then offered the other to Rupert. Rupert, heavy-eyed, took his post, dropped it beside his plate, and then ignored it, chewing steadily through game pie, kidneys, and buttered rolls. But Henrietta picked up an envelope, then pounced on the postcard beneath.

"From Penny!" She sounded relieved to have a topic of conversation. "You remember my cousin Penelope, Aubrey? You met at the Devonshire's ball, season before last."

Aubrey cast his mind back. "Blonde hair, green eyes?"

"Mmm. Just got back from the continent yesterday."

"And sent a postcard already?"

"To invite me to visit. I've got an NUWSS meeting this morning: might go directly from there." Henrietta cut the envelope open with a letter knife and slid out a gilt-edged card. "And the Pevenseys are hosting a musical recital. 'A great talent,' it says."

"Aren't they all, until you hear them." Rupert stabbed a kidney with his fork.

Henrietta laughed. "Certainly!" She slid the invitation towards Rupert. "We might go, my dear? Make up our own minds?"

Aubrey's throat closed.

"If you like." Rupert peered at the card. "I'll check my diary."

"Will you come, Aubrey? You're bound to be invited."

Of course he'd be invited. He mightn't be the catch of the season, but he was reasonably attractive, had good breeding and excellent connections, and would secure a respectable settlement from his father when he married. Any number of eligible young women had subtly indicated their interest in becoming Mrs Fanshawe.

Aubrey laid his cutlery on his plate and choked down a mouthful of tea. "Depends on the date. I'll check when I get home."

Home to Albany. Because Hernedale House could never be his home. However long and passionately he loved Rupert and Henrietta, he'd never share their name, nor they, his. There'd never be an invitation inscribed to 'The Earl and Countess Hernedale and The Hon. Mr Fanshawe'. He'd never openly share a bed with them.

He'd been Rupert's lover since they were a pair of lonely misfits at school, but Rupert and Henrietta belonged together in a way he'd never belong with either of them, let alone both. In a way he could only ever belong with his wife: a woman he had yet to meet.

Henrietta discussed the rest of her post with increasingly strained cheer. Rupert was qui— No. He damned well *was* sullen.

And Aubrey tried to reassure Henrietta with reflexive social niceties and practised smiles, barely hearing what she said past an ache that hadn't lessened in six years.

— Chapter Seven —

LUCIEN CARRIED HIS report on the season's hats downstairs, tensing further with every step. Hernedale's letter should've arrived by now, and, since Jameson never overlooked an envelope embossed with a crest, he'd have read it.

"Regarding the WSPU story, Mr Jameson." Lucien placed his copy on the editor's desk. "Miss Enfield has kindly agreed to collaborate with me. Her knowledge of the history of the movement is invaluable, and she can speak to them woman to woman and get the inside story."

"Load of nonsense." But Jameson's expression was assessing. "They'll talk politics to anyone: can't shut 'em up. And a woman'll much sooner confide in a charming fellow than a shrewish spinster."

Confide. Jameson wanted a gossip piece, not politics. How had Lucien missed that?

"Up to you, though. Long as you deliver good, reliable copy, I don't care how you manage it. If you can persuade her to do your drudge work…" Jameson shrugged.

"That's not—!"

"Don't care, Saxby." Jameson creaked back in his chair. "You have some interesting acquaintances, by the way." He lifted a sheet of dense cream paper from a drawer, and laid it on the desk between them. "The Earl Hernedale, for instance."

Lucien glanced from the coat of arms embossed at the top of the page to the neat, narrow signature at the bottom.

"Seems Lady Hernedale's brother mistook the situation Friday night."

"He did." Lucien skimmed the letter discreetly.

...appreciate your concern and prompt action in...

"Apparently, Mr Lowdon is not sufficiently intimate with their household to have realised you are, in fact, well acquainted with them both."

Lucien stared at the letter. Hernedale had *lied*? For him?

...should be deeply disappointed ... any negative repercussions on Mr Saxby as a...

"Saxby?"

"Er. Certainly, I hadn't met the gentleman before that night."

...ignore any further communication regarding my family from this source.

He'd discredited a family member on behalf of a virtual stranger? Even as the beneficiary, Lucien wasn't sure how he felt about that.

"Which accounts for the misunderstanding." Jameson cast a lingering glance over the coat of arms before restoring the letter to its drawer. "It appears you're a considerable asset to your department."

"I'd like to think so," Lucien said reflexively.

"Hmm. Well. Don't hide your light under a bushel. Keep me informed of your contacts."

"There are contacts who..." Lucien trailed off delicately. "They value discretion, Mr Jameson. Don't like to have their names bandied about."

"Ahhh." Jameson folded his hands over his belly. "In that case, you'd best protect your sources."

"Quite, Mr Jameson. One doesn't kill the goose who lays the golden eggs."

"No, indeed. Good man."

Lucien trudged up the stairs to his office, light-headed with relief and weighted with guilt and anger with himself.

Jameson clearly wouldn't reduce Miss Enfield's assignments to account for her covering the Women's Procession, but Lucien could help with those. What rankled was that he hadn't defended her against Jameson's slurs.

On top of that, he shouldn't have suggested he had Society contacts. Panic over his job, combined with his facility with words, had pitched him into almost as bad a mess as the one he'd just escaped. He couldn't produce the stories Jameson was even now imagining.

William would be no help at all, even supposing Lucien was prepared to use him, which he wasn't. The Hernedales were putting themselves out to help him. What kind of rat would take advantage of their confidences, or of gossip overheard in their company? And as for Fanshawe…

They'd parted on poor terms, but Fanshawe had helped him, immediately and unstintingly, when he had nothing to gain by it. He'd poured him brandy and reassured him. He'd let Lucien stay in his home practically unsupervised, eating dinner he'd provided, while he solved his problem for him. Without Fanshawe, Lucien might be walking out of New Carmelite House for the last time.

No. He'd promised he wouldn't betray Fanshawe, and though they'd been talking about sex, he wouldn't betray him in anything else, either.

Autocratic snob though he was, the fellow'd more than earned that.

THE BRUTAL DEMANDS of common courtesy drove Lucien to walk to Albany immediately after work, missing dinner-time at his boarding house. By quarter-past six, he was tapping at Fanshawe's front door, braced to acknowledge aloud, for the second time in three days, that, despite all his skill and hard work, his judgement was so bloody poor he couldn't keep his job without assistance from the nobility.

Fanshawe opened the door, looking tired and a bit surprised, and then expressionless.

"Apologies. I don't mean to stay," Lucien murmured. "Only to say—"

"Come in." Fanshawe let him pass, and closed the door behind him.

"Sorry." Lucien shook the offered hand. "Sorry, I know one's not supposed to talk outside the sets. Only, I didn't want you to feel obliged to ask me in."

"Quite all right." Fanshawe gestured towards the drawing room.

Lucien controlled a wince. "I really don't mean to stay. Just to let you know my editor received Lord Hernedale's letter, and accepts that I didn't harass Lady Hernedale. And to thank you for your help."

"You're very welcome. I'm glad it's resolved."

"From my editor's point of view, it is. And thanks to Lord Hernedale's offer of continued assistance, it may soon be completely resolved. I went to Hernedale House first, actually, but they weren't at home."

"General election, you know. They were only in London for the weekend."

"Ah. Of course. Don't s'pose you know when they'll be back? I should thank them in person as soon as possible."

"Not till Friday."

"Righteo." Lucien offered his gloved hand, and Fanshawe shook it. "Thank you again, most sincerely." He squeezed to indicate strength of feeling, and Fanshawe flushed. "That was an uncomfortable spot of bother: couldn't have resolved it alone." Releasing Fanshawe's hand, he turned to the door.

"You—wouldn't care to stay for a drink?"

"Oh. No, thank you. Must—" Lucien turned back, and saw what hadn't been clear while he was grinding gratitude through humiliation.

"You're a busy man, of course." Fanshawe's tone was light, but his flush darkened with embarrassment.

"Not too busy for you." Lucien reached for his hand again: not to shake, but to hold. "But this… interview has been difficult. Perhaps you might honour me with an invitation another time?"

"I should've realised." Fanshawe's face softened. "This'll be a strain on you all week, I imagine."

"Until I've cleared the air by thanking Lord and Lady Hernedale."

"I'd suggest Saturday, but you'll probably talk to Ru— Hernedale and Lady Hernedale on Friday night. So you mightn't…"

"Saturday night, after dinner?" Lucien offered. "I should've recovered my equanimity by then." He'd have reassured Noel by then, too. And Noel worked Sunday mornings, so he could safely stay overnight, if things worked out that way.

"I could finish dinner early." Fanshawe's dark eyes held his. "Might we say, nine o'clock?"

"Might *I* say—" Lucien lifted Fanshawe's hand, and bowed to kiss the inside of his wrist "—how very much I look forward to that time." Fanshawe's pulse raced under his lips. Pressing his fingers, he straightened. "Until Saturday."

He let himself out, rather than disturb Fanshawe's moment.

It seemed unkind to set the fellow into a fever of want then strand him, but want must be better than the hurt he'd recognised moments before. It was pleasantly anticipatory, at any rate, unlike rejection.

As for himself, he was leaving the interview less humiliated than he'd expected, and a good deal more optimistic. Looking up from Fanshawe's wrist had been a treat in itself. Recalling the flush on his smooth-shaven cheeks, dwelling on his half-lidded eyes and parted lips, put quite a spring in Lucien's step. Anticipating Saturday would make Friday's interview a lot less miserable.

— Chapter Eight —

A month later, Lucien sat, uncomfortably damp, in the Press Gallery of the House of Commons, above and behind the Speaker. Outside the Strangers' Entrance, perhaps four hundred women—most of them impoverished—stood in a freezing February downpour, waiting for news. So much for London women being reluctant to march.

A short, stocky Scottish woman had led them from the railway station to Caxton Hall, where they'd cheered speech after speech, and then, on a wave of enthusiasm, followed Mrs Pankhurst and her daughters to the House of Commons.

There, police had refused them entry to the Ladies' Gallery. Several women sent their cards in to private Members of Parliament, which embarrassed the government into mitigating the ban. But still, they admitted only twenty women at a time: a fraction of the Gallery's capacity.

Lucien tapped his pencil on his thigh. He'd feel less guilty if he were out in the cold with them, but Miss Enfield, shoulders hunched against the chill, had been crystal clear.

"Listen, Saxby, I appreciate your concern, but this is no time for outmoded chivalry. When people are so desperate to be heard that they'll stand in the rain, the least we can do is tell their story. Go in, stay for as long as women are admitted, and get that story. I'll stay here and get the story of the women who waited."

But so far, none of the MPs who'd held the floor had mentioned women's suffrage, and the Ladies' Gallery above him remained silent. If he'd been in the long Strangers' Gallery, he might at least have *seen* the Ladies' Gallery; might've glimpsed a flicker of movement behind the brass grille which hid the women from public view. As it was…

Dawlish sat among other political journalists, taking copious notes, but Lucien's story had stalled, and his mind wandered, inevitably, to Fanshawe.

A pattern had evolved, in which they spent every Saturday evening sipping Fanshawe's excellent brandy and making uncontentious small-talk, then retired to his canopied bed—saved from ostentation only by clean lines and plain-dyed, heavy silks—and had equally excellent sex. By unspoken consensus, Lucien always stayed the night. And woke on Sunday morning to the second part of their pattern: where Fanshawe spoke with exaggerated courtesy, and washed under a nightshirt, and said goodbye with a self-consciously firm handshake.

There were proper ways to part, even after a casual encounter. A peck on the lips or cheek was much less intimate than whatever had gone before, and left a fellow with a feeling of general goodwill. Fanshawe's anxious discomfort left Lucien feeling like a mistake.

Shoving that thought aside, along with the hurt, Lucien leafed through his notebook, adding impressions from the procession through the rain and noting questions to ask the organisers.

Probably, he should go home on Saturday nights. But by the time they'd finished, he didn't relish the walk. And… Fanshawe's bed was soft and broad, and his rooms were warm, and his big, bony body curled around Lucien's was a sublime comfort—the sort of comfort that was hard to come by, for a fellow like himself.

Maybe Fanshawe drank to free his passion, only to regret it in the morning. He clearly wasn't inexperienced with men, obviously enjoyed sex with Lucien, but—

Lucien folded his notebook over the pencil and shut his eyes. He should stop visiting the chap altogether. Why associate with someone who was ashamed of him, whatever the reason? He mightn't be the best-looking chap in the world, but he wasn't short of fellows delighted to have his company. And yet...

Hour after hour, nothing distracted him from his thoughts. Above him, the women held their peace, perhaps afraid protest would lose them their small concession. Below, MPs puffed through self-aggrandising speeches, chortling at the sneers that passed for wit in the House. Each party celebrated its own pronouncements with growls of approbation, and censured its opposition with howls and jeers.

But not a single word was said, by any member of parliament, about women's suffrage.

LUCIEN STEPPED OUT of the House behind the last damp, frustrated group of women to leave. It'd stopped raining, but the afternoon was grey and cold.

The group outside the Strangers' Entrance was smaller than the one he'd left, but still substantial. Tired, hopeful faces turned towards them, hats and hair bedraggled and limp, clothing dark and heavy with rain.

Several of the emerging women shook their heads.

Shoulders slumped and Mrs Pankhurst's face tightened. "Well," she said.

Lucien followed the women into a chilly fug of wet wool and perfume and slightly rancid pomade, but stood against the wall of the House, trying not to intrude.

"Now then, ladies!" the small, round Scottish woman called. "It mightn't look like it, but we've done very well today."

Lucien tucked his riding cane under his arm and took notes.

"You can be proud of this day's work. We *will* win one day, partly because of what you've done today. Your daughters, and your daughters' daughters, will thank you. For now, go home and gather your strength, but look out, ladies, for notices of our next meeting! Every one of you fine folk will be needed to win this battle. Votes for Women!"

"Votes for Women!" the crowd called. But they sounded weary and defeated.

Christabel Pankhurst and Annie Kenney—a thin ex-mill-worker who'd delivered a passionate speech about impoverished women—edged through the dispersing crowd to join Mrs Pankhurst.

"Now then." The Scottish woman gestured Lucien further from the Pankhurst group. "Were you looking for an interview?"

"I was, but—" Lucien glanced around. "You might already have spoken to my colleague? Miss Enfield?" He spotted her walking towards them, shoulders hunched against the cold. Damp had frizzed the hair below her hat brim into a fine dark halo, softening her face and the severe line of her chignon.

"Ah, yes."

Water dripped from the cuffs and hem of Miss Enfield's thin coat. Her face looked pinched and yellowish, and her eyes, bruised. Lucien glanced down his list of questions, mentally discarding most: he'd keep this brief.

"Mrs Drummond," she said. "May I introduce Mr Saxby, of the Daily Mail. Mr Saxby, Mrs Drummond of the Women's Social and Political Union."

Lucien shook Mrs Drummond's firm, wet, gloved hand. "Please stop me if I repeat anything Miss Enfield's asked: I expect she's already covered everything I can think of, and more besides."

"Wouldn't surprise me." A gleam of approval in Mrs Drummond's eye.

"At Caxton Hall, Miss Kenney described mill workers and sweated labourers who work every waking hour while enduring violence at the hands of their husbands and fathers and supervisors. How does the WSPU imagine *eligible* ladies gaining the vote will help these impoverished, ineligible ladies?"

"A vote is a voice. Governments will pass laws to protect women if they know they'll gain votes thereby."

"But the WSPU only campaigns for ladies to be enfranchised on the same basis that men already are—that is to say, those with property or a reasonable income of their own. Most ladies here today wouldn't qualify to vote under those conditions."

"Our ultimate goal is for all women to have the vote, regardless of wealth. All men, too, for that matter. But for now... We're a community of *women*, Mr Saxby. Wealthy women will vote in support of those who don't qualify."

Lucien stared at her, pencil suspended above the page.

"You needn't be so cynical, Saxby," Miss Enfield said irritably. "Women have things in common that men don't. We feel an affinity with one another."

"I don't dispute that." Lucien folded his notebook over his pencil. "On an individual basis. It's just—"

"Don't let it trouble you, Mr Saxby. A man can't understand the sisterhood of women."

"No, of course," Lucien agreed. "And certainly I've seen an astonishing sense of community among you today. It's quite inspiring."

Mrs Drummond smiled. "I'm very fortunate to be a part of it."

"But— What about ladies *outside* your movement? Don't you think they might view things differently?"

"They're still women," Miss Enfield pointed out.

He turned to her gratefully. Disagreeing with familiar Miss Enfield was infinitely easier than disputing Mrs Drummond's blade-sharp certainty.

"It's just... I grew up around wealthy ladies."

Miss Enfield and Mrs Drummond stared at him. "And?"

"Hardly any of the ladies here today would qualify for the vote. The ladies who could most easily assist them, with or without the vote, weren't here."

"The Cause has wealthy supporters," Mrs Drummond argued. "Wealthy *women* supporters."

"But they don't walk with the poor ladies. Will they vote on their behalf, or only in their own interests?"

"You don't think they'll help?" Miss Enfield demanded.

"I think most don't even notice poor ladies exist until they need a service. I think poor ladies won't benefit from women's suffrage under current conditions, but they're being encouraged to think they will, and that's why they walk."

Silence, but for the shuffle of women leaving, but for the quiet hum of a few remaining groups, and the rumble and clatter of a cart passing in the street beyond.

Mrs Drummond laughed, hard and tight. "You're a cynic, Mr Saxby. And generalising beyond your experience."

He offered her a charming smile. "I daresay."

"This is only the first battle of a war. Do you not think, Mr Saxby, that women should have the same rights as men?"

"I do, actually. Just don't see how this will help poor ladies."

"Because you lack *vision*, Mr Saxby. Fortunately, we do not."

The vision appeared to be for the poor to deplete themselves serving the wealthy, as ever. Meanwhile, wealthy women—whose fathers and husbands and brothers and sons squabbled and jeered in the House behind them—fussed over menus and dynasties, and made no effort whatsoever to convince their men to support women's suffrage. A handful of easy guineas, necessary though they were, could never make up for that.

Still, he'd antagonised Mrs Drummond enough for one day, so he deflected the topic with his most charming smile. "Sincere congratulations on your historic procession."

Her round face softened. "It was historic, wasn't it?"

"A triumph. Thank you for your time, Mrs Drummond, particularly at the end of a long day."

She barked a laugh. "Take more than a wee procession and a drop of rain to tire me. Interesting to meet you, Mr Saxby. By the bye, don't think your flattering jergon'll cast your words from my mind: I'll remember, and when all's done, we'll just see, won't we?" She turned away to join the other organisers.

So much for women preferring a charming fellow.

Lucien tucked his notepad and pencil away. "Shall we, Miss Enfield?" They walked out of the courtyard together. "Which way to your rooms?"

"No need to escort me." She started to retrace the route of the procession.

"Part-way, at least? You look very pale. I understand if you're worried about my intentions, but there's truly no need."

"I know. Nor need you worry about mine." She glanced at him from under the sagging brim of her hat. "If you catch my drift."

Lucien stopped walking. She stopped, too, and raised an eyebrow.

"Ah," he said softly.

"Quite. Now. That's more comfortable, isn't it?"

"Much." The day looked inexplicably brighter, and his shoulders loosened. "Good Lord, that really does feel better."

She laughed. "Felt much the same when I realised about you."

"Er. Am I that transparent?" Prison beckoned, if so.

"Not at all."

Thank God for that.

"I only caught on when you let down your guard." She shrugged off a shiver. "Even then, probably only because I'm similarly inclined."

"Not likely to let down my guard with any of the others, whatever their inclinations."

She snorted. "Why on earth would you?"

They strolled in companionable silence past boot-blacks and the occasional street vendor, overtaken by more urgent pedestrians.

As they passed the brick and sandstone façade of Caxton Hall, Miss Enfield said, "The Pankhursts are quite genuine, you know."

Lucien glanced at her.

"Not taking advantage of poor women. Recall: Christabel Pankhurst's been imprisoned for the cause."

The Pankhursts were middle class—wealthy only by working class standards—but it wasn't worth quibbling over. "It just seems wrong. Persuading poor ladies to fight for wealthy ladies' interests, when they already work so hard, and in appalling conditions. They'll exhaust themselves winning this battle, then still have to fight for their own right to vote. Probably with less financial support."

"And yet it is their battle, too, since if they don't win this one, they can't ultimately win voting rights for themselves. *My* battle."

Lucien met her gaze.

She smiled wryly. "I'm a woman, Saxby: I earn significantly less than you. I'll only gain the vote if we win the second battle."

"Ah."

"And if wealthy women won't stir themselves to fight the first, then I must. I've been thinking about what you said. You're not wrong; and at the same time, you are. You can afford to debate the fairness of individual contributions because you already have the vote. I can't. For the first time in years there's some genuine forward impetus for women's suffrage. We can't afford to lose that squabbling over whose responsibility it is to lobby Parliament."

"Ah. You may have a point."

She glanced at him sidelong. "Thanks very much for your approval."

He laughed. "As though you need it."

She nudged him, grinning. The walk seemed to have loosened her muscles, but she was still alarmingly pale.

"Have you someone to look after you when you get home?"

Her face closed. "Have you?"

"No."

They walked on.

"There used to be someone," she said at last. "She left about a year ago."

Oh. "Difficult working hours?" Lucien asked sympathetically.

"Basic incompatibility. We're better off without one another. You tend to hold on rather too long when the alternative is loneliness."

"Do you?"

"Don't *you*?"

"Wouldn't know. There's never been anyone for me. Not that way."

She watched him a fraction too long before she said, "By choice?"

He mustered a smile. "No."

A few quiet minutes later, they arrived back at St James Park District Railway Station.

"I'd still like to walk you home."

Miss Enfield patted his arm. "That's very decent of you, but I'm a lot less frail than I look. Have to be, really."

RATHER MORE THAN half an hour later, Lucien let himself into his rooms, chilled through and regretting his promise to visit William later. He built and lit the fire—hoping Miss Enfield had a hearth and could afford coals—washed and dressed, then sponged and ironed the morning's clothes and arranged them on the clotheshorse he'd set at the fireside. Warmed by activity and the fire, he opened his writing desk and settled to work.

As half-past six approached, footsteps and voices drifted in from the hallway. He locked his work into the desk and changed his dressing gown and cravat for a jacket, collar, and tie. His boots were still damp. Sighing, he pulled them on anyway, combed his hair, and went downstairs to the dining room.

He was over-tired and disinclined to chat, but made conversation with his fellow boarders over dinner anyway, wearily cementing his reputation as a good bloke. Afterwards, he hauled himself upstairs, where he'd have liked to stay, at his own quiet fireside with a good novel. Since he *had* to go out, he really ought to shave and change into dinner clothes. Instead, he shrugged into his overcoat—also damp, damn it—put on his bowler and gloves, tucked his riding cane under his arm, and went to visit William, who wouldn't mind taking him as he was.

He should've taken the tube. Instead he walked through London as twilight turned to lamp-lit dark, retracing his steps towards Albany where he'd left Fanshawe the previous morning, imperfectly cleaned and wrapped in figured silk, after a night of tender-savage lust.

He dismissed memories of the stilted meetings establishing him as Hernedale's acquaintance. Dismissed the reflexive anxiety they brought—unreasonable now he had a home and income of his own—at his fate lying in the hands of powerful others who'd reward him if he pleased them, drop him like a defective toy if he didn't. He dismissed the memory of Fanshawe, cold as polished marble, gliding away with his noble friends to a place Lucien could never belong.

That wasn't the Fanshawe he wanted, anyway.

Have you someone to look after you when you get home?

Lucien paused in a shadowed shop doorway, gazing across Vigo Street, past the night doorman, down the lamp-lit Ropewalk. In a world where Fanshawe was a working man, he might've been Lucien's someone, and Lucien, his. The silks and satins, the luxurious bed, they were... delicious. But unnecessary. What he wanted was the weight of Fanshawe's head on his shoulder, the generosity of his lust, the warm, dark delights of his receptive body. He wanted to soothe the terrors that made Fanshawe weep and tease his down-turned lips into laughter, into gasps and moans of want sweetened by confidence that his need would be satisfied.

A man strode into the Ropewalk.

Shit! Lucien hurried on. Imagination insisted the man was Fanshawe, but imagination would, wouldn't it? Because it was the most embarrassing possible outcome.

Behind him, quick footsteps rapped the paving stones.

"Saxby!"

Buggery! Lucien turned as Fanshawe drew level on the opposite pavement. "Oh, hullo!"

"Bit of luck, seeing you pass." Fanshawe, overcoat unbuttoned over formal evening dress, crossed the street to stand in the white halo of an electric street lamp. "Don't s'pose you'd care to join me for dinner?"

Dinner? They'd never dined together. Lucien gazed at Fanshawe's absurdly elegant face, half-shadowed by the brim of his top hat. "Thank you. I wish I could, but I've already eaten."

A flash of hurt and suspicion.

"Boarding house," Lucien explained. "My landlady doesn't work late."

"I—see." The polite incomprehension of a man who'd always had service as late as he liked.

"And I'm on my way to visit a friend. A prior commitment."

"Oh. Well." Fanshawe stared at his bowler and took a step back. "Quite all right."

Clearly, it wasn't.

"If I finish early, I might knock on your door? If you'll be in, that is. You look as though you're going out yourself."

"Oh, it's not— That is to say, just a turn around the block, you know."

In evening dress?

Fanshawe held his gaze. "I'll be at home, should you happen to pass."

Lucien stared at the vision of perfection: burning white carved with sharp-edged black shadows. An eldritch visitor to soot-smudged old London. "How late is too late?" he heard himself say.

"Oh goodness." Fanshawe forced a laugh. "I'm always up late. It's worth a try, whatever the time."

"In that case—" Lucien stepped forward, dream-like, offering his hand "—I'll see you later." He pressed his thumb into Fanshawe's hand, rubbing a small, firm circle. And watched, mesmerised, as he swallowed. Gloves weren't the same as skin— not even Fanshawe's fine kid-skin gloves—but pressure was pressure, and he'd noticed Fanshawe liked pressure with his tenderness.

The rasp and jangle of a shop-keeper locking up brought him to his senses: they shouldn't stand staring at one another in the street. Giddy and breathless, he tipped his hat and strode away without a backward glance.

The euphoria gradually dwindled on the walk to Park Lane. As he reached for the brass knocker of Camberhithe House, it burned out entirely, and he lowered his hand without touching it.

What the hell was he thinking, messing about with a nob? A quick roll was one thing. Even a weekly arrangement could be safe, provided they kept it friendly but distant. *This*, though… This would hurt.

Lucien leaned against the glossy doorframe, boiling with embarrassment, sucking in deep, careful breaths.

He could blame the conversation with Miss Enfield for the turn his mind had taken. He might blame the theatrical lamplight, or the allure of well-fitted evening dress. But these were superficial. This was far worse than holding onto a lover too long. Fanshawe only wanted to enliven a dull evening, while *he…*

Lucien wrenched his mind from Fanshawe. Had William slept? Had he eaten? He drove his thoughts into familiar pathways of concern until his face cooled. Then he lifted the weighty knocker and let it fall.

WILLIAM WAS ON the chaise longue in the library, *Don Quixote* beside him, as though neither had moved since the day before, the month before. But when Lucien ghosted across the Turkish carpet and picked up a chair, he opened surprisingly alert eyes.

"You're awake." Lucien set the chair beside the chaise longue and sat.

"And much better," William agreed. "Had an egg for breakfast, and it didn't hurt at all. Boiled chicken for lunch, and barely a cramp."

"Delighted to hear it." Profoundly relieved, too. But Lucien took a deep breath and reached for reserves of patience.

William had every reason to be self-absorbed: he'd cheated death again, at least for now, and was delighting in the energy food brought. But listening to him ramble was frustrating, especially when Lucien was shaken, his mind filled with Fanshawe. And that was selfish and unjust. Selfish, to have asked Fanshawe to wait for him when he might've gone to his evening engagement. Selfish, to have hoped William was already in bed. Unjust because he was self-absorbed, too, and because he was irritated in anticipation, not because of anything William had yet said or done.

The bald fact was William was easier company when he was almost well, and could pursue a few interests; and when he was very ill, when he was quiet and dreamy and too weary to fear death—when Lucien could look after him in simple, material ways, and read or write or think while William dozed. This in-between stage—when William grew frustrated as he tired and concentration failed, when trivia assumed disproportionate significance because he had nothing beyond himself to occupy his mind, when ordinary tasks seemed urgent because his time felt short and precious—this stage was annoying and demanding.

Lucien felt guilty for thinking it.

William ate a few shreds of boiled chicken for dinner, and Lucien joined him in a cup of fruit jelly.

"Lord, I'm stuffed." William lay back and closed his eyes.

Lucien's stomach leapt and trembled with a mixture of frustration, and appalled disbelief at his own cheek—and budding hope. Because he hadn't asked Fanshawe to stay in, had he? Fanshawe'd volunteered.

A pair of footmen collected the dishes, brought in the tea tray, and eased out of the library.

"Might be strong enough soon to eat in the dining room." William's eyes were still closed.

"Perhaps next week?"

Fanshawe'd chosen to miss his evening engagement. For Lucien.

"It's wonderful not to be tired all the time." William's eyes were still closed.

Lucien's chest tightened with awkward tenderness. If anyone knew what it was to live with frustration, it was William. Surrounded by beloved books he often couldn't read. Invited to every Society event, but seldom able to attend. He stocked his house with gourmet food, but his bespoke dinner jacket bagged on his reduced frame. Even Lucien's lounge suits, self-altered as his muscles developed, fit better than that.

Which reminded him—his stomach tensed—he had a theatre engagement with the Hernedales in less than two weeks, and nothing suitable to wear. And there'd be other formal evening engagements, too, now the election was over. The Hernedales might overlook his dinner jacket, but Society hostesses would frown on the infraction, especially if Lowdon had maligned him to them.

Probably, he should buy a second-hand set of evening dress. But then if Jem—

"Oh!" William's eyes opened. "Remembered what I'd heard about Hernedale."

"Remembered?"

William huffed impatiently. "When you first said you were meeting him, remember? I said I'd heard—"

"Oh yes. It's not important though. Seems a decent chap."

"Leopards and spots, you know. This story goes back to Eton, and a chap called Aubrey Fanshawe, of the Letchworth Fanshawes."

Lucien's weariness vanished under a chill wave. "He's a good fellow, too."

"Had a bit of a reputation at school, actually. Charlie told me, years ago."

Lucien could cheerfully have throttled Charles when they were younger, and the impulse returned with renewed force. "It really doesn't matter."

"No, listen: you should know. He said Fanshawe was the first chap any older boy looked for when he wanted a bit of relief."

William looked at him meaningfully. "Never a popular sprout, as you can imagine. Bit of a crier, too."

Lucien's head pounded. He wanted to slaughter the cruel, contemptible little ticks: casting the blame for their own urges and actions on Fanshawe.

"Now here's the connection: Hernedale was a close friend of Fanshawe's, and never dropped him. Made chaps wonder whether he was quite the thing himself, of course."

"School must've been—over a decade ago." Lucien's throat was thick with fury. "And Hernedale's been married for years, so that can't be—" He felt a little queasy at reinforcing that prejudice. "And boys do ill-advised things that—that get misrepresented." Heat crawled up his face: he knew he was offering too many justifications. "Besides, gossip always exaggerates reality."

"Can do." William's eyes were alert and curious.

"Can't believe Charles anyway: probably none of it ever happened." God! If William reminded Charles of this, he'd revive the story. It could destroy Fanshawe, and it'd be Lucien's fault for jogging William's memory. So much for promising not to betray him.

"You esteem the chap, then?"

"Not— Well. He's a decent fellow, is all. And it's a bit much to have malicious playground gossip dog one all one's life, don't you think?" William would hate to be considered a gossip. Or gullible.

"Oh, naturally. One wouldn't want to…"

Lucien let out his breath.

"Anyway, speaking as one who's never had the opportunity to attract gossip…"

Feeling as though he was lifting a boulder, Lucien tried to divert William's attention. "Only think: your reputation would be in tatters, if people had known. Lurking in libraries. Painting scandalous Latin quotations on walls—"

"Weren't that damned scandalous." But William eyed him thoughtfully.

"Were, in Potter's opinion."

"Oh, well. Potter." William's tutor had been desperate to impress the marquis. "Anyway, it was only watercolours."

Lucien knew that, since he'd cleaned the walls.

William sank back and closed his eyes. "Those arty chaps get away with scrawling quotations all over the place."

"You might've been the next William Morris."

"Kempe," William murmured.

"Was it?"

"Mmm. Working for Morris. Wightwick Manor."

Having distracted William and lightened the atmosphere, Lucien shut his own eyes. He felt injured and soiled, as though William had slashed open something fragile and terribly personal, and then trampled it. It hurt that he hadn't properly defended Fanshawe, but he couldn't without endangering them both.

His own youthful adventures had been covert but friendly and uncomplicated, and he ached for young Fanshawe, trying to please boorish ingrates who humiliated and gossiped about him afterwards. No wonder he feared gossip. No wonder he didn't part with a kiss. He wasn't afraid of his desires, but of the aftermath.

Lucien liked Hernedale better for standing by Fanshawe. Even supposing they'd been lovers, it'd have been easier to turn Judas than face accusations and contempt born of propinquity. It was admirable, especially in someone so young.

As for the scandal… Provided everyone involved had been willing, allowances ought to be made, at that age, for the volatile combination of erratic judgement and near-compulsive urges. And the bloody school certainly should've protected Fanshawe from exploitative older boys: what the devil did parents pay exorbitant fees for, if it couldn't even manage that?

William sighed. "How's work?"

Lucien dragged his mind back. "Fine, thank you."

"Still enjoying it?"

He ignored William's hint that he should stop working and move back to Camberhithe House. "Mostly. I like the Society reporting. Less keen on the domestic politics my editor's got me covering at the moment."

"Politics?" William's eyes opened. "Man must be mad. You're a natural-born valet."

Lucien stared at William, breath trapped in his throat.

William smiled and closed his eyes. "You're clever enough to carry it off, though."

As though he was no more than the embodiment of his training. As though valets, by definition, cared for nothing but clothes and social events and gossip.

But William was too ill to argue with. And he shouldn't be surprised. That William thought birth was destiny, and that servants were naturally stupid—would've been better-born in the first place, if their parents hadn't been stupid. It was a common belief, among the nobs.

Somehow Lucien had assumed that, through growing up with him, William knew that was wrong. He'd had uncomfortable moments with William before, but they'd been minor, and he'd chosen to overlook them or find excuses for him. *This* though—

"Is there anything you need?" William asked.

Lucien's lips shaped a furious, reflexive 'no', but relaxed before he voiced it. He'd made a point of never taking advantage of their friendship, but William's habitual question now sounded more like a lord of the manor rewarding diligent service than the natural concern of a friend.

Very well. Since he was regarded as a valet, he'd claim a valet's dues: friendship couldn't survive this, anyway. Assuming there'd ever been a friendship outside his own mind.

"When you next get rid of evening dress, would you toss a set my way?"

William's eyes opened. "You'd better get a new set, properly fitted. Put it on account at my tailor's."

Shortly after they'd moved to Camberhithe House together, William had persuaded Lucien to have a full wardrobe made to measure. He was still wearing those clothes; still felt burdened by the debt he could never repay. Not that William would ever accept payment. "No thanks. I don't need that."

"You're ridiculously stubborn."

Lucien's jaw tightened. "Born that way, I suppose."

"Wouldn't be surprised." William's eyes slid shut. "I'll send it along tomorrow. Got a new wardrobe arriving next month anyway."

"Thanks. I appreciate it."

William half-raised a listless, dismissive hand. "I'll send day clothes, too, when the new things arrive."

"I don't need—"

"Dear *Lord*, Lucien, just shut up and take them." William sounded exhausted; miserable. "It costs me nothing, and God knows I'd do more for you if only you'd *let* me."

Lucien swallowed past a thick lump. William did care, in his way. And he cared for William. Of course he did. He'd come out to visit him on a cold night, after a working day, in a damp overcoat and boots. He'd turned down an evening with Fanshawe for him.

From the age of seven, he'd prioritised William's interests above his own wishes. He was lucky, his parents had reminded him, to share the meals cooked for William, sit in on the education provided for William, play with the toys bought for William, sleep in rooms furnished and heated for William. Lucky to wear William's elegant cast-off clothes. He'd known the marquis might take it all away if he didn't earn his place every hour of every day. But he'd also known he was William's friend.

Now William's casual assumption of inborn inequality, overriding a lifetime of daily intimacy, dragged a long-lurking question into the light. Did he love William because they'd have become friends anyway, under other circumstances? Or only because he'd been trained to feel precisely that?

— Chapter Nine —

AUBREY WASN'T SORRY to cancel his arrangements for the evening. The concert looked promising, but the prospect of meeting debutantes and their hopeful families was significantly less so. Anyway, he'd be wasting their time: they'd have better luck with other chaps. He'd much rather spend his evening with Saxby. Anticipation coiled, pleasantly uncomfortable, in his belly.

Grieve helped him into a dressing gown and settled him on the sofa with a glass of wine, the last post, and the latest issue of the *Athenaeum*, then went to buy dinner from a restaurant.

Enjoy it while it lasts, Rupert had said, because any damage was already done. But where Aubrey's casual encounters usually ended within the hour, this one was lasting and lasting. He'd hardly know what to do with himself on a Saturday night if Saxby wasn't there to share brandy and conversation by the fire; to share the unique delights of their joined bodies in the quiet dark. To share—unless only Aubrey felt it—a... fondness; an ease in one another's company. An ease that evaporated by morning.

He'd loathed his weakness in bringing Saxby home. He'd feared contempt when Saxby tired of him; betrayal when Saxby no longer needed his help. He'd told himself over and again to have some pride, to drop the fellow before that happened. By the time he'd begun to trust his kindness, Saxby'd stopped offering to share the basin, and now Aubrey didn't know how to cross the dressing room to join him.

It'd feel like an admission that he'd misjudged and insulted Saxby, even though his fears were rational. As though he'd be intruding on Saxby's territory, even though it was his own. It'd expose him to derision and righteous indignation.

He simply couldn't do it.

After dinner, he was too restless to read, let alone write, so he brought out his sketchbook and returned to the dining table. In the absence of an interesting subject, he sketched his sideboard—an old-fashioned, carved Victorian thing—and the cut crystal decanters and glasses on their silver trays, while a light but persistent drizzle hissed against his windows.

His attention drifted to the mantelpiece. Almost ten o'clock. He wrenched his gaze from the clock. It wasn't late. Not really. An evening engagement might end much later. It was unreasonable to feel Saxby had preferred someone else's company to his: a prior engagement was a prior engagement. Besides, Saxby had every right to prefer someone else's company.

A diffident tap at the door brought him to his feet, but it was only Grieve with the tea tray.

It'd be easier if Grieve provided washing facilities for two on a Sunday morning, but he still couldn't claim Saxby as an overnight friend. Who'd get caught out late every Saturday night? It wouldn't stand up to even casual consideration.

"That's all for tonight."

Grieve drifted out, and Aubrey carried a cup of tea and the plate of macaroons to the sofa.

Saxby'd been walking west. Who could he possibly know in those exclusive areas, let alone know well enough to call 'friend'? And who, in those areas, would accept an evening visit from a man in a bowler hat?

He touched the backs of his fingers to the china cup, then snatched them away. Too hot.

Actually, *he'd* invited Saxby to visit this evening, and even to dine with him. He'd welcomed evening visits from Saxby for weeks, regardless of what he wore. So other gentlemen mightn't object either.

Aubrey's stomach tightened, and he took a cautious sip of his too-hot tea. He didn't like that thought. He had a rather... *particular* interest in Saxby, and while he didn't expect him to abstain from others, the idea that Saxby might've left him here, marking time, while he went to fuck another man was—

Well. He didn't quite like to think he was waiting his turn.

He stared into the leaping flames, chewing his bottom lip, then stood. Bugger it all, anyway. Putting his tea on the dining table, he sat and picked up the sketchbook. He shaded a detail on the side of a decanter, then dropped the pencil and rubbed his face.

The sketch wasn't very good. Like many things, he liked to do it, but was mediocre in the execution. If he could just set his mind to it...

But it was difficult to concentrate on drawing decanters when memory overlaid them with Saxby's hand reaching for a glass— *Better give me your coat, as well*— With the coat sliding from Saxby's muscular shoulders. With the scent of thyme over soft, dense wool.

Aubrey picked up the pencil and stared at his sketch. He'd never been the possessive sort. He had two lovers himself, for God's sake, and didn't want Saxby any less for that: why should Saxby feel differently? But he also had a comfortable income, a permanent home, security. Saxby didn't. If someone were to offer Saxby comfort and security in exchange for exclusivity... it might be tempting for a fellow in his position.

Aubrey reached for his tea, and knocked the cup. He grabbed it before it fell, but warm tea sloshed over his fingers, over the saucer, onto the table. Damnation! He laid a linen napkin over the spill on the table, then wiped his fingers and the teacup with another and laid it across the puddle in the saucer before draining the cup.

It was ridiculous to be upset that Saxby might end their arrangement. They weren't lovers, just occasional—well, all right, *regular*—bedfellows. You couldn't miss a chap you barely knew, especially when he hadn't even gone yet. Besides, Aubrey had no right to Saxby's company, and no wish to be anyone's damned albatross even if he had. If Saxby chose to be exclusive with a lover, for whatever reason, he ought to shake his hand and wish him well: it'd be the decent thing to do.

He picked up the stained napkins with trembling fingers, mopped up the remaining spill, and threw them on the tray.

It was sheer selfishness to want to hold onto Saxby when the fellow might do better for himself. But Aubrey wished he could afford to give him that better life. He wouldn't demand exclusivity in return, either: he wasn't a bloody barbarian. He just wanted to be the chap who clothed Saxby in bespoke cottons and silks and soft wool blends; who housed him; who brought him security. Wanted, guiltily, to keep him far from anyone who might offer an exclusive arrangement.

It was far from the spirit of the unspoken agreement that guided their nights together: so far it felt almost as though he'd drawn Saxby in under false pretences.

One thing, at least, was perfectly clear: he couldn't impose his unsolicited emotions on Saxby. The fellow deserved better from him than that.

BY MIDNIGHT, AUBREY had drunk enough brandy to feel rather too warm and very sleepy. He sank deeper into the sofa. He ought to go to bed, but... Lucien might yet turn up—it was possible— and he didn't want to miss him, even at the expense of his dignity.

His eyelids slid shut, sheltering him in dull red half-light that flickered with the leap of the flames. He was an utter fool. But he was a fool at peace with himself. He knew what he wanted, he realised it was completely one-sided, and he was willing to accept that, for as long as Lucien wanted him, because the alternative was unthinkable.

A quiet tap. He sprang across the drawing room, bounced off the door frame into the hallway, and snatched the front door open.

It was Lucien, looking exhausted and a bit damp. He stood aside to let him in.

"Awfully sorry I'm so late," Lucien murmured, stepping past him. He hung his riding cane and bowler on the coat-stand while Aubrey closed the door. "William took ages to go to sleep."

Aubrey choked on a breath.

"You all right?" Lucien turned, overcoat half off.

"Perfectly." Aubrey coughed, hand over his mouth, and waved at the coat-stand.

Lucien hung up his coat.

"William?" Aubrey hoped it sounded casual.

"Earl of Camberhithe."

And there it was. Why else would a working man be on first name terms with a nobleman? But he'd stayed only till Camberhithe slept. Probably not love, then—unless Camberhithe couldn't share a bed.

Aubrey mentally dredged through a haze of brandy and anxiety. "Isn't he that sickly chap? Hardly ever in society?"

"That's right."

God knew if you *had* to be sick, a fellow like Lucien would certainly take your mind off things. Camberhithe ought to have done more for him: man of his wealth wouldn't even notice the cost. But perhaps he'd only provide security in exchange for exclusivity.

"I hope he's well."

"Thank you." Lucien's face lightened: a tired smile. "He's been very ill, but improving."

He cared, then.

"Brandy?" Aubrey walked into the drawing room, snatched his glass from the occasional table, and retreated to the sideboard. His head and eyes throbbed, and his throat felt thick.

"Thanks."

"Have a seat." He poured the drinks, then handed Lucien a glass and sat at the opposite end of the sofa. "Macaroon?"

"Ta." Lucien helped himself. "I'm really awfully sorry for being so late. Nearly didn't come, in case I disturbed you, but then I worried you might be waiting up for me."

"Quite all right," Aubrey murmured, only slurring a little.

Lucien stilled, then sighed. "You always say that when it's not all right at all."

"Do I?" Heat flooded Aubrey's face.

"Ah, no." Lucien put the macaroon and glass down. "I'm sorry. I've lost my manners." His cool hand closed around Aubrey's. "I'm so tired I might as well be drunk."

"Quite all—" Damnation! Aubrey fumbled his glass onto the table.

"Let's agree, shall we, that it wasn't, particularly as you only said it to spare my feelings. I won't do it again. I won't keep you waiting so long, even if it means disappointing someone else." Lucien gently squeezed Aubrey's hand. "And I'll be more considerate of your feelings." He squeezed again.

Each squeeze arced along Aubrey's arm and settled, warm and trembling, low in his belly. He pressed his cheek to the antimacassar and stared at their joined hands. At Lucien's thumb describing languid circles over his knuckles.

One day, Lucien would leave him, but while he was here, Aubrey wanted more than stolen nights and awkward, hurtful mornings. Be damned to pride and fear alike: they were only keeping him from what he wanted.

He held Lucien's hand to his cheek, then pressed his lips to his knuckles, inhaling scents of clean skin and of leather, from his gloves.

"There now, beautiful." Lucien cradled Aubrey on his shoulder. "I won't speak anymore, because I'm bound to say something else stupid." He disengaged his hand, passed Aubrey his glass, and picked up his own.

Surrendering to a desire for simple closeness, Aubrey hesitantly nuzzled the underside of Lucien's chin and jaw, kept from his neck by his high, starched collar. It was one thing to do this in the heat of passion—most chaps made allowances, up to a point—but to do it in a quiet moment, and not as an advance, was to risk ridicule or appalled rejection.

But Lucien's arm tightened around him, and he pressed his lips to Aubrey's forehead, then the bridge of his nose. Aubrey closed his eyes, ecstatic, and stroked Lucien's fingers, his knuckles, the ridged strength of his hand.

The clock chimed two, and Lucien sighed. "I'd better go. Got work in the morning."

"You're leaving?" Tension pooled in Aubrey's throat and the pit of his stomach. "I mean— Of course you must, if you want to. But you might stay, as usual."

Lucien stilled. Then: "We seem to be better friends at night than in the morning. I'd rather part as friends."

Aubrey straightened to stare at him.

"I don't like making you anxious."

"What if—" Aubrey forced the words through stiff lips "—I want you to stay more than I want to avoid anxiety?"

"What if that's not how you feel in the morning?"

"What if—" Oh God! "—it always is?"

"Damn it!" Lucien tipped his head back on the antimacassar.

Aubrey watched the long line of Lucien's throat, the tightness in his face.

"I hate feeling like an intruder."

"You're not intruding." Aubrey reached for his hand. "I'll do better."

"Don't. Don't pretend. I'm too old to enjoy make-believe."

"Well then I won't."

Lucien held his gaze, then blew out a long, brandy-scented breath. "Bloody hell. Come here, then." He drew Aubrey back onto his shoulder.

Aubrey went gladly, pausing to kiss Lucien's stubbled cheek.

"Let's hope we don't regret this, eh?"

"Well I won't, at any rate." Aubrey snuggled closer.

Lucien peered down at him with a wry smile, then sighed, stretched out his legs, and eased his fingers into Aubrey's hair. His lips rested on Aubrey's head between sips, breath warm above lulling, blunt fingertips.

It seemed only a moment later that Aubrey's glass drooped in his hand, startling him awake.

Lucien put his glass on the table, then took Aubrey's. "Time for bed, beautiful."

Tranquil and half-asleep, Aubrey let Lucien lead him to his bedroom, where he undressed him with practised efficiency, buttoned him into a nightshirt, and tucked him into bed.

Aubrey drifted off to the clank and light, dry rattle of Lucien banking the fires for the night. He half-woke when the mattress dipped; when Lucien's bare body pressed, warm and undemanding, along his. Comforted, he kissed the corner of Lucien's mouth. "G'night, sweetheart," he mumbled, nestling closer.

Lucien held him, still and silent. It seemed a long time later that his voice vibrated through him.

"Goodnight, beautiful."

LUCIEN WOKE TO a cool draft on his shoulder and the red glow of a banked fire in darkness. Fanshawe was gazing at him, propped on an elbow, letting cold air under the covers.

He'd called him 'sweetheart'.

Lucien cupped Fanshawe's stubbled jaw in his hand. He must've mistaken him for someone else in his sleep, but it was touching all the same.

"You put me to bed." Fanshawe leaned into his palm.

"You needed it."

Fanshawe touched the tip of his tongue to Lucien's thumb, watching his face.

Smiling, Lucien stroked him from hip to shoulder through the silk nightshirt, then back again.

Still watching him, unnervingly intense, Fanshawe licked Lucien's thumb, then sucked it into the wet warmth of his mouth.

121

Lucien clutched his hip, his own lips parting as he watched Fanshawe's, as Fanshawe licked and sucked his thumb deeper.

Then Fanshawe lifted his head, releasing him to the cold air. "Do... you want this?"

"Yes," Lucien whispered, watching his lips.

"I mean... You want this because you like it? Not..."

Lucien stared up at him. "Are you still drunk?"

"No. I just— It occurs to me you really do need Rupert's support. So you might think you need to— Well. To keep me sweet. And—"

"Bloody *hell*, Fanshawe!" Lucien was sitting bolt upright without quite knowing how he'd got there.

Fanshawe knelt beside him. "I wouldn't blame you. Won't, that is. It's your livelihood at stake: perfectly understandable. But—"

"You think I'm fucking you for access to Hernedale?"

Fanshawe's eyes closed. "You don't have to— Look. Just... I'd understand, all right?"

As though he'd ever sink to that! And yet— He'd seen good men driven to appalling extremes. If Hernedale was the only way to keep food in his belly, mightn't he be tempted? And why wouldn't Fanshawe suspect he was being used? He'd had years of being despised by fellows who bedded him.

"Fanshawe. I'm not that bloody desperate."

"It's all right. Honestly. I'll help anyway."

"Shit." Lucien flopped back, arm over his eyes, trying to line up words that would cut through this tangle.

"I'd much rather you didn't have sex with me, actually." Fanshawe's voice quivered. "If you don't really want to. I'll still help."

"It's not *like* that. Not that I— Listen. I appreciate your offer. But it's two separate things, d'you see?" Lucien lowered his arm and stared up at the tester. "There's the help Hernedale offered, which I value. And then there's our—association. Which has *nothing* to do with Hernedale, understand? Nothing. Anyway, we started this before I ever asked for help, remember?"

Fanshawe folded, face-down, into the pillows, his breath uneven, and they lay side by side, not touching.

"D'you want me to leave?" Lucien murmured at last.

"Only if you want to." The words were muffled by the pillow.

Lucien stared at Fanshawe's huddled form, then laid a careful hand on his shoulder. He didn't flinch away. "Then I'll stay."

Fanshawe sighed, muscles relaxing. "Hernedale and Lady Hernedale—they'll help you till this is resolved. Even if—after you stop visiting me."

"Thank you for that."

"I'll keep helping, too. Regardless."

Lucien closed his eyes, aching with affection and appreciation and humiliation. "That's... more than generous."

"Not at all. Lowdon's a damned disgrace." Fanshawe burrowed into the pillow, and his voice grew muffled. "Look here. This... between us. It's not transactional—not on my side, anyway."

"Nor mine."

Fanshawe rolled over, opening puffy eyes. "I'm sorry. Truly. I know it's insulting. Just... didn't want you to feel obliged; and didn't want to feel like an obligation. But I'm sorry."

"No, it's—" Lucien sighed. "Well, obviously, it's insulting, but I'd rather we were straightforward with one another. And I appreciate the reassurance."

Can't have been easy for Fanshawe, either, to ask whether he was merely a means to an end, and offer support anyway.

Fanshawe's long fingers slid between his and squeezed. Lucien squeezed back. That single point of contact was astonishingly soothing, and Lucien found his thumb stroking the side of Fanshawe's hand, his head turning to face him. A growing urge to kiss his hand was horribly counter-balanced by revulsion. Fanshawe'd offered to protect him with his higher status: to kiss his hand now would feel like offering fealty to an overlord.

Tension built inside him, until Fanshawe brought their joined hands to his lips and kissed Lucien's knuckles. Lucien squeezed his eyes shut as Fanshawe rolled towards him and kissed his cheek. It was what Fanshawe didn't do, as much as what he did, that brought a lump to Lucien's throat. He didn't lean over him: his head lay on the pillow beside Lucien's, keeping them on a level. He didn't grab at his body, but stroked his hair, his temple. He didn't part Lucien's lips, but pressed soft kisses on each of his eyelids, tenderly lipped the tips of his eyebrows, his hairline; kissed his cheek and jaw and lips.

Tension melted from Lucien's body. He drew Fanshawe closer, burying his nose in his hair. Fanshawe lay quiescent in his arms, finding, Lucien hoped, as much comfort in their closeness as he did. Only when he kissed his forehead did Fanshawe move. He tipped his head back, offering Lucien his lips, and they shared gentle, careful kisses across the abyss between them.

The kisses deepened. Fanshawe stretched his body along Lucien's, warming him through the delicate, absurdly expensive silk of his nightshirt. "You all right?" he whispered.

Touched by his concern, Lucien drew the tip of his tongue along the seam of Fanshawe's lips, then nipped up his jaw to his ear and sucked the lobe. "Does that answer your question?"

"Mmm." Fanshawe shuddered as Lucien breathed into his ear and nuzzled the soft skin behind the lobe; as he slowly sucked his way down his neck. He gasped and clutched Lucien's head as he licked and sucked the junction of neck and collarbone. And when Lucien sank his teeth gently into the side of his neck, Fanshawe moaned, his shoulders and hips curving closer. Lucien held the pressure till Fanshawe subsided, then suckled the spot, nursing him through gasping reaction to calm.

He rubbed his cheek along Fanshawe's jaw, and murmured, "Convinced yet?"

"Just— Don't feel we have to have sex. For any reason."

"You think this is obligation?" Lucien knelt up, over Fanshawe's thighs, and let the covers slide back. "Behold! Was there ever a keener stand?"

Fanshawe's hands fastened on his hips. "It seems… unlikely."

"And yet, no keener than your own." He gripped Fanshawe's hips, and watched the taut white silk twitch and leap between them. Smiling, he pressed the flat of his tongue to the covered crown, breathing warmth over it while Fanshawe moaned and clutched his wrist. He grazed parted lips over the tip, then drew them in small, slow circles down the length of Fanshawe's shaft. It pulsed against him, enticingly warm and rigid; responsive under silk.

He lifted his head, and Fanshawe, looking heated and dazed, released him. "It appears—" Lucien stroked his shins "—we're both quite pleased to be here." He slid his hands under the hem of the nightshirt that separated them, moving slowly up Fanshawe's thighs, then over hips and belly and chest, his wrists rucking the fine, light fabric up to Fanshawe's throat. He seized his shoulders, and when Fanshawe gasped and arced his hips towards him, he brushed his open mouth with his lips.

He held Fanshawe until his body relaxed, then undid his buttons, slid his arms free of the wide sleeves, and lifted the nightshirt over his head to puddle in gleaming folds around him. Leaning forward, he sucked on his lower lip, gasping as Fanshawe stroked feather-light fingers along his flanks and offered him his throat.

Would it be so foolish to imagine, for just one night, that Fanshawe was his someone?

For a single, shining instant, before common sense asserted itself, he'd been certain of it. Fanshawe had reached for him with sleepy, unhesitating trust; had held him with unqualified affection.

Had named him sweetheart.

Fanshawe's tongue explored his mouth. Warm palms drifted over his back, his shoulders, his neck, drawing reflexive shudders and spasms from his body. Gentle fingers eased into his hair.

Closing his eyes, Lucien lost himself in the tenderness of skin on skin, in the pressure of Fanshawe's firm-soft belly beneath his cock, in the warm nudge of Fanshawe's shaft along his balls and crease as they rocked together in languid rhythm.

125

'In vino veritas', they said, and Lucien had known men to spill heart-felt secrets in their cups. But even in this blissful moment he wasn't fool enough to believe Fanshawe loved him. At best, he might fulfil a fantasy: the plebeian lover who appeared at night, slaked Fanshawe's desires, and vanished with the dawn, taking his inconvenient social deficits with him.

But… mightn't he dream, too?

Slow, languorous kisses lifted Lucien into an otherworldly space where nothing existed but the liquid slide of tongue on tongue, the satin of Fanshawe's skin, and the crisp friction of his body hair. He kissed and nipped down Fanshawe's chest, sucked one small, hard nipple into his mouth, and rolled it between his teeth.

Gasping, Fanshawe clutched Lucien's head and arched his chest closer. So Lucien circled the nipple with his tongue, then did it again. And again. Until the response seemed weaker. And then he lipped the other one and started over, exulting as Fanshawe gasped and writhed under his hands and tongue and teeth. *This* was what a sweetheart did—could do—for his someone. But the room was lightening; his time of sacred darkness was short.

He stroked Fanshawe with firm hands; sucked and nipped along the base of his ribcage as Fanshawe moaned and clutched his hair and stroked his cheeks and neck. He lingered on Fanshawe's belly—teasing him with delicate bites and careful passes of his stubbled cheek and chin, soothing him with lips and tongue and hands—until Fanshawe shuddered and moaned almost without ceasing.

He dipped his nose into Fanshawe's groin, between thigh and pubis, then lower, nuzzling around and beneath tight-drawn balls.

"Oh God!" Fanshawe sobbed.

"That's the way, beautiful," Lucien whispered. He drew the tip of his nose the length of Fanshawe's cock, from straining base to taut-skinned crown, as Fanshawe clutched his shoulder. Then he slowly licked the weeping tip. Fanshawe moaned and tensed, and his cock swelled further.

Resting his forehead on Fanshawe's belly, Lucien breathed warmth across the crown. "Not yet," he murmured. Please. Let it not end. Not yet.

"Oh God! *Please!*"

Lucien brushed parted lips along Fanshawe's straining shaft. "Pass me the oil," he murmured.

Groaning, Fanshawe reached into the bedside table and handed him the bottle.

Lucien poured oil into his palm, then handed it back. Tipping his hand to trickle the oil down to his fingertips, he slowly massaged the tight ridge behind Fanshawe's balls, then slid into the cleft of his buttocks.

Fanshawe sighed, drawing his knees up, stroking Lucien's arm, and Lucien increased the pressure: rubbing over and around his ring as Fanshawe's arm and hand grew lax, as the muscle beneath his fingers eased.

"Lucien."

It was barely a whisper, but his battered spirit soared. It was almost 'sweetheart'.

Aubrey. His name filled Lucien's mouth, tender and hopeful, pressing at his teeth, but he swallowed it: he couldn't speak that name. "I'm here, beautiful." Blinking back tears, Lucien stroked his oil-slick hand over his own cock, and pressed the head against Fanshawe's relaxed muscle. "Yes?" He watched his face.

"Yes."

He steadied himself with a hand, pressing against him and easing off, until Fanshawe's body welcomed him, and the head of his cock was encompassed by smooth, clinging warmth. A circle of muscle clamped around him, and he paused, giving Fanshawe time to adjust: leaning forward to mouth his nipple, massaging the ring stretched tight around his cock with careful, oil-slick fingers.

"Oh," Fanshawe sighed. His eyes were dark and soft in the pre-dawn light, his lips parted, his face relaxed and peaceful as a man on too much laudanum. Silver trickled from the corners of his eyes, down his temples, and into his hair.

Lucien pressed inward. "Yes?"

Fanshawe licked his lips. "Yes. Oh yes. Please."

Still massaging the muscle, Lucien pulled out a fraction, then sank deeper. Closer.

"Oh yes," Fanshawe breathed.

Lucien withdrew, sank deeper. "Like that, my love?" He wanted to kiss the tears from Fanshawe's face, but he wasn't tall enough.

"Oh yes. Just like that."

He paused to move his hand.

"Lucien. *Please*."

His heart ached and exulted. Wrapping his arms around Fanshawe, he surged slowly into the enclosing warmth of his body.

"Yes." The word was breathless, but he heard it. He withdrew, and Fanshawe's muscle clung to him; urged him back. He pressed into welcoming depths, and Fanshawe's arms and thighs slid around him, whisper-light; finger tips drifted across his back.

"Please."

Tucking his forehead into Fanshawe's shoulder, holding his someone close and tight and safe, he rocked him slowly, ecstatically, into drawn out, sobbing release. Into the bright and merciless morning.

— Chapter Ten —

Tuesday, 20th February 1906

"Saxby."

"Here," Lucien mumbled reflexively. Floating to awareness, he opened his eyes. Fanshawe leaned over him, his hand warm on Lucien's bare shoulder. He stared up, disoriented.

"You have to get up."

He must've slept after coaxing Fanshawe to completion, because everything between then and now was blank and dark.

"Oh. Oh yes. Grieve."

Fanshawe flushed. "Won't come in till ten unless I ring for him. I—er—exaggerated a bit. Before."

"Oh."

"I wasn't— It's a work day. I don't know what time you start."

"Ten. I'm supposed to be there by ten."

"It's only eight." Fanshawe collapsed back into the pillows.

Lucien rubbed his face, then propped himself on an elbow. "It's all right. I'll go."

"You don't have to." Fanshawe closed his eyes.

Lucien gazed at the perfect angles of his face; at long, thick, dark eyelashes and arched brows; at the lock of brown hair he daren't brush back, in case Fanshawe took it as an unwelcome advance. "Wouldn't like to impose."

"You're not." Fanshawe's hand slid into Lucien's.

129

Lucien folded his hand around Fanshawe's, half-expecting him to pull away. When he didn't, he pressed his lips to Fanshawe's fingers.

Fanshawe drew Lucien's knuckles to his own lips, then sighed and rested their joined hands on his chest. "But don't stay if you don't want to."

Bloody hell. Lucien understood most of the coded language the nobility used; even used it by reflex himself, when he was around them. But this was—

What it *wasn't* was, 'Want to go somewhere, Luce?' or, 'I'd better be off now.' What it wasn't, was straightforward. It sounded as though Fanshawe wanted him to stay, and the unprecedented morning affection seemed to bear that out. But he couldn't ask that, because nob etiquette—assuming Fanshawe was applying it to him, which he did, sometimes—would dictate that Fanshawe agree, even if he didn't want to.

"You... want me to go?" he hazarded instead.

"No."

That was clear enough. A circuitous, 'Naturally, you're welcome to stay as long as you'd like' would've meant, 'Please leave'.

Fanshawe rubbed Lucien's fingers. "Your editor. Hasn't given you any more trouble since Hernedale wrote to him, has he?"

Lucien's stomach tightened. A month since Jameson had read Hernedale's letter, and he still didn't have a Society scoop to justify his boast. "No. But the situation isn't over yet."

"Oh." Fanshawe's thumb paused. "Poor choice of topic, in that case. Apologies."

"Never mind, beautiful. Thank you for your concern."

Fanshawe met his gaze, eyes so full of yearning that Lucien's chest ached.

"Ah, no." Compulsively he drew Fanshawe close, curling his body around him. "What's the matter?" His nob dialect was slipping, but, even knowing it might discomfort Fanshawe, he couldn't seem to regain it: the language of family was the language of reassurance.

Fanshawe laid his prickly cheek on Lucien's chest and stretched a tentative arm over him.

"Want to tell me about it, beautiful?"

Fanshawe huffed a laugh. "It's nothing you can help with. Nothing anyone can help with."

Lucien knew the sound of a door closing when he heard one. It was unreasonable to feel shut out, though: Fanshawe didn't owe him an explanation. Stifling a sigh, he held him, since it seemed to soothe him. And because it was lovely, to hold Fanshawe in his arms in daylight.

"You know—" Fanshawe stroked his flank. "We've never talked about anything personal."

He'd got the impression Fanshawe had purposely kept their conversations general. "That has occurred to me." The door between them had shifted his dialect back to nob.

"So, er… What d'you do like to do? In your spare time?"

"We seem to share a taste for theatre, given where we met."

"*Two Naughty Boys*?" Fanshawe sounded dubious.

Lucien laughed. "A ridiculous title for a ridiculous play."

"I assumed you were only there to report. Once I knew you were a journalist."

"I was, for that one. But I enjoy theatre in general, and musical theatre in particular."

"Henrietta persuaded us to go. Said she wanted to see the sort of thing Rupert and I got up to at school."

Fanshawe's easy use of the Hernedales' Christian names, his volunteering of a personal anecdote, were so intimate they made Lucien's chest ache. "And did she?"

"Lord, no." Fanshawe's smile was a light pressure on Lucien's skin. "She was teasing. We'd have been caned raw if we'd got up to a tenth of that mischief."

Lucien brushed a finger across Fanshawe's lips, upturned for now, and his heart lightened. "You have good memories of school?"

Fanshawe kissed his finger, but his back tensed. "Just smiling over Henrietta's tease. I loathed the damned place. Chock-full of boys who loved cricket and the Field Game and despised anyone who didn't. Thank God for Rupert."

"He seems the quiet sort," Lucien agreed. Hard to imagine Hernedale enjoying anything more energetic than a leisurely postprandial stroll from drawing room to terrace and back.

"What else do you like to do?"

Lucien hesitated. What if Fanshawe resented him as the cricket and Field Game sort? But he'd better know that sooner than later. "Boxing." Fanshawe didn't flinch. "I instruct at a club in Lincoln's Inn Fields."

"Accounts for the muscles." Fanshawe stroked Lucien's shoulder.

Lucien relaxed, smiling at the compliment. "Partly. Single-stick accounts for the rest. Sabre, really, from my time in the army, but the club can't afford sabres, so we teach single-stick. Same principles."

"You were in the cavalry?"

"18th Hussars. Discharged in 1902."

Fanshawe raised himself on an elbow and stared into his eyes. Then: "Ladysmith?" Evidently, he kept up with the news.

"Yes."

"I'm sorry."

Lucien mustered a smile. "So was I."

Fanshawe sank back into the pillows. "Do you ride much now?"

"When I can. I've always loved horses."

"I ride, too, though I wouldn't go so far as to say I love horses. Is that why you carry a riding cane?"

"I don't ride often enough for that."

"Oh?"

"I tell people it's for self-defence. Nowhere's entirely safe, even in the day."

"But that's not true?"

Lucien kissed his forehead. "Something longer would be more practical, but it's not altogether untrue. I'd rather rely on my fists, though. Unless I was facing a knife."

A waiting silence.

He could change the subject: Fanshawe'd follow out of ingrained courtesy. Instead he said, "It's a memorial. To friends who died in a pointless war; who'd never have signed up, if they'd known the horrors we'd support, and how stupid some officers could be. And a reminder to myself, to be careful what I support in future."

Fanshawe's lips lay against Lucien's jaw for a long moment; then he kissed his cheek, and the corner of his lips. Then settled back on the pillows in silence.

It was up to Lucien to restart the conversation: God knew Fanshawe couldn't, after that revelation. "What do you enjoy?"

"Nothing anywhere near as—"

Lucien closed his eyes, anticipating 'adventurous' or 'exciting'.

"—active or varied as you."

He let out his breath. "Things don't have to be active to be interesting."

"Are you patronising me?" Fanshawe was grinning.

"No. At least, I don't mean to."

"I'm quite accustomed to it. Well, not from—"

'The lower orders,' Lucien's mind supplied.

"—you, of course, because we don't know one another well enough yet. But in general."

Was there a promise in those words? "I hope I won't patronise you even when we know one another better," he said carefully. Fanshawe didn't flinch at 'when' rather than 'if'. "And I hope you'd tell me if I did."

Fanshawe cupped his cheek in a warm palm, and gazed at him with what his deluded mind insisted was affection. "I like the theatre, too. And fencing."

"You fence?"

"Not well, nor as frequently as I should."

"Sabre?"

"Yes. Otherwise, I draw quite badly, I play the piano quite badly, and I write mediocre fiction."

Lucien's interest sharpened. "Published?"

Fanshawe hesitated. "A few short stories."

"Which magazine?"

"Er. The *Athenaeum*."

Lucien stared at him. "I doubt they're mediocre, in that case."

"Well, they're not exactly Wilde."

"Who is, except Wilde? I'm no Dickens myself. What name do you write under?"

Aubrey hesitated again, then sighed. "Avery Edmonton."

"I'll keep an eye out for your work."

"Look, don't expect greatness, will you? You'll only be disappointed."

"Don't worry so much." He kissed Fanshawe's narrow lips. "Excuse me." Rolling over, he reached for his pocket watch on the bedside table. Quarter to nine. He snapped it shut, sighing, and sat up. "I have to go."

When he came out of the WC, Fanshawe was standing at the washstand, naked, the lines of his body tense. Lucien paused, then slowly joined him.

Fanshawe held up a soaped facecloth. "Shall I wash your back?"

Lucien searched his eyes. "We're... not pretending, are we? I'd rather you were honestly frosty than—"

"I said I wouldn't." A wave of crimson swept up Fanshawe's neck and face, and bled down his chest.

"Thanks: I'd like that." Lucien turned.

The cloth was brisk and business-like and cold. Lucien bowed his head and rolled a shoulder, hoping to ease Aubrey's anxiety. The cloth paused, then resumed more slowly, spiralling up his spine, sliding over the nape of his neck.

That was better.

A hand joined the cloth, gliding over soapy skin, soothing and sensual.

Fanshawe kept at it much longer than necessary—till the cloth felt almost warm—then smoothed a palm down Lucien's spine, sighed, and rinsed the cloth. He returned to wipe the soap from his back with long, cool strokes.

When Lucien turned, it was to clear evidence that Fanshawe had enjoyed the experience every bit as much as he had. "Your turn," he murmured.

He soaped a clean facecloth to thick, soft slickness, and slid it across Fanshawe's broad-boned back, circling over his shoulder-blades and ribs, working slowly down to his buttocks. "Lean forward a bit."

Fanshawe leaned on the washstand, and Lucien soaped his buttocks, then slid the cloth into the cleft between them. Fanshawe gasped, and his head drooped.

"That's it," Lucien murmured into his shoulder. "Relax. This might take some time."

"Mmm. Might it?"

Lucien warmed to the smile in his tone. "If you want it to." He kissed his shoulder blade. "There's a lot to clean up, after last night."

"Is there really?" Fanshawe's legs parted. "How much?"

"Oh, it's just... everywhere." Lucien slipped the cloth over and around his balls, and Fanshawe gasped and pressed closer. "You were so beautiful. So thrilling. You couldn't possibly have held all I had to give you."

"Lucien..." Fanshawe's thighs trembled.

Aubrey. Lovely Aubrey. Lucien stroked the soft, soapy cloth the length of Fanshawe's rigid shaft, sliding the fingers of his other hand along Fanshawe's soap-slick cleft and down to massage his balls. "You emptied me," he whispered, touched by Fanshawe's ragged breathing. "I shot so hard and long my spunk must've soaked your balls. Must've spilled down your cleft as I fucked you."

"Oh God!" Fanshawe's shoulders hunched and his hips arched forward.

"That's it, beautiful." Lucien rubbed his jaw along Fanshawe's shoulder blade and slid his fingers higher, massaging Fanshawe's ring as he slowly worked his cock. "You did so well. I had so much to give you, and you did your best. You took as much as you possibly could."

Fanshawe moaned and pressed back against his fingers.

Lucien flattened them, to glide over him. "Sssh. Not inside. Not with soap. It might sting. But you've already got me inside, from last night, filling you up." Fanshawe gasped and quivered. "You'll hold me deep inside you all day." Was that too much? Apparently not, because Fanshawe moaned and jerked, and his cock pressed hard into Lucien's hand.

"That's the way." Lucien laid his cheek on Fanshawe's shoulder blade, feeling him fuck the smooth, slick cloth, watching his buttocks work, watching his own fingers slide along his crease. "That's how you took me last night." He wet and soaped his hand again, massaged the relaxing muscle. "That's how you pumped me dry."

Fanshawe groaned and bent lower, resting his head on his folded arms, pressing back and spreading his legs. Irresistible.

"Is this what you need, beautiful?" Lucien rested the shaft of his straining cock along Fanshawe's warm cleft.

"Yes!" Fanshawe gasped, working harder, and Lucien joined his dance, sliding between his buttocks, pressing closer, working his own hips.

"Ah God, but you feel beautiful underneath me. Beautiful around me." They picked up speed.

Fanshawe began to lose rhythm. Lucien closed the cloth over the head of his cock, clamped a firm hand on his hip, and thrust, strong and regular, along his cleft.

"Oh God!" Fanshawe shuddered. Lucien increased the pressure. "Oh!"

Lucien was close to the edge, his cock filling and his balls tightening. "Come on, beautiful," he urged. "Let me have it. Please let me have you!"

With a moan that grew to a bellow, Fanshawe did, ramming tight and hard into his fist, his ring clenching with spasms Lucien felt along his shaft. Lucien fingered Fanshawe's cock lightly through the soapy cloth, coaxing the last dregs of pleasure from his quivering body as he rode his flushed buttocks to ball-knotting, groaning completion.

The world went black and silent, and when it returned, he was resting on Fanshawe's long, slippery back, his belly in a pool of his own semen. With trembling fingers, he eased the cloth from Fanshawe's cock, careful to hold in his issue, and put it on the washstand. Wrapping both arms around Fanshawe's belly, he nuzzled his back. "You all right, beautiful?"

"Shit. Yes. Dear *God*." Fanshawe rocked his forehead on his folded arms.

Lying over him, Lucien kissed Fanshawe's back; stroked his hips, his flanks, his shoulders.

At last, sighing, he straightened, picked up his cloth, and cleaned Fanshawe's back and buttocks and crease. Fanshawe shifted, and Lucien laid a gentle hand on him. "Stay there a moment." He helped himself to a clean cloth from the wardrobe—just as well Fanshawe had a good supply there—and washed Fanshawe again, from nape to thigh.

"Thank you." Fanshawe straightened.

"Just a sec." Lucien fetched another cloth, and carefully washed Fanshawe from head to toe. "There, now." He dropped the cloth on the washstand and kissed his cheek.

Fanshawe fetched a clean facecloth from the wardrobe. Lucien reached for it, but Fanshawe wet it, then swept it across Lucien's cheek. "Your turn." His voice shook, uncertain, but his lips were firm.

So Lucien stood, a hard lump growing in his throat, while Fanshawe lathered the cloth and washed him, gently and thoroughly.

When he'd finished, Fanshawe bent and pressed his lips to Lucien's for a long moment. "There," he whispered. He sounded calmer, more sure of himself.

"I can't—" Lucien swallowed. "I have to go. I don't like to leave so abruptly after— That is to say, assuming you actually wanted me to stay, but—"

"You have work. I understand."

Lucien sighed. "Yes."

Warm palms cradled Lucien's neck. Fanshawe leaned their foreheads together, his eyes closed, then sighed. "You'd better dress."

Lucien flung on his clothes, glancing at his watch. Not enough time to get to his rooms before work. Just as well his stubble was pale and slow-growing. With any luck, his suit wouldn't look as creased and stained to anyone else as it did to him. And the shirt... He sniffed it discreetly. Could be worse. Just as well he'd changed after the procession.

Fanshawe, wearing nothing but a plum-coloured figured-silk dressing gown that made him look altogether too appealing— particularly with his hair rumpled, and his face shaded with morning stubble, and his body full of Lucien—kissed him as he turned the key in the lock, then whisked out of sight as Lucien opened the door. Like a startled fawn, Lucien mused fondly.

Once past Noel, on Vigo Street, reality intruded. He flipped his watch open: he'd just missed a tube, and it'd be quicker to walk than wait for the next. Abandoning poise in favour of speed, he hurried across London, the pace of his body outmatched by the pace of his mind. Fanshawe had washed him, and not as a sexual approach. Had *served* him. Sober, and standing in the plain light of day.

What the devil was he to make of that?

LUCIEN PUFFED INTO an almost deserted office. He was early, though not by much.

"Morning, Miss Enfield." He hung up his outdoor things and sank into his seat. "Are you well, after yesterday?"

"Perfectly, thank you." She looked at him over the top of her reading glasses. "Wake up late this morning?"

"Something like that." He pulled out his notebook and stared at it. Damn. "Can we look at your work for now? Left mine at home."

She watched him a fraction too long, then slid her work towards him. "Hope he's worth it," she murmured.

Lucien shot her a grateful smile. "Me too." He picked up a page and skimmed it, and his heart sank. "Er. Bit militant," he suggested. Damn it! She *knew* Jameson wanted a gossip piece.

"I know. I was too tired to correct for tone last night."

At least she wasn't wedded to it. "We might make it heart-tugging instead?"

Miss Enfield sighed. "Thought of that. 'Brave little ladies endure bad weather for a hopeless cause'."

"Sentimentalised character sketches," Lucien agreed. "Flower of British womanhood. Family unity and loyal friendships."

"I suppose it's better than Jameson's approach: 'Selfish, feather-brained harpies attempt to disrupt the serious business of Parliament'."

"He might tolerate a bit of politics, if we present it the right way."

"Damn it." She looked wistfully at her work. "All right. We'll give him big hats and flowing skirts and pretty faces upturned in shy supplication."

Lucien cocked an eyebrow. "Mrs Drummond?"

She half-choked on a laugh. "Oh Lord, she'll be appalled, but they need publicity, and we need a story for Jameson. Ah, dash it all, Saxby." She laid her glasses on the table and rubbed her eyes. "I'm never getting out of this damned niche, am I?"

Lucien fumbled for an appropriate response.

She jammed her glasses back on her face. "If Jameson wanted a serious political story, he'd have sent political hacks, regardless of how well they communicate with women."

"That's... more or less what he said."

"Right." She closed her eyes. "Did you note clothes and hats? Because I was more focussed on the politics."

"Style and colour for each of the speakers and organisers." He tapped his notebook. "And general impressions of the rest. It's all written up at home."

Miss Enfield stared at his shoulder. "Look, there's no point reprising work you've already done. Go home and get whatever you need: I'll cover for you. And Saxby?" She leaned closer and lowered her voice. "Pomade stain on your jacket. Shoulder and collar."

"Righteo!" His face felt hot enough to melt spoons.

Once outside, he set a quick pace, but the scent from a coffee stall, still open from the night before, dragged him to a halt. A tired-looking woman leaned over a basin behind the stall, washing cups and plates.

"Morning!"

She looked up, sighed and dried her hands on her apron.

"Coffee, please," Lucien said. "And—" He glanced over the food. "A slice of currant cake." It'd be less dried-out than the bread.

He blew on the drink she handed him.

Fanshawe'd called him 'Lucien'. Only during sex, but didn't it mean something, that a formal sort of fellow used your Christian name?

He balanced the plate on the edge of the stall and bit into the cake. Like sawdust, despite the currants. A scalding mouthful of over-brewed coffee helped it down, and brought him to his senses.

Fanshawe could use his Christian name without invitation because he was a nob and Lucien was a working man. But Lucien couldn't use Fanshawe's Christian name, however senseless with pleasure he might be, until Fanshawe invited him to.

You'd invite a friend to use your Christian name, wouldn't you?

Except—he hadn't behaved like a friend last night.

Lucien's throat closed. "Thanks," he rasped. He handed back the half-empty dishes and hurried on.

Fanshawe had looked soft and sleepy, rosy-cheeked with brandy: more endearing than a chap his size had any right to look. Lucien had just wanted to look after him and pet him. And Fanshawe'd obliged, since he was accustomed to being looked after.

By Grieve.

William was right: Lucien was a natural-born sodding valet. McHenry was right: he wanted his bloody duke. Or rather, an earl's son, which was just as impossible.

He slammed the front door of the boarding house open.

"Hoy! Who the bloody hell's that, then?" Mrs Emmott stormed into the hallway, blacking brush in hand.

"Only me. Sorry."

"I should bloody well think you are sorry." She nudged the front door shut, inspecting the wall while he stood guiltily on the bottom step. "No harm done this time, but you mind my bloody walls, Mr Saxby!"

"Will do. Sorry."

"Why're you here, anyway?" She looked him up and down. "Lost your job?"

"No, no. Just fetching some paperwork. In a bit of a rush, actually."

He darted up the stairs, but Mrs Emmott thundered close behind him. Damn it. Not that he blamed her—a single default on the rent would cut her income by a fifth—but he wasn't going to be that sort of problem and didn't want to waste half an hour reassuring her.

The door opposite his own stood open. Mrs Emmott's daughter crouched at the fireplace, ash-pan in hand, pale and watchful.

Grim-faced, Mrs Emmott pushed past him to join her, and slammed the door.

Oh.

His rooms had been cleaned, and the early post lay on the table. He retrieved his pages from the desk, folded them into his pocket, and turned to leave. Then remembered the pomade stains.

He stripped, shaved quickly, and dressed, trying not to dwell on Fanshawe washing him; on Fanshawe watching him dress, his face smooth and bright with the aftermath of pleasure Lucien had brought and taken. Probably just as well he couldn't use the fellow's given name: God knew if any more social boundaries were removed, he'd be lost entirely.

The hallway was blessedly Emmott-free when he left. Reluctant to invoke her again, he crept downstairs and out, closing the front door quietly enough to satisfy even Dad. But Fanshawe haunted him all the way back to work.

He didn't need to get attached to another nob who'd require endless care and attention and never return them. What he needed was someone like Ben, but unmarried. Someone to share lodgings with; share friends and a life with. Even if Fanshawe felt as Lucien did—and he doubted the irresistible, self-involved blighter did—a wealthy earl's son could never justify living with a working man.

And yet, he wanted him. He just... wanted him.

Trudging into the office, he hung up his outdoor things, raising an eyebrow at Miss Enfield, who'd moved to the chair beside his.

"Bridges swapped seats, since we're working together."

For the next hour, they cut out paragraphs, then wrote and cut more, arranging them into a narrative leavened with description. They scribbled in bridging phrases, then finally wrote the whole thing out again, correcting for tone.

"Bloody hell." Miss Enfield slumped over the table. "Cosh me, before Mrs Drummond reads that travesty in the morning paper."

Lucien grinned. "I take it you don't want to do the honours?"

She waved a feeble hand. "Take it away, Saxby. Before I immolate it and myself with it."

So Lucien found an unoccupied typist and dictated their copy, then trudged downstairs, hoping today wouldn't be the day Jameson demanded his scoop.

— Chapter Eleven —

IN THE EVENT, Jameson had been engrossed in an article, and only grunted when Lucien put the report on his desk. Relieved, he'd escaped to the familiar comfort of writing fashion news for the remainder of the day.

His walk home provided more time to think than was healthy, and he opened the boarding house door torn between a heady sense of freedom and a heavy sense of loss. On the one hand, William was well enough that he needn't visit as often, so he wouldn't miss club tonight. On the other, he wouldn't miss club tonight because he wasn't visiting Fanshawe.

This moping was absurd: he'd woken up with the fellow just this morning, for heaven's sake! But, flawed though it'd been, he wanted to cement the morning's warmth and intimacy—its sheer friendliness—before Fanshawe retreated to the brittle awkwardness of their previous mornings together.

The mood still dogged him when he climbed the stairs after dinner. He found his fire dwindled to a red glow and a few small, yellow-tipped blue claws, so he eased the poker into the bottom of the grate and levered upward. Coals rose and tumbled, and the flames gasped and leapt free. A shame it wasn't as easy to relieve his own claustrophobic thoughts.

A quiet, deferential tap. So out of place that Lucien jolted upright, staring at the door, before putting the poker in its stand.

One of William's footman stood outside, holding a valise and a leather hatbox.

The evening dress. Which he wouldn't need, if he'd never met Fanshawe and the Hernedales.

"Hullo Frank."

"Evening, Mr Saxby."

Everyone had their rung on the cast-iron ladder of the social hierarchy. But surely the fellow who'd voluntarily washed his semen-streaked body shouldn't be Fanshawe to him. Mightn't they... step aside? Together?

"Landlady let me up cause it's just a quick delivery."

"Thanks." Lucien tipped him. "Camberhithe well?"

"Bout the same as yesterday." Frank's gaze darted to the stairs. "Can't stop: Mr Dawson said not to dawdle." He probably hoped to snatch a minute with a friend or lover before going back to work.

"Righteo." Lucien shut the door, carried the luggage to his bedroom, and unfolded the evening dress, item by item, onto his narrow bed. A complete set, from silk top hat to gleaming, ribbon-laced dress pumps. Magnificent. Barely worn.

His.

William had sent everything he'd need. Except he hadn't: McHenry would've selected and packed it all.

Lucien yearned to put it on. And flinched from wearing William's cast-offs once more: redundant clothes for the second-class child.

He closed his eyes, reaching for rationality.

He needed this. William hadn't meant to hurt him; had only kept his word—sent what he'd asked for. And when he sent more in March, it'd be absurd to reject them only to spend hard-earned money on clothes which wouldn't look as good or last as long. He was *lucky*. Lucky that so much was his for the asking. Time to stop feeling sorry for himself over his good fortune, and pass some along.

He'd repaired and altered his own clothes since his youth, but, skilled though he was, he couldn't do the evening dress justice. It'd take a professional to fit it perfectly, and he knew just the woman.

Taking a deep breath, he cleared the top shelf behind his clothes rail, then picked up the shoe box. It felt oddly unbalanced, so he opened it again.

Tucked behind the tissue paper at one end of the box was a burgundy leather jewellery case. He stared, then sat on the bed to open it. A matched set of conservative pearl studs on gold backings—shirt studs, collar studs, and cuff links—nestled in the white silk lining.

Even nobs didn't dispose of jewellery as they disposed of clothes.

Lucien touched a cool, smooth pearl with his fingertip. From William, directly. Not a careless cast-off or a gift of money. This was... thoughtful. Meaningful. The perfect gift, chosen with care; with his express wishes in mind.

Closing his eyes, he swallowed the rough lump in his throat. Then stood and carried the jewellery case to the living room, and locked it in his writing desk.

Back in his bedroom, he re-wrapped and boxed the accessories and stacked them on the top shelf. Then he hung the suit and shirt, straightening and smoothing each item to perfection.

Because he was a natural-born sodding valet.

LUCIEN'S MUSCLES RELAXED as he stepped into the lobby of the church hall. Through the open hall doors came the smack of fists on bags, hoarse shouts, and a thick reek of leather, sweat and sawdust, underlaid with the sharp nip of vinegar and a hint of mould. He sucked in the air as though it were a sea breeze.

The side room which stored the club's equipment between meetings doubled as their changing room, though most members couldn't afford exercise clothes and trained in their long underwear and bare feet. Lucien pulled on the vest, leggings, and soft training shoes from his army days, then stood in the hall doorway, assessing where help was needed.

Nearby, an instructor supervised bare-fisted men working through drills in pairs. Both punch bags, suspended from beams in the middle of the room, were in use. Beyond them, three men pummelled punch-balls with varying degrees of skill, while another instructor helped a daunted-looking young bloke with the fourth.

In the far corner, Ben, stripped gloriously to the waist, demonstrated basic strikes with a single-stick. "Watch my bloody *feet*, will you?" he said. "Swinging the stick's the easy bit." Lucien grinned. His mind cleared, and his body lightened.

Someone yelped. Dragging his gaze from Ben, Lucien sighed and made for Tommy. The new lad Ben had described in St James' Park had turned out to be a disastrous combination of inept and alarmingly keen.

"I told you: mind how you punch that bag!" Ben yelled. "You'll strain your wrist and elbow."

"S'only pain." Tommy punched again.

"Right. That's it." Ben strode across the room. "Stop." He shoved his stick at Lucien and grabbed the bag. "Either you're here to learn, or you're here to show off. And if you're here to show off, you can piss off."

"I'm not!" Tommy's fists fell to his sides. "Just ain't going to be put off by a few bumps."

"We ain't a children's club, Tommy. We're grown men with families relying on us. And if you think anyone'll train with you when you don't even mind your own safety, you got another think coming."

"I ain't—!" Tommy's thin shoulders sagged beneath his old, misshapen undershirt. "I ain't going to hurt anyone."

"You ain't going to get the bloody chance!"

"Watch the others for now," Lucien suggested. "And think about what Ben said. We're all busy men, and we're not paid to teach. We won't waste time on blokes who won't listen."

Tommy slunk away, and Lucien turned to Ben. "You all right?"

"Bloody grumpy, is all."

"Jem all right?"

"No worse, at least." Ben turned to watch the drills. "Cath's auntie says he should live in the country. I told her the sodding manor house'd have to wait till I next get paid." Lucien laughed, and Ben slid him a wry, grateful look. "What can you do, eh? Sodding countryside."

"Got a job for your Cath, actually, if she's not too busy."

"What's that then?"

"Set of evening dress to alter."

Ben stared at him. "Ain't taken to house-breaking have you?"

"Heh. Cast-off from a—an acquaintance." He'd almost said 'friend'.

"An acquaintance," Ben echoed flatly.

"Nob acquaintance. Tell you about him sometime."

Ben's face closed. "Won't bloody know you, time you're done."

If someone gave Ben a set of evening dress, he'd sell it to pay for a doctor. Horror at his own thoughtlessness arced through Lucien's chest and deep into his belly. "Don't be daft: course you will. Unless you don't want to."

Ben's grin didn't reach his eyes. "Won't get rid of me that easy. I'll camp on your palace doorstep and embarrass you."

"You bloody well won't. You'll come in the front door like everyone else."

"Mind there's swanky cake when I come round." Ben clapped him on the arm, but his face was remote. "When d'you need that suit done?"

"Within the week, ideally. But if you'd rather not—"

"A week?" Ben whistled. "Don't ask for much, do you? All right. I'll let you know tomorrow."

After class, the instructors sparred. By the time Lucien unlaced the gloves, his shoulders felt loose and light, and Ben's smile looked warmer.

"Nearly as good as a nice hard shag, eh Luce?"

Relieved, Lucien laughed. "If you say so."

The instructors cleaned and oiled the equipment, swept the floors, then locked up.

Ben clapped Lucien on the arm. "Till tomorrow night, then, your swanky lordship."

Lucien sighed.

"Now then, don't get the hump." Ben laughed like shattering glass. "You'll only make it harder to fit in your fancy new togs."

Lucien trudged home alone, aching for Ben, but also, selfishly, for himself. Ben's 'your lordship' tease stung almost as much as William's 'natural-born valet' comment. Both said he didn't belong and never would; that when they looked at him, nobs and working people alike saw only a flawed imitation of themselves.

Long as a man knows himself. And doesn't forget where he come from.

He knew exactly where he came from, thank you very much, McHenry: a long line of diligent, determined working people. He took pride in their achievements.

But he also knew himself. He was a working man, but, thanks to Mum and Dad, he hadn't been raised as a working man: not really. He'd always known he'd never be homeless, nor starve, nor watch his family starve. He'd taken risks—chosen and changed careers—confident that feather beds lay ready to break his fall. Even his dialect made people listen to him in a way they wouldn't listen to Ben.

Ben liked him—Lucien didn't doubt that—but it'd be hard not to be at least a little bitter when you couldn't offer your family a fraction of the security your friend had been born with.

Lucien unlocked the door to his rooms, tireder than a day at work and an evening at the club could possibly justify.

It'd be hard not to be at least a little bitter when the clothes on your friend's back could save your child's life, if only they were yours.

— Chapter Twelve —

A bit after seven the following evening, Lucien ushered Ben into the dining room of his boarding house.

"How's Cath?"

"Well enough. Busy."

Ah.

"But not too busy for my mate Luce, she says." Ben clapped him on the arm. "So pack up your nob togs and come along: Cinderella's going to the bloody ball."

William's evening pumps, gloves, and collar hadn't fitted, so Lucien had sold them. The proceeds had covered a new collar and evening gloves. Pumps would have to wait.

He packed the suit and shirt into the valise, then folded payment—generous, but not so much as to look like charity—into a sheet of paper and slid it down the side.

Then he and Ben walked companionably through dark, narrow streets, almost as though nothing had happened to crack their friendship.

Lucien brushed the back of his gloved hand against Ben's. "I meant what I said last month. About the doctor."

"I know." Ben unlocked the door to a shabby house on Great Wild Street.

Lucien laid a hand on his arm.

Ben stilled, then sighed. "I'm just grumpy, Luce. Ain't your fault. I'll get over it." He locked the door behind them, sealing them into a narrow, dark hallway thick with the smell of cold boiled mutton and onions. Opening the door to their left, he showed Lucien in to a busy room, warm with gaslight. Two women behind a long table at the back of the room looked up from their sewing.

"Cath and Mary, meet Luce." Ben hung Lucien's outdoor things on a peg beside the door.

"Wotcher, Luce." Cath, thin and pale with straight blonde hair pulled back in an untidy bun, stood and shook hands. "Let's have these togs, then."

"Dad!" A small, fluffy-haired, golden-brown boy hurled himself at Ben.

"Sam!" Ben pinned on a smile and swung the boy high. "Whoops!" He pretended to drop him. The boy shrieked with glee, then grunted as Ben caught him and set him down.

On the floor, two more small children played with a rag doll and a rag ball. A fourth, older—perhaps five or six years old—sat on a rag rug at the hearth, supporting a pale baby against her body. A cloud of black hair covered her shoulders and half-hid her tired, sallow face. The baby, in a flannel dress, gnawed a glistening fist which clutched a knot of rag ribbons, and stared into the small, curling flames, coughing lightly after every few breaths.

Lucien laid the clothes on the scrubbed table.

Mary—taller than Cath, with neatly braided light brown hair—folded a trouser leg back. "Nice broad seams."

"Have you tried it on?" Cath asked.

"No point. Chap I got it from is about my height, but thinner." William had never grown even as tall as his sister Marjorie, let alone his brothers.

"All right. Let's measure you. Chuck me the tape measure, Mary."

Lucien took off his jacket and laid it over a chair back, feeling uncomfortably exposed. It was one thing to undress for

William's tailor, quite another in front of women. By the time he put his collar and tie on the table and his collar studs in the bowl Cath offered, he felt naked.

"Waistcoat, too: let's get a good fit."

Appalled, Lucien turned to Ben.

"Don't look at me." Ben, holding the baby to his shoulder, poured boiling water into a teapot on the hearth table. "They're the experts."

The girl who'd been minding the baby was playing with the others, and looking a lot less tired. He felt a painful affinity with her that almost eclipsed his embarrassment.

Almost.

Reluctantly, he unbuttoned his waistcoat.

Cath's hands, wielding the tape measure, felt alarmingly intimate with just his shirt between them; worse when she measured his wrist and neck, her thin fingers cool and dry on his bare skin. He gritted his teeth when she looped the tape around his hips; and when she knelt in front of him and stretched the tape up his inside leg, he flinched.

She dropped her hands to her lap. "Don't worry, love: I ain't interested in your family jewels." Heat flooded Lucien's face and neck. "What with kids and work, I barely got time to keep my own polished." She grinned up at him, and then at Ben, behind him.

Lucien's face boiled, but— Somehow, Cath's words didn't feel as intrusive as they should. Probably because, unlike Chiddicks, she meant to be kind.

"Ben says it was you wrote in the paper about the women's procession." Mary didn't look up from unpicking the trouser waistband.

"Miss Enfield and I did."

"That's the lady journalist I saw there?"

"You were there?" He gritted his teeth but held still as Cath stretched the tape up his inside leg.

"All day."

Cath re-measured, then stood and patted his arm. "All done, love."

"Were you there, Cath?"

"No time, or I would've been." She fastened the collar to the back of his shirt with practiced efficiency, and offered him the front stud. "You can put your jacket back on if you like."

Lucien did bloody like. He wanted his waistcoat, too.

"Cath looked after the kids for me."

"S'what big sisters are for." Cath pencilled a note on a scrap of paper.

"I meant to sew while I was there—you can do plain sewing while you walk, you know, just a bit slower—but it didn't work out. The hall was too packed, and then it rained, so I hardly got a bloody thing done."

Lucien's fingers paused on his tie. "Must've been difficult to make up that time."

Mary laughed the painful, slightly manic laugh of the permanently overstretched. "Stayed up late four nights, sewing under a lamppost. Saves on gas, and they're bright enough for plain work."

In February. Lucien shrugged into his jacket and felt dressed again.

"Worth it, though," Mary added.

"Was it?" This was a perfect example of poor people serving the interests of the wealthy to their own detriment.

"You maybe don't see it, being a bloke. But it was something, to watch women stand up and speak, as bold as any man. And to see them listened to, and all, even if it was only by other women."

"*I* listened."

"But you was paid to. Probly wouldn't have been there, else."

True.

"Seeing women like your Miss Enfield was something, and all: women with jobs as good as any man's."

"She does the same job I do," Lucien agreed. "Exactly the same."

Ben put a cup of weak-looking tea on the table in front of him, then turned back to the hearth, where he'd left another three. Jem coughed on his shoulder.

"I'll get them." Lucien fetched the other cups, hoping he wasn't drinking the last of their tea, while Ben settled at the table.

"Thanks." Still holding the trousers, Mary sipped her scalding drink. "It's a relief, knowing there's more chances for my girls than working their fingers raw at fancy sewing till their eyes get too old, then scraping by on plain sewing till their eyes get too old for that; or else street-walking and maybe dying young."

Cath cast her a sharp glance.

"Well I ain't wrong!"

"I bloody well know you ain't."

Ben glanced between them, and stood. "Right, kids! Let's get you to bed. Dolly and Lizzie, you're sleeping here tonight: your mum's staying late to get some work done." The two little girls squealed, thrilled. "Winnie, come along darling, we got to plait your hair."

"I don't want to. It hurts!" The eldest girl trailed miserably towards him.

"I know, pet, but it'll only be worse in the morning, else."

Lucien gazed at her cloud of thick, curly, longish hair and winced at the potential for tangles. "Shall I look after Jem while you do that?"

"You?" Ben stared at him. "You ever held a baby?"

"Can't be that hard. And it looks as though you'll need both hands."

"Could do with at least three, if you ask me." He draped a cloth over Lucien's shoulder, then laid Jem on it, face down. "Keep him leaning a bit forward, all right? He coughs more when he leans back."

Jem was surprisingly heavy for someone so small. A soft-skinned, warm forehead pressed against Lucien's throat, and fluffy hair tickled his jaw. This close, he heard the quiet wheeze of every breath, felt the rattle in the small chest, and the whole-

153

body convulsion of each cough. A plump starfish hand rested on his starched collar, fingers clenching and opening.

"Suits you." Ben's eyes were soft when they met Lucien's, and his smile, warm. "Be wanting one of your own, next. Come along, Winnie love."

While Cath and Mary measured and pinned, Lucien laid his cheek lightly on the fluffy hair and listened to the baby fight for breath. He stroked the hand on his collar with a fingertip, and Jem grabbed it and pulled it towards his mouth. Afraid of choking him, Lucien crooked his finger and let him gnaw on a knuckle.

The toothless gums were unexpectedly hard. And Lucien hadn't known babies—let alone sick babies—could have such strong jaws. Between that and the warm drool flooding down his finger into his palm, he'd have pulled away if Jem hadn't been enjoying it so much.

But this child, of all children, should have every possible thing he wanted. Unlike William, he didn't have the best doctors, nor servants to attend him night and day; just struggling parents and a diligent sister barely out of infancy herself. Who knew how long he'd survive?

"Does he have a godfather?" he murmured.

"Who? Jemmy?" Cath glanced up from pinning. "No."

"I'd be his godfather. If you and Ben want it."

Cath and Mary stared at him, then exchanged glances.

"I'll talk to Ben about it," Cath said at last.

— Chapter Thirteen —

Miss Amory gazed up with parted lips as Aubrey drew her close and whirled her into another turn. Her cheeks flushed and, over her décolletage, her small bosom rose and fell more quickly than the exertion of the dance justified.

She felt wrong. He wanted Henrietta's frankness and energy, Rupert's quiet self-containment, Lucien's deep sensuality and easy physicality.

The debutante was feather-light in his arms: an insubstantial blend of over-tutored civility and inchoate need lent temporary shape by a whalebone and satin casing.

Lucien had called him 'love'.

Aubrey might be mistaken—he'd been drunk on emotion and sensation—but he seemed to remember he'd even called him '*my* love' that night. That... particular night.

He spun through the dance with practised ease, drawing the debutante with him.

But Lucien hadn't called him 'love' when he'd seen him again, three nights ago, two mornings ago. Maybe he called every chap he bedded 'love' now and then: nice and easy; no name to mistake. The idea was a blunt ache in Aubrey's chest.

He led Miss Amory through the last steps with flawless grace and a reassuring smile. Amazing what relentless tutoring could achieve: he might knock over drinks, but he could waltz with the best. When the music ended, he escorted her back to her mama and left her with a murmur of gratitude and a disagreeable suspicion that he was abandoning her in a shark pool. Not that he could do anything about it: she'd been restored to the bosom of her family and would have to take her chances. He edged towards the terrace doors, smiling and greeting.

"Fanshawe!"

Oh hell. "Lowdon." Aubrey adjusted his smile to polite but distant and kept walking. Liberating though it was not to have to socialise with the fellow anymore, the actual avoiding was desperately uncomfortable. But he was close to the doors, and within a few steps, he escaped.

That poor girl. Resting an elbow on the balustrade, Aubrey took a deep breath of cold night air. She knew nothing about him beyond his name, rank, and, probably, approximate expected income. But she'd glowed at his smile, and melted when the dance required their bodies touch. She'd easily confuse her physical yearnings for love, and swoon into the hand of any man who didn't seem entirely objectionable, because she didn't know what would suit her. Couldn't. She'd been over-sheltered to produce this precise result.

Unlike Lucien, who knew exactly what he wanted, and had a personality Aubrey couldn't overlook. Who, far from trying to transform himself into aether, knew how to use his weight and strength to thrill.

But what future could they have together? Nobody'd invite a gossip journalist even to lunch, let alone a house party.

A shadow part-blocked the light from the open doorway.

"You all right?" Rupert leaned on the balustrade beside him, elegant in evening dress. "You left in a bit of a hurry."

"Oh. Well. Fresh air, you know."

Rupert waited.

"They just— The girls are too young."

"If they were, they wouldn't be here."

"In experience, not years. Miss Amory, for one. Handing her over to fellows to be guided around and flattered and— Well, it's obscene. She doesn't understand."

Rupert studied his face. "She's aware she's trying to marry a wealthy nobleman."

"She's being encouraged to resign her entire life to a chap based on his rank, wealth and company manners. How will she feel when she realises he isn't a delightful dream?"

"Most of us take that chance."

"You and Henrietta didn't."

"Well. Not everyone can marry their childhood friend."

"Not everyone *has* a childhood friend of the opposite sex," Aubrey pointed out. "And those friendships often end at puberty."

Maybe he should've married young, like Rupert. The debutantes hadn't seemed so child-like then. He and a wife might've grown together. But he'd always had Rupert, and then he had Henrietta, too, and either of them was more interesting than any debutante he'd ever met, let alone both together.

"Try someone around our age," Rupert suggested.

"You mean, someone who married within a couple of years of her debut?"

"They don't all. Hettie didn't marry till she was twenty-three."

Aubrey laughed. Henrietta'd had a reputation for being too lively. Society had disapproved her easy flirting and frank speech, especially as she was only a baron's daughter. The number of aristocratic young fellows who'd courted her passionately, regardless of parental disapproval, had been salt in the wound. "Lucky for you she didn't want any of those other chaps." As far as Aubrey could tell, he and Henrietta were the only people Rupert had ever been attracted to.

Rupert sucked in a deep breath and sighed.

Aubrey met his troubled gaze. "Lucky for both of us," he murmured.

He wanted to slide an arm around Rupert; to kiss the small, worried wrinkle from his forehead. Instead he stared out at the shadowed grounds. "Anyway. Name me someone around our age who isn't yet married."

"Penelope Heatherton."

"I don't like clothes enough to play second fiddle to her wardrobe."

"Sophia Duleep Singh. Good company, serious-minded—"

"A princess. And Queen Victoria's goddaughter. Why on earth would she look at me twice?"

"She likes you." Rupert's fingers tapped restlessly on the balustrade. "And she's thirty and unmarried."

"Maybe she doesn't want to marry. She certainly won't want to marry a mere honourable mister."

"Her mother wasn't noble."

"But it's different for fellows."

Rupert sighed. "Hermione Blakeworth."

"Kittens," Aubrey said firmly.

"They're not all—"

"She *gets* them because she can't resist a kitten. She *keeps* them because they were all kittens once. She needs an in-house carpenter to keep her furniture in good repair, and she lets them *wash themselves* on the dining table. I like her, but no."

Rupert looked away. Eventually, he said, "You just don't want any of them."

Well they weren't Rupert. Or Henrietta. They weren't Lucien.

Aubrey'd called him 'Lucien' during sex again, on purpose. He hadn't seemed offended, but nor had he taken the hint to invite Aubrey to use his Christian name. And since he hadn't, Aubrey didn't like to offer his own. Might be difficult for Lucien to refuse, given their relative social positions.

He sighed. "Look. Suppose one of them was willing, and we married. I'd do my best to make her happy, but we'd both be miserable. I'm sure they want to be as vital to the person they marry as I do. Besides, they're not like Henrietta: they wouldn't understand about…" He stared at Rupert meaningfully.

Rupert glanced around for eavesdroppers.

"Wouldn't be right to keep it up if my wife didn't know," Aubrey pointed out. "And I won't end it: not for anything."

Rupert didn't suggest anyone else. They stood, side by side, carefully not touching, and stared into darkness together.

"Aubrey?" Rupert murmured.

"Mmm?"

"D'you actually want to marry?"

Aubrey stared at him. The worried crease in his forehead had deepened. "When I meet the right woman. No point before then."

"S'pose not."

Aubrey gazed at his lovely profile, but found no clue as to what he was driving at. "Might take a while," he admitted.

Rupert sighed. "When your brother inherits…"

"I know." Father wasn't hale anymore, and Bertie would use Aubrey's allowance to make him toe the line.

"You know I'd—"

"Of course." Rupert would happily support him. "But it'd raise questions." Unless… "S'pose I could start a career: work till I marry."

Rupert stared at him.

"Something more lucrative than writing. You know: pull Bertie's teeth before he can bite."

"But you've never wanted to do anything but write."

"Well. Home or Foreign Office might be all right. Provided the work's in London." He'd loathe it, but it'd be easy enough to get a leg up to a half-decent position.

"You wouldn't earn even as much as your allowance, let alone the income from the settlement you'll get when you marry."

Aubrey huffed a laugh. "There's the rub. But Bertie's less likely to cut me off if he knows I'm not desperate." He'd start saving, though, just in case.

Rupert looked out at the grounds, his lips pressed into a straight line. "Times like this," he murmured at last, "I wish I smoked."

Aubrey managed another laugh. "You hate the smell."

"Just seems the time and place for it."

It did. If he ignored the music and chatter behind them, Aubrey might almost pretend they were alone with the night.

The voices in the ballroom rose with excitement. Rupert eyed the bright doorway like a condemned man. "S'pose we'd better go back in."

"Probably." Aubrey scrunched every muscle in his face, then relaxed them, ready for another round of smiling. "Ready?"

Side by side they walked back into heat and light and noise, and the thick, over-perfumed air of the crowded ballroom. Back into the cramped generative heart of their world.

— Chapter Fourteen —

The crush-room of the Adelphi was living up to its name. Half an hour before curtain-up, Aubrey couldn't move a step in any direction without colliding with four other people. Despite its considerable size, the room was too warm; dense with the breath of hundreds of people. Counterpointing the background hum of conversation, an irregular muttered chorus of, "Excuse me. Excuse me. Dreadfully sorry, didn't see you there. Do excuse me." And he couldn't see Lucien anywhere.

"Let's go to the box," Henrietta said. "He knows where it is, doesn't he?"

It seemed awfully rude, but Lucien wasn't tall: they mightn't see him until the crowd thinned, near curtain-up, and then they'd have to dash to the box.

Holding his programme, Aubrey followed Rupert and Henrietta up the central staircase, still searching the crowd. The crush-room's lilac and pale yellow colour scheme, occasional features picked out in gold, seemed too frail to contain the crowd of patrons. Men in evening dress and top hats stood like iron rails, while women in pastel gowns drifted, like loose-petalled blossoms, beside them.

An upturned face beneath a top hat drew his attention.

Lucien met his gaze, and smiled: such an open, sunny smile that Aubrey's breath caught in his throat.

The hat hid Lucien's face as he edged out of the crush and onto the stairs. He held his left arm stiffly, but his tailcoat clung to the lines of his body as only bespoke clothes could. Aubrey's chest tightened. Surely he'd have worn evening dress when they first met, if he'd owned it then.

"How do you do?" At the warm pressure of Lucien's kid-skin-gloved hand on his own, Aubrey's bones turned to butter, but Lucien was already stepping past him to greet Rupert and Henrietta.

"Lovely to see you again, Mr Saxby." Henrietta offered him her hand. "And looking so *very* well!" she added mischievously.

"Indeed, Lady Hernedale, I had thought so myself." Lucien bowed over her hand. "But this simple candle can't retain its foolish vanity in the sunlight of your presence."

Dear God! No wonder he couldn't keep his head around the man.

Henrietta laughed, delighted. "Lend me your arm, Mr Saxby. I can't possibly dispense with your company just yet."

Lucien shook Rupert's hand before offering her his arm.

Henrietta and Lucien were much of a height, but they looked very well together. Lucien's golden-brown hair showed to advantage beneath the black top hat. Aubrey, walking behind them with Rupert, desperately wanted to press his lips to the spot where his hairline curved up towards his ear.

From behind, too, it was clear why Lucien held his left arm stiffly. Cradled in his hand was the handle of his riding cane; the rest was up his sleeve. He might've left it at home just this once, but Aubrey ached with inappropriate tenderness anyway.

They passed through a private retiring room and into a spacious box. Four upright chairs, upholstered in fine-corded yellow silk, stood in the bow-fronted balcony. Lucien laid his riding cane on the table at the side wall, then held a chair for Henrietta.

Below, the stage's asbestos curtain was still closed, and the orchestra had yet to take its place. A few dozen people wove through the seats in the circles and stalls.

Aubrey took the seat at the far end. The point of this evening was for Lucien to be recognised as Rupert's acquaintance: best if he was seen sitting beside either Rupert or Henrietta.

Rupert slid a miniature volume from his tailcoat pocket and settled to read on the end chair beside Henrietta.

Lucien took the remaining seat, between Aubrey and Henrietta, and proceeded to flirt outrageously with her, while conversing on everything from jewellery to literature. Even Rupert interjected a comment from time to time.

The orchestra filed into the pit and began tuning up, and people flooded into the auditorium, squeezing past patrons who'd already found their seats, raising the background hum to a subdued roar.

"There must be a better way," Aubrey mused.

"Nobody minds it much." Lucien smiled into the crowd. "They're looking forward to the show."

Aubrey stared at the heaving stalls, then up into semi-circles of seething chaos. "*I'd* mind."

"Yes. Well."

Aubrey turned at Lucien's tone.

"I suppose we're used to it." Unsmiling, he held Aubrey's gaze until heat rushed from his collar to his cheeks.

When Aubrey looked away, Henrietta was speaking to Rupert, courteously ignoring Lucien's outburst.

A rap on the retiring room door heralded an attendant. By the time he returned with a tray of drinks and canapes, the orchestra was playing. Soon afterwards, the electric chandelier and side lights darkened, and music swelled as the curtain rose on a farmhouse kitchen scene. Rupert closed his book.

Lucien leaned towards Aubrey. "I'm sorry," he murmured in his ear. "Shouldn't have ripped up at you like that, especially in front of your friends."

"No, it's... You made a fair point."

Lucien stared at him, then glanced away. "Manners aren't optional. I hurt you and embarrassed us both."

Aubrey considered this. "You might speak your mind in priv—"

"Marnin' to 'ee, Jan'fer!"

Aubrey flinched.

Onstage, a roughly dressed farmhand leered at a maid plucking a goose.

In the ordinary way of things, he mightn't have noticed the exaggerated—probably inaccurate—dialect, but with a working man beside him, it loomed into appalling significance.

"You'm lookin' uncommon graand, Jan'fer."

Lucien's gaze locked on the stage as the city audience shrieked with laughter.

Dr. Wake's Patient was billed as a comedy romance. Surely—surely!—this pair weren't the romantic leads. Aubrey scrabbled for his programme. And—thank God!—'Janifer (a farm servant)' was near the bottom of the cast list.

The farmer and his wife were rather less dreadfully portrayed. Until they discussed their son, the Oxford-educated doctor.

"You've no brains," the farmer told his wife kindly. "Women have no call to have brains—it bean't their province. No, it's not the brains he gets from you."

Movement at the corner of his eye: Rupert gripping Henrietta's arm. As the farmer extolled his wife's virtues—"a sweet nature, a noble spirit, and a pure heart"—Rupert leaned in to murmur to her, but she glared at the stage, tight-lipped.

"You're always right, Andrew," the wife agreed.

The farmer patted her shoulder. "I'm as proud of him as I am of you."

Lucien slid a small notebook and pencil from his tailcoat pocket. Onstage, the couple welcomed their son home.

"Perhaps we should leave," Aubrey whispered, glancing between Henrietta and Lucien.

They exchanged a glance he couldn't interpret.

"I think not." Henrietta leaned back in her chair. "I feel a letter to the Times coming on."

Lucien gave her a devastating grin, then turned its full effect on Aubrey. "And I—" he unbuttoned his gloves "—am writing a review." He folded the gloves neatly into his tailcoat pocket, then flipped his notebook open, past screeds of incomprehensible shorthand squiggles, to a blank page. "It will include the offence tendered to Lady Hernedale and to all ladies in the audience." They shared another smile.

Aubrey met Rupert's gaze past Lucien and Henrietta. Staying was a mistake, he was sure of it, and he saw his own concern reflected in Rupert's eyes.

"The pigs!" the young doctor exclaimed. "Oh I say! What about Henrietta?"

Aubrey turned to the stage with a dreadful hollow in the pit of his stomach.

"Th' old sow?" the farmhand asked. "She be there still."

Rupert leaned towards Henrietta. "We should leave."

"Oh no." Henrietta folded slender arms encased in long evening gloves. "I am bloody well seeing this abomination through to the end."

Rupert eyed Lucien askance.

"I'm sure Mr Saxby's heard worse," Henrietta said.

"Much worse." Lucien made an indecipherable note. "Don't mind me: I shan't put that bit in."

"You *are* a dear." Henrietta rewarded him with a dimple and a smile. He grinned back as though he knew perfectly well what she was doing and was amused by it, and she laughed.

Once it moved away from the servants and their mangled dialects, parts of the play weren't terrible. The doctor caring for his injured sweetheart was endearing, and some of the dialogue was smart. But then the heroine's noble parents sent a dinner invitation to the doctor's bucolic parents, ignorant of their class.

Lucien's pencil paused.

It was awful. Not as awful as it might've been, since a half-decent speech had been written for the farmer, and the doctor stayed loyal to his parents. But still awful.

Of course, the young couple was separated, but eventually found happiness. They even gained the blessing of the heroine's hectoring father, but only after the doctor was unexpectedly honoured with a knighthood.

The curtain fell at last, to thunderous applause, and Aubrey forced his head round to face the others.

"You noticed, I trust," Henrietta said, "that every woman over the age of twenty-five is presented as either well-meaning but bumbling, or downright unpleasant?"

"Or unpleasant *and* bumbling," Lucien agreed.

"And that the same behaviour presented as charming high spirits in young women is excoriated as shallow selfishness in older women?"

"Thank you. I'd missed that." Lucien made a quick note. "Did you observe that the young couple could only become engaged after the working man abased himself before the noble?"

"Presented as Christian humility, of course."

"Indeed. But the aristocrat isn't expected to display the same virtue."

"That," Rupert said, "was abysmal. And I'm understating the case."

The curtain closed on the last, triumphant curtain call, and the lights came up.

A tap on the door heralded the attendant with a tray full of silver. "Souvenir of the play?"

Aubrey froze.

"Picture frame? Lovely cosmetics jar here. Or a Vesta case, with the name of the play embossed on—"

"No, thank you." Rupert waved the fellow away an instant before Aubrey leapt to his feet.

"It's rather late to continue this conversation, Mr Saxby," Henrietta said, "but perhaps we might discuss your review and my letter at a later date."

"Thank you: that's most generous." Lucien regarded his notebook ruefully. "I shan't be able to write this as I'd like—have to get it past my editor, you know—but if you'd permit me to quote one or two of your points, I might get away with more."

"I'd be delighted." Henrietta paused. "I suppose I'll have to be circumspect myself, or the Times won't print my letter."

"Your position allows you considerable leeway, of course." Lucien tucked his notebook and pencil into the tail of his coat. "But, should you wish it, I could help you develop an approach that will make most of your points and still satisfy the Times' editor." He smoothed his gloves on.

"Perhaps you'd call on me? After working hours, naturally. Tomorrow or the next—" She exchanged glances with Rupert. "Ah no. I'm engaged the next evening, and tomorrow might... I'll check my diary and write to you. Aubrey, you'll come too, of course."

"Thank you." Lucien stood, tucked his riding cane up his sleeve, and offered her his arm. "There's no urgency: the play's scheduled to run for some time."

Aubrey and Rupert followed them past the untouched snacks—canapes curling at the edges from the heat—through the retiring room, and into the corridor. Thank God they'd be out of this miserable situation soon.

"Good evening, Henrietta. Hernedale." Lowdon's grave tones sounded behind them. "Fanshawe." He stood just beyond the door of their box, his wife, looking exhausted, beside him. Must've been waiting for them.

Lucien began to turn, but Henrietta visibly gripped his arm. "Let's go on, please, Mr Saxby." She barely tilted her head to glance back. "Lovely to see you, Violet. Do, please, visit me soon."

It was disgraceful that Lowdon had used his wife to try to force Henrietta and Rupert to an amicable public encounter. Appalling that he'd ostentatiously snubbed Lucien, to whom he'd been formally introduced, while demanding acknowledgement from the rest of their party. He'd absolutely earned this public humiliation. But Aubrey's face burned, and Violet Lowdon looked ready to collapse with mortification.

"Evening, Mrs Lowdon," he managed.

Rupert flicked a dismissive glance over his brother-in-law, then smiled kindly at Mrs Lowdon. "*Always* lovely to see you, Violet." He turned away, and Aubrey followed him, hoping his face would cool on the stairs.

AUBREY REFUSED RUPERT and Henrietta's offer of a lift. He owed Lucien an apology and a listening ear.

"Bit of a hoof back to Albany," Rupert said dubiously.

"Not much above fifteen minutes," Aubrey pointed out.

"Saxby?"

"Thank you, but no. My rooms are even closer than Fanshawe's."

It was only as Rupert and Henrietta left that Aubrey remembered Lucien's rooms were in the opposite direction to his own.

"Might I stand you a drink?" he asked.

"Here?" Lucien glanced around the emptying crush-room.

"If you like."

"The Nell Gwynne's just around the corner."

"All right."

They stepped into the chilly night together, passing young men loitering near the door.

"Meant to tell you." Lucien adjusted his hat. "I read your stories."

"Really?"

Lucien glanced at him, grinning in a way that lightened his heart. "Is it so unlikely? I said I would."

"Er, which ones?"

"Maybe all? I looked through back-issues at the library: found five."

Aubrey's stories had been published months and years apart. How far back had Lucien searched, before deciding five was all he'd find? "That... must've taken some time."

"I'm a journalist." Between his top hat and the street lamp behind them, Lucien's face was bathed in shadow. "Research is part of the job."

"I'd have shown them to you. Saved you the bother. I didn't realise you were serious. About reading them, I mean."

"They were good. I particularly liked the twist in *Lady Dorothea's Drawing Room*. Not exactly Wilde, as you said, but... more not-yet-Wilde than never-could-be-Wilde."

It was so obviously a genuine assessment. So obvious that Lucien had read and thought about his work. "Thank you. That means a lot, coming from you." His voice was husky. "From... a very good writer."

Lucien's head turned and their eyes met.

"I've been reading your articles."

Lucien stood stock still. "*You've* been reading the Mail? *You* have?"

"Is it so surprising?"

"Yes! Good Lord! You're hardly the target demographic."

Aubrey couldn't help but laugh. Lucien's astonishment was utterly endearing. "I'm the target demographic for any publication you write for."

The moment he said it, he knew it was too much. He should've said it teasingly, flirtatiously, if he said it at all. Darkness had left him unguarded.

Lucien's face stilled. "Well," he said softly. "Can't say I'd usually scour the *Athenaeum*, either."

Aubrey held his breath, searching Lucien's semi-visible eyes for... something. Something impossible.

Lucien inclined his head to the road ahead. "Shall we?"

The weight of things half-spoken settled between them as they walked, binding them with the deep complicity of wilful ignorance. Aubrey wasn't sure how Lucien felt about him. He wasn't certain how he felt about Lucien, either, except that he very badly didn't want to be without him. Instinct mapped the hidden shape, and flinched from exposing it.

But there were words it was safe to speak; words that, in courtesy, should be spoken. "Just wanted to say: dreadfully sorry. Lowdon's a damned disgrace."

"Not your responsibility, but thank you. Lady Hernedale, though…" Lucien's voice crept higher, astonished. "She took my side against her brother."

"Well you did nothing wrong, whereas Lowdon…" Aubrey shrugged his disgust.

Lucien stared ahead thoughtfully.

"Apologies for the play, too. I'd have suggested another, if I'd known, and so would Hernedale."

"Quite all right," Lucien murmured.

Aubrey raised his eyebrows.

After a puzzled moment, Lucien laughed. "Oh! No, I mean it. Can't say I enjoyed the play, but it really is all right now. It's given me material for work, and Lady Hernedale and I found a bit of common ground. Which was… unexpected. And pleasing. To me, at least."

"Well, if you say so. I haven't been that dashed uncomfortable in public since I was a child, and it seems to me it'd be much worse for you."

Silence.

He glanced over to see Lucien watching him.

"I didn't expect you to notice how dreadful it was, let alone how I might've felt about it."

Heat flooded Aubrey's face. "I'm surprised the audience liked it so much."

Lucien sighed. "Town will look down on countryside. It's easy to mistake another person's interests for your own, when you live and work closely with them; hard to see the interests you share with someone you've been raised to despise."

"I—can't say I've ever given the matter much thought."

"Whereas, lately, I've been giving it altogether too much thought."

The bitter edge in Lucien's tone wrenched Aubrey's heart. He wanted to hold him, but settled for a hand on his shoulder.

Lucien paused to look at him, and a wry grin hooked his mouth up on one side. "Don't worry so," he said. "It's not materially important: just self-indulgence."

Aubrey stared down into his face—at the fine creases of tension around eyes and lips thrown into relief by unforgiving electric light—and his throat swelled and ached. That Lucien, emotionally bruised and vulnerable, should be alone tonight was— It was— "Would you consider coming home with me?"

Lucien drew breath.

"Not to— I won't trouble you with any demands. Just... We might share a drink and conversation, and then sleep."

Surprise slackened Lucien's face. "That's very kind, but I don't think—" He glanced down. "I can't walk home tomorrow in evening dress."

Aubrey dropped his hand from Lucien's shoulder before they became conspicuous. "Borrow my clothes. You could bring them back on Saturday."

Lucien stared at him. "That's a generous offer—extremely generous—but... For one thing, they'd be too big."

He ought to let it go there. "Mightn't they'd do just to get you home?"

Lucien's eyes closed. "Fanshawe..."

"Aubrey."

Lucien looked at him blankly. "Pardon?"

"Er. Don't feel obliged, obviously. But if you wouldn't dislike it... do call me Aubrey. Please."

Lucien's mouth twisted. "Oh shit," he said helplessly.

It sounded like the opening line of an unpleasant revelation. A weight plummeted from Aubrey's chest and lodged in his belly, leaving him half hollow, unbalanced. "What's the matter?"

"Never mind." Lucien took a deep breath and turned back the way they'd come. "All right, then, love. We'll go to yours." His accent hovered in an indeterminate space between his normal speech—or what Aubrey'd assumed was his normal speech—and Cockney.

Aubrey stared after him, then fell into step beside him.

Lucien had only ever called him 'love' on one particular night. If it was a habitual bedroom endearment, wouldn't he have heard it more often?

It was easy—too easy—to say words in the dark one would never speak in the light. But those words… they weren't casual. They could only be spoken when your companion's face was half-hidden; when you needn't see reaction in their eyes; when, if necessary, you could both pretend they'd never been said. They were words that laid you bare. They were terribly, terribly risky.

"Lucien?"

Lucien met his gaze. Shadow hid the expression in his eyes, but lamplight showed a face taut with conflict. As Aubrey watched, he hitched his lips into a smile. "No point wasting money in a pub when your brandy's so much better, is there?"

Aubrey held his gaze, face to face in white lamplight, and spoke words neither of them could deny. "No, sweetheart," he murmured. "None at all."

— Chapter Fifteen —

Friday, 2ND March 1906

"Lucien? You have to get up."

Lucien woke to Aubrey curled around him; to Aubrey's arm across his chest; to the light prickle of stubble on the nape of his neck. It felt blissful, and strange, and soul-deep familiar.

Slowly, he turned, tipping his head back to see Aubrey's face. They'd spent a peculiar, comfortable night, sipping brandy and talking into the early hours. Aubrey'd held him and pressed occasional affectionate kisses on his forehead and cheek. And when at last they flagged, Aubrey'd undressed him—"Your turn"—buttoned him into a silk nightshirt, and held him till he slept.

"It's eight o'clock." Aubrey's hand slid to Lucien's hip. "You have to be in Downing Street at ten, remember?"

"Tell me something." Lucien covered the long hand with his own. "Are you Fanshawe this morning?"

"Not to you, sweetheart."

'Sweetheart'. Sober, and in daylight. And definitely meant for him. Lucien crushed into Aubrey's bony shoulder.

"Not in private anyway. We'll have to be Saxby and Fanshawe in public."

Lucien snorted softly. "Be a bloody scandal if we weren't."

Aubrey's cock, morning-hard, jutted into his hip through silk nightshirts. His own, equally interested, pressed between them.

Lucien stroked Aubrey's flank and lingered over the swell of his buttock. "Eight," he murmured, regretful. "I have to get up."

"*I* told *you* that." Aubrey's smile tickled his head. His arm tightened around Lucien, then he released him, flinging back the covers. "Go, Lucien! Fly free!"

Lucien braced himself on an elbow. "You're absurd."

"Frequently."

Lucien stared into his big face, framed by sleep-rumpled hair and a dark drift of morning stubble. "And altogether too damn lovely."

"Strange: I was just thinking the very same about you." Aubrey's eyes were dark and dense as midnight in the dim room.

Lucien swept back his hair and kissed him slowly, thoroughly, losing himself in the languid slide of tongue on tongue; in Aubrey's long, gentle hands stroking his back, his shoulders, his head.

Eventually, he rested his forehead against Aubrey's, heart over-full, aching with tenderness and terror.

Aubrey was like a magnet, like bloody *gravity*: Lucien couldn't tear himself away. He lay cradled in a blissful ecstasy he'd barely dreamed possible, but woven through it, inseparable as the pattern in figured silk, was the agony of future loss. He could barely encompass the depth of either, let alone both at the same time.

"Lucien?" Aubrey murmured. "Sweetheart?"

Lucien's eyelids and nose heated; his eyes prickled. "Have to get up." He dropped a brisk kiss on Aubrey's lips, rolled over, and stood.

By the time he came out of the WC, Aubrey had poured water into the basin in the dressing room, put a facecloth beside it, and was half-hidden in the wardrobe.

"I wonder whether you could get away with the tailcoat." He picked out a shirt and hung it on the valet stand. "Your overcoat's long enough to hide the tails. And my jacket shoulders might be too broad for your overcoat."

"Bound to be." Lucien wet and soaped the cloth, and started washing.

"A scarf to hide the fit of the collar…"

"If I can borrow a scarf, I won't need the shirt."

"But the trousers…" Aubrey dived back into the wardrobe.

"Unless you have some from your childhood, love, forget it. Even if you keep a needle and thread—"

"I'd have to ask Grieve," Aubrey admitted.

"Don't bother: they'd be more conspicuous than my evening trousers anyway."

"Could you hem them with shirt studs?"

Lucien almost choked. "Dear Lord, I can see it now: me walking down Piccadilly with the sunlight flashing from a dozen gemstones around my ankles."

"Oh." Aubrey grinned. "No, I quite see." He picked up another facecloth and joined Lucien. "You sew, too. A multi-talented man."

Or just a natural-born valet.

Lucien's amusement evaporated like water spilled on a stove, but he mustered a grin. "Something like that."

The silence suggested his comment hadn't rung as blithely as he'd have liked.

Aubrey put his cloth down. Cool arms slid around Lucien from behind. "What do you need, sweetheart?"

Lucien rested an arm over Aubrey's. "Everything's here, thanks. I'll shave at home."

"I mean— If you need help with anything…" Aubrey rubbed his cheek on Lucien's hair, snagging it with short bristles. "Anything you can't afford… You can come to me."

Lucien squeezed his eyes shut, sucking in careful, shallow breaths.

"I'd like you to," Aubrey added.

Lucien dropped his cloth. He became aware that he was clutching Aubrey's arm far too tightly. Carefully, he peeled the arm from his waist and turned, but Aubrey didn't step back. They stood so close that skin slid over soap-slick skin with every breath, but Aubrey's body seemed as little affected by that as his own. This was important to him, then.

"Listen." Lucien strove for a calm tone. "Obviously I'm not as wealthy as you, but I'm not poor either. Thanks for your offer, but I don't need financial help. And if I did, I wouldn't feel comfortable asking you for it."

"Why ever not?"

Lucien sighed. "Because I want you to know I visit you purely for the pleasure of your company. Because I don't want to owe you anything. Because I don't want to have to feel grateful to you."

"You don't have to—"

"No. Listen." He brushed Aubrey's cheek with the backs of his fingers to soften his words. "I don't want to feel as though I always have my hand out, and I would, if you gave me things, even if I never asked for them. I can't return your gifts with gifts of equal value, so if I accept them, I put myself in your debt; if I ask you for something, doubly so."

"You wouldn't be in my debt. I just don't want you to suffer."

"I'm not suffering." He paused. "Do you have an allowance? Or a settlement?"

"Allowance. For now."

"And do you feel equal to the person who pays your allowance?"

"Well, no, but he's my father."

"But regardless, you couldn't feel equal to someone who might stop your income. You'd take care not to try his patience. Since it's unearned, you'd also feel a debt of gratitude."

"No I damned well wouldn't!" Aubrey stepped back. "When my brother inherits, I'll still feel like his equal. They're family assets: it's only luck he was born first. And... and *bugger* Bertie's patience, actually! I'll get a job before I let him dictate to me. And as for feeling grateful to my father for maintaining me... Why would I?"

Lucien stared at him. "Why... wouldn't you?"

"It's his *duty*. Even if he wasn't fond of me, he'd pay my allowance, just as Rupert pays his vile cousin's. It's no more than his father did, or his grandfather; no more than I'd do, if I was head of the family."

Lucien glanced around the dressing room. "A very generous allowance," he suggested.

"Much the same as he had, as a young man. He doesn't miss it. My allowance is a drop in the ocean of the family estate. Just as buying you things from time to time would be a drop in the ocean to me."

Lucien closed his eyes against the ache in his chest. "Listen to yourself. Just listen. D'you think I want to hear that you buy bespoke suits like I buy pen wipes? D'you think I don't already know that? I work hard for—"

"I *know*!" Aubrey's hands locked on his. "That's why I'm offering."

"Well don't! D'you suppose I want you to be some sort of paterfamilias to me?"

Aubrey's grip slackened. "Of course not."

"Well that's what you're suggesting. Don't. I don't want that from you. And I don't want to be reminded that, however hard I work, you'll always earn a hundred times more than I can, simply by *existing*." The ache swelled into a painful knot.

"Oh." Aubrey's fingers slid between his. "I see. That *would*—"

"As for family assets—" Lucien wrenched away from him, opening his eyes at last. "Your bloody ancestors raked up the assets of this country and a dozen others, so you can sleep in silk while the rest of us watch our babies die by inches because we can't afford a *sodding* doctor!" Tears chilled his cheeks in narrow tracks. "I don't want to *remember* that while I'm with you, Aubrey!"

"*Your* baby?" Aubrey whispered, only his lips moving. "You had a—"

"No." Lucien wiped his face. "Shit. Shit. My friend—"

"His baby died?"

"Not yet. Not bloody ever, if I have anything to say about it."

"Let me help. Please."

"Got it in hand for now." Lucien took a deep breath. "But if it comes to it, yes. For Jem, I'd ask." Aubrey's hands slid into his, and Lucien didn't have the heart to shake him off again. "But that's— It's not the point, don't you see? A child's life shouldn't depend on someone's whim. On whether they'd rather buy him his life or buy themselves a suit. You said it's only luck your brother was born first: well it's only luck that you were born Aubrey Fanshawe and not Jem Evans, or any one of a hundred other Jems." Or that he was Lucien, not Ben.

"I see that." Aubrey rested his temple against Lucien's.

Lucien's heart pounded, hard and angry and aching, but he leaned into Aubrey anyway, craving the comfort of his touch, of his skin. Aubrey couldn't possibly fully understand, but he was listening, and he was trying to understand, and that was more than any other nob had ever done.

"Damn it!" Lucien snarled. "Why isn't it our government's duty to provide for the people who need it, the way your family provides for you? Why?"

Aubrey didn't reply. His fingers smoothed up and down Lucien's arms; his breath rushed, warm and cool by turns, beneath his ear and along the side of his neck.

Gradually, Lucien's heart calmed.

Giddy with grief and the aftermath of anger, he kissed Aubrey's cheek. "I'll take care of myself, love. I need to."

"I see that." Aubrey stepped back, lifting Lucien's fingers to his lips. "But I'm here if ever you should need me."

Ever. As though they had a future together; a future so obvious it didn't need discussion.

Lucien stared at the naked aristocrat kissing his hand—his working man's hand—and promising to be there for him. Not out of obligation, nor to create obligation, nor trap him in dependency, but simply because he wanted to. Even though Lucien had raged at him and insulted his ancestors, when all he'd done was offer to help.

His head swam and the room blurred at the edges, casting his plain hand and the big, sleep-mussed head into improbable clarity. This couldn't be real. It felt as strange and distant as a fairy-tale. Maybe he really was bloody Cinderella.

Hysterical laughter swelled inside him. He choked it down, wrapping his arms around his long-boned prince. Holding Aubrey, who felt solid and right in his arms, whose arms folded around him in turn, pressing him to his new-familiar bony chest.

Lucien clutched him until he felt anchored in his body again—sure of who and where he was, if not of his place in Aubrey's life—then he sighed and kissed Aubrey's neck.

And turned back to the washstand, because the WSPU wouldn't delay on his account.

NOEL DIDN'T WORK Fridays. But Lucien breezed past the strange doorman, knowing the risk, and hardly caring. Though exhausted from an almost sleepless night, he felt oddly light and energised. Walking seemed effortless, and everything looked bright and fresh: cause for boundless optimism. It made no sense. Less than half an hour before, he'd been so furious he'd forgotten the painfully-learned imperative to be likable; to coax rather than argue.

But Aubrey had comforted him anyway.

Aubrey Fanshawe—who saw no reason to feel grateful to a man who kept him in opulent luxury—could never be his someone. Gratitude and obligation had been etched into Lucien's bones from his earliest years, had burned deeper every year till he'd escaped into the army. There was no bridging that chasm. But, deeper than conscious thought, a small, fearful murmur insisted he had a place in Aubrey's affections, at least for now, and that obstinate voice made him unreasonably happy.

He stepped into the boarding house as Mrs Emmott tramped down the stairs with a tray of dirty dishes. She surveyed him from head to toe, pausing for a significant moment on the dress trousers beneath the hem of his overcoat. "Your breakfast'll be cold."

He grinned. "Thank you, Mrs Emmott."

Her eyes narrowed. "Are you drunk, Mr Saxby?"

"Not a bit of it. It's just a particularly invigorating morning."

"If you say so. I ain't had time to see it." She trudged past him.

The first post, on his breakfast tray, included a note from Lady Hernedale, inviting him to dinner later.

Aubrey would be there.

His absurd smile grew wider, but he hadn't time to dwell on Aubrey. He laid and lit the fire, threw off his clothes, shaved, and scrambled into a lounge suit. Then sponged down and ironed his evening dress and set it by the fire to air, because he'd need it for tonight.

In between draining his teacup of cold tea, he wrote a quick postcard accepting Lady Hernedale's invitation, and another notifying Aubrey of his acceptance, then blotted and stamped them and put them in his pocket: he'd drop them in a pillar box along the way. At last, grabbing his bowler and riding cane, he dashed out to Downing Street, aware that he was still grinning from time to time, but unable to stop.

He was on time. In fact—he tugged his watch from his waistcoat pocket as he walked along Downing Street—six minutes early. The WSPU deputation hadn't arrived yet.

Journalists, press photographers, and policemen dotted the pavement on both sides of the street. A crowd of curious onlookers swelled around them, distracting the police with demands to know what was going on.

Lucien struggled not to laugh. The old music hall song, *If you want to know the time, ask a policeman,* played in his mind, then started over again. The police must've wished the pestering onlookers at Timbuktu: Lucien hoped they kept it up, and made the bastards' lives as awkward as possible.

"Morning." Miss Enfield looked at him over the top of her spectacles. She stood on the pavement beside Number 10, her back to the black iron railings, making notes. She must've arrived early to secure that prime spot. A photographer from the Daily

Mirror stood on the other side of the broad doorstep, looking smug.

"Morning." Standing beside her, he started noting impressions.

"If you want to know the time—" he hummed.

Miss Enfield nudged his arm and glared.

"Whoops, sorry. Thought that was just in my head."

"Well for goodness' sake, keep it there."

Grinning, he tipped his bowler with his pencil. "Will do."

She eyed him in silence, then said, "You've met someone new. Or things are going unexpectedly well with an existing someone."

He stared. "How on earth would you know?"

"Either that, or someone's left you a generous lifetime annuity, which seems less likely."

"Oh." He struggled to control the grin, and lost the battle when she grinned back.

"Nice to see you happy, Saxby. Long may it last."

— Chapter Sixteen —

BY MIDDAY, AUBREY had received Lucien's postcard and had written to let Henrietta know he'd arrive earlier than expected. He left Albany promptly at half-past six.

It was a pleasant enough walk in the twilight—busy along Piccadilly and Curzon Street, but quieter along Park Lane with Hyde Park drowsing on his left—and his thoughts turned to Lucien.

He'd never have guessed charming, considerate Lucien would hold such pain and rage: righteous anger, in all fairness. Aubrey's ancestors *had* stolen land and assets and labour from people poorer and less well-connected than themselves, though he'd never thought of it that way before. He'd never do anything of the sort himself, but it was undeniable that he directly benefitted from his ancestors' depredations, which was— No, it wasn't almost as bad, but it was quite bad enough, when babies were dying.

It was one thing to know the statistics—and he'd avoided even those, as best he could—it was quite another to witness Lucien's grief for a particular child. But weren't they all particular, to the people who loved them? To themselves?

If he had Rupert's resources, or his father's, he could fund a foundation to pay impoverished children's medical costs. If he had his settlement, he could start a charity and encourage donations. As it was, in a few years he mightn't even have his allowance.

As it was—

He had enough to do *something*, if not everything. If Lucien, on his meagre income, was funding a doctor for a baby, then he could certainly do at least as much. He felt small and selfish for never having considered it before; he admired Lucien more, that he had. If buying the occasional gift was a drop in his ocean of income, then he could regularly donate at least that sum, for as long as he had his allowance. And if funds were needed for Jem, he could do without a new suit or two, or whatever was necessary, for as long as necessary. It was hardly a sacrifice, when set against a life.

If only it was as easy to take care of Lucien. But Lucien didn't want him to. And Lucien's happiness mattered. His dignity mattered. So that was the end of it.

He trod up the familiar steps of Hernedale House. A footman took his hat and coat and cane, and the butler offered him a seat in the oak-panelled drawing room.

Rupert came in soon afterwards, and closed the door. Leaning down, he dropped a kiss on Aubrey's lips.

"You look very debonair."

Rupert kissed the tip of his nose. "You're rather lovely yourself."

Henrietta swept in, glamorous in shades of cream and peach contrasted with black, and closed the door behind her.

Aubrey stood and took her gloved hands. He kissed the back of each one, and then her cheek. "Ravishing, as always."

"Thanks. But never mind that." She steered him to the sofa, where she sat in the middle and patted the seat beside her. "What's up?"

Aubrey sat next to her, and Rupert drew up a chair on his other side.

"It's about Lucien. Saxby."

"Lucien." Was there an edge to Rupert's tone? "Go on."

"I think… Well, you know that that sort of—of encounter—has always been a casual thing for me."

"But this is different?" Henrietta took his hand. "You've been meeting at your set; spending nights together. You're using his Christian name."

"And I've asked him to use mine. Yes. I hope to spend more time with him, not just— Well, he's important to me."

"And are you important to him?" Rupert's tone was sharp. "Does he ask you for things?"

"He won't let me give him anything." Aubrey slid his hand from Henrietta's and took Rupert's. "He cares for me: I'm certain of it."

"Aubrey." Rupert squeezed his hand. "What does this— When you say more time. What does that mean for us? For Hettie and me?"

The 'us' that didn't include him lanced his heart, as always, though it shouldn't. What other word could Rupert use for himself and another person? *Any* other person. "Maybe— I might miss the odd evening event I'd usually attend with you. I'd let you know in advance, of course."

"Daytimes?"

"Well, he works every day but Sunday, you know, so that won't be an issue."

"Aubrey." Rupert's voice was tight. "Nights? Will you still spend some nights with us? With—me?"

"Oh Lord, yes, Rupert! I didn't mean— Good God, no! I don't mean to end things with you." He drew him closer and kissed him hard on the lips.

Rupert rested his forehead against Aubrey's.

"Sweetheart. I just meant—in the same way I'm committed to you and Henrietta, I've also become committed to Lucien. Also. Not instead. Never that."

"Don't—" Rupert drew a deep breath. "Don't do this out of pity for me."

"Damn it, Rupert!" Aubrey pulled away and glared at him. "How could you think that? I love you! I want you!"

Rupert searched his eyes. "All right."

Aubrey wanted to plaster his face with kisses, but Rupert would hate that. Instead he said, "I wish I was staying here tonight."

"Not a chance." Rupert's lips twisted. "Not with Frederick arriving at some inconveniently unspecified hour of the morning."

Aubrey avoided Rupert's cousin and heir as much as discretion allowed. He was, as Rupert observed, 'inconsiderate, profligate, and over-astute'. Best if that sort of fellow seldom saw them together: he had too much to gain if anything happened to Rupert.

"I shouldn't have raised it tonight."

"Nonsense," Henrietta said from behind him. "You should've raised it as soon as you were certain."

Aubrey looked at her over his shoulder.

"Which you did," she added. "It affects us all, so it's important that we all know how you feel."

"*You* know that—" Aubrey turned back to Rupert. "Can we all sit on the sofa, please?"

Henrietta moved over so Aubrey could shift to the middle, and Rupert sat on his other side. Aubrey held his hand, and faced Henrietta.

"You know I love you, don't you? That I don't mean to—to swap you for Lucien?"

"Well you often say so." She kissed his cheek. "And I know you wouldn't leave Rupert for anybody."

"I wouldn't." Aubrey turned back to Rupert. "I truly wouldn't."

Rupert approximated a smile.

"I probably shouldn't have told you when he's due for dinner, but it never occurred to me you'd think I wouldn't want you. Never, sweetheart. Because I always have, and I'm sure I always will. I'll be a burr on your sock all your life."

Rupert laughed shakily and leaned his head back on the antimacassar. "I'm sorry."

"Nothing to be sorry for." Aubrey kissed the corner of his mouth. "Feeling better?"

"Might take me a while to think it all through. But I s'pose it's not very different, in practical terms, than when you were seeing him casually. Except that you care for him."

"*And* that we'll want to meet him with friendship, not just courtesy," Henrietta said firmly.

Despite the 'we', Aubrey cast her a grateful look.

She brushed the backs of her fingers across his cheek. "It's not a hardship, darling: he's very good company."

"Seems like a decent fellow," Rupert murmured.

"He is," Aubrey said. "Kind. Considerate."

Rupert reached for his hand. "That's good."

"Rupert." Aubrey stroked his fingers. "Sweetheart. Never doubt that I love and want you."

"Really don't see why you would."

Aubrey drew breath to speak, irritated but needing Rupert to feel better. But Rupert got there first.

"Don't. Don't, beloved. I'm not fishing for compliments."

"Burr on your damned sock, Rupert." Aubrey squeezed his hand. "Can't imagine life without you."

"That mightn't be a good thing." Rupert met his gaze. "For you."

"Hard to see how not, sweetheart." Aubrey pressed their cheeks together. "What's so terrible about happiness?"

"Nothing." Rupert's breath ghosted along his hairline. "Not a thing in the world."

"Well there you go. I'm not fool enough to amputate a large portion of my happiness and graft misery in its place."

"Rupert. Darling." Henrietta reached past him to hold Rupert's other hand. "It's not loss. It's only change."

"Yes. Of course." Rupert took a deep breath. "I don't mean to be melodramatic."

"It's not melodramatic to feel. Only human." Henrietta's tone firmed. "But we all know where we stand now, and it's time for a bit of common sense. Aubrey, Rupert and I will go through our diaries and let you know which events we'd especially like your company for. Mr Saxby should do the same. We'll negotiate any clashes."

"That makes sense."

"I'm sorry." Rupert kissed Aubrey's forehead. "I wish you joy. Truly."

Tears prickled behind Aubrey's eyes. "Be more worrying if you didn't mind losing me. But I do love you both, and I could never replace either of you."

Rupert lifted Henrietta's hand to his cheek. "My sensible psychopomp: lighting my path."

"Darling." She cupped his cheek. "Mr Saxby will arrive in around ten minutes. Time to pour some iron in the spine. We need Aubrey's lover to know he's among friends."

"Quite right." Rupert kissed her palm.

Aubrey caught her hand on its way past and turned to kiss her cheek. "Thank you, sweetheart."

She looked tired, and... something else. Exasperated? Bitter? But her lips curled into a smile before he could interpret it, and she patted his hand. "One for all."

"And all for one," Aubrey and Rupert echoed.

"That's the ticket. We'll be all right, all of us, as long as we remember it."

DINNER WITH THE Hernedales was a peculiar affair. So undemanding that Lucien kept forgetting they had no reason to have his interests at heart.

After dessert, Lady Hernedale stayed in the dining room, sipping port with the men: so informal as to be almost scandalous. But since Lucien had no desire to talk politics with Aubrey and Hernedale—he and they were bound to disagree—or, God forbid, to swap off-colour jokes, he was rather pleased about it.

They retired to the drawing room together. Aubrey and Hernedale retreated to the piano at the far end of the room, while Lucien and Lady Hernedale settled beside an occasional table.

Lucien, over-conscious of his need to appease Jameson, felt guilty asking to cite her on so many statements, but Lady Hernedale seemed as eager to have her views published as he was to publish them.

Aubrey lifted the piano lid and, propping a knee on the stool, stroked soft, desultory chords from the instrument one-handed while chatting with Hernedale. Eventually he sat and set both hands to the keys. He didn't use a score, or play anything through from start to finish—phrases from one melody segued into a chorus from another—and his playing lacked passion. But that was probably because his attention was more on his conversation than the music.

"He plays well," Lady Hernedale murmured.

Lucien turned to see her watching him watch Aubrey. "He says not."

She smiled wryly. "That's Aubrey all over."

Lucien watched Aubrey's long fingers dance over the keys, then gazed at his peaceful face. "He doesn't have a piano at home."

"Albany's Board of Trustees doesn't permit musical instruments in the sets."

"Ah." Pity. Lucien looked back at his notebook. "Are you sure I should cite you on all this? It's awfully radical stuff."

Lady Hernedale laughed. "Worst it'll do is make people eye me askance, and reduce my circle of friends to people who either agree with me or are open to discussion: that's not a hardship. I don't have a daughter to marry off, and even if I did, Hernedale's daughter would never be completely ostracised. Anyway, I'd much rather any daughter of mine didn't marry a stick-in-the-mud like my brother."

That decided it: he'd make the article as outspoken as he dared. Jameson might demand he water it down, or decide it was too radical to print at all, but at least he'd be reassured that Lucien had the sources he'd claimed.

While Aubrey played, they discussed possible angles for her letter to the Times.

"You have to consider the viewpoint of the editor and of the paper's readers," Lucien explained, "which aren't quite the same thing. And also who the editor thinks his readership is, which isn't necessarily the same thing as who it actually is. And then work out how to make them care about what you want them to care about, starting from something they already care about."

"A bit like persuading a vicar to hold a charity event for a cause he's not sure he supports, and thinks half his parishioners will disapprove?"

Lucien stared at her. "I imagine so."

"That's all right then." She began jotting notes.

"'Dignity' is often a good one," Lucien murmured. "'Insult to the dignity of British womanhood', sort of thing."

"Oh yes, I like that." She noted it. "Speaking of British womanhood: Aubrey showed me your article on last month's WSPU procession."

Heat flooded Lucien's face. "Miss Enfield's more than mine. But we couldn't write it quite as we'd have liked."

Lady Hernedale looked up. "M. Enfield is a woman?"

"M for Madeleine. She'd have preferred a more… rousing approach, but we had to get it past our editor, and what he thinks the paper's readers will stand. We started from the angle of ladies' safety and fragility, because the Mail's readers care about that. Strong men shutting ladies out in the freezing rain, while they sat in the warm." Tension built at the memory.

"You genuinely disliked that, though." Lady Hernedale was watching him. "It wasn't just an angle."

"Who wouldn't?" Lucien managed a brief laugh, but it sounded curt. "Miss Enfield was terribly pale by the end: I worried she'd become ill."

"She's a… *particular* friend of yours?"

Lucien stared. That question wasn't just inappropriate, it was intrusive. Offensive. "Not… in the sense I think you mean, no. More a colleague who's becoming a friend. But one didn't need a friend affected to be outraged. Most of the ladies there were working ladies. Even those who have fireplaces in their rooms—

and not all do, you know—can't always afford enough coal for their needs."

"Yes, I see. A lot of suffering even after the event."

"Indeed." Lucien's chest knotted at the thought of Mary sewing under a lamppost on cold February nights. "And someone with just one saturated overcoat and no fire can't get it dry for the next day. Not even in June, let alone February. But—" Lucien shifted the topic with an effort and a tight smile "—to get back to the point. We hoped to garner a little sympathy and attention for women's suffrage, though Miss Enfield worried that Mrs Drummond wouldn't quite like the article."

"Flora Drummond? Did you meet her?"

"Briefly."

Lady Hernedale capped her pen and put it down. "What's she like?"

It turned out Lady Hernedale belonged to the National Union of Women's Suffrage Societies. Lucien's heart sank—he already knew more than he'd ever wanted to about the conflicts between the various women's suffrage groups—but she only asked about the procession, and about the WSPU's failed attempt to meet the prime minister that morning. They spent the next hour in unexpectedly interesting conversation about women's rights, and about the plight of working women in London. "Though, as a single man with an adequate income, my understanding of it is necessarily limited."

"You might speak to Hernedale about the difficulties facing women, if it's an interest of yours," Lady Hernedale suggested.

Lucien wasn't sure it was, though the more he learned, the more outraged he became. Perhaps that counted as an interest. "Might he speak for ladies in the Lords, if I raise it with him?"

Lady Hernedale laughed. "He does little else. His particular interest lies in protecting women and children from violence at home."

Lucien looked at Hernedale with renewed interest. "Miss Kenney spoke of violence at home. And at work."

Hernedale seemed to feel his regard: he looked up from watching Aubrey play and offered him a flicker of a smile.

Lucien smiled back. For a ghastly moment he worried Hernedale would think him over-familiar, as altogether too many people did, but Hernedale only returned a courteous smile, and turned back to Aubrey.

Lucien relaxed. "I'm not a political journalist," he told Lady Hernedale, "so I don't really know which interests are whose."

"Hernedale founded the Children in Poverty and Aid For Women charities, and mostly funds them himself. Children's education is his other interest."

Bloody hell! Who'd have thought it?

"I wonder whether…" Another article quoting the nobility would keep Jameson off his back, and this was in a good cause. And he'd be doing Hernedale a favour, not using him.

"An idea, Mr Saxby?"

"My editor's not likely to print an article on poverty and violence in England, but if Lord Hernedale would like it, I might write a Society article about him. And if the only quotations he consents to have published regard his charities and the necessity for them, well, my editor won't remove many, since they come from an earl."

"Interesting."

"But Lord Hernedale mightn't like to be featured in the Mail, in any case."

A soft tap at the door heralded the arrival of the tea-tray. Aubrey and Hernedale joined them, and the conversation turned to more general topics. Hernedale touched the tail of his coat often, where an imperfection in the hang betrayed the presence of a book, but he didn't take it out, which Lucien suspected was an unusual courtesy.

As the clock chimed half past eleven, the butler tapped on the door and announced the carriage. Lucien stared as both Lord and Lady Hernedale rose to shake hands with him.

"You must join us for dinner again, Saxby," Hernedale said cordially.

"We look forward to it," Lady Hernedale agreed.

Ingrained habit drew Lucien through the parting courtesies, putting on his outdoor things, and walking to the carriage. Why invite him to dinner again? A private dinner wouldn't restore his reputation; and, though he'd always made an effort to charm them, he doubted they'd want him purely for the pleasure of his company.

The carriage started to move, and he looked up to see Aubrey watching him from the opposite seat. He summoned a smile and a topic of conversation. "You play well."

Aubrey's mouth lifted at a corner. "You don't have to flatter me, sweetheart: we're not in the drawing room now."

Sweetheart. Lucien's heart leaped. "I'm not a musician, and you clearly weren't putting your whole heart into it tonight, but it seemed very accomplished to me."

Aubrey huffed a laugh and looked out of the carriage window. "I'm no Mozart."

"Does it ever occur to you that you hold yourself to impossibly high standards in everything?"

Aubrey startled. "Not really."

"Wilde wasn't also a Mozart. Mozart wasn't also a Rubens or a Michelangelo. Why do you consider your craft inadequate if you can't match the genius of three people in three separate fields?"

Swaying with the carriage, Aubrey stared at him in silence. Stark white lamplight glared through the windows, then faded into darkness, over and again. White shirt and pale face gleamed between the black coat and tall top hat, then disappeared into shadow: perfect symmetry revealed and snatched away in regular, tantalising rhythm.

"I haven't seen your sketches," Lucien said, "but you're very good at writing and playing the piano: better at both than many are at either. Can't it be enough that you strive to improve? Must everything you produce be perfect?"

"Maybe." Aubrey sighed. "I can see where the thing looks or sounds wrong, but I can't always see how to correct it."

"An advantage of writing for a newspaper: you have to do your best then let go. Like it or not, your stories have to be edited and ready when the presses start rolling."

"It amazes me that you can write at all under those conditions, let alone so consistently well."

Lucien warmed under his admiration.

"I couldn't do it," Aubrey added.

"You could, and you would if you had to. You already write well, and you'd soon be as quick as anyone. I'm willing to bet at least part of your problem is the leisure to brood over every comma and semi-colon."

Aubrey snorted an undignified laugh and clapped a white-gloved hand over his mouth. When he moved it, lamplight gleamed from a bright grin. "You've never seen me write, and yet you know me."

"Not as well as I'd like to," Lucien murmured, watching his smile, appreciating the nob who could take criticism without taking umbrage.

Between one lamppost and the next, Aubrey's smile faded. He leaned forward, reaching for Lucien's hand. "Would you consider coming home with me? For conversation and sleep, or— Well, whatever you want, really. I know you gave me your time just last night, but— Well, I wish you would. If you'd like it."

Lucien curled gloved fingers around Aubrey's hand and squeezed. And watched his lips part in bright glimpses.

He shouldn't. He really shouldn't. He'd be walking home through the morning city in evening dress again: Dad would be appalled. And he was ashamed of the part of himself that exulted in an aristocrat begging him to visit, for whatever he might want to offer or take; that gloried in his ability to move an earl's beautiful son to desire with no more than a murmur and the touch of a gloved hand.

After all—he looked beyond the parted lips to dark eyes fixed on him in the close, leather-and-pomade-scented carriage— this was Aubrey, who'd helped and cared for him at every turn, when he might have had all he wanted without that.

This was Aubrey, who wanted him. *Him*, not some other fellow. A man seeking impersonal satisfaction didn't swoon at a simple touch: he found a willing bloke and a quiet spot, and they exchanged brisk courtesies, then buttoned up and went their separate ways.

But Aubrey... Aubrey liked Lucien enough to invite him home just for conversation and sleep. Liked and trusted him enough to open more than his body to him. Enough to allow himself to be moved by Lucien's most subtle touch.

Watching his face, Lucien lifted Aubrey's hand to his lips and breathed on the fine, soft kidskin. Aubrey's hand clutched his, and his breathing grew loud and quick over the rumble of carriage wheels. Desire quivered low in Lucien's belly as he inhaled the dense scent of skin-warmed leather, as Aubrey clung to his hand, his erratic breath shivering the air between them.

Lucien raised his head, slipped finger and thumb beneath the starched cuff onto soft, tendon-ridged skin, and brushed Aubrey's pulse point with his gloved thumb.

The warm give of yielding flesh through kidskin; the sight of his own fingers thrust beneath perfectly-tailored wool and cotton; Aubrey's dazed eyes and parted lips; the willing—no, *eager*—surrender to his tender invasion...

Lucien closed his eyes as reaction arced up to his throat and down to his groin.

"I'd be honoured," he whispered.

LUCIEN HUNG UP his overcoat and went to pour the brandy. When he turned, Aubrey stood in the drawing room doorway, his expression a peculiar blend of joy and fear.

"What's the matter?" He put the glasses back on the tray.

"I don't—" Aubrey joined Lucien at the sideboard and reached for his arms. His head drooped towards Lucien's shoulder, then jerked up. "Let's—let's get you out of that coat before I ruin it."

Lucien followed him to the dressing room.

Aubrey slipped the tailcoat from Lucien's shoulders and hung it on the valet stand. He unfastened his collar, put it in the valet stand drawer and its studs in a bowl. Then he slid a silk cravat around Lucien's throat. Taking an indigo silk dressing gown from the wardrobe, he held it for Lucien to put on, straightened the collar, and belted it while Lucien folded the too-long sleeves into deep, precise cuffs. "There." He kissed his cheek.

Lucien reached for Aubrey's tailcoat in turn. He eased it from broad, bony shoulders and hung it over his own. Tucking gentle fingers between Aubrey's starched collar and his stubble-roughened throat, he undid the studs. The collar sprang free, and he laid it and the studs with his own. Then he reached for the plum dressing gown.

Standing behind Aubrey, he slid it up his arms and settled it across his shoulders, heart pounding because— hadn't he wanted precisely this since watching Grieve help Aubrey with his overcoat? He smoothed the collar and reached around to enfold him in silk, pressing his lips to the side of his neck. Aubrey leaned in to him as Lucien smoothed the silk over his belly and hips from behind; as he tied the silk cord, nuzzling the delicate skin beneath Aubrey's ear lobe. Yes. He'd wanted this, every bit as much as he'd wanted sex. And if that made him a natural-born valet, so be it. He wanted to care for Aubrey.

True, Aubrey could be a bit of a mink at times—he took his valet for granted, and used his position to bite back and overwhelm—but it was only when he was uncertain. Lucien could help him be less frightened. And—and even if it wasn't just fear, well, everyone had their flaws, didn't they?

Shit.

Lucien dropped his forehead between Aubrey's shoulder blades, trying to steady his breathing. Shit. Why a bloody aristocrat? Of all the sodding people in the world.

"Lucien?" Aubrey murmured.

Lucien squeezed his eyes shut and hugged him fiercely. "Oh, *shit*."

Aubrey tugged his arms until he loosened them, then turned and held him. "What's the matter?"

"*This* is." Lucien sucked in a deep breath, and the scent of Aubrey's skin unknotted his neck and shoulders, set his mind floating. "Us. It's a bloody disaster waiting to happen."

Aubrey huffed a quiet laugh. "Oh Lord! Isn't it though?"

"Ah, shit." Lucien rubbed his face along Aubrey's throat. Knowing Aubrey saw the problem as clearly as he did helped, in an odd way.

"Lucien?" Aubrey murmured into his hair. "Is it safe to assume that—that you might care for me the way I care for you?"

Lucien sighed. "You wouldn't be wrong."

Aubrey held him tightly, face pressed into his hair, breathing too deeply, too slowly. "It's been too short a time."

"It doesn't feel safe." This crushing, uplifting obsession might vanish as unexpectedly as it'd appeared.

"I don't—" Aubrey's breath hitched. "I don't know where this is going. Where it's taking us."

"Straight to hell," Lucien muttered into his throat.

Aubrey huffed a shaky laugh into his hair. "Don't indulge your optimism too far."

They clung to one another like seaweed in a raging ocean; Lucien despairing, but drunk on Aubrey, and on his acknowledgement that he cared.

"I don't see how we can fit into one another's lives," Aubrey whispered.

Lucien rocked his head along Aubrey's neck: acknowledgement and agreement.

"But, at this point—" Aubrey's lips pressed Lucien's head "—I have to try. If you'll let me. If you want to. I can't *not*."

Lucien squeezed his eyes shut. He didn't see it. There was no obvious way for men of differing social status to have this. Unless… Unless he became Aubrey's valet.

Every feeling revolted. To displace a man who'd worked for Aubrey for years. To be dependent on his lover for an income, even if he worked for it. Worst of all, to be at his beck and call, if only in company. That could easily spill into their private lives, especially as Aubrey was so accustomed to servants. There'd be times Lucien wondered whether he was genuinely wanted, or merely a convenient, comprehensive service. No. Absolutely not.

"Lucien?" Aubrey murmured. "Can we try? Please, sweetheart."

"Oh, buggery." Lucien held Aubrey's arms, his grip slipping on the cool, smooth silk. "What's the bloody alternative? Only seeing one another as acquaintances, when we happen to cross paths? Because let me tell you, I won't enjoy that."

"It'd be miserable," Aubrey whispered into his hair.

Lucien shuddered at the delicate warmth. "Can we… agree that, even if we come to hate one another, we'll never purposely harm one another? That I won't use journalism to damage you, and you won't use your position to damage me? Or any other influence either of us might have."

"I can't imagine ever wanting to harm you."

Lucien sighed. "Not now. But hurt feelings often lead to anger."

"Well, I agree, at any rate."

"So do I."

It felt like a larger commitment than the words expressed. Lucien wrapped his arms around Aubrey with new confidence; certain that his affection was wanted—that *he* was wanted.

"So…" Aubrey kissed his head. "Would two evenings a week be too much for you?"

"Not at all, and we already have Saturday, for one."

"Mmm. And, not to be greedy, but that's tomorrow." Aubrey kissed him again. "How about Sundays? You don't have work, so—"

"I visit William every Sunday, and sometimes get stuck there till quite late."

Aubrey stilled in his arms.

"You all right?"

"Perfectly. A prior obligation's a prior obligation."

"I could…" Lucien leaned back to see his face. "If Sunday's important to you, I can make a point of coming by afterwards?"

"Oh no, it's not important. Which day suits you?"

"Are you sure?" Lucien tried to read his expression.

A slightly forced smile. "Of course." Aubrey's eyes closed, and he pressed his lips to Lucien's temple for a long, quiet moment. When he raised his head, his eyes were calm and his smile warm. "Name your day, sweetheart: I'll try to fit in with you."

What must it take, for a dyed-in-the-wool aristocrat to admit to himself that he wanted a working man for a lover, not just an occasional roll? What must it take for him to be the first to say he cared, and ask for more meetings? To accept the day Lucien named rather than insist on his own preference? To face the possibility of rejection by a social inferior at every step, and decide the risk was worth it?

"Wednesday?" Lucien suggested. "It's about halfway between Saturdays." And Noel guarded the Ropewalk on Thursday mornings.

"Wednesday it is, then."

He was wanted, and for more than his bedroom skills. The hand sliding up his spine to cup the base of his skull, the cheek that rested on his head: they spoke of affection as much as passion; of a desire to cherish that might match his own.

"Might have to miss or alter a day sometimes." William would get worse again, and Mum and Dad needed a hand whenever they hosted large events at the hotel.

"Me too. But in general. Saturdays and Wednesdays."

They held one another in silence while the fact sank into Lucien's bones. There was no need to claw all he could from this moment, this night, for fear it might be his last. He'd be back tomorrow night. And the Wednesday after that. And the Saturday after that.

"Shall we have that brandy?" Aubrey murmured.

"Be a shame to waste it."

On the sofa, Aubrey took Lucien's glass from him and urged his head onto his lap.

Lucien laughed, stretching out and hanging his feet over the arm of the sofa. "How can I drink like this?"

Aubrey stroked his hair. "I'll help, sweetheart." He dipped a long finger into his glass and held it above Lucien's lips, an amber drop trembling at the tip. "In you, or on you?"

"Now there's a question." Lucien opened his mouth as the drop fell, and caught the burning spark on his tongue. "That," he observed, "is going to take forever."

Aubrey offered him his finger, and he sucked the brandy from it. He urged Lucien to a half-sitting position, cradled in his arm, then sipped his drink and pressed his lips to Lucien's.

Lucien opened his mouth to a wash of liquid fire and the delicate probing of Aubrey's tongue, which seemed hesitant to intrude too far. He touched Aubrey's tongue with the tip of his own, coaxing him further in.

A tug at his waist, and then a release, as his dressing gown cord opened; another tug, and his shirt tails slid free of his waistband. And then Aubrey's hand slipped between folds of silk, beneath stiff-starched cotton, to lie on his belly. The warm hand spanned his abdomen, then stroked from hip to flank. Lucien groaned and tipped his head back.

Aubrey rested his cheek along Lucien's. "Let me love you," he whispered, his breath warm in Lucien's ear.

Lucien shuddered. *Do you?* But he didn't ask. This thing he felt for Aubrey—the disproportionate delight in quite ordinary things; the bone-deep reluctance to part from him; the soothing, opium-like daze of touching him, of being touched by him... He didn't have a name for that. He didn't know whether he loved Aubrey, and he wouldn't ask for those words from him. He only knew that he wanted him like he wanted sunlight and warmth and shelter. That he could live without him, but it'd be a bleak, stunted existence. That the way he felt was too much—too extreme—to burden another fellow with.

Aubrey untied Lucien's cravat and tugged. It slid from his neck in a whisper of cool silk, tightening his skin to gooseflesh. Pressing his lips to Lucien's forehead, Aubrey plucked out the top shirt stud.

"Wait." Lucien gripped his wrist. "Where are you putting that?"

"On the table." Aubrey lifted his head. "Why?"

"It'll fall off." Lucien sat up. "They need a box or a bowl or—" He looked around.

Aubrey brushed a finger down the back of his neck, and kissed the side. "I have other studs. You can have those."

"No. I don't— I mean, thank you. But I'd rather look after these."

Aubrey stilled. Then he kissed his cheek. "I understand."

Lucien had no idea what Aubrey thought he understood, but the fact that he wanted to, and the tenderness in his tone, made his eyes sting.

"Let's go to bed." Aubrey folded Lucien's fingers around his shirt stud. "I'll find you a box in the bedroom."

He brought Lucien's collar studs from the dressing room, along with an empty navy blue leather jewellery case.

Lucien held it, irresolute. "Is this for the studs you're wearing?"

"Usually." Aubrey dropped his collar studs into a small ivory pot on the dressing table and tugged out a shirt stud. "But I'd rather you used it, for now."

Lucien flinched as Aubrey dropped the gold and sapphire stud into the pot. "They'll get scratched, bumping one another like that."

"They'll be all right." But Aubrey put the next one in more carefully. "I'll have them polished."

That wasn't the point.

Lucien opened the case and set his studs and cuff-links into recesses in the pearl-grey silk lining. By the time he closed it and turned, Aubrey's starched shirt hung open over pale, bare skin, and his shirt cuffs hung loose under his dressing gown sleeves.

"Thank you."

Aubrey cupped his jaw in a long hand and kissed him.

"Listen. Would you make a point of tipping the doormen? I would, but your trustees might think they're taking bribes."

"Already do." Aubrey brushed his lips over Lucien's again.

"Especially Noel."

Aubrey drew back. "Why? And which one's Noel? I only know their surnames."

"Because he's been turning a blind eye to me leaving here in the mornings." A thread of exasperation wound through Lucien's happiness. "And I only know his *first* name. He's on duty daytimes: Saturday to Thursday."

"Right-ho." Aubrey straightened. "Want a nightshirt?"

Lucien tugged him closer. "Why? D'you mean to leave me wanting?"

"Just didn't want to assume anything." Aubrey's hand slid along his throat and under his clothes, nudging shirt and dressing gown from his shoulder.

Lucien tilted his chin to let Aubrey nuzzle his throat, then cool, hard teeth pressed into the side of his neck. He gasped and clutched Aubrey's head, holding him in place. "Harder," he whispered.

Aubrey folded long arms around Lucien and sank his teeth deeper.

Giddy and weak-kneed, Lucien groaned, swaying into the support of his body.

Aubrey's bite eased, was replaced by his warm tongue tip, then by soft lips beneath Lucien's ear lobe. Lucien dropped his hands to broad, bony shoulders.

"Have I ever told you—" Aubrey lipped the shell of his ear "—how beautiful you are?"

"No." Nobody had, because he wasn't. His charm attracted people, and his friendliness; not his looks, which were very ordinary.

"This." Aubrey trailed his lips along Lucien's hairline behind his ear and down to his neck, then paused, and nuzzled. "This spot." He kissed it. "This... delicious curve." A soft, damp tongue tip. "I could kiss and lick this spot for hours. You have no idea how it tempts me."

"You're daft," Lucien told him.

"But what sublime folly."

Teeth nipped at his hairline, casting tingles down his spine, and Lucien clutched silk-covered shoulders as his body arched and froze. Warm lips soothed the spot, and he dropped his forehead to Aubrey's shoulder, slipping his arms beneath his shirt, leaning into his warmth.

"This spot," Aubrey murmured into his neck, "hidden by your collar till you turn or bow your head. And then... a glimpse of perfect, soft bare flesh. And I could—could stroke it, just with a fingertip."

"Oh God!"

"Or trace it with the very tip of my tongue. Or feel the shape of it with my parted lips and breath. That perfect junction of cropped hair and naked skin; that exquisite curve, like a Michelangelo statue."

"Dear *God*!" Lucien half-collapsed against him. "And you think you're a mediocre writer? Dear God, Aubrey!"

The damp touch of a careful tongue tip. "But I can't, in public. So I only watch you. And I wait. Until you come to me, and bare your throat and the nape of your lovely neck to me, and show me what you want from me, and let me please you."

"Aubrey..." Lucien clung to him.

"Have I told you," Aubrey whispered, "about the line of your jaw?" He nuzzled it.

"Look. Can we go to bed? I don't think I can stand up much longer."

"Shall I undress you?"

"I think—" Lucien carefully stood away from him. "I'd better undress myself. Otherwise it'll be time to go to work and you'll have barely started describing the curve of my arse."

"Mmm. About that..."

"Damn you." Lucien laughed. "You're impossibly seductive."

"Not with just anyone."

"Just as well, or you'd never leave your bedroom."

Lucien stripped, hung his clothes carefully on the valet stand in the dressing room, and climbed into bed beside Aubrey, who was already naked.

Aubrey rolled on top of him, supporting himself on his elbows, and kissed him. Lucien opened his mouth to him, the solid weight rendering him breathless and yearning, and let Aubrey's kiss take the last of the air from his lungs. He wound his arms around Aubrey's broad, bony back, and wrapped his legs around narrow hips.

"You asked me a question earlier," he gasped.

"Did I?" Aubrey gazed down at him.

"The answer is 'in me'."

Aubrey brushed soft lips across his eyelids, and Lucien clung to him.

"I want to hold you as close as I can. So close that we forget the morning."

— Chapter Seventeen —

A week later, at ten o'clock on an unseasonably warm, sunny morning, Lucien stood beside Miss Enfield and watched another WSPU deputation process up the road towards Number 10, past police, onlookers, and a full complement of the Press.

The deputation was larger than last time: thirty-five to forty women in all, Mrs Drummond and Miss Kenney among them. Lucien made quick notes on hats and clothes as they approached the dark green—almost black—door, and wondered whether it was still accurate to describe the WSPU as 'militant'. It was bold, but hardly extreme, to approach the prime minister directly, even if it was only a week since their previous attempt. Perhaps the imprisonment of Christabel Pankhurst and Annie Kenney last year had made them all more cautious. He hoped so. Reading accounts of the arrests had turned his stomach.

If you don't know where she is, ask a p'liceman! / For he's 'in the know' he is—

Mrs Drummond seized the ring of the black lion's-head knocker and rapped loudly.

The hall porter opened the door.

"WSPU deputation to see Sir Henry Campbell-Bannerman, as advised in our letter three days ago."

The hall porter looked the women over. "I'll advise the prime minister's secretary that you're here." He closed the door.

The deputation stood on the broad step and on the pavement, speaking to journalists, while the crowd of onlookers swelled, plying the police with questions, shouting unsolicited observations, and exchanging loud, frank opinions.

A carriage rumbled towards the crowd. Lucien glanced over: it was bound to turn and try a less busy road. But it drew to a halt and Hernedale descended the steps. He looked around, adjusting his top hat, then turned to offer his hand to Lady Hernedale.

Lucien's heart clenched painfully as Aubrey, sleek in morning coat and top hat, followed her.

Tomorrow. He'd see him tomorrow night.

Aubrey's eyes met Lucien's across the crowd. He smiled, and Lucien smiled back helplessly, far too warmly. Thank God they weren't in Piccadilly Circus or Oxford Street: that smile was enough to get him arrested, where police were looking out for it.

Aubrey spoke to the Hernedales, who turned to face him, each nodding acknowledgement. He wrestled his face under control and touched his bowler.

Miss Enfield nudged him. "Friends in swanky places, Saxby."

"Yes and no." He returned his attention to his notebook.

"Are they here on purpose? Why else stay?"

Lucien said nothing. He wasn't sure whether Lady Hernedale supported women's suffrage publicly. The carriage retreated, drawing up at the side of the road, the crest clearly visible on the door.

"Hernedale," Miss Enfield mused. "Now how would they have known to come here this morning?"

Heat rose up Lucien's neck. "I might've mentioned it to Mr Fanshawe," he admitted. "But I didn't expect him to pass it on, or for them to come here."

"Interesting." She made a note.

Lucien touched her sleeve. "Don't put them in your notes. Please."

Miss Enfield raised astonished eyes. "My dear Saxby, if it isn't Society news that The Earl and Countess Hernedale turned up at a WSPU event, then I don't know what is!"

"They may not like it."

"Then they shouldn't have come. Take a look along this street, Saxby. What do you see?"

Journalists. Press photographers.

"What do you think Jameson will say if the Mail is the only paper in the city not to mention their presence?"

Buggery. "Will you at least let me speak to them first?"

"Get an interview, you mean?"

Lucien paused. He hadn't meant that, but he should have. Damn it, this was getting complicated. "You recall Lady Hernedale's statements on that awful play?"

"You mean, the review you'd never have got past Jameson if he hadn't been dazzled by your countess' name dropped into every other sentence?"

"Not my countess." He didn't own her, for God's sake; yet he felt like a Judas, denying someone who'd been nothing but kind to him.

"Point is, Saxby, no one could forget the dashed countess' statements on the play."

"Right. So... she might want to help the WSPU."

Miss Enfield stared across the crowd at the Hernedales. "You've changed your tune. What about wealthy women getting the poor to do their work for them?"

"That point still stands. In general. In this specific instance, however, I draw your attention to the fact that the lady is actually *here*."

She gave him an old-fashioned look. "You try to get that interview, but I'm taking notes. They don't have to go in the final copy if you get something better, but I won't be hampered by your scruples when no one else will be."

The door to Number 10 opened. Lucien slid his watch from his waistcoat pocket. Almost three quarters of an hour since the hall porter offered to take a message to the PM's secretary. He snapped it shut and looked up as two men, neither of them the hall porter, emerged.

"You'd better be off," one said to the WSPU deputation. "You mustn't stand on this doorstep any longer."

"Any idea who that is?" Lucien muttered to Miss Enfield.

"None whatsoever."

"The porter took our message to Mr Ponsonby," Mrs Drummond said. "We're waiting for a reply."

The men exchanged glances, then the fellow who'd spoken glared down at her. "There's no answer." He shut the door in her face.

"Oh, how disgracefully rude!" A woman seized the knocker and rapped sharply at the door.

"Irene Miller," Miss Enfield murmured. "Miss. WSPU organiser." Lucien noted it.

The door opened almost immediately, on the same pair of men.

Miss Miller set her fists on her hips. "You might at *least* have—"

"Constable!" One of the men raised an imperious hand. "Take this woman in charge!" He slammed the door shut.

Lucien's heart stopped, then leapt into his throat, hammering at double pace.

"What!" Mrs Drummond turned, outraged. "What *for*?"

Two large policemen approached the deputation. "You'd better come along nicely, Miss," one suggested.

This couldn't be happening. Not over knocking on a bloody door.

"Open this door!" Miss Miller banged her hand on the glossy green paint.

"Now then, none of that, Miss."

"We only want to speak to the prime minister." Mrs Drummond's face was reddening. "We should not be so rudely dismissed."

Miss Miller banged on the door again. "I support you with my taxes!" she shouted.

The policemen reached into the group of women, half-lifted her out onto the pavement, and propelled her down the road.

"Where are you taking her?" Miss Kenney demanded.

"Canon Row, Miss," the second policeman called over his shoulder.

"This is a disgrace!" Mrs Drummond, crimson-faced, whirled round. "*Nothing* will prevent me from seeing the prime minister!" She yanked violently at a small brass knob that looked like a door bell.

The door swung open onto an empty entrance hall, tiled in black and white. The crowd silenced. Mrs Drummond teetered on the threshold, her round face slack with shock. Then she dashed inside. "Where is the Cabinet Council Chamber?" she bellowed.

The door swung to behind her, and the crowd erupted with cheers and jeers and whistles. Mere moments later, two men marched her, struggling, back out.

"Police!" The men holding her didn't let go until a tall, broad policeman muscled past the women on the doorstep. He seized her by an arm and the back of her neck and propelled her along the street in the same direction as Miss Miller.

Shit! Lucien gritted his teeth.

The tiny woman didn't even come up to the policeman's shoulder, but she flung up her free arm, yelling, "Votes for Women!"

A concerted gasp and shout from the edge of the crowd turned Lucien in time to see Aubrey bend then straighten with Lady Hernedale, hatless, in his arms.

"Bloody *hell*!" He shoved his notebook and pencil into a pocket and pushed frantically through the crowd towards them.

Miss Kenney's voice rose above the renewed clamour. "We are only here to speak to our prime minister, as notified in—"

"Why don't you arrest that woman?" a man shouted. "She's one of the ring-leaders. Take her in charge!"

An interested section of the crowd had gathered around Aubrey, who clutched Lady Hernedale, looking desperate. A quick glance showed Hernedale running for the carriage, waving to attract the coachman's attention. The police were doing absolutely nothing to help. Useless sodding malletheaded fuckers. They'd have pitched in if a nob told them to, but since the nobs had lost their heads...

"Move back there!" Lucien yelled. "Give the lady some air." He pressed people aside without striking, but kept his riding cane in hand, in case tempers ignited. "Come *on*! Clear the way." They moved reluctantly, staring at the tableau. "Tommy!" Lucien spotted the youngest club member with relief. "Help me clear a path to the carriage."

The lad's eyes lit up.

"Gently!" Lucien added. Maybe this wasn't such a good idea.

Tommy slithered through the crowd past Aubrey and Lady Hernedale, careless of elbows that poked, of feet that trod on his or barked his shins, extending Lucien's reach. They pushed towards the approaching carriage, clearing people out of the way.

Lucien glanced back to see Aubrey following. Lady Hernedale leaned on him, chalk-pale, but on her feet, thank God, and with no obvious sign of injury. Hernedale and a footman were leading the horses towards them.

The remainder of the crowd between Lucien and the carriage simultaneously gave it up as a bad job and moved aside. The alarmed-looking footman soothed the horses while Aubrey helped Lady Hernedale into the carriage. Without discussion, Lucien, Tommy and Hernedale formed a semi-circle in front of the door, facing the crowd, warning them off by their presence.

Lucien glanced over his shoulder to see if Lady Hernedale was settled. And Aubrey—

Aubrey had his arm around Lady Hernedale. Her head lay on his shoulder. And he was kissing her forehead.

Lucien stared as Lady Hernedale pressed a lingering kiss to Aubrey's jaw, then slowly opened her eyes. He wrenched his gaze away. But when Hernedale turned towards them, he couldn't help but glance in again.

Aubrey and Lady Hernedale were sitting a respectable distance apart. She leaned against the window, very pale, but managed a shaky smile for her husband.

Hernedale—Aubrey's closest friend; the fellow who'd stood by him through scandal and contagious disgrace—climbed into the carriage and sat opposite his wife. "Thanks, Saxby." He leaned out, offering his gloved hand. "*Very* much appreciated."

Lucien shook hands, keeping his eyes strictly on Hernedale. "Anything else I can do?"

"No. Thank you. We'll just get Lady Hernedale home."

Mind you, there was something about the wife...

"Righteo." Lucien stepped back and closed the carriage door. He watched till it was out of sight, then turned to Tommy. "What happened?"

"Don't know. She just flopped. When the peeler dragged that dumpy woman out the house. Just bloody flopped. Like in a play or something."

"She *fainted?*" Impossible to imagine Lady Hernedale fainting.

Tommy shrugged.

"Well. Thanks very much for your help." He dredged a shilling from his coin purse and handed it over.

Tommy's face brightened. "Thanks!"

"See you Tuesday." Lucien shook his hand, then wove through the crowd to Miss Enfield's side. "What did I miss?"

"Annie Kenney's been arrested, the deputation's about to leave, and I've got an interview. D'you want to go to Canon Row and cover that part of the story?"

Did he want to wait in a building full of officious sods who, if they realised he was Uranian, might arrest him just for making eye-contact with another fellow? He sighed. "All right."

"I'll join you when I've finished."

Lucien turned to leave.

"By the way, what happened there?"

"Tell you later," Lucien promised.

"Tease!" She grinned.

But it wasn't funny. What the hell was Aubrey playing at? Surely he'd never— Anyway, Lady Hernedale didn't seem the sort to—

Sitting in the corner of a bare waiting room gave him plenty of time to think, and none of his thoughts was pleasant. Big, blue-jacketed policemen tramped in and out, talking in loud, self-important tones, and gazing around with a smug, proprietary air that set his teeth on edge. He kept his head down, fiddling with notebook and pencil to justify not meeting anybody's bloody eye. It only needed a copper to decide Lucien'd taken a fancy to his uniform to cap the misery of his day.

Miss Enfield joined him, proudly bearing shorthand notes which added nothing to what they already knew.

"Except quotes from primary sources"—she snatched her notebook back—"confirming our story and saving it from being purely narrative."

"True."

"What the devil's wrong with you, anyway? Between that theatre review, and the way you took off when she fell, and the way you're moping now— If I didn't know better, I'd think you had a particular interest in the woman."

He leaned his head back against the drab wall and closed his eyes. Try to convince a court *that's* importuning, you big blue turds.

"You— *haven't*, have you?" she whispered.

He rolled his head on the wall as far as his bowler allowed, and glared at her. "Considerably less than you have," he muttered, "and you've never even met her."

She laughed. "That's better."

"Look. D'you think you could just—subdue your journalistic curiosity for now? Please?"

"Well, all right. For now."

But Miss Enfield's curiosity was the least of his woes. Surely—*surely*—he couldn't have been so horribly mistaken in Aubrey's character. "Actually—" He straightened. "Now you're here, d'you think I might go and see how she is?"

"The woman you don't have a particular interest in."

"Not—" He sighed. "Look. Society news and all that. Add a bit of drama to our story. Other papers will have the basics, but I might get follow-up news."

"Oh." She paused. "All right, then."

"Meet you at the office around four? No later than half past, at any rate."

"Cutting it a bit fine, isn't it?"

"I'll bring polished paragraphs ready to collate."

She eyed him thoughtfully. "You're a bit flighty, you know that?"

Flighty? Lucien stared at her.

"No, you are. But all right. No later than half past, mind."

THE HERNEDALES WEREN'T at home to visitors, so Lucien left his card and polite inquiries after Lady Hernedale's health with a footman, then walked on to Albany. By the time he got there, he'd been walking for nearly an hour, was rather too warm, and didn't want to walk any further. He knocked on Aubrey's front door. And then again.

It remained resolutely closed.

Buggery.

He turned away as Grieve reached the top of the basement stairs.

"Afternoon, Grieve. Sorry if I disturbed you."

"Afternoon." Grieve pulled a set of keys from his pocket. "Mr Fanshawe's not at home. I'll let you in to wait for him."

"Er, thank you." Surely Aubrey didn't let all his acquaintances in when he wasn't there? Unless… Grieve might assume Lucien was welcome because Aubrey'd let him wait here while he dined with the Hernedales. But it wasn't good practice, and such a skilled valet ought to know better.

Tension slid from his shoulders as he crossed the threshold of Aubrey's home, despite the upcoming conversation. He hung up his bowler and riding cane, bizarrely at ease in a place he'd first entered just two months before. Grieve flowed past him into the drawing room as he took off his gloves and coat.

The set was cooler than outdoors—too cool for comfort without a cardigan or dressing gown—but it couldn't be helped. He walked into the drawing room to see Grieve building up the fire.

"Oh. Thank you, but please don't trouble yourself if it's just for me."

Grieve slanted a sardonic look over his shoulder. "I'm certain Mr Fanshawe would want me to ensure your comfort."

Lucien stilled. What was that supposed to mean?

Grieve slid a final shovelful of coal onto the fire, closed the purdonium, and slotted the coal shovel into its holder on the back. "Pot of tea, Mr Saxby?"

A pot of tea would be perfect, after the morning he'd had; maybe a biscuit, too. But he'd intruded on Grieve's day quite enough. "Thank you, but no."

"You prefer brandy?" Grieve eyed the decanters.

"Good Lord, no. Not at this hour."

Grieve turned unsettling pale grey eyes on him. "You're Henry Saxby's son?"

Startled, Lucien smiled. "You know him?"

"I surmised, as it's an uncommon name. I know *of* him. A skilled and hard-working man."

Lucien warmed with pride. "That he is."

"So you'll have grown up in The Marquess of Erthingleigh's establishments."

"That's right."

"That being the case—" Grieve folded his arms "—you'll know how fast news travels among those in service."

Lucien's smile froze. "Yes, of course."

"Consider the size of Albany, Mr Saxby. Sixty-nine sets. Now consider: every set has at least one servant; most have more. And we're always up before the nobs, as you well know."

Lucien dropped the smile. "Please speak plainly."

"*So far*, nobody has enquired about the chap who leaves Mr Fanshawe's set before breakfast, wearing evening dress."

Lucien's heart clenched, turning him breathless, then started pounding at double-time. Of all the *sodding* days for this to happen! Could he pay Grieve off? How much would—

"Perhaps no other servants have spotted this chap yet. Let's hope so."

Lucien stared.

"But you might consider the doormen, who are bound to notice you."

"The doormen are... not a problem," Lucien managed through stiff lips. He hoped he wasn't betraying Noel.

Grieve tipped his head like a curious vulture. "Demonstrating more caution and sense than I credited you with. However, since this is becoming a regular occurrence, you might consider leaving morning dress here, or a lounge suit and bowler. You will, at least, be less remarkable."

The room was far too hot. Lucien's neck and palms were damp with sweat. How could Grieve stand in front of a blazing fire? "Thank you. I'll—try not to disturb your arrangements."

Grieve smiled thinly. "So far you've been admirably tidy, and very little trouble."

"I'll make sure I keep it that way."

Grieve glided past him, then turned in the doorway. "Any particular times you'll be here? It's more convenient if I know in advance."

Lucien paused, wary. But Grieve already had enough information to damn both Aubrey and himself, even without this. "Assuming nothing changes—" And it might, it truly might, after the conversation he had to have with Aubrey "—Wednesday and Saturday nights. Something unexpected came up today, or I wouldn't be here."

Grieve waved his explanation away. "Will you take your dinner here on those nights?"

"Depends whether he asks me to."

"Probably, then." Grieve eyed Lucien. "You'd better stay for breakfast on Sundays, if his nibs'd like it. Best if you're not seen sneaking out early on a day of rest, but rather assumed to have visited early."

Lucien blotted his palms on his thighs. "Don't like to put you to any trouble."

Grieve waved this away, too. "One more for breakfast is hardly any bother. Just—don't take his jewellery and pin the blame on me. And don't clean him out."

Outrage swamped fear and embarrassment. "Bloody *hell*, Grieve!"

Grieve's narrow face shut like a trap. "None of that, Saxby. Cards on the table. I've a sister and niece to provide for, and I hope to retire in relative comfort. So do me a favour and don't clean the bugger out entirely."

"I won't take any of his sodding stuff! I haven't accepted a single thing from him, and I won't."

Grieve raised his brows. "More fool you, then. Doubly so if it's because you're getting attached."

Lucien deflated. "Probably."

"Though now I think of it, you can afford scruples, can't you? You might be living on brass for now, but you've a silver spoon of your own to retire on— unless you've got a dozen brothers I never heard of to split it with."

"No, there's just me. And you're right. Look. You... don't mind? About me and Fanshawe?"

"Time you get to my age, you know what's important and what's not. I want things to stay clean and tidy, and I want the retirement I've worked for. This—" he gestured at Lucien "— is no worse than most nobs get up to, and a deal better than many. Better than violated, pregnant maids who'd still be in the schoolroom if they were nobs." Bitterness edged his tone. "At least you're old enough to know which way's up. And you're not trapped between starving or staying in his manor taking his shilling. Though if you ask me, you've ditched whatever bloody brains you were born with."

"Been wondering that myself," Lucien muttered.

"Keep wondering: it'll do you good. End of the day, a nob's a nob." Grieve turned to the hallway and then back again. "Just be careful, will you? I don't want the fool getting himself arrested. I'd have to start over again with another nob who won't feel obligated to me for years of good service. Besides, they all want young, fashionable sorts. His nibs is tolerable, and doesn't expect any fancy nonsense; that suits me."

"And yet—you didn't warn him when you thought I meant to clean him out?"

"Eh, you're not a bad sort. And he's fair game." Grieve grinned a narrow, shark-like grin. "You can't really clean out a nob like his nibs. He's got a very indulgent daddy. Worst that could happen is he'd have to move back to the family manor, so daddy could keep a closer eye on his spending. Less independence, but he'd never lack. It's me who'd lose out: Daddy Nibs won't care much about pensioning me off properly."

"I bet." It was one of many reasons Lucien had never wanted to go into service. Despite the potentially huge rewards of valeting a wealthy aristocrat, you might end up with nothing more than you'd managed to save along the way, and the wealthiest men weren't always the most generous. He met Grieve's gaze in perfect sympathy. "I'll be careful."

Grieve gave him a cynical look.

"More careful than I have been."

"Glad to hear it," Grieve said. "And work out a reason for visiting so often. Maybe you're teaching him writing or something."

"Ha!" Lucien smiled. "No, he's—"

"You're missing the point, and I have work to do. Make it up, but make it convincing."

Lucien sobered. "Yes. I see."

"Good. Now. D'you want that pot of tea?"

"I'll come and make it. You don't have to."

But Grieve waved him off. "Sit your arse on the nice sofa, Saxby: you're doing none of us any favours. If this is going to work, you'll have to mind your bloody place. For now, that's upstairs, as his nibs' chum. Anyway," Grieve added, "I was just making myself a pot when you turned up. No bother to bring you one, as well. Want a sandwich with that?"

Lucien's stomach growled.

"I'll take that as a yes."

Rather than settle on the sofa, Lucien sat at the table and pulled out his notebook. His mind was full of Grieve, and of Aubrey and Lady Hernedale, but he had to get copy onto Jameson's desk today, and it was already—he glanced at the mahogany mantel clock, sighed, and turned back to his notes— twenty past one. In three hours, including walking time, he had to be in the office with polished paragraphs, and he had to fit in a bloody horrible conversation with Aubrey, too. He glanced around the room. Aubrey was a writer: there had to be paper here somewhere.

The bookcase on the right caught his eye. At waist level, beneath the bookshelves, a deep, elaborately carved drawer ran the width of the unit. Almost certainly a secrétaire, but he didn't like to dig through Aubrey's things without permission. He'd ask Grieve when he came back.

Grieve, who was right, God rot him.

Messing about with a nob could only lead to grief. For him, of course, not the nob. Lucien had become caught up in Aubrey's fears because they were a reflection of his own. But nobs slid out of their legal difficulties on gold-plated rails slicked by social connections, facing nothing worse than humiliation and social censure, while parliament drew a discreet veil over their offences. Working people had no such resources.

More immediately, Lucien did not bloody well need to get caught up in complicated aristocratic games of betrayal. But he already was. He dropped his head in his hands. Hernedale had gone out of his way to help him: he couldn't betray him by not telling him what he'd seen. But he didn't want to betray Lady Hernedale either, who'd demonstrated more understanding than he'd have believed possible for a woman of her class. And he very badly didn't want to betray Aubrey, who he—who he—

A tap on the door. Grieve glided in and set a tray on the table. Chicken sandwiches, fruit jelly, biscuits, and a pot of tea.

Lucien mustered a smile. "Thank you. That looks delicious." His stomach groaned agreement.

Grieve smiled his narrow smile. "Anything else, while I'm here?"

"Is there any paper I could use? I've got to wait for Fanshawe, but I've also got to work."

"In here. He doesn't lock it."

He probably should. Lucien followed Grieve to the bookcase and watched him open the broad drawer.

"D'you need the writing surface?"

"No thanks. I don't want to intrude, and the table's just as good."

So Grieve didn't unlatch the front of the drawer, just pointed to the cubbyholes and small drawers at the back. "Ink in that section if you need it. Envelopes over there. You want to watch the paper: some of it's embossed with his family coat of arms."

Of course it bloody was.

"Use the plain stuff at the bottom of the stack." Grieve patted it. "Blotting paper here. Most of the rest is personal."

"Right." Lucien's gaze settled on 'the rest'. Somewhere in there might be evidence of Lady Hernedale's over-friendliness with Aubrey. "Thanks." Wrenching his attention away, he picked up the ink and a sheet of blotting paper.

Grieve gave him a knowing look. "I'll leave you to it, then."

"Would you mind getting me some plain paper?"

Grieve lifted it from its mahogany bed, and turned cool grey eyes towards him. "Shall I leave this open?"

"Close it, please."

He eased the drawer shut and laid the paper on the table.

"Thank you," Lucien said. "That's very helpful."

Thin lips twitched. "Ring if you need anything. Don't you set a bloody toe on my stairs, hear me? It's not worth it."

Then Grieve slid out of the room, leaving Lucien alone with his lunch, his work, and his unsettled thoughts. And an unlocked secrétaire full of highly tempting personal correspondence.

— Chapter Eighteen —

By THE TIME Aubrey let himself into his set, it was well after two. It'd been a hectic day, and he wanted the quiet of his rooms. He also wanted to be with Rupert and Henrietta—and felt rather as though he ought to be—but it'd seem dashed odd to stay in their house while Henrietta was in bed and Rupert supporting her. Aubrey forced down resentment that he couldn't support her, too. She'd have had him there if she could, and before he left, she'd sent a message that she'd be up later, and he should join them for dinner.

He hung up his outdoor things and sorted through the post on the shelf under the hall mirror.

A handful of invitations he'd open tomorrow.

A picture postcard from his niece in Kent, written in a careful, uneven cursive that made him smile: she hoped Uncle Aubrey was well, and wished he was here.

A letter from his contact at the Home Office. He unfolded it, already mourning the hours and energy the job would devour. He skimmed it. Paused. Re-read it with growing outrage. The damned fellow looked forward to meeting Aubrey again, briefly and discreetly, but couldn't recommend him because he daren't have their names associated.

Like hell would he meet him! Aubrey threw the letter back on the shelf. And what the devil was wrong with his name?

A note from Mother, inviting him to dinner tomorrow night. No. He put it down. She'd be disappointed, but tomorrow was Saturday: Lucien's evening.

A letter from his father's old friend, an avuncular chap who'd always had a shilling for him when he was a boy. Aubrey'd asked him to speak to the Home Secretary on his behalf. The letter was a cold dismissal, no reason given, and no hint of the old indulgence. Aubrey's hands trembled as he put it down. What had he ever done to the fellow?

A letter from his man of business, confirming his instruction to send a regular donation to Dr Barnardo's charity.

He turned from the mirror, and his breath caught in his throat. Lucien, looking tired but unspeakably lovely, stood in the wide doorway between the hall and the drawing room. Grieve must've had the sense to let him in.

"Wondered what was taking you so long," Lucien said.

Aubrey reached him in two long steps, and wrapped his arms around him. "Thank you," he whispered into his hair. He took a deep breath, inhaling thyme, and the ache in his throat eased. "I just— I didn't know what to do. And you fixed it. Thank you."

Lucien's arms settled loosely around his waist. His head drooped, and his forehead rested on Aubrey's lapel—a welcome weight. "How is Lady Hernedale?"

Aubrey huffed a laugh into his sleek hair. "Pregnant."

"*What?*" Lucien's arms dropped; he took a step back.

"Confirmed by her doctor. Apparently, it's fairly common for women to faint in early pregnancy. She thanks you for your concern—" He tugged a note from his pocket and offered it to Lucien "—and sent a statement. I was going to post it to you later. She said you can add it to your article, or quote from it. If you want to."

Lucien took the note, his gaze fixed on Aubrey's.

"Six years!" Aubrey told him. "Six years she's been trying. And now, somehow, she's pregnant."

Lucien took a deep breath. "By—" He cleared his throat, but his voice was still husky. "By you?"

"By *me*?" Aubrey stared at him. "Of course not! What on earth makes you think that?"

"Oh thank God!" Lucien sagged back against the door frame. "In the carriage today— You were— It looked as though she was—"

"Damnation!" The information was safe with Lucien, but who else might have seen them? "I panicked. But no, the child's not mine. We've always been very careful."

"You've—!" Lucien clutched the door frame. "Dear *God*, Aubrey!" He stumbled across the drawing room, dropped Henrietta's note on the occasional table, and collapsed onto the sofa, his head in his hands.

"Er." Aubrey hesitated in the doorway, then crossed to sit carefully beside him. "Lucien?" He laid a hand on his knee. "You and I—we never agreed to be exclusive. It never occurred to me you'd want that."

"That—! That's not the—!" Lucien's fingertips whitened as he pressed them into his scalp. "Bloody *hell*, Aubrey! Your best friend's wife!"

"Well, yes, but she's—"

"What kind of— Dear *God*! You're fucking your best friend's wife behind his back, and all you can say is, 'We never agreed to be exclusive'?"

"Well I mean, it's not exactly behind his back."

Lucien turned to stare at him.

Aubrey rubbed soothing circles on his knee. "More—er—under his nose. As it were."

"Just because he's oblivious doesn't make it—"

"Or... beside him," Aubrey ploughed on, horribly uncomfortable. Clearly, he was going to have to be explicit. "And—er—sometimes underneath. Or on top of him. It varies."

"Jesus sodding *Christ*!" Lucien was chalk-pale. "Please say she wanted that."

"Of course she bloody did! *Does*!" Aubrey snatched his hand away. "D'you really think I'd— Good *God*, Lucien!"

"And— Hernedale? He wasn't persuaded, or—or urged or any—"

"*No*, damn it!" Aubrey sagged into the sofa. "What the hell kind of pleasure could anyone gain from a reluctant lover?"

"I don't know." Lucien took another deep breath. "But somehow, people do, with dismaying regularity."

"Just— Listen. Please. Rupert and I have been lovers since we were thirteen years old. It was— Well. Eton was—" He shut his eyes and blew out an impatient breath, battling the tension that gathered in his stomach and back whenever he thought too closely about school. "We didn't fit in, he and I; couldn't, really." He opened his eyes. "Maybe it was just the boys there at that time, but that's how it was for us. It's one of the reasons we became friends, from our first year there. Then we... discovered ways to soothe and please ourselves, and showed one another what we found. You must've done that, with other boys, when you were a boy?"

Lucien tilted his head in agreement, but his face was tight. "Most boys do, I think."

"Well. By the time we were fifteen, we'd become... very attached to one another."

"You don't think you should've grown out of that by now?"

"No, sweetheart." Aubrey brushed his tense cheek with the backs of his fingers. "We've just grown up together. Grown closer. We suit much better now than when we were fifteen or eighteen or twenty-one. We've been lovers more than half my life, and I can't imagine being without him. Don't want to."

"Right. Understood." Lucien slumped back into the sofa. "What about Lady Hernedale?"

"She and Rupert were childhood friends. Grew up as neighbours in the country and played together since forever. I met her when I visited Rupert one holiday, and, after that, I holidayed there quite often. She'd sometimes cover for Rupert and me when— Well, she was a broad-minded girl."

Lucien stared at him. "You— dragged a young lady into—"

"'Dragged'? I doubt it." Aubrey essayed a grin. "When they were children, she often got into trouble for leading Rupert into mischief. She's a couple of years older than us—which makes a big difference when you're barely more than children—born and raised in the country, and always was a lot wilder. The despair of her parents. And her brother: Lowdon was forever trying to keep her in line."

"So when they married, it was just assumed you'd—join in?"

"Not at all! By then we— I mean, it all started because we thought—" How to explain it? "Well. It was Henrietta's idea, actually: most things are. She couldn't seem to get along with most Society bachelors. Gave it a jolly good try for almost two years, but it didn't work out. Said some were well enough to flirt with, but they were all a bit tedious and managing, and er... Well. She was already rather attached, you know. To Rupert and me. And that feeling was mutual, or rather, unanimous. So she decided to join us when we were eighteen. Or—no, Rupert would still have been seven—"

"Wait. Stop." Lucien paled. "You're telling me the pair of you ruined a—"

"I'm telling you nothing of the damned kind!" Aubrey glared at him. "None of us did anything that could damage her prospects, if she'd decided to marry someone else. And that's all I'll say on the matter."

Lucien flushed. "Quite right. I sincerely apologise for making personal enquiries about a lady."

Damn it all to hell, anyway: it was hardly Lucien's fault that he didn't understand. He was extraordinary, really: most wouldn't even try. "No, it's—" He dropped his head back on the antimacassar. "Look. I know it sounds... well, not the sort of thing one would expect. But there's no— We were friends *first*: close friends. Nobody has to do anything they don't want to, not then and not now. If I could, I'd have married her the day we all chose one another, and so would Rupert. Henrietta said she'd marry either of us, provided we could all be together."

"So then—"

Aubrey stared at the mantelpiece. "Neither of us had attained our majority. Rupert's mother and his guardian disapproved the match."

"And you…"

"Didn't have a title. Or an independent income. No point even asking. I'll have a very comfortable settlement on marriage, but wealthy, titled men were pursuing her, so her parents were holding out for both."

"She couldn't put them off? The pursuers?"

"Some of them. A few wouldn't take no for an answer. Kept proposing. She hated them by the end."

"Seventeen and eighteen." Judgement hovered in Lucien's eyes. "It's not *very* many years till twenty-one. Three years. Four."

"Almost a quarter of your lifetime, at that age. Too long, when you want one another desperately; when she knew Rupert and I weren't waiting for one another, and she'd be left out. Women have needs, too, you know, and she'd turned twenty. Why should women be expected to—to turn themselves into marble or what have you until they marry? Nobody really expects men to."

"That's different."

"Only because society says so."

"*And* because—" Lucien's eyes closed and his lips tightened. "We're getting off the point. Just…" He rubbed his face, then opened tired-looking eyes. "All right. Please go on. I don't mean to interrupt."

Aubrey wanted to kiss each heavy eyelid. Instead, he sighed. "That's all, really. Rupert posted the banns the first Sunday after he attained his majority. No one to stop him once he was head of the family, you know. Well. They kept talking, but it's not as though they could do anything about it."

"And her family didn't mind that his opposed it?"

"He met their criteria." Aubrey smiled wearily, still bitter after all these years. "And by then, they were beginning to worry she'd never marry well, partly because she wouldn't have anyone else who'd proposed and partly because Society was finding her a bit, er… lively. They were only too delighted Rupert still wanted her."

"I'm sorry," Lucien murmured. He really did look sorry, too.

Aubrey tried to brighten his smile. "Probably for the best: Rupert needed to marry more urgently than I did, and had more to offer. And people overlook a lot, in a countess." The words came easily enough: he'd been telling himself the same thing for years. He just—wished they could all have married.

Lucien didn't smile.

"Anyway," Aubrey said, "that's— Well that's it, really. I'm not betraying Rupert, and Henrietta's not being hurt in any way."

"Right." Lucien stared at Aubrey. "Well at least it's—" He sighed and sagged back, hands over his face. "Actually… I'm not sure I'm up to this level of—of sophisticated aristocratic entanglement."

"I'm sure it's not exclusive to aristocrats."

"Oh really?" Lucien glared at him. "D'you think anyone else has the time for this kind of complication? We're a bit too busy earning our daily bloody crust for that!"

"Lucien. Sweetheart." Aubrey laid a tentative arm over his shoulders. "Are you telling me you've never had sex with a married person?"

"Not a married woman: I wouldn't. Anyway, women aren't— I like women, but I've yet to meet a woman I'd want to have sex with. And even if I did… Another man's wife? No."

Aubrey stared into the flames, stroking Lucien's arm through his jacket. "What's the difference, really, between another person's wife and another person's husband? They're both married."

"The difference is she might get pregnant."

"Condom," Aubrey murmured. "Or creativity. No need for a cock to go into a quim just because there's one of each in the bed."

"She might have children to care for."

"So might a fellow."

"And she's... another man's *wife*. And..."

Aubrey let him trail off without comment. Something told him Henrietta would've voiced a strong opinion, though.

"And men are— Well, they're *men*."

Aubrey pressed his lips to Lucien's head and they stared into the fire together.

"So, in that case," Aubrey said at last, "you think it's all right that Rupert's my lover, but not all right that Henrietta is?"

"I suppose... if you have his permission..." A long pause. "And if she wants it, too, of course. Then..."

Aubrey let Lucien's words hang in the air. "But you've had sex with women's husbands?"

"Well, yes. But neither of us'll get pregnant. And I'm not a threat. Even if I tried to persuade them, which I wouldn't, no one leaves his wife for a chap, especially when he can have both. Besides, if a fellow's looking for another fellow, then if it isn't me, it'll be someone else, and at least I'm not going to pass on an unpleasant surprise."

"Might pick one up."

"Does that trouble you?" Lucien craned his neck to look up.

"Not as much as it should, or I'd never have invited you to stay that second night, let alone be sitting here with you today. And I might pick one up, too, I suppose, though I'm always very careful." He huffed a laugh. "Not with you, though. Demonstrably."

Lucien settled back on Aubrey's shoulder. "I tend to stick to fellows I know are careful, and mostly they do, too."

"I stick to hands during casual encounters: not likely to catch anything from them."

"—But I can't control what others do, and as for myself... Well, I'm lonely, love, and since there's no marriage in my future I suppose I always will be."

Aubrey squeezed his eyes shut against the ache in his heart.

"And there isn't—" Lucien sighed and slid a hand, warm and soothing, over Aubrey's belly. "A friendly fuck can take the edge off the loneliness for a while, but it doesn't cure it. A self-deluding part of me hopes to find a lover to settle down with, but I never have, so I don't suppose I ever will. It's made it harder to resist the occasional risk in the past, though I'm more careful now."

"There's supposed to be a marriage in my future," Aubrey admitted. "But I don't think I'll ever have the kind of marriage I want: the kind Rupert and Henrietta have. The women I meet... they don't interest me, and I doubt I interest them, but they have to marry, and they have to manage it quite young. So they pretend to like me, or delude themselves, and I can see the pretence and delusions, but I can't see who they are underneath that, so I don't know if we could ever be friends, let alone companions. Or— anything, really, other than business and social partners who sometimes share a bed and might not even like or trust each other very much."

"Good God. That's miserable."

"What I'm thinking is, if I need Rupert's permission to be Henrietta's lover, shouldn't I need Henrietta's permission to be Rupert's, even though we were lovers for years before they married? Shouldn't you need my notional wife's permission to be my lover, even though you were my lover before she was ever my wife? Even if she doesn't like or want me? Wouldn't she have a moral right at least to know about you, and about Rupert and Henrietta, even though it could put all of us at risk?"

"Probably you just shouldn't marry someone you can't trust. I can't imagine a wife you don't trust being happy with you anyway."

"Well." Aubrey sighed. "I won't. I'd rather do without than have that sort of marriage. But I'm currently under a lot of pressure to marry."

Lucien sat up and stared at him. "Bloody hell, Aubrey! Just get a job. Then it won't matter what anyone else sodding well wants anyway."

Aubrey laughed. The way Lucien's accent sometimes hovered between aristocratic and almost-but-not-quite Cockney was ridiculously endearing. Unspeakably intimate, too, since

Aubrey'd only ever heard it when they were alone; when Lucien was emotional.

"I'm bloody serious!"

"I know. I'm looking into it. You're a man of many talents, you know. Unlike you, I've been educated to be almost perfectly useless."

"You write very well: that's a skill. You could perform as a pianist, too."

"Dear *God*! No. I definitely couldn't. And I can't support myself by writing, either: it doesn't earn enough."

Lucien muttered something that sounded suspiciously like, "Bloody nobs!" and added aloud, "*I* make my living by writing. But you've made your choice, haven't you?"

"I'm not naïve enough to think I could live in penury. Not long-term."

Lucien's eyes softened, and he sighed. "Not that it's penury. But I don't suppose you could, at that."

"If worse comes to worst, Rupert'll tide me over till I find a solution, but it shouldn't come to that." Aubrey tugged Lucien closer.

Lucien leaned towards him, then flinched away. "Damn it, I'm ruining your coat. And you look bloody handsome in it, too."

"Do I?" Aubrey preened a bit.

"You know perfectly well you do, you beautiful peacock." Lucien laced their fingers together and kissed Aubrey's wrist.

Aubrey stared down at the nape of his neck, at the smooth curve of cropped hair and soft skin. He slid his other hand down Lucien's head to cradle the base of his skull. "After all," he murmured, "it's marked already."

Lucien sighed, slid his arms inside Aubrey's morning coat, and settled his head on his shoulder. He lay quiet and still as Aubrey pressed his lips to his forehead. At last he said, "This is bloody complicated, that's all, and it feels like it should be simpler."

"It'd be simpler if I met a woman who could be a friend as well as a wife. Who I could tell about you and Rupert and

Henrietta before we married and trust she'd understand, and either still want to marry me, or else not marry me, but also not betray us all."

"That's not quite what I meant. But… you don't think that's a bit naïve?"

"Well, Henrietta always understood, so there must be other women who would, but how can I tell who they are?"

"And that's precisely what I mean about aristocratic complications."

"In that case, yes. But when it comes to Rupert and Henrietta, our relationships predate their marriage: it was all agreed in advance. The alternative must be more complicated. If you're having sex with someone's spouse—well, a wife might feel just as threatened, if she found out, as a husband would."

Lucien sighed. "Mostly, I don't know who's married: they don't say. But Cath, for example… I don't think Cath'd be threatened."

"Cath's husband is your lover?"

"My friend. With the sick baby."

Aubrey peered down at him. "You have sex and you're also close enough that you know his family?"

"Friendship plus, I suppose. I imagine Cath'd be disgusted, but not threatened: Ben clearly adores her. Anyway, I wouldn't harm her for the world. I don't expect most people to understand. We're all taught to be disgusted, aren't we? Must be hard to get past that without personal experience."

Aubrey's heart turned over. He cradled Lucien's head in his hand. "Sweetheart," he whispered.

Lucien tightened his arms.

"I have to say, though," Aubrey murmured, "that sounds a lot more complicated than my arrangement, and no less fear of discovery. And she might feel hurt, you know, even if she's not threatened."

Lucien lay still and silent. Aubrey stared into the fire and let him think.

"I wish I'd known they were your lovers," Lucien said at last.

Aubrey's chest ached. "I know."

"I mean, I assumed you had other fellows on a casual basis: most blokes do; *I* do. I even thought you and Hernedale might meet one another's needs now and then."

Aubrey stared down at him.

"But it never occurred to me he was your lover, let alone Lady Hernedale. Besides, I assumed you'd tell me if you had a lover, once we became close."

"I can see why," Aubrey husked.

Lucien said nothing.

Aubrey swallowed the lump in his throat. "I couldn't tell you at first: I hardly knew you. And there was your job. And then... Well, it wasn't my risk to take: they haven't learned to trust you the way I do."

Lucien said nothing.

"I am sorry. Truly. I can see it'd be a shock."

"You might've said. Even if you didn't mention names or details. At least I'd have had an idea where I stood."

"That... didn't occur to me. It should have."

"If I'd been a duke, would you still have left me in the dark?"

"Yes." That was an easy one. "You're the first person I've ever told."

Lucien tensed. "D'you think I should be flattered, when you only told me because I'd already discovered half the story?"

Aubrey squeezed his eyes shut. "No. No, you're right, of course."

Lucien fell silent, and his head grew heavier on Aubrey's shoulder, but his body was still tense. Aubrey stared into the fire, afraid to move or speak; afraid he'd tip the fragile balance between them towards rejection.

"Tell me something," Lucien murmured into his coat. "How do I fit into your arrangement?"

"You fit because I—" Aubrey closed his eyes, acknowledging it at last. "Because I love you. And I love Henrietta. And I love Rupert. So you all fit."

"And I love you." Lucien's voice was rough and uneven.

Those words should've filled Aubrey with delight, but all he felt was qualified relief and painful hope and a growing lump in his throat. "I'm sorry. So sorry I hurt you."

Lucien took a deep, shuddering breath. "I just don't see— I mean, it can't be the same, can it? You've loved Hernedale since you were thirteen, and Lady Hernedale since you were eighteen and however long you cared for her before that. And me for—for what? A couple of months? How can it be the same?"

"It's not," Aubrey admitted.

Lucien flinched.

"Sweetheart, let me finish. It's all different. I love Rupert with all my heart, because he's Rupert. I love Henrietta with all my heart, because she's Henrietta. And you and I— Well, we haven't known one another very long, but I absolutely do love you with all my heart, just because you're you."

"That's three hearts," Lucien pointed out.

"It's a glorious mystery." Aubrey nuzzled his hair. "I have a whole heart for everyone I love, every time. And I know, from the way I've felt about Rupert and about Henrietta, that the longer we love, the more love will grow. And I know it'd break my heart if you left me, even now."

"But that means less, doesn't it, if it grows over the years, and you've loved them for more years?"

"How can it be less, when it's all yours? When every bit of it's yours and can never belong to anyone else? I can't love Rupert the way I love Henrietta, because he's not her. But he hasn't lost anything by it, because even if I'd never met her, I could never have loved him the way I love her, any more than I can love her the way I love him. And I can't love Rupert or Henrietta the way I love you, because they're not you. I don't know how to explain it any better than that. It's just different. Everything. There are different things I admire or find beautiful or touching about each of you. I speak about different things with you than with Rupert or Henrietta. I'm a bit different with each of you, because I respond to who you are. I'm even different in bed with each of you, and in the ways I express affection. Because you're all different, and there are different things you each like and dislike. Different ways I want to touch and be with each of you."

Silence filled the room, but for the gusty hiss of the fire and the occasional gritty sigh of coals shifting in the grate. Lucien lay quiet and still for so long that Aubrey began to wonder whether he was asleep.

"Lucien?" he whispered.

Lucien's hand brushed the starched front of Aubrey's shirt, then stilled. "I want to believe that; I do. But it sounds like the consolation you offer the child who came last in the race. 'But nobody else has such pretty hair, pet.'"

Aubrey slid his fingers into Lucien's hair. "Well, you *do* have very lovely hair. But it's not that. Not for an instant."

"But here's the thing." Lucien twisted to look up at him. "How many years have you been Hernedale's lover?"

"Around fourteen. We weren't paying much attention to the date at the time, so I can't be more specific."

"So suppose you and I— Look, I'm not assuming anything, but..." He paused. "No, wait, try this. Say you meet someone tonight, who you come to love. Say you continue to love one another, and you also keep on loving Hernedale. Even after twenty years, that new person is still going to be fourteen years behind where you are with Hernedale, aren't they? There's never a point where they catch up."

"It's not about catching up. Relationships aren't comparable that way: not for me, anyway. It's about how that one particular relationship grows between those two particular people. Besides, Rupert and I may suit one another better now than when we were fifteen, but that doesn't mean what we had then wasn't worth having, or that I didn't love him enough. Because I did. I wouldn't be without that time, and I wouldn't be without the way we loved one another then. It was complete in itself."

"But if you had to choose between—"

"But I don't." Aubrey held him tighter. "I don't want to, and I don't have to, and quite honestly, I couldn't, any more than a parent could choose which of their children to sacrifice."

"Except they can," Lucien pointed out, "and they do. All the way back to Iphigenia and to Ishmael and Isaac."

"Well, you'll have to assume I'm not that kind of damned rotten parent. Or lover. Because I couldn't. Unless one of you tried to force me to choose. Because— Look, someone who loved me wouldn't purposely hurt me or people I love, so I'd have to choose against whoever did that."

"There's got to come a point, though, when you have so many lovers they barely see you. A lover might simply be desperate for your company."

"It wouldn't be very loving or responsible to commit to so many people that I couldn't meet their needs. I don't commit lightly, and I'm willing to give up other things to make time for my lovers."

Lucien turned his head away.

"What about your needs?" he said at last. "Shouldn't your lovers meet your needs, too?"

"Of course. And you all do."

Lucien lay in tense silence.

"What is it?"

"I don't mean to—" Lucien blew out a long breath. "All right, look. You were lonely, the night we met. How were your needs being met?"

"We have to be careful. I can't live with Rupert and Henrietta, and I can't stay the night too often, any more than you can stay with me too often. That's not to say— Well. Either or both of them would've met that need if they could. They do, as much as they—"

The clock chimed four.

"Shit!" Lucien scrambled to his feet and launched himself at the dining table.

Aubrey shot up, heart pounding. "What's wrong?"

"Got to be at the office at half-past at the latest." Lucien shoved his pen and notebook into his pockets and scrambled several sheets of paper together. "I'll barely make it."

"I'll get you a cab." Aubrey made for the doorway.

"Don't! Damn it, it's too obvious." Lucien dashed across the room with a bottle of ink and a sheet of blotting paper and tugged at the handles of the secrétaire.

"What on earth are you doing?"

"Tidying up." The drawer opened, and he stared into it.

Aubrey took the things from him and put them in their proper places. "Grieve would've done it, you know."

"He's not paid to tidy up after me."

"He's paid to tidy up whatever's untidy in my set. Or the maids are, if they get to it first."

Lucien stared at him. "Oh, *bloody*— Look, can we talk about this tomorrow? I've got something to tell you, but no time." He snatched up the unused sheets of paper from the table and held them out. "Please, love. I haven't time to work out where he got these from."

Aubrey slid them into place while Lucien folded his written pages and shoved them into his jacket pocket, then fled into the hallway. Aubrey grabbed Henrietta's note from the occasional table and followed him.

Lucien was struggling with his overcoat.

"Wait." Aubrey took it from him and hung it back on the coat-stand. "You can't go out like that: I spoiled your hair."

"Shit!" Lucien stared into the hall mirror.

"Henrietta's statement." Aubrey tucked the note into Lucien's pocket. "Hold still." He slipped Lucien's comb from his inside pocket and combed his hair into place. Tugging his own shirt from the waistband of his trousers, he wiped the comb on his shirt-tail.

"Bloody hell, Aubrey! That's a good shirt!"

"No time to get a cloth."

"Could've used my hankie."

Aubrey tucked the comb back beside Lucien's pen. "It's only the tail." He picked Lucien's overcoat from the coat-stand and held it for him. Lucien slipped his arms in, and Aubrey settled it on his shoulders and smoothed the collar.

"Oh Lord! Thank you. Why is one all thumbs when one's in a hurry?"

"Because one's utterly endearing." Aubrey plucked Lucien's bowler from the coat-stand and put it on his head, then handed him his riding cane.

Lucien patted his overcoat pocket. "Got my gloves. Damn it." He tipped his face up. "Kiss me; I have to go."

Aubrey made the most of the invitation without delaying him unduly. "See you tomorrow, sweetheart." He tucked his shirt tail in as Lucien turned away. "Seven o'clock too early? We could dine together."

"Damn it." Lucien paused with his hand on the door handle, then turned, grabbed Aubrey's head in both hands and kissed him fiercely. He leaned back to stare into his eyes. "Seven. Tomorrow."

"Yes."

"Right." Lucien pecked him again, then wrenched the door open and ran.

Aubrey closed the door and leaned against it, heart pounding, pulse leaping. Grinning foolishly, because he couldn't help it.

LUCIEN PANTED INTO the almost empty office at twenty-five to five.

Miss Enfield turned from the long table beneath the window and glared at him over her spectacles. "Half past four *at the latest*, you said."

"Sorry," he gasped. "Just—give me a minute."

He hooked his riding cane on the coat-stand at the second try and his bowler at the first, then struggled with his overcoat. Every inch of the sleeve lining clung to his hands: he'd need to sponge it down when he got home.

Chiddicks strolled over, slid into his own overcoat, and settled his top hat on his head. "Nose to the old grindstone, Saxby?"

Lucien ignored him, peeling his hands free of the coat at last. He was revoltingly sweaty, which shouldn't be possible in early March.

"I'm off to the Olde Cock, myself." Chiddicks glanced at Miss Enfield. "Might see you later, if you escape the old battle-axe." He neighed at his own wit.

"God. Just shut up, Chiddicks." As though he'd visit any pub that blighter haunted. Chiddicks sauntered out, grinning, as Lucien slung his coat at a hook. To his amazement, it caught at the shoulder, and stayed. He ought to hang it properly. Instead, he wobbled to his seat on quivering legs and collapsed.

"Sorry. Truly. I know you have better things to do. How're the ladies at Canon Row?"

"Released."

He sucked in a deep breath. "Thank God!"

"By the PM's direct instruction. *And* he's offered to meet a WSPU deputation to discuss the matter of votes for women!"

"Oh good." Lucien folded his arms on the table and dropped his head on them. His entire body thumped with his heartbeat.

"You do understand the significance of this, Saxby?"

"Course." This meeting—supposing it ever took place— might result in women's suffrage being discussed in the House. "Jolly good news. It's just— I ran all the way." He sniffed. "Probably smell horrible. Sorry."

Miss Enfield sighed sharply. "Pages, Saxby."

He shoved his hand into his pocket, fought the lining for the pages, and slid them onto the table. "Here. And—" He battled another pocket. "Statement from Lady Hernedale. No idea if it's any use. Haven't had a chance to read it yet." Parking his arm back under his head, he tried not to pant.

"Oh, *Saxby!*" Miss Enfield breathed.

"Here." He briefly raised an overheated, throbbing hand.

"This statement is pure gold."

"Oh good."

"I'll just—" Pages slid against one another. "If I alter this and move the description of Annie Kenney— Except... no. I like your description better, and it'd fit..."

He stopped listening.

Probably, he should sit up. Probably, he'd get his breath back faster if he did. But for now, he wanted to rest with his face where nobody would see or comment on it, and try to reconcile confusion and anxiety with the inappropriate, irrepressible joy that squeezed through them, despite every rational argument he could throw at it.

The last person to comb his hair had been his mother, when he was—what? Eight? His scalp tingled with lines of pressure where Aubrey'd gently raked his hair into order. He couldn't possibly still feel that; somehow, he did.

But... His best friend's bloody wife, for God's sake!

How can it be less, when it's all yours? When every bit of it's yours and can never belong to anyone else?

God damn all fiction writers to everlasting sodding perdition. How was a fellow to think straight when they used words that way? When they sounded so sincere?

Every ounce of common sense told Lucien this situation was an appalling risk. One nob who could tear his heart to bleeding gobbets. Two more with reason to hate him for diverting Aubrey's attention; who might turn Aubrey against him, and follow it up by destroying him in more material ways. Or even just abandon him to Lowdon's spite.

He should end this now.

But he wouldn't. He was going to visit Aubrey tomorrow. And when he did, he'd kiss him, not leave him. Because, when it came to Aubrey, he had all the self-control of a small child with a bag of sweets.

Gradually the thunder of his pulse quieted. His breathing eased. He began to feel unpleasantly damp and cool.

An earl's wife. And the sodding earl, too. At the same bloody time.

And a considerate kiss, from a fellow who'd wanted him to stay, but helped him leave because it was what he needed to do.

Buggery. He sighed.

Beside him, Miss Enfield shifted closer.

"Saxby." Her whisper stirred his hair.

"Here." He lifted a finger.

"The Honourable Aubrey bloody Fanshawe, Saxby?"

"Oh God!" Lucien shot upright. It sounded so much worse with his title on the front.

She sat back, grinning.

"How—how did you work that out?"

"Ha! I'm right, then."

Lucien stared at her. "That was damned sneaky."

She leaned in again to murmur, "Confirm, Saxby. I already know, but satisfy me to make up for keeping me waiting... The Honourable Aubrey bloody Fanshawe is the chap you met? The fellow who's got you smiling and singing about policemen?"

"Fine. Yes. How did you know?"

"You said you'd told someone called Fanshawe about the event. That's a bit of a swanky old name, Saxby, in case you didn't realise."

"Course I bloody did."

"So I looked him up in the clippings files. Found a few Fanshawes with an 'e', one or two Fanshaws without the 'e', and a couple who're so aristocratic that the rules of proper spelling don't apply to them, who spell their Fanshawe 'Fetherstonhaugh'. For some reason, you'd inconsiderately neglected to provide the correct spelling."

Lucien summoned a guttering spark of wit. "I don't regret that, in case you wondered."

"Ha! I believe you. Don't mind telling you I despaired a bit at that point, but I'm nothing if not a good journalist. I remembered you saying you hadn't expected Fanshawe to tell the Hernedales. So I looked up Hernedale, and there he was—Aubrey Fanshawe, The Hon.—almost always mentioned in company with Hernedale, The Earl and Countess."

Of course he was. Lucien's throat closed. "All right. I've confirmed. You're jolly clever and all that. Now, where are we with this copy?"

Miss Enfield leaned back, took off her spectacles and folded them onto the table. "Doing very nicely, in fact. Your paragraphs are good. Very good. Which I didn't expect, given how distracted you've been today. And Lady Hernedale's statement is better than good."

Lucien hooked it off the table.

Apparently, Lady Hernedale had 'happened to be passing through Downing Street'.

"Ha!" Lucien muttered.

...the shock of seeing policemen and government officials—men whose duty it is to protect us from violence—the shock of seeing these men stand upon the literal doorstep of a symbol of our democracy, and lay violent hands upon mothers and daughters who had caused no injury; whose only intent was to speak and to be heard by their government... This shock was so extreme as to cause me to fall into a dead faint, from which I have still not properly recovered. Any lady who saw this scene must have been deeply distressed by it; and any man of common decency, outraged.

I implore Sir Henry to rectify this terrible wrong which he permitted to be visited upon noble-spirited British ladies, upon his very doorstep! And I call upon every lady of conscience, and every man of honour, to deplore the actions of these violent, power-mad knaves.

Lucien laid the letter reverently on the table and closed his eyes. She was impressively strong-minded, to have penned this so soon after fainting and learning of her pregnancy. And, oh God, but she was quick to learn. He'd told her himself that the Mail's readership was concerned with women's safety and fragility, and that his editor was likely to print almost any quotation the nobility cared to provide.

Why the hell hadn't he read this before giving anyone else so much as a glimpse of it? He couldn't explain that the police probably hadn't caused her to faint: what legitimate reason could he have for knowing that extremely intimate information? Certainly, he had no right to share it.

Opening his eyes, he stared at the firm, confident script. "You don't think— I mean, Jameson wouldn't print this, would he?"

Miss Enfield stared at him. "Has that run shaken your brain? Lady Hernedale and Jameson—the countess and the snob: it's a match made in heaven. And it's sensational *and* involves the nobility: our readers will positively lap it up. The papers will be flying off the newsstands. We're going to be on the front bloody page, Saxby!"

"Right." Shit.

"Heading." Her hands framed an imaginary banner. *"Supplicant Women Assaulted at Number 10.* Sub-headings—and we can spread ourselves a bit here, because Jameson will want a nice long article—*Countess in Distress* and *'Power-Mad' Police, Complicit Officials* and *PM Permits Violence on His Doorstep.* Footer, in bold: *See Page 3 for Letter from a Countess."*

"Dear *God!"* The suffocating reek of sickness in tropical heat, of horse-meat boiling down to sludge to feed a starving army, caught in his throat. He'd seen what a struggle for voting rights could lead to. "We can't print this. There'll be riots!"

"Dashed well ought to be." Miss Enfield leaned back, lacing her fingers behind her head. "But there won't."

"God! I hope not."

She threw him an exasperated, affectionate glance. "Don't worry. The government can't ignore this: not when it's on the front page on every newsstand."

"I hope you're right."

"And we needn't tone down our copy, or write about clothes. Saxby, I'm in heaven. I could almost kiss your spiky, sweaty cheek."

"Please don't." He glanced around the office. Empty, thank goodness, but for them. Everyone else must've left while he was wallowing in a puddle of sweat and sentiment.

"I said 'almost'." Miss Enfield put on her spectacles. "You're safe: I'm not quite so lost to sanity as that." She laid Lady Hernedale's statement high on the table, between their seats, and smoothed it with reverent hands. "There. Our inspiration. Pen and scissors out, Saxby: I'm looking forward to this one."

— Chapter Nineteen —

THE BAND PLAYED quietly in the Savoy's restaurant as Aubrey swallowed his last mouthful of crêpe in orange sauce. "I don't think I can eat another thing."

"I'm perfectly stuffed," Henrietta agreed.

"Merely perfect," Rupert murmured.

Only seven hours after she'd discovered she was pregnant, she had a serene glow. A glow which had nothing to do with the physical fact of pregnancy, and everything to do with relief that she'd conceived at long last.

In her position, after the shocks of the day, Aubrey would've wanted to dine at home or Hernedale House, but Henrietta had wanted the Savoy.

A silent waiter laid a tray of coffee and a plate of delicate chocolates on their table, then evaporated.

Leaning back to ease his belly, Aubrey glanced around. Halfway across the room, moustache bristling, Edgar Lowdon glared at him, while his wife paid exaggerated, merry attention to the woman beside her. Aubrey arranged his expression to neutral and continued his sweep of the room.

Henrietta put down the coffee pot. "Spotted Edgar, have you?"

"Glad I didn't notice him before." Aubrey took the cup she handed him, rather shaken. "Enough to put a chap off his feed."

"He's the spider in our soup," Rupert sighed. "The slug in our salad. The self-important serpent in our summer pudding."

"The fellow inspires you." Aubrey managed a grin.

"He moves me to an ecstasy of sheer loathing." He glanced at Henrietta. "Saving your presence, beloved."

"Oh, don't apologise on my account."

Lowdon caught them as they were donning their overcoats in the lobby. His furious glare swept past Aubrey and Henrietta and settled on Rupert.

"Hernedale, I really must speak to you."

Rupert ostentatiously focussed on easing a skin-tight glove over his fingers. "I doubt the necessity."

"It is," Lowdon said between gritted teeth, "a matter of *vital* importance."

Rupert looked up from his glove buttons to pin Lowdon with a cold stare. "Permit me to doubt that your issue is remotely as important to me as it is to you."

"I *assure* you that—"

"If it even approaches the degree of urgency you suggest, kindly convey the matter to your parents: I should be delighted to listen to *them* at any time." Rupert offered Henrietta his arm— "My dear?"—and they swept out of the lobby, drawing Aubrey in their wake.

Later, none of them in the mood for sex, they sprawled across one another in Rupert's bed, talking. Aubrey lay in the middle, where he always started his nights with Rupert and Henrietta. It was their way of showing he was important to them, since he couldn't have their attention as often as they had one another's, but at times it made him feel like embroidered cushions in a carriage: an optional luxury. Which was particularly uncomfortable when he had something to confess.

"Got to tell you both something."

Henrietta tickled his foot. "Enlighten us, O Great One!"

Aubrey twitched his foot away. "Wait, sweetheart. Listen. Lucien saw us in the carriage."

"Should think the—" Rupert yawned, his fingers pausing in Aubrey's hair "—'Scuse me—whole damned street saw you."

"No, I mean— Well, I rather panicked, and once we were in the carriage, I—er—may've kissed Henrietta."

Rupert jerked upright. "Where the whole damned street could see you?"

Henrietta sat up at the foot of the bed and stared down at him.

"I hope not. I mean, obviously, if I'd thought anyone could see us, then I wouldn't—"

"Oh God! I kissed you back, didn't I?"

"Erm. Yes. But obviously, you weren't well, and I really should've been more careful."

"So should I! Can't go around losing my blasted head just because I fainted like a maiden in a bad novel!"

Rupert flung himself off the bed and stalked into the dressing room.

Damnation.

Aubrey met Henrietta's gaze—best to let Rupert cool off alone, when he was miffed—and she turned and dropped into the pillows beside him, sighing.

"Damn it all. All right, who else could've seen?"

"I've been racking my brains, and I don't think anyone could. I mean, between the angle of the door, and the sun glancing off the window, and Rupert and Lucien and the boy in front of the doorway, I don't think they could have. Unless I didn't notice the boy looking in. God knows I didn't notice when Lucien did."

Rupert strode back into the bedroom. "*And* I didn't tip that boy, or even thank him. After all his help, I completely damn well ignored him." He threw himself onto the dressing stool and sank his head in his hands.

"Lucien obviously knew him," Aubrey said. "I'll give him a tip for the boy."

"Seems we all panicked." Henrietta slid out of bed and padded over to stroke Rupert's hair.

He wrapped his arms around her and leaned on her chest, sighing, then flinched away. "Oh God. Is that—"

"You're not hurting me." Henrietta guided his head down again. "They're a bit tender, but I'm told that's normal."

Aubrey watched from the bed. He shouldn't feel isolated—had Rupert felt left out when he'd brushed Henrietta's hair? Probably not—but it was hard not to when he'd made such a hash of things.

"I'm sorry," he mumbled.

Rupert sighed. "I'd probably have done the same."

"Yes, well, it wouldn't have mattered if *you'd* done it, since you're married." His tone was meant to be light but practical; somehow it came out appallingly bitter.

Rupert and Henrietta froze, then stared at him.

He tried a quick laugh, to prove he hadn't meant it the way it sounded. "An advantage of the shackled state."

"Now that's a point." Henrietta turned to Rupert. "You're both dark. You have much the same build. You were both wearing morning coats. You might easily be mistaken for one another, even in a photograph, if the photographer wasn't very close. And it wasn't a Society event: how many people there would know it wasn't my husband who helped me to the carriage?"

Aubrey and Rupert exchanged glances.

"It'd only take one person who did know," Rupert suggested.

"I'll tell select acquaintances how Aubrey held the crowd off while you helped me into the carriage. Give it a few weeks, and anyone who did see it will assume they were mistaken."

"Aubrey's damned Saxby won't!"

"No," Aubrey agreed, "but he won't betray us, either."

"For God's sake, Aubrey! He's a gossip journalist! And it's not as though we'd inform on him for exposing you and Hettie: it'd only draw *you* to police attention."

"That's not the—!"

"I wish we'd never taken him on! Then he wouldn't know us any better than anyone else. He couldn't destroy us now if we hadn't saved his bloody job for him."

Aubrey choked back anger. Rupert didn't know Lucien the way he did, and he'd just had a shock. And this crisis was entirely Aubrey's fault.

"Look," Henrietta said. "First of all, we had a *duty* to help, since his job was only endangered because of me; and secondly, he can't be certain we wouldn't inform on him. Besides, I really don't think he'd betray us."

"He wouldn't, sweetheart," Aubrey said. "When he challenged me about it, his only concern was that I was betraying you, and then, when I explained the situation—" he looked at Henrietta "—that *you* might be being coerced into something you disliked."

"He's got a damned cheek!" Rupert shot up from the stool. "As though you'd ever— As though *I* would, either! It's—"

"Rupert." Henrietta laid a hand on his arm. "He was protective of you and of me. Does that sound like a man who'll expose us?"

"I suppose not. But now—"

"It's what we'd hope for from a friend, isn't it? He ran to help as soon as he saw we had a problem; and he insulted Aubrey to his face to defend you and me, even though he cares for Aubrey and barely knows us. He won't expose any of us, darling."

"But, damn it, don't you see? He *could* expose us now. *All* of us."

"I didn't know what else to do," Aubrey admitted. The bed was beginning to feel like a witness box. "He was so horrified that I would betray you that I—" His mind cleared. "Oh! Oh God! You think I should've let him keep thinking that, don't you?"

"Of course. If he'd come to me, I'd have thanked him for his concern or damned his cheek. The worst we'd have faced is gossip and bloody Frederick: simple infidelity doesn't carry a prison sentence."

Aubrey fell back on the pillows, his hands over his face. "I do see that. But what if I'd lied to *you* about something as important as this, Rupert? Even early on in our relationship? D'you think we'd still be here today?"

"This," Rupert pointed out, "didn't risk just you."

"Oh *God*." Aubrey buried his face in a pillow. He'd told Lucien the truth to reassure him, and out of fear of losing him. But he owed loyalty to Rupert and Henrietta, too, and he'd broken their trust. "I'm so very sorry. I didn't mean to— I mean, I wouldn't have, if I hadn't been certain he was safe. And... he asked if Henrietta's baby was mine, and that— Well, that couldn't be allowed to stand, obviously. But I shouldn't have, anyway. Not—until I'd cleared it with both of you."

"No, you bloody well shouldn't." Rupert flopped onto the bed. He tugged Aubrey roughly into his arms and pressed a hard kiss on his head. "*Damn* it, Aubrey!"

"And I snarled at you over a condom!" Aubrey wrapped his arms around Rupert. "I'm so sorry. For everything: beginning to end."

"Damn it." Rupert sighed into his hair, his arms loosening. "Bloody horse has bolted now. I'll cultivate a few acquaintances in case we need to shut down a prosecution, but we'll hope for the best."

Henrietta settled on Rupert's other side. "Aubrey? Did you think Mr Saxby would be less shocked by the truth than by thinking you were betraying Rupert?"

"Yes, of course."

"And... was he?"

Aubrey huffed a laugh into Rupert's familiar, comforting chest. "He was appalled. Thought Rupert and I must be hurting you. And then that you and I had persuaded Rupert into something he didn't want. Oh, I don't know: he just couldn't seem to understand."

"It's the strangest thing." Henrietta slid an arm behind Rupert, and he rested his head on her shoulder, still holding Aubrey. "It feels perfectly ordinary and rational to me, and then I remember that beyond this bedroom door is a world full of people who don't understand, and don't want to, either."

"Except Lucien does want to understand," Aubrey pointed out. "He's trying, anyway. And that same world doesn't understand that Rupert and I can love one another, either. Didn't, even when we only had each other."

"True." Henrietta sighed. "What if I invite Mr Saxby to dinner?"

Aubrey and Rupert craned to look up at her.

"Is that… a good idea?" Rupert asked.

"Oh ye of little faith! Each of us knows, now, where the others stand in relation to Aubrey, but only he has seen Mr Saxby since then. You and I are uneasy because we don't know how he'll react to us, and I imagine he's uneasy, too, over how we'll react to him. The longer we don't see one another, the more uncomfortable it'll get, and the more—well, the more *significance* we'll attach to meeting again. Better get it over and done with. Clear the air."

Aubrey and Rupert exchanged glances.

"And—you think dinner's the best way to do that?" Aubrey asked.

"Nothing huge: just the four of us. Dinner's a familiar situation for everyone. And there'll be servants, so we won't be able to talk about anything personal till everyone's shared a meal and had a glass or two of wine. By the time the servants leave, we'll all be a lot more comfortable with one another."

"Actually, that makes a lot of sense," Aubrey admitted.

"Of course it does, darling." Henrietta stroked his cheek. "Just leave it to me."

"Our marvellous Minerva," Rupert murmured.

"You forgot 'modest'." Henrietta kissed his temple, then rested her cheek on his hair. "It'll be all right, darling: he won't betray us."

"He appreciates what you've both done to help him." Aubrey laid a hand over Rupert's. "So he wouldn't harm either of you. But he's not the sort who would, anyway."

Rupert sighed. "Seems like a decent chap."

"Besides, he told me the night we met that he never writes about Uranians."

"I wish the government put as much damned effort into stopping men beating their wives and children as they do into persecuting us. If they're going to interfere in what a Briton does in the privacy of his own damned home, why not include that?"

"That's a long-term goal," Henrietta said. "In the meanwhile, Mr Saxby'd better have the reassurance of staying with Aubrey after dinner, since it'll be on our territory, not his. When does he next visit you?"

"Er. Better be Wednesday. I'm seeing him tomorrow, but I invited him to dine at my set, and—"

"Wednesday it is, then."

"That's only five days," Rupert pointed out.

"Sooner the better, my darlings." She put her hand over theirs. "Let's get it over with, so we can all be comfortable again."

— Chapter Twenty —

A quiet, diffident tap at the front door.

Aubrey looked up from his newspaper, wondering what Grieve wanted at this time of day. Then leapt to his feet. Why on earth did he always mistake Lucien's knock for Grieve's? Usually he had no difficulty telling the difference between his valet's knock and a visitor's.

Aubrey closed the door while Lucien hung up his bowler and riding cane, then held his overcoat for him.

Lucien's head bent as he slid his arms out of the sleeves, and his hairline emerged above his starched collar.

"Mmm." Aubrey pressed his lips to the junction of hairline and soft, untanned skin.

Lucien laughed. "Let a fellow get in the door, will you." But he arched his neck, offering better access.

"I would, but I can't seem to get past this spot." Aubrey nuzzled his hairline. "I've told you what it does to me."

"And your appreciation for it does some rather delicious things to me. However—" Lucien turned, kissed him, took the coat, and hung it on the coat-stand "—I'm sure we'll be more comfortable without an overcoat between us."

Aubrey followed him into the drawing room.

Lucien picked up the abandoned newspaper. "Still reading this?"

"No."

Lucien folded it neatly and put it on the dining table. "Listen. Before we relax, I haven't yet told you—"

Another diffident tap at the front door. After a courtesy pause, Grieve appeared, carrying two glasses of lemonade on a silver tray.

"Good evening, sir; Mr Saxby. It occurred to me you might welcome some refreshment." He put the drinks on the occasional table. "Dinner will be served at eight." He left as quietly as he'd arrived.

"That was thoughtful." Aubrey handed a glass to Lucien, then sipped from his own.

"Possibly." Lucien's forehead was creased.

Aubrey caught Lucien's eye.

"No, well, obviously it was thoughtful." Lucien put his glass down. "But it was also a reminder I didn't need. To tell you Grieve knows about us."

"*What?*" Aubrey's glass thumped onto the table rather harder than he'd meant it to.

"No, listen. Let me explain."

As Lucien spoke, Aubrey's heart sped up, till it was a regular, painful thud in his ears.

"Grieve—" He took a deep breath. "Grieve is *blackmailing* me?"

Lucien stared at him. "No. He's helping us."

"Then why tell you he knows about us? 'Helpful' would be turning a blind eye!"

Lucien's hand wrapped around his, warm and solid and comforting. "Because we weren't being careful enough."

"Dear God! And now I can't sack him!"

Lucien's hand withdrew abruptly. "Why would you want to?"

"*Because*—" Aubrey sucked in a deep, shuddering breath. "He *knows!*"

"And he's acknowledged an interest in keeping you safe. Isn't that better than a new valet with less to lose? Who might be horrified, or blackmail you? Someone younger, who could easily find another position if anything happened to you? Someone with fewer years of service; less claim on a retirement arrangement to keep him committed to you?"

"That! *That's* what he's after! Making me pay for the rest of my life!"

"Stop it Aubrey! Think for a minute, will you? I know this is a shock—it was a shock to me, too—but *think*. Grieve's good at his job: excellent, in fact. You've kept him on for years, so you must be satisfied with his work. And you don't strike me as the miserly sort, so I assume you meant to give him a generous pension or retirement settlement anyway."

"Well of course!"

"Then what have you lost?"

Aubrey closed his eyes. "Peace of mind?"

Lucien sighed. "Come here, you daft nob."

A firm tug on his arm, and Aubrey was on the sofa, cradled in Lucien's arms.

"Right. Now *listen*. He's not asking for anything you wouldn't have done anyway, except for us to be more sodding careful. That's in our interests, too. In return, he's offered to tolerate my clothes in your wardrobe, which—"

"Shouldn't that be up to me?"

Lucien took a slow, deep breath. "Of course. Which is why I didn't turn up tonight properly dressed for dinner and carrying a valise. I meant to ask you first. But your wardrobe is also Grieve's territory: he'll take pride in keeping it in order, and satisfaction in the quality of the clothes in it. Anyway, you couldn't have offered to keep my clothes if Grieve didn't know about us."

Aubrey sighed.

"He's also made it plain he doesn't care what we get up to, so we can relax a bit. He's even offered to make us breakfast every Sunday, to share companionably after what he probably assumes is a night of rampant debauchery. Now, if you don't think all that's a *princely* bloody gift for a pair of law-breaking degenerates—"

"For God's *sake*, Lucien!"

"—then I don't know what to tell you."

"We're not degenerate!"

Lucien sighed and stroked his cheek. "I know that, love. But the law doesn't. Most people don't. And Grieve's willing to help us. Or rather, to help you. I know—I *know* it's embarrassing, and alarming, and difficult to face him, but it's less risky than the alternative, and it won't always seem so awful: you'll get used to it."

"Oh God." Aubrey folded his knees up, wrapped his arms around Lucien's waist and pressed his face into his belly. After a moment, he muttered, "Damned buttons."

"Just a sec." Lucien nudged his head back and unbuttoned his waistcoat. "Shirt buttons are smaller."

Aubrey nuzzled into smooth, unstarched cotton that barely separated him from the cushioned warmth of Lucien's belly. Sighing, he slid a couple of fingers between shirt buttons onto soft, lightly furred skin.

"There you go." Lucien stroked his hip. "There's an advantage straightaway. You'll still jump when Grieve knocks, but it won't be the end of the world if I can't do up my waistcoat before he comes in. See?"

"S'pose so." Aubrey flexed his fingers. "What if... I were to open this shirt button? Just the one."

Lucien laughed. "That might be taking things too far. I'm sure he wouldn't want to see that from a married couple, either."

"S'pose not. But it's not about that, actually. Just—your skin is very comforting."

"So are you, beautiful," Lucien murmured.

Another thought shattered Aubrey's peace. "Dressing! Oh God! I don't want to be naked in front of him if he's going to think I'm aroused by it."

"Since you'll be naked, it'll be clear enough that you're not. Besides, he's obviously known for a while; the only difference now is your knowledge. I wouldn't worry about it."

Easy for him to say.

Lucien's hand massaged the base of his skull. "Look, Grieve strikes me as a man who likes a quiet life. I'm sure you've nothing to fear from him, provided you treat him fairly and don't throw too many shockers his way."

"What about the maids?"

"Grieve said nobody'd enquired about me yet," Lucien pointed out. "And he wouldn't have suggested I keep clothes here if he let them so much as open your wardrobe doors."

"I don't trust him. He's never warmed to me."

Lucien's fingers stilled, then were removed. "Look. He's helping, but you can't expect him to like you."

Aubrey leaned back to eye him.

"Well, you can't. Not unless you've made a much bigger effort than I think you have to befriend him."

Aubrey sighed and burrowed back into Lucien's belly.

"But you *can* trust him to have his own interests at heart, and he's told us what those are. It's a transaction: make sure he's confident you'll meet his needs, and he'll meet yours." Warm fingers rested on his neck again.

"And you said aristocratic relationships were complicated," Aubrey muttered.

"This *is* an aristocratic bloody relationship, my sweet man."

Aubrey melted into him as Lucien's fingers tightened on his neck.

"D'you think the rest of us need to worry about someone dressing us or poking around in our wardrobes? Assuming we even have a wardrobe, that is. You're just not used to thinking of his specific needs. You know what 'a servant' is entitled to, but you're not considering your servants as individuals. If you can negotiate with earls and dukes, you can negotiate with your valet: you just haven't yet. But he's made the first move now, and it's in your interests to meet it."

He was probably right.

"And, speaking of people poking around, you really ought to lock your secrétaire."

"What for?"

"To protect your privacy, of course. You have maids and—"

"Nothing in there but stories and letters from my editor and man of business and so on."

Lucien's hand paused on his neck. "Bloody Grieve was playing me, then. He told me it was personal correspondence."

Aubrey twisted to look up at him.

"I admit it was tempting, since I'd just seen you and Lady Hernedale together in the carriage and we hadn't spoken yet. But I didn't look, of course."

"No. Well, if you had, you'd have known there was nothing personal in there, wouldn't you? Wonder what he hoped to achieve."

"Probably wanted to know if I'd snoop. Which should be reassuring for you, my love, since he wouldn't care unless he genuinely meant to protect you. And really, I don't mind either, since I've nothing to hide. Only... yesterday was a bad day for it."

"I'm sorry." Aubrey reached up and cupped his cheek. "You understand, though, why I couldn't tell you, unless you'd found out yourself?"

Lucien's lips brushed Aubrey's palm, and he pressed his cheek into his hand, sighing. "Reputations, prison sentences, etcetera."

"Heirs," Aubrey added softly.

Lucien raised an eyebrow.

"Rupert's cousin Frederick is his heir: he'd love to get Rupert out of the way. Things are safer now Henrietta's pregnant, but, till the baby's born, Frederick's next in line. Even afterwards, it'd make trouble if he could cast reasonable doubt on Rupert's children being his."

"Ah." Lucien grinned down at him. "Aristocratic relationships, eh?"

Aubrey huffed a laugh. "S'pose so."

"Enemies before you're even born, and within your own family, at that."

"Advantage of being a younger son. A lot of the benefits and fewer drawbacks." Aubrey slid an arm behind Lucien's back. "What you said earlier. Would you want to stay for breakfast on Sundays?"

"If you want me to."

"Tomorrow?"

Lucien bent and kissed his head. "Love to."

Aubrey closed his eyes. "D'you know, I think I'm beginning to see some advantages to this situation."

— Chapter Twenty-One —

SUNDAY, 11TH MARCH 1906

"Good morning, Mr Saxby."

"Morning." Lucien looked up as Grieve carried a steaming ewer through the drawing room without a trace of consciousness. As though Lucien, reading on the sofa, had merely dropped in for breakfast.

After shaving and dressing Aubrey, Grieve laid their breakfast on the table and left the set.

It was glorious, but harder than ever to leave. Sharing after-breakfast coffee and kisses without fear of discovery tempted Lucien to stay longer than he should. But it was Sunday—William was expecting him—so he tore himself from the sofa and the hypnotic fire and the comfort of Aubrey's arms.

"We should go riding together sometime," Aubrey said. "I'm sure so much time on the sofa and in bed is debilitating."

"I get plenty of exercise," Lucien pointed out. "And you don't keep horses. Back in a tick." In the dressing room, he used the WC, scrubbed his teeth again with Aubrey's toothpaste on a finger, and combed his hair. His suit was limp—and, on closer inspection, rather marked by Aubrey's pomade—and he needed a shave, but there wasn't time to go back to his rooms. With any luck, William wouldn't notice. He'd just have to weather McHenry's criticism.

When he walked back into the drawing room, Aubrey was standing, waiting for him.

"Rupert and Henrietta keep horses."

Lucien eyed him. "I noticed."

"They're happy for me to ride them. Saves the grooms taking them out."

"Pardon me for pointing this out, my love—" Lucien checked that his cuffs extended the correct amount from his jacket sleeves "—but I am not you."

"They won't mind me bringing you along."

Lucien paused. He should be leaving, but— "They wouldn't mind you bringing anyone along? Or they wouldn't mind me, specifically? Because I've been wondering whether they might mind me, specifically, very much indeed."

"They don't, sweetheart. Honestly."

"But they know about us, don't they? That second morning, you said—"

"They knew from the moment I followed you at the Gaiety."

"And I assumed they didn't mind, because they kept inviting me places, but I didn't know either of them was your lover, let alone both. If they don't mind, it's probably only because they think it's casual. And I very much don't want to benefit from their generosity under false pretences."

"You wouldn't be. I mean, I told them that, too. That I care for you. The night we all had dinner together."

Lucien paused while his brain caught up with his ears. "You *told* them?" Aubrey'd acknowledged him? Had *told* his aristocratic lovers that he cared for a working man?

"Well, yes."

"Wait a minute. You must've told them before dinner, because I came home with you afterwards."

"Just before you arrived."

Lucien closed his eyes, holding onto calm. "You mean I spent all evening thinking I was visiting your friends, while they were reassessing me as your lover, and—and maybe as competition, and... I was the only one there who didn't know the whole story?"

"No! That's not how— Well, it's not how I *meant* it. I had to tell them how I felt about you, so... so that..."

Lucien opened his eyes to watch horrified realisation crawl across Aubrey's face. "So you wouldn't be going behind their backs."

"Oh God! I'm sorry. So sorry."

"But it was all right to go behind my back, wasn't it? What happened to loving me with a whole heart? Is the heart I get less loyal till I've served a year? A decade?"

"No! Of—"

"Will there *ever* be point when you value a working man equally with your aristocratic lovers?"

"Oh God, Lucien, please let me think! I'm panicking, and I don't want to say all the wrong things."

Lucien took a deep breath. "Do you mean to think of the best story to tell me? Or find words for the truth?"

"The truth. I swear it. Please."

"Sodding hell." Lucien dropped onto the sofa and closed his eyes. "I can't be your—your occasional entertainment, Aubrey. Your twice-weekly hiatus from real life. I didn't mind when we both felt that way, but not now. And even at the start, humiliation wouldn't have been an acceptable price."

The sofa sank beside him, and a cold, bony hand slid into his. The instinct to chafe Aubrey's hands, to make sure he was all right, was a searing imperative.

"Don't," Lucien murmured. "I need to think about what's best for me. Don't ask me to look after you now."

"I didn't—" Aubrey's hand slipped from his. "I only wanted to touch you."

Lucien let his head fall back.

"You're not just entertainment. Not at all. I *love* you."

Lucien's throat swelled. "I was honest with you," he husked, "from the moment I set foot in your set."

"But you had the upper hand in that situation!"

Lucien cranked his head round to stare at Aubrey in disbelief. "In your home? With a man of your class?"

Aubrey's face was pale and tense. "That... was difficult for you?"

"Bloody hell." Lucien dropped his head back again. "Courting disgust and rejection? What do you think?"

Aubrey's hand brushed his, then flinched away. "You seemed so confident."

Silence, but for the sigh of the coal fire, and the hollow tick of the clock.

"Before I—" Aubrey swallowed audibly. "I have to tell you something else."

"There's *more*?" Lucien stared at Aubrey.

"I told Rupert and Henrietta that you know about us. About us all."

"What?" Lucien jolted upright. "*Why*? I'm a bloody Society journalist! Now they'll worry about that, when they needn't."

"Because they had a right to know. If someone knew about you and me, wouldn't you want to know?"

Lucien's jaw tightened till his teeth creaked. "Oh, bloody, sodding hell. I suppose you'd better know that Miss Enfield knows about you and me, then."

"*What*?"

"She already knew about me, and worked out about you after Lady Hernedale's indisposition in Downing Street. But she's perfectly safe."

"Dear *God*! That—that one bloody day is—is—"

"She's safe. I swear it." Lucien leaned back, closing his eyes against the horror in Aubrey's face.

"I'll... have to trust your judgement, since I don't know her."

"As I've had to trust your judgement concerning the Hernedales, who have a great deal more influence." It came out more biting than he intended, but it was true, damn it.

Aubrey was silent. The silence went on for so long that Lucien began to regret his tone. He swallowed, about to apologise, but Aubrey said, "Henrietta's going to invite you to dinner."

Lucien rolled his head on the antimacassar to stare at him.

"Erm. On Wednesday."

"Aubrey. Why?"

"She wants us all to get along."

"Jesus sodding Christ." Lucien closed his eyes again.

"She wants us to be comfortable with one another."

"Comfortable." He couldn't afford to refuse the invitation, either professionally or in common courtesy: the Hernedales had helped him more than he could ever repay. He took deep, even breaths. At least humiliation didn't leave visible scars.

Aubrey's hand slipped into his. "This—is worse for you than telling me your job the night we met, isn't it?"

"Much." He had so much more to lose. But he felt heartened: Aubrey'd taken his hand to offer comfort, not to seek it.

"I can cancel it."

Lucien sighed. "Don't." All else aside, he wouldn't embarrass Aubrey.

"Are you sure?"

"Positive." He should leave. William would be waiting. But he felt stunned and adrift, and Aubrey's bony hand was his anchor.

"I'm sorry," Aubrey said at last. "For everything. I never meant to humiliate you. I should've realised how you'd feel, but I didn't. Looking back, I can see anyone would feel the same: like the outsider at the club. That's partly why I— Well, I wanted you *in* the club. And that meant telling Rupert and Henrietta how I feel about you, so they'd respect you and our relationship."

Lucien sighed. "And what about not going behind their backs?"

"That's— I mean, obviously I owed them both the courtesy of— They had a right to know I had a new commitment."

Commitment. Delight and wonder swelled his chest and throat, but they couldn't completely cushion the hurt. "But you didn't owe me the same courtesy?"

"Well, I did, yes. And you're right that how long I've been with a lover shouldn't make a difference. Doesn't: it's about commitment, not number of years. Telling them was— It's partly habit: I'm used to taking them into consideration. But also, they already knew you were Uranian, so there was no risk to *you* in me telling them how I felt. But you didn't already know about them, so it would've increased the risk for *them*, and although I trust you, they don't yet know you well enough."

Lucien said nothing.

"I absolutely am committed to you, and I'd have told you about them sooner, if I could. I mean, if I took another lover, I wouldn't tell him or her about you, either. Not unless they already knew you were Uranian."

"Right. So. Any other lovers you haven't mentioned?"

"No, not—"

"I understand you want to protect them. I'm not asking for names, just—quantity."

"Lucien. *No*. None. No other lovers at all. Not even casual encounters since I met you. And I swear I'll tell you if there's someone in future, even if I can't give you their name."

"I should think three lovers would keep you quite busy enough."

"I do like to keep busy." Aubrey's tone was tentatively teasing. Every instinct in Lucien screamed to soothe his anxiety, but he couldn't let him smooth things over again: not before they were properly settled.

He stared into the fire. "It feels as though I'm making all the compromises. I have to understand about your other relationships; I have to make allowances for your habit of prioritising other people over me; I have to accept being the oblivious stranger at the table."

"I'm sorry," Aubrey murmured. "I do see. And I swear I'll try not to do it again. I never meant to hurt you."

"It can't help but hurt." Lucien rubbed his hands over his face. "I don't belong in your circles. I'm the working man at your ball: I can watch and report on the event, but I can't dance. It's where you belong—you and your other lovers—but I can't follow you there. And you can't follow me, either: you'd feel even more out of place in my world than I do in yours."

"And yet… I belong with you anyway," Aubrey husked.

"Damn it, Aubrey! How can I know what's best for me when you say things like that?"

"How can you know whether you want me if I don't speak?"

"That, at least, isn't in question. It's whether staying with you will destroy me."

"I mean," Aubrey whispered, "I'd much rather it helped you thrive. And—I'm willing to work awfully hard towards that goal."

"Oh, for God's sake!" Lucien grabbed Aubrey's shoulders. He went along without a hint of resistance, letting Lucien draw him across his lap and cradle his head in the crook of his arm. Lucien gazed down at him. "As though I could leave you anyway, at this point."

Aubrey's clammy hand cupped his cheek. "Is it terrible that I'm pathetically relieved?"

Was it terrible that Lucien delighted in the beautiful aristocrat lying meekly in his arms? Not that he didn't love Aubrey just for being Aubrey, but even through misery and anger, he thrilled to the aristocrat yielding willingly to his direction; exulted in the implicit trust and acceptance.

He shouldn't enjoy it so much. But he wanted what he wanted, and he wanted Aubrey desperately, for everything he was. No point eternally questioning the reasons for his attraction to a fellow who returned it.

He pressed a kiss into Aubrey's palm. "Not at all." Aubrey couldn't help being a nob, any more than Lucien could help being a working man. Was it terrible that he was attracted to the whole man, not just the parts he approved of?

"I'm more sorry than I can say for hurting you," Aubrey murmured. "I'll do better. I swear."

Lucien laid his head back on the antimacassar. Aubrey's weight, his closeness, were an extraordinary comfort. "This won't be easy."

"However hard it is, it'll still be easier than losing you."

Lucien peered at him. "Sweet words can't fix everything."

"Well. It wasn't a fix, you know, only the simple truth. But if it sugars the pill a bit, I'm glad of it." Aubrey's eyes were closed; his forehead and the bridge of his nose tucked into Lucien's body.

Lucien sighed. Aubrey was clearly doing his best. He'd listened. He'd recognised the offence. He'd apologised. He'd promised to do better.

Closing his eyes, Lucien let his head fall back and his mind empty of everything but the moment and Aubrey's warm presence.

The clock chimed the half-hour, and Lucien startled. "Damn it! I've got to go."

Aubrey pressed a kiss to his belly, and sat up.

The hall mirror told Lucien that Aubrey's head hadn't improved his suit; and reflected the man himself, watching him comb his hair.

"Wait a minute." Lucien turned, wiping the comb on his hankie. "You're telling me the Hernedales invited me to dinner again *after* you told them you care for me?" He slid it into his pocket. "When they might've been expected to hate me?"

"Partly they invited you *because* I told them, you know, because they want us all to get along. But only partly. They wouldn't have invited you if they didn't like you, and I wouldn't have expected them to, any more than I'd expect you to socialise with them if you disliked them."

Lucien stared at him.

"Henrietta invited you to dinner before, didn't she? After that god-awful play. And Rupert invited you to join us the first evening we met."

"Which makes no sense at all. He was reading."

"But not oblivious. He'd have noticed Henrietta was enjoying your company, and that I was attracted to you, and he must've been reasonably comfortable with you himself."

"Right." He had no idea what to make of it all.

Aubrey offered a farewell kiss. And, since he was dressed, he didn't dash into the drawing room when the door opened, but waved Lucien off as he might a friend.

Lucien walked to Park Lane through Sunday-quiet streets feeling oddly disconnected from his body. To become friendly with the Hernedales was to dine with wolves. Wolves like William, who could hurt him without even meaning to, or destroy him on a whim. And Aubrey was part of that pack.

But the invitation was a declaration that they didn't mean to harm him. For Aubrey's sake, of course—he wasn't fool enough to think they had any personal attachment to him, or that the acquaintance would last if he and Aubrey fell out—but it was as safe as any contact with the nobility could be.

He'd never have made that impulsive proposition to Aubrey at the Gaiety Theatre if he'd understood the situation, and yet he couldn't wish it away. Then, his life had been stable but lonely; now it was unstable, but no longer lonely. He'd have liked more than two nights a week, but the risks were too high, and ultimately, he'd rather have two nights with Aubrey than share a home with anyone else. His path was set.

"How is he?" Lucien let Frank the footman take his outdoor things.

"Good morning, Mr Saxby," Dawson said. "Lord Camberhithe's—"

"A demmed nuisance." McHenry closed the door to the basement behind him. "See if you can't do something about that, would you?"

Dawson drew himself up and glared down his nose at McHenry.

"Stow it, Dawson," McHenry advised him. "When you've wiped his arse as often as I have, then you can tell me how to speak about him. Until then, just shut up and let the people who know him best speak."

Frank glanced between them and discreetly left the room.

"That bad?" Lucien ignored Dawson's pale, thin-lipped fury.

"Eh." McHenry, grey pouches under his eyes, seesawed a hand. "Just... ongoing. And I've had about enough of it."

"I'll see what I can do. Go put your feet up, if you can, or punch something, if that'll help."

McHenry almost smiled. "He's in the drawing room."

Lucien watched him leave. He should move back in, if only to help McHenry, who wasn't getting any younger. Besides, Camberhithe House was infinitely more comfortable than his boarding house, with excellent food and service which wouldn't cost him a penny. And—he almost laughed—he'd have a wardrobe again, which, as he'd reminded Aubrey, not everyone had. William would be delighted, even if he didn't give up work.

But he desperately didn't want to. And how the devil would he explain sleeping elsewhere twice a week?

William was upright on the drawing room sofa, a book in his lap. The fire was lit, but the terrace doors were open, and the air in the room was fresh and as clean as it got in London.

"Morning," Lucien said. "What're you reading?"

"If you can call it reading." William slammed the book shut and shoved it onto the table beside him. "I've just read the same sentence four times and can't understand it."

"You're still recovering." Lucien craned to see the title. "Maybe Marcus Aurelius is a bit ambitious for now?"

"Shouldn't be."

"Something in English?" Lucien suggested.

"Damnation, Lucien! Don't you patronise me as well."

Lucien settled into a chair beside him and reached for patience. "As well as who?"

"McHenry." William leaned back and closed his eyes. "As though I didn't have enough limitations."

"How've you been sleeping?"

"Badly. And before you suggest laudanum, McHenry keeps offering it to me and I'd rather be in pain than trapped in nightmares."

"Fair enough. Does he stay awake with you?"

William's lips tightened. "I know what you're going to say, but I don't call him or anything. He just wakes up and comes in."

"Well, tell him he needn't, now you're a bit better. He's bound to be on edge if he's overtired."

"*I'm* overtired, too."

"But that can't be helped if you'd rather not have laudanum. Besides, you don't have to work."

William drew breath.

Lucien leaped in before he could say something really annoying. "Every day, he cleans and irons and folds and mends your clothes till there's not a single loose thread or fragment of fluff on anything. He keeps your dressing box and jewellery in good condition. He washes and shaves and dresses and undresses you twice a day. He makes sure you're comfortable throughout the day. He's awake before you every day, and doesn't go to bed till you're settled. *And* he's awake in the night with you, because you won't have a nurse. William, you can't get good service from him if he's exhausted. He's not a young man anymore."

William glared at him. Lucien bore it patiently.

Eventually, William blew out a long breath, closed his eyes, and thumped his head back on the antimacassar.

Lucien waited, listening to blackbirds sing in the garden. Who'd want to lie awake for hours in a silent house, alone with pain and fear of the future, or with a paid stranger? This situation… It was too much for McHenry, and not enough for William. McHenry needed his tasks confined to valet duties. William needed friends who shared his interests, and a lover.

A lover who didn't have to work; who delighted in his company. A lover who'd want to hold him through the night, sleeping or waking; who'd sympathise with his frustrations; who'd give him something to smile about and be someone to laugh with. A lover with whom he could explore the varied pleasures his body might experience and bestow, to offset the pain and frustration it inflicted. A lover whose happiness he wanted, too.

He'd often spoken of marriage when they were younger, but seldom mentioned it anymore. Lord Camberhithe would never lack for women eager to marry him; but what he needed was someone who loved him, and that was more difficult, especially as he seldom left his house.

"Damn it," William said at last. "I knew that."

"It'll make things easier for both of you, if he gets enough sleep."

"Look. I'll—"

A light tap at the door, and a polite pause.

"I'll tell him to stay in bed, unless I call him."

Dawson entered, and set a tray on the table between them. "Seed cake, my lord, and madeira." He poured them each a glass, and left.

It was on the tip of Lucien's tongue to ask whether William should drink madeira when he was still ill, but that really would've been patronising: William was capable of making his own judgements. Instead, he handed him a slice of cake, and ate a forkful of his own. "Warm from the oven. Delicious."

William stared at his plate. "Do you have any idea what it's like to be afraid of food?"

"No."

"I want this cake. And I'm afraid it's going to hurt later, even though food hasn't hurt much for days."

"Then it probably won't hurt."

"I *know* that. I just said so." William sliced into it with the side of his cake fork and put a piece in his mouth. "Good Lord, that's lovely," he mumbled.

Lucien watched him chew each mouthful. There was something deeply satisfying about watching William enjoy food. More satisfying, even, than eating his own. William was getting better. With any luck, he'd be relatively healthy for weeks, maybe even months.

When he'd eaten half the slice, William put his plate down and leaned back. "Wish I could manage more."

"Madeira?" Lucien offered him his glass. William took it, sipped, and closed his eyes. Lucien gazed at his thin wrists and hollow cheeks. "I wish you could eat more, too," he murmured.

"I know." William half-opened his eyes. "I can hardly remember a time you weren't there, you know."

"Well." Lucien remembered the moment they'd met with agonising clarity. He'd been seven years old, taken to a luxurious room filled with thrilling toys, under strict instruction from Mum to play whatever games the pale, listless boy wanted, and leave the rest alone if he hoped to be invited back.

"You're like a brother to me."

Lucien stilled. "I... sincerely doubt that."

"You've always been there for me. More so than my real brothers. Much more."

"Well, then." Lucien pressed William's hand gently and managed a smile in return.

You wouldn't consider your brother a natural-born valet. Your brother wouldn't be your unpaid servant. Your brother wouldn't grow up following your commands; obliged to be your sickroom companion, day and night. Your brother would never have despised himself for pleasing you out of fear of what he'd lose if he didn't.

Of course he'd always been there for William: he'd had to, when they were children, and love and habit and responsibility had driven him since. No wonder William thought him the embodiment of a valet: what had he ever done, in William's presence, but serve William? Even when he argued with him, it was in William's own interests.

But why crush his fantasy? William's servants cared more for him than his family and acquaintances did, and it was true enough that Lucien loved him, for a painful, conflicted value of love. And that William loved Lucien, too, for—well, probably for being who William needed him to be.

He wouldn't love the real Lucien: the Lucien who was messy with loneliness and self-doubt and conflicting loyalties. The Lucien who'd been a soldier, but now lived in unmanly fear of the horrors of conflict. The Lucien who found peace and ecstasy in sex with men. The Lucien who loved Aubrey Fanshawe and held him blissfully through the night.

William could never trust that Lucien, and William needed to trust the people who cared for him. So Lucien would be the person William needed him to be, for as long as necessary.

He sipped his madeira but couldn't swallow another mouthful of cake.

William picked up his book.

"How about the *Aeneid*?" Lucien suggested. "Instead of the *Meditations*? Still Roman, but less dry." In Latin, too, rather than Greek, which might ease things a bit for William without seeming patronising.

William's lips tightened, but then he sighed. "Yes, all right."

So Lucien found it for him, then scanned the shelves for something for himself. What he wanted was Edward Carpenter's *Sex-Love: And its Place in a Free Society*, which he'd borrowed from Aubrey, and which was waiting for him in his desk, but William would never allow it in his library, supposing he even knew it existed. So he settled for Eliot's *Middlemarch*, since he'd liked *Silas Marner*.

"Where did that come from?" William eyed it as Lucien brought the books in. "Did Marjorie leave it here?"

"No idea." Lucien handed William the *Aeneid*, then sank into his own chair, resigned to reading a book he didn't quite fancy in the hope of escaping conversation he wanted even less.

Lucien stayed as the sun climbed the clouds. He stayed for lunch. He stayed as the sun slumped lower, casting desperate rays through the terrace doors, clinging to the carpet and curtains.

A little before sunset, he closed *Middlemarch*. "I'd better go."

"You might stay for dinner," William suggested.

Boarding house dinner would be over by the time he got back. And Mrs Spence would provide an elaborate spread. And William would like it. But Lucien looked at his hollow, hopeful face, anticipated an evening of complaints and oblivious, insensitive comments, and lied. "Awfully sorry: I've got to be somewhere." He'd buy a pie on his way home and eat it in his rooms. That sounded all right. He could read Carpenter in peace over dinner and into the evening. That sounded even better.

"Oh." William's face closed. "Right-ho."

Guilt knotted his stomach. Without him, William had nothing to look forward to but a delicious meal he couldn't properly enjoy. And God knew William had reason to complain, not just daily, but over his entire life. It wasn't as though he had many visitors, or went out much, which might give him something to talk about beyond his own circumscribed thoughts and how he felt from moment to moment. And, since Lucien disliked his prejudices, he should've challenged them years ago, as he'd challenged Aubrey. A chap like William, over-sheltered and replete with social advantages, couldn't learn it alone. But William wasn't well enough for that conversation, and Lucien couldn't bear another instant of gritting his teeth.

"Is there anything you need?" William asked.

A reward proffered to the almost-brother-not-quite-servant, in return for his visit. The muddle of gratitude, guilt, and outrage at William's condescension threatened to close his throat. "No. Thank you, William."

William glared at him, then leaned back and shut his eyes, his jaw tense.

Lucien laid a hand on his shoulder. "See you next week."

Reaching up without opening his eyes, William patted his hand. "See you then."

Lucien escaped to the entrance hall, then stepped through the basement door and followed the smell of roasting beef and onions down to the kitchen. McHenry sat in a wooden chair at the fireside, feet up on a low stool, a folded newspaper and a pair of steel-rimmed spectacles in his lap. In the chair beside him, and sharing his footstool, Mrs Spence had hiked her skirts partway up to toast her narrow shins and swollen ankles. Voices from the scullery suggested the kitchen maids were preparing vegetables.

"Pull up a chair, pet," Mrs Spence suggested. "These stone floors are shockingly cold."

"No thanks. Been sitting all day."

McHenry eyed Lucien's jaw and his limp suit, gaze settling on the pomade stains on his jacket. "He in a better mood now?"

"Got a book he can concentrate on and enjoy, at least." Lucien leaned against the chimney breast, folding his arms over the stains.

"Well that's something." McHenry switched his attention to Lucien's eyes. "And I've had most of the day off, thanks to you. Might just stay here till I'm needed: catch up tomorrow."

Mrs Spence patted his sleeve. "You do that, McHenry: you could do with it." Sighing, she flipped her skirts down and stood. "Better make a start on that pudding." She crossed the room, peered inside the gas oven, then turned to the table. "Mabel! Get the flour."

McHenry opened his newspaper and shook the pages straight. Even taking his ease beside the kitchen fire, he wore a spotless morning coat. Waistcoat buttons strained slightly across his comfortable, barrel-like belly.

"I had a thought," Lucien said. "William sending me that evening dress, and planning to send more clothes: you won't lose out by it, will you?"

"Course I will."

Shit. He should've realised. "Look. I can—"

"Don't let it bother you." McHenry flipped a corner of the newspaper down and looked at him over his spectacles. "You deserve a bit of something after all these years. Besides, I've already got my nest egg—more of an ostrich egg now, as it happens. Could've retired comfortably years ago, even without a pension."

"Why didn't you?" Lucien had a feeling he knew the answer.

"Can't just leave the poor blighter. You know as well as me that the marquis'd assume any valet would do the same job I do. He'd install a new fellow then swan off to the Continent for a month or three. Wouldn't give tuppence for our lad's chances of surviving the first year."

"So you'll... what? Stay on till he dies?"

McHenry smiled grimly, folding the newspaper. "Him or me. He might outlive me yet, and I'll do my best to make sure he does, though I won't deny it's a worry, that I might leave him behind."

Lucien swallowed the lump in his throat. "Best look after yourself, then, hadn't you?"

"Heh. Do my best."

"I've asked him to let you sleep, and he's agreed. But you need to stand your ground, too. Don't go in at night unless he calls you. Please. He's not eight anymore: he'll let you know if he can't manage."

McHenry snorted. "Old habits, eh?"

"Don't let those habits kill you. Why not sleep in your bedroom instead of his dressing room? Then you won't wake whenever he does. Get a bell installed in your room, connected to the pull by his bed."

"That's not a bad idea."

"And you know where I am if you need me; for *anything*, all right? And... thank you. For the clothes. And everything."

"Pfft." McHenry waved it off.

Lucien straightened from the chimney-breast. "I'll be off then. Get out from underfoot."

"As though you were ever underfoot."

Lucien stared. McHenry had been sharp enough with him at times, especially when he was a boy.

"Can't think what I'd have done without you all these years. Don't mind admitting the time you were in the cavalry was rough."

Oh Lord. Lucien swallowed hard, then drew breath to lighten the moment.

"And not just cause I worried you'd end up drilled through like a colander and buried in some demmed place I'd need an extra tongue to pronounce."

Lucien snorted. "They're not that difficult. If you can pronounce 'colander', you can pronounce 'kopje'."

McHenry fixed him with a severe eye. "Some of us are plain men without a fancy education. Once you can read your heathen demmed Greek, you can probably pronounce anything you like."

Lucien laughed.

McHenry grinned back, then sobered. "Damme, Lucien, you wouldn't move back in, would you? *He*'d like it, too: he's kept your rooms for you."

Guilt swept through Lucien like a heated sickness that'd never be conquered, only retreat temporarily. William needed him, and McHenry was giving his bloody life to care for him, while Lucien— "I'm sorry. So sorry."

McHenry's gaze dropped. "Never mind."

"I can't. I just— No. Not if he offered me the keys to Paradise, and the alternative was sleeping in a flooded ditch."

"Right. Can't say I blame you." McHenry hauled himself up and dropped the newspaper onto his chair. "Don't want you cooped up here if you wouldn't like it, anyhow."

"I could visit more often, if it'd—"

"As you're doing is more'n good enough. I didn't know you disliked it so much."

"No, but—"

"Off you go. No point wasting a nice evening here when you've already lost the day."

Lucien shook his hand. "See you next week."

"I know I will." McHenry clapped him on the shoulder. "I've always been able to rely on you."

It'd be rather nice, Lucien thought as he picked up his hat and cane, to have only the responsibilities he'd chosen, instead of those chosen for him in childhood. In fact—he trod down the steps into Park Lane—it'd be rather nice not to be relied upon by anybody at all. Just for a while.

— Chapter Twenty-Two —

Lucien arrived at Albany just after half-past six on Wednesday evening. The days were growing longer and, though Aubrey's curtains were drawn, it was still fairly bright outside.

Theoretically, there was no reason to worry about dining with the Hernedales. He'd dined with them after Aubrey'd told them he cared for him, and they'd invited him back, so they weren't likely to bite his head off now. He should've been anticipating a pleasurable flirtation with Lady Hernedale: few people knew how to enjoy a dalliance without taking a fellow seriously, and it was a delight not to have to watch every word and smile; a delight to amuse and be amused by overblown compliments signifying nothing but fun.

He tapped on Aubrey's door, knowing precisely why he was tense. Tonight, he wasn't dining with Aubrey's friends, but with Aubrey's influential lovers.

Aubrey, in dress trousers, plum dressing gown, and cravat, let him in, glancing at his valise.

"That your lounge suit?" Aubrey slid the overcoat from his shoulders and kissed the back of his neck.

"Mmm." Lucien shuddered and angled his head forward. A warm, damp tongue tip traced his hairline to his ear. "I should hang it up. As soon as possible, so it doesn't crease any more than it already has."

276

"S'pose so." Aubrey's silky-smooth cheek rubbed his neck.

"Aubrey. My love." He laid a hand on Aubrey's head to still him, then turned, took the overcoat, and hung it up. "We're going out to dinner, remember?"

"Not for almost an hour." Aubrey's lips tugged the corner of his mouth. "And I haven't seen you in days."

"You're impossibly alluring. But I need to look presentable tonight. And I should hang this suit up."

In the dressing room, he opened the valise, took out his jewellery case, and put it on the washstand.

"For the studs you're wearing?" Aubrey asked from the doorway.

"Mmhm."

"Could've borrowed mine: my studs weren't damaged last time."

"Let's keep it that way, eh?" Lucien opened the wardrobe doors. "Where should I put my suit?"

"Don't mind. Put it in the middle, if you like."

Lucien stifled a sigh. "Very generous of you, but since annoying Grieve isn't at the top of my list today, I'd rather put it somewhere unobtrusive." Lounge suits were on the right-hand side of the rail; his had better go on the very end. He tucked his folded shirt beneath a snowy stack of Aubrey's, then found a spare hanger, slid Aubrey's clothes aside, and hung up his suit.

"You're awfully good at that," Aubrey observed from behind him. "I'd be all thumbs."

Lucien paused. They didn't have enough time for this conversation. But it was such an obvious opening that if he avoided mentioning his history now, it'd look as though he'd deliberately concealed it when it finally came out.

He closed his eyes and took a deep breath. After all, this might turn out to be a very short conversation indeed: too many nobs regarded servants as lesser even than other working men. "Yes. Well." He opened his eyes and checked the hang of the trousers, purposely not looking round. "I was trained as a valet."

"Oh."

After that single word: silence.

Hands quivering with tension, he smoothed his jacket and redistributed Aubrey's clothes evenly along the rail so they wouldn't crush one another. Then he closed the wardrobe doors, blew out a long, slow breath, and turned.

"From childhood." He met Aubrey's gaze and folded his arms.

"But… you're a journalist."

"Much to my father's disappointment," Lucien acknowledged. "Valeting a nobleman pays much better, and includes bed and board. And you work in fancier surroundings, though servants' quarters typically leave a lot to be desired, if you ask me."

"So… why didn't you? Become a valet, I mean."

"It was the obvious path: between my training and my father's reputation, I'd have obtained an excellent position. But there are more opportunities for working men now than in my father's day. Just as well, really, since I loathe arbitrary rules, and don't like to serve."

"But that night. You put me to bed…"

Lucien sighed. Might as well admit it. "I wanted to look after you." He held Aubrey's gaze. "It's not a thing I'd do for just anyone."

"You didn't mind?"

"I chose to do it." Lucien paused. If realising he'd served a servant was going to tip the nob into outright rejection, he'd better know it now. "Just as you chose to put me to bed a few nights later."

Aubrey's narrow lips twitched a brief smile. "I wanted to look after you."

"Right." Lucien took a deep breath. "Are we— Is this a problem? Should I have told you sooner?"

"No! No, I'm just—" Aubrey stepped closer, and his bony hand covered Lucien's. "I'm reorganising my thoughts, that's all. Understanding things differently."

Lucien slid his hand free of Aubrey's. "Things like—my *nature*, and the kinds of things you assume might interest me?"

"Things like the care you take with my clothes. Like the way your suits are always immaculate. Like the way you understand how Grieve might feel."

"There's that," Lucien acknowledged.

"And that—it might hurt you, to think I'm taking Grieve for granted."

"That, too. I know how hard valets work. My dad was an excellent valet. So good that the marquis kept him on after he married the marchioness' lady's maid. Even though it put the marchioness to the profound inconvenience of finding another maid, and the marquis to the profound inconvenience of hearing her complain about it." Hard not to sneer at the nobs' utter bloody self-absorption; at their conviction that any employee who prioritised a personal life was a traitor.

"Have… I upset you?"

"Not—" Lucien unknotted tense arms and rubbed his face. "Nothing you've said. It's more… anger at my parents' employers. And anger that my parents weren't angry with them, and still aren't." That they were *grateful*. Grateful that Dad hadn't been sacked. Grateful, later, that the marquis magnanimously tossed Dad the retirement settlement he'd earned with decades of flawless service. It burned in his bowels like Greek fire.

"You're angry because… their employers didn't want them to marry?"

"Because they didn't see them as *human*, with needs the same as their own."

"Ah. Yes, I see."

"And because they never learned to."

"Hard to forgive."

Lucien offered Aubrey a wry smile and a small, ironic head tip. "As you observe." He sighed, and admitted the rest. "I worried you might think less of me, for being raised in service.

That you'd assume it made me a certain sort of person. Or non-person. That you mightn't be able to see *me* past it."

Aubrey swallowed and dropped his gaze. "I mightn't have, I suppose, if I'd known. When we first met, you know. But now, well... You're just... *you*."

Lucien's throat ached. "My parents and friends are themselves, too. So's Grieve." Bad enough William slighting his people and background: he couldn't bear it from a lover. "They're no less intelligent or caring or... or *worthy* just because they didn't have a classical education, or because they don't speak the way you do. I'm no better than other working people, and we're no lesser than the nobility. Income and influence make the difference, not worth."

Aubrey stood silent, looking wary, then— "Yes. I see that."

"And yet you wouldn't have brought me home that first night, if you'd known."

"I didn't say that. As I recall, I didn't ask about your job until we were already here."

"You didn't assume I was a working man at all," Lucien pointed out. "I told you."

Aubrey paused. "Well. I doubt it would've mattered. I followed you very much against my better judgement that night. You really are irresistibly attractive."

"Aubrey." Lucien watched carefully, but he didn't flinch at the use of his Christian name. "I'm really quite plain."

"Not to me, sweetheart." Aubrey reached towards his face, and hesitated.

Lucien seized his hand, feeling Aubrey's gasp shiver through his own body, watching his eyes darken and his cheeks flush. Beginning to feel more confident.

Tension in his shoulders eased. "Is that right, my love?" he murmured.

Aubrey's eyes closed, and he rested his forehead on Lucien's. "Oh Lord, you're so lovely. And ridiculously competent and clever and honourable. Which, granted, I couldn't have known that first night, but maybe I did, somehow."

Lucien snorted disbelief.

"I liked your eyes. You have such kind eyes. And— Well. I don't make a practice of bringing strange fellows home, you know. Which is to say, you were the first."

"Really?" Surprise slackened Lucien's grip.

Aubrey's other hand slid between Lucien's tailcoat and waistcoat to rest, warm and solid, in the small of his back. Lucien drew him closer—and relaxed.

Because Aubrey's response to him was the same. Because he could still move him with a touch of his hand. Because, in an ocean of uncertainty, this, at least, was still reliable.

Anxiety lurked like a shattered sword-point deep in a scarred-over wound: ready to pierce again at the slightest disturbance. But as Aubrey helped Lucien off with his tailcoat, to keep it fresh until they left; as he fetched the indigo dressing gown and wrapped it around him—it began to feel as though things really might be all right.

THE WALK TO Hernedale House was peaceful, but Aubrey's mind was anything but.

For one thing, he'd declined yet another invitation to dine with Mother and Father. If he didn't visit them soon, they'd start to feel neglected, but a prior engagement was a prior engagement, and, short of a crisis or inescapable obligation, all his Wednesday nights were Lucien's.

For another, while it didn't particularly bother him that Lucien had been raised in service, it bothered him a great deal that he might've discounted him entirely, and for no better reason than a stupid habit of thinking.

"D'you really think we can all be comfortable with one another?" Lucien asked.

"Hmm? Henrietta thinks so."

Lucien sighed. "And what do *you* think?"

"I—" Ah God, what a question. "Sweetheart, I hope we can. I don't want to be pulled in different directions. I'd rather we could all be together."

"Not—" Lucien stopped in the street. "Aubrey, *not* in the bedroom. Because—"

"Good Lord, no!" Aubrey laughed and tugged him on. "They wouldn't want that any more than you do."

"Thank God!" Lucien said devoutly. "It wouldn't suit me at all, and not just because Lady Hernedale's a woman."

"I just meant— I'd like us all to be friends." He tried to crush the note of yearning in his tone. "I'd like us to enjoy evenings together, with everything above-board between us all."

"Pleasant evenings together should be possible, with effort on all sides. But as for friendship... Look. I'm just— I'm not a nob, d'you see?"

"I *know* that."

"No, listen. I might look or sound like a nob at times, but don't be— Don't assume I think the way you do, all right?"

Aubrey twitched his shoulders uncomfortably. "People are— I mean, we're all the same at heart, aren't we?"

"No. We are not. You assume everyone thinks like you, but we don't; we can't. We have to worry about things you barely consider. Your voices are automatically heard and respected over ours. Some of us can't even vote! You get respect and deference wherever you go, just for existing, while we're expected to provide that deference, regardless of how you treat us. It affects the way we think and the way we see the world and the way the world sees and treats us. I'm never going to think like a nob, Aubrey, and I don't want to. I'll never pass for a nob—not under close scrutiny—and I don't want to. I'll never fit into your social world, however much you want me to. And I don't really want to."

Aubrey walked in silence a while, thinking. Then, "You know, I like you as you are. I don't need you to fit in. And I don't particularly like my social world either."

"You're entitled to it anyway, and I'm not, even if I wanted it." Lucien sighed. "I'm trying to explain that the problems I have are not the problems you have."

"Yes, all right: I understand."

"You *can't* fully, not with the best will in the world. How can I be friends with people who use their position to crush their social inferiors? Even if I didn't care about them crushing others—and I do—*I'm* their social inferior: I could be next if I offend them. If they were really vicious, they could target my family, too, and there's nothing I could do to stop them. Besides, they can't see me as a friend, because they can't see me as an equal. I don't make a habit of developing friendships with people who think they're better than I am."

"I don't think..." Aubrey couldn't honestly say Rupert regarded Lucien as an equal. *I'd have thanked him for his concern or damned his cheek* wasn't the sort of thing you'd usually say of a peer. And Henrietta... Well she might be a bit patronising. That could make friendship awkward, if you minded it. "Shunning Lowdon wasn't a casual decision, you know. Henrietta wanted to prevent him damaging other men's careers over her the way he tried to damage yours."

"That does make a difference." Lucien paced quietly beside him for a while. "But she could only do it because she outranked him. She might as easily have destroyed him on a whim, or because she'd mistaken his actions, just as he tried to destroy me. It isn't right."

"I—do see that, when you put it that way."

"I shouldn't need to be under anyone's protection. I didn't do anything wrong. But Lowdon's words carry more weight than mine, even though my editor's known me for years and doesn't know him at all. It's wrong. It's wrong when anyone does it. A person can't feel safe."

"They wouldn't crush anyone without good reason, but I take your point."

Aubrey's pumps and Lucien's boots struck the pavement in unison, counterpointed by the light tap of Aubrey's ebony cane.

"I do like Lady Hernedale," Lucien said at last, "as much as I can afford to. Lord Hernedale... I respect him, and he's been pleasant to me so far, but he was quite cruel to Lowdon, the night we met."

"For a start, Lowdon disturbed his reading," Aubrey pointed out reasonably.

Lucien turned to stare at him.

"You might as well drag a man bodily out of his lover as disturb Rupert while he's reading. In either case, it's only polite to wait till a chap's finished what he's doing before you interrupt."

"All that, over a *newspaper*?"

"Well. That was just an aggravating factor. It was mostly because Lowdon was policing Henrietta again. Even if he had a right to, which he damned well doesn't anymore, he'd no reason to humiliate her. And he never listens when she stands up for herself, so Rupert had to step in and—er—show him the error of his ways."

"Rather brutally," Lucien suggested. "Considering he was just trying to protect his sister. You said yourself that I was over-familiar."

"But Henrietta wasn't upset: she was enjoying it, and she was perfectly safe. It wasn't up to him to stop her. Or anyone, really."

Lucien frowned. "I suppose so."

"And courtesy hadn't worked in the past, you see. Rupert's put up with a lot from Lowdon—since he was a child, because Lowdon's twelve years older than we are—and he'd had enough. Besides, when a chap's humiliating your wife in public and simultaneously questioning your masculinity... Well, he was asking for it, really."

"I agree it wasn't polite."

"Anyway, Rupert isn't usually that sharp with people. Not unless they've really annoyed him."

Lucien stopped walking. "By, for example, knowing about his relationships?"

"Oh." Aubrey stopped, too. "No, he wouldn't— Rupert's fair-minded, you know. He was quick enough to see where the responsibility lay and damn me for a fool."

"And... you don't mind that?"

"Lord, no." Aubrey urged him on. "It was well-deserved, and I've snarled at him for less. I was damned careless in that carriage. And then, to cap it all, I told you about him, which— well, it wasn't my place to tell, especially when the consequences could be so severe. Anyway, I apologised, and he got over it."

"When you put it that way, he sounds more than reasonable."

Aubrey warmed. "He is. Truly. I do think you'll like him, when you know him better."

Silence. He turned to see Lucien watching his face.

"You love him a lot," Lucien murmured.

"Oh Lord, yes: absolutely adore him. I told you that."

"You did," Lucien faced forward again. "He's your sort. So is Lady Hernedale. You share a long history, and it's uncontroversial for you to spend time with them. And they're handsome people. I wonder whether you'd have noticed me at all, if you'd been able to live with them."

"Can't imagine being oblivious to you for long." He brushed the back of his gloved hand against Lucien's.

Lucien's lips twisted in a wry smile. "'But nobody else has such pretty hair, pet.'"

Aubrey held his gaze. "But nobody else is you, sweetheart. Nor ever could be, in all of time and space. I could never love anyone else the way I love you. And I do love you quite desperately."

Lucien's eyes glittered in the lamplight, and he turned his head away. "Bloody fiction writers," he muttered.

"Except this isn't a fiction." He brushed Lucien's hand again. "Not for me, anyway. It's as certain as death. And as sweet as your body in mine."

"You don't stop, do you?" Lucien laughed, but his voice was thick.

"Not until I convince you. And maybe not then. You inspire me."

Lucien snorted. "I'm a bloody odd-looking muse."

"You're the perfect muse for me."

Lucien stopped on the pavement outside Hernedale House. "Give me a moment, will you?"

Aubrey waited while he pulled out a perfectly pressed handkerchief, wiped his face, and took a deep breath.

"Henrietta arranged it so we we'll go straight in to dinner. No—no awkward chat beforehand, you know, and it'll give you all a chance to get comfortable with one another in a relatively neutral setting."

Lucien shot him a grateful look. "That helps." He took another deep breath. "Right, Aubrey. Let's go have dinner with your other bloody lovers."

FROM THE MOMENT they crossed the threshold, Lucien's charm was in full flow. It seemed almost reflex, though, and Aubrey was sure he was uneasy. But over the course of the meal, his manner eased from brittle and glittering to resilient and smooth, and by the time the Eton Mess and strawberries in madeira were served, he seemed almost relaxed.

"I meant to tell you," Henrietta said mischievously, "how much I enjoyed your report on the suffragist deputation to Downing Street last week."

"Miss Enfield was pleased with it," Lucien said, a slight edge to his tone.

"Speaking of which—" Rupert helped himself to a few more strawberries "—there's a petition circulating in the Commons over it."

Lucien and Henrietta stared at him.

"Over... the report in the Mail?" Lucien asked.

"Rather, *because* of the report in the Mail. MPs are upset by the way the ladies were treated, and a few of the Lords are absolutely up in arms. I've had question after question about your health, my dear."

"Good!" Henrietta said. "I hope they care about the women who were actually manhandled, too."

"None of the Lords mentioned them. But, of the Commons... Keir Hardie, of course: he's their champion and knows several of them personally. And the Mail report gave him sufficient ammunition to recruit others."

Aubrey watched Lucien's hand drift towards his tailcoat pocket, then return to the table.

Rupert must've noticed it, too. "Feel free to take notes, Saxby, though I'd rather you didn't quote me on anything."

Lucien flushed. "Sincere apologies for the discourtesy. And, naturally, I'd never quote any part of a private conversation without first clearing it with the source."

"No need to apologise: I wasn't just being polite. Nor snide. God knows I read in inappropriate places myself."

"No! Do you?" Henrietta asked innocently.

Rupert grinned at her. "It's an informal dinner, Saxby, and, under the circumstances, I hope we're becoming friends. So go ahead. With Lady Hernedale's permission, of course."

"Please do, Mr Saxby." Henrietta put her spoon down. "I very much want this news printed."

While the servants removed the last of the dishes, brought the port, and left them to their conversation, Lucien took notes. "What does the Commons petition request?"

"For the prime minister to fix an early date to receive the signatories' representatives, so they can discuss the necessity for women's suffrage with him."

Henrietta raised a sceptical eyebrow. "Is he likely to do that?"

"Hard to say. But over a hundred MPs from all parties have already signed, and the petition was only started four days ago."

"A hundred!" Aubrey poured his and Henrietta's port and put the decanter in front of Lucien.

"Mmm. Not sure when they mean to present it to Campbell-Bannerman, but it's already impressive."

"I worried there might be riots over that article," Lucien admitted. "But Miss Enfield said not, and that the government couldn't ignore it." He placed a final loop and point, closed his notebook, and filled his glass. "She has better political instincts than I do."

"That doesn't trouble you?" Henrietta asked.

"Good Lord, no." Lucien put the decanter in front of Rupert. "She's a colleague, not a rival, and a superb working partner. Besides, I never meant to go into political journalism: the suffrage thing was rather thrust upon me."

"While Miss Enfield has achieved greatness?" Henrietta murmured, a little cruelly, Aubrey thought.

"No." Lucien tilted his glass, watching the crimson liquid sway. "Probably would have if she were a man, though."

"Ah." Henrietta's eyes softened. She watched Lucien a moment longer, then turned to Rupert. "D'you think Campbell-Bannerman will pay much attention to this petition?"

Rupert picked up his glass. "Hard to say."

Aubrey concentrated on filling uncomfortable pauses in the conversation, though Henrietta and Lucien smoothed over most of them with practiced skill. This was clearly taking real effort for everybody, but they were trying. And because they were all trying, the evening was becoming a success.

Love was too small a word to describe the immense swell of emotion he felt for them all: for each of them; for them all together. Every one of them was here, struggling to find common ground, for his sake alone. Because they loved him, and valued his happiness.

— Chapter Twenty-Three —

LUCIEN WAS SILENT in the carriage on the way home.

It'd been a particularly difficult evening for him, Aubrey realised. He'd started with fear that Aubrey'd reject him for being raised in service, moved on to anxiety over Rupert and Henrietta, and then to doubt that Aubrey could love him. All before he'd walked up the steps of Hernedale House, prepared to be the outsider at the club.

He might be feeling tired now, or insecure. Or both.

Aubrey reached across the dark carriage and took his hand. "Thank you."

"What for?" Lucien's kidskin-gloved fingers curled around his.

Aubrey huffed a laugh. "Dining with a trio of nobs for my sake."

Lucien held his gaze as lamplight slid into the carriage and away again. Then he raised Aubrey's hand, parted his sleeve from the top of his glove, and pressed a long kiss to the inside of his wrist. "You're very welcome," he murmured.

Aubrey slid to his knees on the carriage floor and wrapped his arms around Lucien. His top hat toppled sideways.

"Shit!" Lucien lunged and caught it before it hit the floor. "What the hell are you doing? Your trousers'll get filthy!"

The carriage floor was hard, and his knees felt every jolt in the road. "I don't care." He crushed closer.

"Well I bloody do, you daft nob! Keep your pomade off my dress shirt."

"All right." Aubrey tipped his head back. "Kiss me, then."

Lucien stared into his face as dark succeeded light. Then he sighed and put Aubrey's hat on the seat, and his own beside it. "Bloody hell, Aubrey." He cupped Aubrey's jaw in both hands, laid his fingers along his neck, and met Aubrey's lips with his own.

Aubrey opened his mouth to him, wanting to drink him in like wine. The carriage rumbled over cobbles, jolting their lips and tongues out of rhythm, jolting teeth into lips, and Lucien drew back.

"I won't suggest," he said carefully, "that this is the *worst* idea you've ever had. But it's some way from the best."

"It didn't work out quite as I'd hoped," Aubrey admitted. "What was the best?"

Lucien's gloved hands cradled his cheeks, and Aubrey nestled into them, gazing into his eyes.

"It might've been when you acted to save my career, even though you hardly knew me." Lucien's thumb brushed Aubrey's lips, and Aubrey parted them. "It might've been... when you waited up for me, even though I was hours later than expected." He leaned forward and brushed his lips over Aubrey's, barely touching. To avoid hurting him when the carriage jolted, Aubrey realised.

"It might've been the first time you washed me." Lucien's tongue tip touched the corner of Aubrey's mouth, then swept towards the middle. "Possibly—very possibly—it was when you invited me to use your Christian name, and first called me 'sweetheart'." He tipped Aubrey's head back with his thumbs, held him steady, and gently sucked the vulnerable flesh beneath his chin while Aubrey's head swam. "Or... when you held me when I was angry, and *listened* when I told you hard truths, rather than dismissing them. When you said you'd be there for me, if ever I needed you." His lips traced the line of Aubrey's jaw to his ear.

"I want to say—" he straightened Aubrey's head "—it was when you first said you loved me. Because *that*, my love—" He tugged Aubrey's bottom lip between his own. "Mmm. *That* was definitely one of the very best ideas you've ever had. But I don't think it would've meant as much without all that'd gone before."

He touched his tongue to the join of Aubrey's lips, and Aubrey parted them again. "No. On balance—" his tongue tip dipped between Aubrey's lips, flicked the underside of his top lip, and withdrew "—I'd say the best idea you've ever had, you big, beautiful, daft, talented nob... was loving me."

He sucked Aubrey's lower lip gently, and released it at the next bump. "Loving me then, before you even knew you loved me." He swiped his tongue along the inside edge of Aubrey's lower lip. "Loving me now, on your knees in a jolting carriage." They hit a series of bumps, and Lucien raised his head. "And showing you mean to love me into the future."

"That—" Aubrey remembered to breathe. "That *was* a rather splendid idea. And—do you mean to love me into the future, too?"

"Provided I don't have to clean your trouser knees or polish the scratches from your studs."

Aubrey huffed a laugh, but watched Lucien's eyes: almost impossible to read in the moving, poorly lit carriage.

Still holding his jaw and neck, Lucien leaned his forehead on Aubrey's. They jolted together, over and over, alternately hidden in semi-darkness and revealed to one another by harsh white light. It hurt a bit, but, engulfed in Lucien's scent, secured by his warmth and pressure on face and throat and head, that didn't matter.

"Bloody hell, Aubrey," Lucien whispered at last. "I don't think I can sodding well help it."

Aubrey sucked in a deep breath of dense pomade, of body-warmed leather and wool, of acrid dye. It smelled like relief, like hope, like the lifting of a burden he hadn't known he'd carried. He tugged Lucien's hand across his mouth and pressed his lips to his gloved palm.

Moments later, the carriage slowed, and the weight of Lucien's head lifted from his. They must be almost there. His knees had stiffened on the hard, jolting floor, but Lucien helped him up, and brushed at his trousers when he sat down.

"Poor Grieve." Lucien handed him his top hat and put on his own. "You're an absolute disgrace."

Aubrey heard the warmth in his voice, saw the tilt at the corner of his lips, and grinned. "But you like it."

"I'm not complaining," Lucien admitted. "Who wouldn't want a clever, considerate, beautiful…" He paused.

"Man?" Aubrey suggested.

"Just… you, my love. Who wouldn't want *you* at their feet, asking for kisses?"

The carriage halted. Aubrey tipped the driver and Albany's doorman, then Lucien and he trod the lamp-lit Ropewalk together in silence. Even once the front door was locked behind them, they didn't speak. Aubrey helped Lucien with his overcoat, and Lucien helped him. When Lucien's fingers brushed the side of his neck, he shuddered.

He turned the hall light off, and, with one accord, they passed through the drawing room, lit only by the leaping flames of the fire, into the equally fire-lit bedroom. Aubrey fetched both stud cases and set them on the dressing table, and they undid one another's tricky collar studs. As each turned to finish undressing himself, Aubrey spoke at last.

"Lucien." He laid a hand on his sleeve.

Lucien met his gaze.

"Who wouldn't want to kneel at your feet, sweetheart, asking for your kisses?"

Lucien's face softened. "Let me undress you."

"If I can undress you."

Lucien smiled. "Forgive me, love, if I don't quite trust you to handle my only set of evening dress with the same care I would."

"Nothing to forgive." Aubrey kissed Lucien's cheek. "I wouldn't know how." He guided Lucien's hand to the top button of his waistcoat. "Undress me, then. But only if you want to."

"Tut, Aubrey. You really don't know how." Lucien tapped the bottom button of his waistcoat. "Button up from the top down, but always unbutton from the bottom up. But first, the tailcoat." He stepped behind Aubrey to slide the coat from his shoulders, then turned away to lay it over the bed. A moment later, arms clad only in shirtsleeves reached around Aubrey's waist from behind.

"From the bottom, up." Lucien slipped the bottom button of his waistcoat open. "Elegance, even in undressing. This way, the garment continues to hang well, even when only one button is closed. Also puts less strain on the fabric." He undid the next button.

Aubrey rested his hands on Lucien's arms, immersing himself in the warmth of his body and the ridged flex of muscle through fine cotton. Lucien took the waistcoat from his shoulders, and, after a moment, his arms slipped around Aubrey again, naked this time. He must be undressing himself, even as he undressed Aubrey. The shirt-tail was tugged from Aubrey's trousers, and then Lucien began to undo his shirt studs. From the bottom, up.

Aubrey slid his palms over forearms deliciously textured with hair; over working tendons in the backs of strong hands; over the hard knobs of knuckles. He spread his fingers along Lucien's as they worked up his shirt to the throat.

Lucien's lips pressed his shoulder blade. "Let me put these away."

Aubrey watched him settle each sapphire stud into place, then put his own pearl studs away.

Lucien stepped behind him again. But instead of lifting the shirt off, his bare hands slipped into the open front, and warm palms glided from waist to chest.

Turning his head, tilting it back, Aubrey offered his lips to Lucien, and was rewarded with a kiss.

Warm fingertips brushed his nipples, then pinched and held.

"Oh!" Aubrey sagged against Lucien, eyes closed, gasping. The pinch eased, and Lucien's arms braced him, but Aubrey's body seemed no more inclined to take his weight than before.

"Turn with me," Lucien murmured in his ear. So Aubrey shuffled on the spot with him, until he stopped. "Now. Open your eyes."

Aubrey discovered himself reflected in his dressing table mirror by amber firelight. His hair was mussed, his cheeks flushed, and his head leaned back to bare the side of his neck. His open shirt-front lay partly over Lucien's bare, muscular arms, and his dress trousers strained over his cock.

"Dear God!" He stared at himself as Lucien braced an arm diagonally across his chest; as Lucien's other hand warmed his cock through his trousers. "I look utterly debauched!"

"You look… utterly beautiful." Lucien kissed the side of his neck as he undid Aubrey's trouser buttons and dipped his fingers inside.

Unquestionably debauched. And yet Aubrey couldn't look away as Lucien drew his rigid cock from his drawers and slowly slid his foreskin over the head and back again. There was something… *something* about Lucien's leisurely massage along the length of his cock—about the pressure of Lucien's arm against his chest, and his warm, strong body pressed to his back—combined with seeing it as he felt it. With seeing Lucien's muscular arm bracing his pale, bony body and Lucien's tanned hand wrapped around his cock, framed by open dress trousers. With seeing the top of Lucien's head over his own shoulder, lying against his shoulder-blade, turning to nuzzle the side of his neck… Something about that combination that—

"Dear God," he whispered. "Do you do this often? With mirrors?"

"Never." Lucien laughed softly into his neck. "D'you think many people have this kind of privacy? The only mirror I've had for love is the lake in St James' Park, reflecting the moon and stars, not me. For silk sheets I've had cool grass. And leaves and branches for a tester." His hand worked smoothly.

Aubrey craned to kiss Lucien's temple. "That sounds… rather lovely."

"Haven't you been?"

"I've tended to brief encounters—" he clutched Lucien's arm, gasping "—as—they cross my path. Haven't gone looking."

Lucien's hand slackened and gentled.

"Strictly in darkness." Aubrey nudged into Lucien's hand encouragingly. "Alleys and so forth."

"Well. The Park has its moments, love, in fine weather. And it's always a relief to be among my own kind after days or weeks of being taken for someone I'm not. But very often the weather's not good. And, while police don't prowl there as often as in Hyde Park, it's sufficiently well-known that you have to be alert." He nuzzled Aubrey's shoulder. "If you want to learn to run," he sang softly, "ask a p'liceman!"

"Bastards." Ignoring the urge to race to completion, Aubrey turned and took him in his arms.

"Bloody, sodding, overgrown, malletheaded bastards." Lucien's arms surrounded him, and he rested his head on Aubrey's shoulder.

Aubrey stroked his back and kissed his hair.

"You know," Lucien murmured into his shoulder, "it's just as well you're taller than me."

Aubrey craned to look down at him.

"Otherwise, I'd be cleaning smears off my dress trousers. Fortunately, skin wipes easily."

"Oh."

"Let me get them off while they're still safe."

Aubrey undressed and got into bed. The mirror had been extraordinary, but its moment had passed: to try to reprise it would feel uncomfortably self-conscious.

Lucien climbed in beside him.

Aubrey opened his arms. "You all right?" he murmured.

"Why wouldn't I be?" Lucien curled into him.

"It's been a difficult evening for you, hasn't it, almost from the moment you arrived here."

"Observant fellow." Lucien leaned up on an elbow. Holding Aubrey's gaze, he slowly lowered his torso, crushing him into the mattress.

Aubrey groaned as languor melted his muscles and weighted his eyelids. "I—should be doing this for you," he whispered.

"Why?"

"To—please you."

Warm lips covered his. Muscular fingers slid between his own and tightened, setting his mind spinning. He moaned into Lucien's mouth, hips canting upward, breathless from the pressure on his chest, but craving it all the same.

"That's the way." Lucien held tight till Aubrey's hips relaxed; then his grip slackened, and he stroked his fingers as reaction faded.

Aubrey's breathing eased back to normal, and Lucien lifted their joined hands. A whisper of breath— And a soft kiss, bordered with shallow stubble, grazed the inside of Aubrey's wrist, setting his heart hammering again. "Aubrey."

Dazed, Aubrey opened his eyes to see Lucien watching him, lips still pressed to his wrist. Firelight cast his face in half-shadow; bronzed the line of brow and cheekbone, lips and chin; gilded otter-sleek hair.

"Do you think it doesn't please me," Lucien murmured against sensitive skin, "to hear you gasp and moan at my touch?"

Aubrey watched, breath quickening, as Lucien, still holding his gaze, suckled on his wrist: a light, wet tightness. "I just— thought you might like to relax."

"Oh Aubrey, my love. Provided you enjoy it, *this*—" Lucien tweaked Aubrey's nipple, making him gasp, then soothed the sting with his tongue and the flats of his fingers while Aubrey clung to his back. "That's it, darling: just like that." He knelt astride Aubrey, and slowly lowered his full weight onto him.

Aubrey groaned. His head fell back, and his groin arced into the soft warmth of Lucien's belly.

"Provided you enjoy it, my love…" Lucien sucked Aubrey's nipple into the tight wet heat of his mouth. An ecstatic eternity later, it was replaced by the dry pinch of broad, blunt fingers.

"After the evening I've had…"

Aubrey opened his eyes to see Lucien watching his face.

"…this… is *exactly* what I crave."

THURSDAY, 15ᵀᴴ MARCH 1906

Aubrey yawned, stretched, and propped himself up on an elbow behind Lucien. Gazing down at Lucien's peaceful, sleeping face, he warmed with happiness and uncomplicated affection.

To wake, relaxed and secure, with his lover, was still a new and extraordinary freedom. Other constraints remained, of course, but the dread that a servant might find them together and betray them to the world was gone. And in its absence he noticed the crushing weight of it in his life all the more. The strain of never daring to sleep too deeply or too long, unless he slept alone. The fear of being discovered as he crept across a dim hallway. Thanks to Grieve, nobody would interfere here: he could watch Lucien in peace. The simple pleasure of this tranquil morning was almost ecstatic.

It was true that, without his animating charm, Lucien wasn't classically beautiful, but he was *Lucien*: Aubrey's heart ached for everything Lucien was. He leaned forward to kiss the fine skin at his temple, closing his eyes against a pang at the softness and fragility of it, then wrapped an arm around him and curled closer.

Lucien covered his arm and hand with his own, almost, it seemed, by reflex. "Time to get up?" His voice was slurred with sleep.

"Almost." Aubrey nuzzled and kissed the nape of his neck.

"Mmm." Lucien arched his neck. "How'm I going to use the WC if you keep doing that?"

"Wait for it to go down?" Aubrey sucked his earlobe. "Otherwise: very, very carefully."

"Neither of those options sounds as much fun as what you're pressing into my spine."

"What? This old thing?" Aubrey nudged his back. "Not enough time for that, sweetheart. Besides, you need the WC."

"I do. Damn it."

Aubrey slid spread fingers into the hair on Lucien's belly, closed them, and tugged lightly. Then rolled onto his back and folded his arms behind his head, staring up at the cerulean tester. "I deserve a medal."

Lucien rolled over to look at him. "For waking me in the morning?"

Aubrey huffed a laugh. "For keeping my hands off you whenever you need to leave."

Lucien stroked a gentle finger down his nose, from bridge to tip. Aubrey tipped up his chin and licked it.

"Mischief," Lucien whispered. He laid his finger tip across Aubrey's lips. "How will I ever get up if you keep doing that?"

Aubrey kissed Lucien's finger. "'Up', you say. From what I noticed—" He sucked in just the tip, watching Lucien watch him "—'up' doesn't seem to be your problem this morning." Sucking Lucien's finger in further, he stroked it with his tongue. "Mmm."

"Bloody hell! You wretch!"

Laughing, Aubrey freed his hands to pop Lucien's finger from his mouth. "Well, you started it."

"*Me*? Who woke me with kisses and a bloody truncheon in my spine?"

"Oh. That." Aubrey waved a hand in airy dismissal. "You were already half-way there."

"It doesn't count if I'm asleep."

"I beg to differ. I was awake, and it was right there. Believe me, it counted."

Lucien surged up, straddled Aubrey's hips and held his wrists down beside his head. Aubrey's bones turned to warm water and his mind floated.

"I have to get up," Lucien told him.

"I'm not stopping you," Aubrey whispered. His hips arched involuntarily, brushing the underside of his cock along Lucien's balls. The second time... wasn't involuntary.

"Aubrey." Lucien leaned his forehead against Aubrey's. "My love. I don't want to leave you wanting."

"You won't. My hands are quite adept, I promise you."

"You don't mind?"

"Not at all, sweetheart. I'd rather enjoy the moment and finish off later, if I still want to, than not start at all because there isn't time to finish."

Lucien's eyes searched his.

"Provided it's not frustrating for you, that is," Aubrey added.

"Might've been if I'd thought we had time for more, but no. It was lovely." Lucien kissed him thoroughly, then laid his prickly cheek against Aubrey's. "I have to go," he murmured.

"I know. It's all right."

Lucien sighed and knelt up, taking the covers with him.

Aubrey gazed at the muscled thighs braced over his hips, looked higher, and whistled softly. "Good luck with the WC, sweetheart."

He was so long in the lavatory that Aubrey had time to fetch out his shaving set and work up a lather, find Lucien's clothes and arrange them on the valet stand, refresh the lather, and stand around getting cold, wondering whether he should put on a nightshirt. He was considering going back to bed when the chain rattled and clanked and the water flushed.

"All done?" he asked with mock solicitude when the door opened.

"Eventually," Lucien agreed. "You do tend to stick in a fellow's mind."

Aubrey warmed. "Have a seat." He indicated the dressing stool. "Let me shave you."

Lucien gave him a long look. But then he sat, and Aubrey did the best he could with a face that wasn't his, when he wasn't accustomed to shaving even himself.

It wasn't bad, in the end. Not as close a shave as Grieve would've given him, but not bad for an amateur.

Which Lucien wasn't.

Aubrey sighed. "You'd have done a better job yourself, wouldn't you?"

Lucien ran his fingertips over his face. "It's well done for the most part, love. Just—" His fingers paused under his jaw. "Pass me the razor?" He slid it over the spot, then another couple.

In the absence of hot water, Aubrey dabbed the last of the shaving soap off with a cold, wet facecloth. "Should I have left it to you?"

"No." Lucien tugged him onto his lap, to sit facing him. "I liked it." He drew his head down for a kiss. "The result isn't nearly as important as that you wanted to do it for me."

Aubrey wrapped his legs around Lucien's waist. "That's what I hoped."

"Then you have your wish, beautiful." Lucien's palms settled on his hips, and his forehead on Aubrey's collarbone.

Aubrey folded his arms around Lucien's shoulders, laid his cheek on his head, and took a deep breath, nerving himself. It was foolish to be anxious. This was *Lucien*: he'd no more mock or belittle him than Rupert or Henrietta would.

"Lucien? May I come along to your club? Just once a week?"

Lucien leaned back to stare at him. "You want to *box*?"

Aubrey huffed a nervous laugh. "No, I don't think— But single stick, maybe? I don't practice sabre enough, and—"

"Then a fencing club might be more—"

"Except I'd lose interest after the first class, whereas I know I'll see you at your club, so—"

"Aubrey. Love. I'm there to instruct everybody. I can't spend the whole evening training just you."

"No, well, I only meant to train alongside everyone else."

"You mean—take instruction from working men you don't know?" Lucien's eyes searched his. "From Ben? He's an instructor, too."

"Why not? They're bound to know more than I do about single-stick."

"True."

"Besides, you said last night that I can't understand you, but how will I learn if I never see you in your element?"

Lucien's hands tightened on his hips. "Aubrey. You don't have to—"

"You dined with my lovers for my sake. Least I can do is step into your world from time to time. Unless you'd rather I didn't."

"It's not a question of—" Lucien sighed and rested his forehead on Aubrey's collarbone again. "I was raised on the outskirts of your world. It's not so foreign to me."

"And I'd like your world to be less foreign to me. As it is, apart from you, the only working people I know are servants, and they're obliged to defer to me."

Lucien snorted. "Don't delude yourself, love. I can think of several club members who aren't in service but who'd defer to you anyway, and I really don't want to watch that."

"Oh." Aubrey paused. "No, I quite see that— Well. I wouldn't want to intrude, or to upset anyone."

Lucien's thumb rubbed his hip, over and over. "I suppose... we might try. After all, anyone's welcome to join the club." The thumb stilled, and Lucien leaned back to meet his gaze. "But— Look. If it doesn't work out... if people are uncomfortable... then—"

"I'll stay away," Aubrey promised.

"Right. But bear in mind you might be uncomfortable, too. Those who don't defer to you will likely be more brusque than you're used to. Ben, for instance."

"I'm sure I've mentioned that I went away to school, and that I'm a *younger* son."

"Oh. Good point."

"Besides, I'd like to meet Ben, if he doesn't mind. After all, you know Rupert and Henrietta."

Warm hands settled on Aubrey's thighs. "Might be a good thing, I s'pose, for certain fellows to see a nob's no better than they are."

"That's the spirit," Aubrey encouraged him. "Anyway, nobody'll defer to me after I drop the blasted stick for the third time in five minutes."

Lucien grinned. "Now you're exaggerating."

"Well. Perhaps a little." Aubrey pressed a kiss to the corner of his mouth. "But I really am woefully inept, you know."

"All right. I'll talk to Ben and the other instructors next week. I ought to let them know about you in advance."

"Thank you." Aubrey kissed Lucien till tense muscles loosened beneath his fingers; till Lucien leaned, soft and relaxed, against him. Then he rested his forehead against his and sighed. "You'd probably better get a move on, or you'll be late for work."

Lucien straightened in a hurry. "Damn it, Aubrey, you're a bad influence. Delightful, but very bloody bad."

Climbing off Lucien's lap was accomplished less gracefully than he'd have liked, but then, things often were. He braced himself on Lucien's shoulders while his legs remembered their primary function, then offered him a hand up. "Let me wash you."

Lucien stood. "Not sure I've got time."

"The clock chimed not long ago. Can't be later than ten past nine." He dropped a clean cloth in the basin of water and wrung it out. "Let me do this for you?"

He helped him with his collar and jacket, too, and knelt to button his boots while Lucien arranged his tie with characteristic precision.

If Lucien left his set without a bone-deep certainty that he was wanted and loved and accepted exactly as he was, it wouldn't be for want of trying.

— Chapter Twenty-Four —

A week and a half later, Aubrey sat at Rupert and Henrietta's breakfast table, contentedly buttering a warm muffin. Life with his lovers was falling into a comfortable pattern. Rupert and Henrietta seemed to have settled into the new arrangements, Lucien seemed happier and more secure with him, and he was to introduce himself at Lucien's club tomorrow. The situation wasn't perfect, but since he couldn't see a way for them all to live under one roof—and doubted any of the others would want to— this was as close to ideal as he could imagine. Laying his knife on the side of his plate, he sipped his coffee.

"Any plans for today?" Henrietta asked him.

"Editing that French Revolution story." He took a delicious bite of muffin and scrambled egg.

"Again?" Rupert put down his cutlery. "You've been working on that for at least four months."

Aubrey swallowed. "Six. But it's still not right."

"You could put it aside, just for now." Henrietta lifted her post from the silver salver Mannings offered. "It's probably better than you think."

"Start something else," Rupert agreed, taking his own post. "Maybe you'll see it more clearly if you ignore it for a while."

"But when I look back on it, I might see it's complete rubbish."

Henrietta turned over a postcard and skimmed the back. "In that case, you'll have saved yourself weeks of pointless work."

"Start something new," Rupert said again. "Your writing's good: you just need to trust yourself more."

Aubrey made a non-committal noise and sipped his coffee. How to explain the terror of 'starting something new'? Of the blank, passive page waiting for the miracle of creative genius to stir it to life? The stories he'd written weren't quite right, but at least they existed. He could fiddle with a name here, improve pacing with a comma there, and alter mood with a single verb-change. And if he didn't like it, he could change it again.

"Aunt Margaret will be in London from next week." Henrietta set a letter aside and opened another.

"That'll be nice." Even flawed as they were, the stories he'd written were daunting. An earlier, wittier version of himself—someone who wasn't him at all—must've penned them, because they were surprisingly good. Not good *enough*, of course, but the poor limping brain he was stuck with now could never have developed those stories, nor told them as well.

He should ask Lucien! It came as a blinding flash of insight, though it should've been obvious all along. Lucien began and finished new material every day, and yet somehow it was all very well written. He managed to make a *living* as a writer, for God's sake!

"Rupert?" The sharp concern in Henrietta's tone made him look up.

Rupert, his face pale and tight, his fist clenched around his fork, was rapidly scanning a letter.

Aubrey put his cup down. "Rupe—"

Rupert's fork clattered onto his plate. He shoved his chair back and stalked out, still clutching the letter.

Aubrey met Henrietta's alarmed gaze. This—was more than a miff. Leaving him alone to get over it probably wasn't—

"Aubrey?" she breathed. "I don't think…"

Aubrey shook his head. "Shall I go, or will you?" Close though they all were, sometimes it was best to speak to just one other person.

She dropped her letter and whisked out of the room.

Nerves jangling, Aubrey poked at his egg, then put his cutlery down and sipped his coffee. What on earth could've upset Rupert so badly? Politics? Some disaster with his charities or estates? Please God his mother was safe: she wasn't old, but accidents happened, and she was his only living parent.

The sideboard was laden with food which had smelled deliciously savoury just minutes before, but which now smelled unpleasantly thick with fat. And his eggs were cold.

He carried a fresh cup of coffee into the drawing room and sat staring out of the window at the low, grey sky. A book, picked up for appearance's sake, lay open on his lap, but he couldn't have named the title. When he next thought to reach for his coffee, it was cold.

Some time later, Henrietta swept into the room. She stopped just inside the doorway, fists clenched at her sides. "Come riding with me, Aubrey?"

"Beg pardon?"

Her face was white and tight, and her eyes glittered. "It's a lovely day for a ride."

He stared out at the darkening clouds, then back at her. "Should I...?" He glanced in the direction of Rupert's study.

"Oh no." She laughed brightly. "Come riding. I don't suppose it'll rain till after lunchtime."

"Er. Right-ho. I'll go home and get changed."

Walking down Piccadilly, Aubrey wasn't sure whether Henrietta had needed him out of the house for a while, or whether she needed to talk to him where servants wouldn't overhear her. Or... where Rupert wouldn't? She couldn't visit him at Albany; not without a scandal.

An hour later, trotting through Hyde Park beside her, her groom following behind, he was none the wiser. Henrietta was frenetically over-cheerful, and the park itself blessedly deserted, thanks to the weather. As they approached the Serpentine at a slow walk, Henrietta gestured for the groom to fall back out of earshot. They were in clear view at the lakeside, but would see anyone approaching before they got close enough to overhear them, which was probably the point.

"Here." She pulled a rumpled letter from her sleeve and held it out.

Aubrey looped the reins around his wrist and smoothed the paper over his thigh. "This is the letter Rupert got at breakfast?"

Henrietta nodded tightly. "From Edgar. Enough to ruin anyone's appetite."

A spot of rain struck the small, cramped writing. Then another three. "Henrietta…"

"Just read it."

"Does Rupert know I'm reading this?"

"Of course he damned well does!"

"Yes, of course. Sorry." Aubrey turned his attention to the letter.

Hernedale,

I regret the necessity of penning such a missive to a man whose birth and breeding must command the respect of every right-thinking individual—to a man I call brother—but duty requires it, and I have hesitated too long.

Had you a sister or a daughter, you would already understand my feelings on this matter. Indeed, in a man of honour, empathy would be unnecessary, since every decent impulse would drive him along the correct path. In the absence of decency, simple recognition of duty or concern for one's social standing would suffice. I can only conclude that you lack all these qualities: a reflection which causes me no small concern.

When my father accepted your suit for Henrietta's hand, I was quietly satisfied. I should have recalled then how, as children, you permitted her to lead you into folly after folly, which any child of normal sense and feeling would have reported to an adult rather than join.

However, as a young man, you appeared unexceptionable. Aside from natural advantages of birth and wealth, you seemed sober and studious, lacking the impulsiveness and immature devotion which characterised too many of my sister's admirers. I trusted you would prove a stabilising influence upon a girl who, encouraged by the uncritical reverence of fools, had developed an unbecoming vivacity.

Dear Lord. He did not want to read this. Besides, the letter was becoming speckled with rain. "Henrietta. The ink will run."

"Just read it."

Damnation. Aubrey returned to the letter, reflexively soothing his horse.

You may imagine my dismay, then, after her marriage, as I watched you indulge every one of her whims, no matter how frivolous or unseemly; no matter how inappropriate to her station. Even so, I could never have envisaged the blatant impropriety which has been flaunted in the face of decent Society over the last few weeks.

Heat flooded Aubrey's face.

I speak not of my sister's disgraceful conduct in employing the very lowest of the daily newspapers to advertise her ill-considered opinion of a frivolous play. I speak not of her appalling want of delicacy in publicising her personal weakness in order to further an unspeakable cause. I speak not of your ill-natured discourtesy when I discreetly drew your attention to your duty, as is the obligation of an elder; nor of your vile attempt to force upon me an introduction and acquaintance you knew I should abhor. I speak not of your unwarranted public shunning of your own brother-in-law when I reached out in a spirit of forgiveness to heal the breach between us; the stress of which led to my wife miscarrying the long-awaited infant who would have been my first-born child.

Aubrey raised appalled eyes to Henrietta. "I didn't know Mrs Lowdon was—"

"Nor did I." Henrietta indicated the letter. "Keep going. He has plenty more to say."

I do not expect a man so lost to every decent feeling to recognise the injuries the object of his fevered devotion visits upon her targets.

"Good God!"

However, I had hoped you would recognise injuries affecting that same object, even when those injuries are inflicted by her own compulsive narcissism. To invite a scrounging, presumptuous office boy into your box at her command; to permit him to dally with your wife in a public theatre, was beyond the pale.

Blood drained from Aubrey's face faster than it had risen, leaving him chilled and shaking.

To subsequently permit her to adopt this contemptible character like a runt puppy could only lead to the kind of speculation which you must surely abhor on her behalf, even if you are too abject to resent it on your own. In fine, my sister is the talk of Society, and over an undersized, ill-favoured, ink-fingered office boy at that, and the responsibility rests squarely upon your shoulders.

Your selfish inattentiveness to a girl who requires a watchful eye, and your reluctance to exercise your natural authority as her husband, have led her to this pass. You have turned a high-spirited girl who only needed a firm hand into a harpy who can brook denial of nothing, from a pretty brooch to a vote of her own; into an immoral disgrace who flaunts her cicisbeos in High Society, while you look on, wearing your horns for all to see.

Aubrey's breathing quickened.

This shameless indulgence is not love, whatever you might tell yourself. It is nothing but weakness. If you loved my sister, you would manage your household—and your wife—in a manner befitting your status; you would take your responsibilities as a man and as the head of a noble line seriously. If you loved my sister, or even held her in respect, you would never allow her to comport herself so; to lose all respectability in the eyes of those she must rely upon for friendship.

As if that were not enough, I have lately discovered what manner of acquaintance you introduced into my sister's circle. I had always considered Fanshawe a weak but otherwise inoffensive character; now I am told he is a blubbering catamite.

A blunt ache stabbed Aubrey's chest and thickened his throat. He stared at Henrietta.

"My esteemed brother disapproves of us all, you see, individually and en masse." She gestured to the letter.

How this information escaped Society at the time is a puzzle: I can only suppose it was deliberately restricted to the environs of Eton. More puzzling yet is why you maintained your acquaintance after his blatant degeneracy was exposed. Or, rather, your reasons are altogether too clear, to me and to Society. You have created an environment in which it is impossible for my sister—for any decent woman—to retain either her modesty or her virtue, and for that, I can never forgive you.

You can never fully understand my feelings on these matters, since you have no sister of your own, and, if you had, you would doubtless have married her to a responsible man. In a spirit of Christian charity, which you ill deserve, I hope you may never experience the disappointment and public humiliation of watching a daughter not only fall among wolves, but be cast to them by the very man who once vowed to protect her.

Sincerely,

Edgar Lowdon

With trembling hands, Aubrey folded the letter carefully along its original creases, trying to banish the revenant of old shame which scalded his face and burned the back of his throat. He should've controlled his urges better. Should at least have had the dignity not to satisfy boys who'd despise him for it later. Shouldn't have brought scandal to Rupert's door. Rupert and Henrietta made endless excuses for him, but he'd never forgiven himself. "Where—did he hear about Eton?"

Henrietta waved his question off impatiently. "Someone's dug up ancient gossip, but it won't stick. I'll tell certain ladies I'm pregnant: that'll distract people and provide Rupert with a bit of respectability. Meanwhile, a quick word with each of those Eton chaps—or a hint to their wives—will get their support, and soon everyone will agree the rumours are spiteful nonsense."

"But… people have *heard* them now."

Henrietta's eyes softened. "You'll live it down, darling, as you did before, and so will Rupert. There's nothing more recent to corroborate it. And look on the bright side: once those chaps realise we're willing to sink them with you, they'll be jolly keen to ensure you're never prosecuted for anything similar."

Aubrey stared across the lake, trying to appreciate the bright side— And remembered he wasn't the person most affected by the letter.

"Sweetheart." He turned to her. "Are you all right?"

"This is a load of rubbish." Henrietta shoved the letter violently into her sleeve. "Edgar was delighted when I married Rupert: hoped it'd boost his status. And poor Violet's miscarried three previous infants that I know of."

"Should think just living with Lowdon would be sufficient strain to provoke it."

Henrietta's laughter was shrill and brief. "He— Rupert—" She wiped a gloved hand over her face "—thinks he's ruined me."

Aubrey's breath caught in his throat.

"Dear God, Aubrey! My husband thinks I'm *ruined*." Her voice was a harsh whisper. "He thinks me debauched."

"No," Aubrey managed at last. "He must know you wouldn't— Or Lucien either, for that matter."

She covered her eyes with her hand. "This—isn't about Saxby."

"But the letter—"

"And it's not— He's not blaming me for it. Or—you."

"*Me?*"

"Just himself, for not being enough for me."

Aubrey stared at her, mind straining. They'd been together before she ever married, so how—

"Dear *God*!" Henrietta sucked in a gasping breath. "My oldest friend, and I've made him feel less than a man!"

"He's not—!"

"I know! You have to talk to him, Aubrey." She dropped her hand at last. Her face was pink and blotchy.

"I... can't," he whispered. Not if Rupert believed he'd debauched her.

"Damn it, Aubrey, *listen* to me. I can't convince him myself. Thanks to bloody Edgar, I can't convince him of *anything* now."

Intermittent spots of rain turned to a steady drizzle, soaking through Aubrey's jodhpurs to chill his thighs and knees. His mind ground to a halt.

He'd trusted Rupert for most of his life, and Rupert had trusted him. How could Rupert think him capable of defiling his wife?

His mind limped a step further along a track of logic. He could. Of course he could. Because after all... Aubrey had. He'd had sex with Henrietta—with Rupert's wife—over and over again. In Rupert's bed.

"Oh God!"

While Rupert watched, and believed himself inadequate.

"Oh God! I'm so sorry. I didn't think. I should've—"

"*Don't*, Aubrey!" Henrietta snatched a tiny, lace-edged handkerchief from inside her glove and scrubbed her face. "For God's sake, don't take that away from me. As though I'd have fucked just anyone who happened to be Rupert's best friend!" She crammed the handkerchief back into her glove. "As though I was a puppet, to do my husband's bidding."

"I didn't mean—"

"Well don't! I chose, too. *I* chose to be with you. Maybe it was the wrong decision, but it was mine. I wanted you. *You*, not just some—some—*stud* to satisfy an urge. So don't— Just *don't* take that from me."

"I—" Aubrey's head bent under a crushing weight "—won't. I won't."

Maybe it was the wrong decision. Of course Rupert must come first with her. He was her husband: she was bound to him by law and by daily habit and affection. Aubrey... had simply been a mistake.

But there were more urgent things to address than his hurt. "What... can we do about the gossip about you and Lucien?"

"What gossip? Edgar imagines what he believes should happen—what, in his spiteful heart-of-hearts, he wishes *would* happen—and then makes himself believe it. That's why it sounds convincing. But there's no bloody gossip about Saxby and me. Violet didn't lose her baby because of me. And socialising with Saxby will do my reputation no damned harm at all, as long as Rupert's always with me when I do."

That was something, if she was right, and she often was.

Aubrey straightened and sucked in a painful breath. "But Rupert—"

"Rupert's sitting in his study, riddled with guilt over things that haven't happened—that won't happen—and I can't convince him he's wrong."

"I'll talk to him."

"Aubrey."

He met her gaze.

"My *husband*—" she closed her eyes "—thinks I'm *debauched.*"

"I'll talk to him, sweetheart. And—we shouldn't stay here any longer. Not if he thinks that. Not even with your groom." He turned his horse's head towards the park gate.

"We could stay if *I* was the man." Henrietta almost snarled the words. "If *I* was the bloody husband."

The drizzle turned to rain. By the time they reached Hernedale House, they were both drenched, and Aubrey was chilled to the bone.

"I'd better go home." Aubrey dismounted and helped Henrietta down. "Get dry and then come back and see Rupert." He had dry clothes here, but it felt wrong to make free with Rupert's house now.

The saturated skirt of Henrietta's riding habit clung to her legs and to itself, hobbling her, resisting her attempts to button the long side up out of the way. Aubrey could only watch, helpless. He couldn't touch her, or even her clothes.

"After all," Henrietta said, as though answering him, "whatever happens about me, *he'll* still have you. And you'll still have him."

Aubrey froze, but the groom was already leading the horses away, and the pavement was blessedly empty in the rain.

"And that's what's always been most important to either of you." She yanked at a doubled-over fold plastered to the calf of her boot.

"What?" he whispered.

She looked up, her face damp and pink, her eyes hard. "It's not as though I didn't know from the start."

"Then you knew wrong. Being with you is also the most important thing to me."

"'Also,'" she said flatly.

"There can be more than one most important thing, can't there? Food *and* drink. Shelter *and* warmth."

Her eyes filled with tears. "Dear Lord, Aubrey. You're such a bloody dreamer. And yet I do know exactly what you mean, though I wouldn't have put it quite that way myself."

"But—earlier you said, 'Maybe it was the wrong decision'."

"Because Rupert's my *husband*. I gave him authority over me in law, and now he's wielding it. But I chose you, too. I'd have married you, too."

A hard lump lodged in Aubrey's throat. "Is it all right that— that I'm glad of that? Even under current circumstances?"

She stepped away, putting more distance between them. "Be glad, darling: it's all I can offer you now."

"Only until—you think of a plan."

"There's no plan." She tipped her face up, blinking hard against the rain. "I can't see my way out this time. And you can't dream me out. Whichever way I turn, all I see is closing doors."

"Then I'll *talk* us out of it, sweetheart." He reached for her, then forced his hand back to his side. "I'll break every damned door and smash every window till you can rest or fly as you will."

"If only you could, darling." Henrietta pulled the inadequate handkerchief from her glove and blotted her face. "If only my hands weren't shackled, so I could do it myself." She poked it back into her glove and straightened her shoulders. "But there it is."

He watched her walk up the steps; watched Mannings bow her into the house. Then he turned and walked away, before he had to watch the door of her own home shut her in.

AUBREY FELT NO better after a hot bath, and no better for clean, dry clothes. By the time he was ready to leave his set, rain was sheeting down, so he took a cab.

Lord Hernedale was still in his study, Mannings told him, as a footman took his outdoor things.

Walking down the hallway, Aubrey tugged his watch from his waistcoat pocket. Almost two: Rupert had been there for well over three hours.

He paused outside the study door, bracing himself to face Rupert, whom he adored. Rupert, who'd hurt the woman he adored. Rupert, who'd been accused of degeneracy because of him.

Rupert, whose wife he'd debauched.

His stomach knotted. It had never been this difficult to face Rupert. Never. But waiting wouldn't make it easier, so he took a deep breath and tapped at the door.

No answer.

The knot in his stomach rose to his throat. Clutching the door knob, he took another deep breath and opened the door a crack. "Only me," he said softly.

A sigh. Then, "You'd better come in."

Aubrey slid into the room and closed the door. Forcing a light tone, he said, "Well don't leap for joy, old chap."

"Heh."

Rupert, hair rumpled and eyes pink, sat behind his mahogany desk. Floor-to-ceiling glass-fronted cabinets lined every wall, over-filled with his collection of ancient Greek and Roman amulets and erotica. Arranged on shelves, suspended from bespoke brackets, or braced on walls were shards of pottery and sections of mosaic, whole cups and vases, statuettes, jewellery and dishes in gold, silver and bronze, and fragile rags of papyrus tracked with fading text and illustrations.

Aubrey stopped behind the visitor's chair. "Shall I—sit over here?"

Rupert stared across his desk at the chair, then at Aubrey's hand on the back of chair. "No." He met his gaze at last. "No, that's ridiculous. Drag it round here."

Aubrey set the chair beside Rupert's, and Rupert shoved his own chair back, so they sat almost knee to knee, half-facing one another.

"Hettie says you've read the letter."

"Er. Was that all right?"

"Of course. It concerns you, too."

"I'm sorry, sweetheart. So very sorry your name's been dragged into things I did in—"

"Well. Hettie has a plan, and if necessary, we'll face the buggers down as we did before. There's no damned evidence. It's all hearsay bar the chaps involved, and I invite you to contemplate how willing they'd be to admit it."

Aubrey huffed a relieved laugh.

"And you and I are hardly going to expose one another. But that's not the—" Rupert picked up the small bronze phallus he used as a paperweight. "Thing is…" He closed his eyes, rubbing his thumb up and down its smooth length.

"Rupert?" Aubrey murmured.

"I know what I ought to do, old chap: it's clear as glass. It's just—" He watched his own hand set the paperweight carefully back in place "—damned hard to do, now I see you. Harder, I should say. It was always going to be hard."

Aubrey swallowed past the rough lump in his throat. "Henrietta… indicated she and I can't go on. As we were."

"None of us can. It'd hardly be fair, to expect of her what I don't expect of myself."

"But Lowdon didn't say anything about Henrietta and me." Aubrey felt oddly removed from this conversation. This impossible conversation. "He was talking about Lucien, and he'd never— Nor Henrietta, either: not behind our backs. You know neither of them would ever—"

"Saxby's not the issue."

"That's what Henrietta said. But then I don't understand why you're—" Aubrey struggled to wrench his words into line: for Henrietta's sake; for his own. "I mean, there's no evidence of what Lowdon's accusing Henrietta of, either, since it's not happening, so—"

"Edgar's a disgusting creature." Rupert's voice was cold, but it quivered. "A crap-spattered cock crowing on a dung-hill. No one could despise him more than I. But even a pebble-brained, shit-scratching chicken can accidentally reveal something that bears consideration."

"Rupert. He doesn't know. He's never going to know."

"That's… not the— Hettie should—should never have needed—" Rupert reached for his hand and clutched it. A dark hand clutched Aubrey's heart, too, and squeezed till he could barely breathe for the crushing pain. This wasn't real. It couldn't be happening.

"I should never have married her, knowing how—" Rupert sucked in a shuddering breath "—how I am. That I can never satisfy a woman." His quivering thumb pressed into Aubrey's flesh, rubbing the side of his hand over and over. "Or anyone, really. You shouldn't have had to find other fellows at school or in the street."

"That isn't why—" It wasn't the good kind of pressure. Breathing through the pain in his chest, Aubrey accepted it, and the friction, too, since it was what Rupert needed. "Look. My satisfaction isn't your responsibility."

"Just as well, really."

"Or anyone's but my own. But, as it happens, you've always satisfied me."

"Always?" Rupert's lips twisted into a sardonic smile. "I've *always* satisfied you?"

"Of course."

"When it actually happens, you mean."

"What else would I mean? It happens when we both want it, and when it does, it's satisfying. More than satisfying."

"And the rest of the time?"

"Is my responsibility."

A polite, professional tap at the door. Their hands slid apart, and each leaned back in his chair. A moment later, the door swung open on silent hinges, and a footman paced in, carrying a tray.

"Tea and plum cake, my lord." He placed the tray beside the paperwork and withdrew.

Aubrey poured the tea. "Have you eaten?" Rupert had had hardly any breakfast, and might've missed lunch, too.

Rupert picked up the cake slice and served himself a wedge of cake. "I've let you down, Aubrey. Don't you see that?"

"Not in the least." Aubrey slid him a cup of tea.

"You always meant to marry."

"And I will. When I meet the right woman."

Rupert wrapped his fingers around the delicate china cup. "Tell me about the right woman, Aubrey. What does she look like? Who is she?"

"She's—" Aubrey reached for a slice of cake. With his fingers, since he'd never had much luck balancing anything on a cake slice. "Well-born, I suppose." He wasn't sure he cared about that anymore, but it'd make things easier. He brushed crumbs from his fingers. "Educated." Rupert passed him a napkin. "Thanks. Good company. Reasonable and understanding." He wiped his hands.

"Like Hettie," Rupert murmured.

"I mean— Not Henrietta herself, of course." Aubrey put the napkin beside his plate. "She's married to you."

"*Stuck* with me, anyway." Rupert's cup rattled onto the saucer. "Especially now she's pregnant."

"She wanted to marry you. I just meant... someone *like* Henrietta."

"If I hadn't married Hettie, you two might've made a life together."

Aubrey's heart clenched painfully. If he'd married Henrietta, he wouldn't be about to lose her. Or Rupert. He took a deep, careful breath. "That's not—"

Rupert stabbed his cake with a cake fork. "Back to the right woman. Your wife. Understanding, you said."

"Yes."

"Understanding that you want Hettie and me. That you love us."

"Why not? You've both been understanding. It's not impossible that someone else would be, too."

Rupert put his fork down and shoved his plate aside. "Been doing a lot of thinking today." He reached out, and Aubrey clung to his hand. "You could marry any woman, really. You're attracted to them in general, not just... specifically."

"I mean," Aubrey objected, "not *any*."

"But you could—could function with most women. If it wasn't for me... and if I hadn't introduced you and Hettie, and then let things go... well, the way I did—"

"You didn't." Aubrey tightened his grip. "It wasn't just your decision. It was mine and Henrietta's too. At that point, it wasn't even certain she'd marry you!"

"But think: if you'd never known her... You'd be married by now."

"You can't know that," Aubrey argued.

"I do see things, you know." Rupert's fingertips pressed into the back of his hand. "When you're at Society events, you don't look at the women. Not the way you would if you really planned to marry."

"There's no rush."

"Not while you have Hettie."

"And you."

Rupert squeezed his hand. "You're stifling your life waiting for the impossible. It won't happen."

"What—are you saying?"

"That things were different when we were younger: we didn't have as many responsibilities. But we lost sight of that and just— carried on as we always had." Rupert sat back, looking around. "Maybe this made a difference." He gestured at the display cases. "Maybe immersing myself in all this… twisted my understanding. I thought it'd be all right, provided we all wanted it."

"It *was*. It *is!*"

"Not when the world's so set against it that one person seeing you and Hettie kiss in a carriage could destroy us all, and call the legitimacy of my heir into question."

"I'll be more careful!"

"Not when Hettie could be disgraced, and lose friends, and even family over it."

"But that's always been—!"

"Not when—" Rupert squeezed his eyes shut "—when you open your eyes one day—or have them forced open, humiliatingly, by a loathsome specimen—and see what you've done. Really see it. How your inadequacy risks your wife's happiness and your child's security. How your selfishness injures your dearest friend."

"You haven't injured me!"

"I'm bad for you. As bad for you as I am for Hettie. What kind of man would let her face disgrace? And yet I would have, to protect you and myself."

"To protect her, too!" Aubrey put in. "If the whole truth had come out, people would've—"

Rupert's grip tightened. "I should've destroyed your Saxby before he could—"

"No you bloody shouldn't! Anyway, he wouldn't—"

"Listen! Hettie can't leave me without damaging her reputation, so I have to start taking my responsibilities towards her seriously. I volunteered for the responsibility of satisfying her, so I shouldn't—shouldn't dissipate what virility I have with anyone else and drive her to need others. I should've—Oh God, Aubrey!—I should've let you go, when you first told me you cared for Saxby, so I could fulfil that obligation to her, and so you could be free of me. I need to—to—stop clinging to you as though we were still misfit schoolboys, and let you build your own life. Your own family."

"You're not preventing me build—!"

"But we'll still be friends. Won't we?" Rupert opened bloodshot eyes. "You'll—stand godfather to our baby?"

Aubrey's heart ruptured at that 'our'. At the finality of his exclusion. Breathing through the pain, he said, "Well of course I will."

Rupert's eyes closed. He tilted his chin up and squeezed Aubrey's hand. "If— you don't mind awfully, old chap, I rather need a moment to myself."

"No, I— Of course."

Rupert patted his hand, then released it. "I'll come and see you. Not tomorrow. Not— Well. Perhaps the next day. Or— Sometime, anyway. We'll stay good friends, Aubrey. Won't we?"

Aubrey stood, swallowing past the lump in his throat. "The best."

"Always."

Aubrey squeezed his shoulder. "Always, Rupert."

He let himself out of Rupert's study and closed the door behind him.

Henrietta had company.

"In the front drawing room," Mannings told him. "Shall I announce you?"

She could probably do with the support. God alone knew how she was coping with callers today. But— "No. Convey my apologies to Lady Hernedale: I have to— I have an appointment."

"It's still raining. Shall I send for a hansom?"

A hot prickle behind nose and eyes made the decision for him. "No, no. Quite all right."

He had to wait for a footman to fetch his things and help him into his overcoat. Then he snatched his hat and cane and fled for the front door. The footman wrenched it open an instant before he grabbed the handle himself.

And then he was outside, in a close, drenching rain that fell straight and hard as stair rods and bounced ankle-high off the pavement, where nobody would notice his tears.

AUBREY'S OVERCOAT KEPT out the worst of the rain, but saturated trouser legs clung to his ankles at every step, and by the time he got home, his shoulders and back were damp and chilled.

He rang for Grieve and stood in front of the drawing room fire, dripping onto the hearthrug.

Grieve arrived and paused in the doorway, staring at him.

Aubrey stared back, stunned. *They left me*, he wanted to tell him.

"Perhaps we might remove to the dressing room?" Grieve suggested.

So Aubrey dripped through the bedroom and into the dressing room, then stopped in front of the washstand and dripped there.

Grieve took the saturated hat from his head and the cane from his frozen fingers, unbuttoned his gloves and peeled them from his hands, then eased the overcoat from his shoulders. "Should I draw you another bath, sir?"

They left me.

"No, I don't—" He squeezed his eyes shut. "I don't want to do anything."

As Grieve removed his waistcoat, it struck Aubrey that this was the second set of wet clothes he'd stripped from him in a matter of hours. They'd have to be cleaned, he supposed. Dried. Pressed. "I'm sorry," he said.

Grieve's hands paused on his shirt buttons. "Beg your pardon, sir?"

"The extra work." Aubrey gestured vaguely along his body.

Grieve held his gaze, his face blank. Then, "Ah." He peeled off the rest of Aubrey's clothes in silence, towelled him dry, and dressed him.

"Pot of tea, sir?" Grieve tied his dressing gown cord. "And sandwiches? In front of the fire?"

"Thanks." *They left me.* He slumped onto the sofa.

"Your post, sir." Grieve laid it and the letter knife on the table beside him, then carefully blotted the damp spots from the hearthrug, built up the fire, and disappeared back into the bedroom.

Aubrey stared into the flames. An instant of inattention in a crisis—which had come to nothing, after all, just a fright—and both Rupert and Henrietta were gone. Despite all his anxiety, he hadn't been careful enough, not just that day, but generally. And now Grieve knew about Lucien and himself, and so did Lucien's fellow gossip journalist. And Rupert and Henrietta were— impossibly, inconceivably—gone.

He'd never anticipated life without Rupert. They'd agreed early on that marriage would make no difference to their relationship. Why should it? They'd never bear one another children, or even be socially accepted as lovers, so neither could be a threat to the other's wife. Then Henrietta'd joined them, and she'd seemed equally permanent. Their mutual relationship had felt inevitable; indestructible.

Grieve ghosted past, his arms full of clothes, and the front door opened and closed.

How had he never before realised how much everything depended on Rupert's approval? Rupert was quiet and relatively undemanding, but when Aubrey thought back, he'd always been in charge.

Rupert had the houses where they met and loved, and the title which induced Society to overlook most of his eccentricities—and those of his wife and friend. They'd agreed they all had the right to love as each one wished. But from the moment Rupert and Henrietta married, it hadn't been a right at all, only an indulgence, granted by Rupert and easily revoked.

And why wouldn't Rupert feel entitled to revoke it? He was accustomed to deciding what was best for other people, accustomed to deference. Aubrey himself almost always indulged Rupert's whims and soothed his tempers, and so did Henrietta. Rupert expected it, and somehow it'd just seemed the civil thing to do.

The fire blazed up hot and fierce, almost to the mantelpiece, but Aubrey was chilled to the core. It'd hurt more than he'd expected, to watch Rupert and Henrietta's relationship socially accepted—*celebrated*—while he stood apart, in the shadows. But this! To be cast out altogether. To be told it was for Henrietta's sake and his own, when he loved her, and had lost her, and she had lost him, too. When he knew even Rupert, who'd inflicted this upon them all, was in an agony of loss and despair…

They'd all lain together in love just the night before: how could they be gone from him? How could they *both* be gone?

He couldn't keep brooding on this: it was tearing him to ribbons. He reached for the post.

Invitations. Never before had his own name looked so bald and lonely. It was a foolish thought—his invitations always looked like this—but now that he wasn't certain to go with Rupert and Henrietta, his lone name held a crushing significance. He turned them over, so he wouldn't have to see it.

A letter from Rendall, the editor of the *Athenaeum*. One from Father. One from his second cousin in Kenya, whom he barely knew, but who was an annoyingly keen correspondent. And one from Allenby, his contact at the Foreign Office.

He stared at Allenby's letter, barely breathing, very afraid he knew what it would say. Then sliced the envelope open.

I find myself unable at this time—

"Bloody *fucking* hell and damnation!" He flung the letter at the table. "Fucking... Fucking..." He clutched his head in his hands, sucking in deep breaths. "Bollocks," he whispered.

Whatever Henrietta's plan might be, it was too damned late for him. The gossip wouldn't have mattered as much if he'd meant to go on in the old way, but for a chap who wanted to start a career...

They left—

He snatched up Rendall's letter. Writing would never cover his expenses, but at least it was something he could do, and was praised for.

...with regard to the commissioned story, The Angel of the Bastille. *We note that this story has already missed two deadlines, and note also a pattern of such delays in the submission of Avery Edmonton stories.*

Editors just didn't understand the demands of Art. Or the crushing terror of putting one's name—even if it was just a nom de plume—to work that would be sent into the world for critics to sneer at.

Late submissions entail significant expense as well as considerable inconvenience for the Athenaeum *staff. However, we are reluctant to end our association with an author of such promise, and so we eagerly anticipate receiving* The Angel of the Bastille *promptly on 9th April.*

Aubrey stared at the words. This story wasn't ready. Might never be ready. He folded the letter with trembling hands and shoved it back into its envelope, then hid it under the pile of invitations.

At least Father's letter wouldn't be a demand. Another invitation, probably, but not a demand. And it'd be easy enough to find time for his parents, now that—

He shook out the letter.

My dear Aubrey,

I hoped we might have this conversation tête-à-tête, but since you have been unable to find the time to accept your Mother's invitations, I must explain my intentions in writing.

It has recently become evident, to both your Mother and myself, that you are unlikely to choose to marry.

Dear God. Surely they hadn't heard that gossip? Surely nobody would be so cruel as to tell them?

Our dearest wish has always been that you might find the peace and contentment which springs from mutual affection in a legal union,

No. Oh no. Now really wasn't the time for this.

however, since it is not to be, we must address the issue on more practical grounds.

Your financial situation is precarious, depending, as it does, entirely upon my goodwill, and upon that of your brother after my death. Three weeks ago, Bertie most earnestly represented to me the propriety, nay necessity, of your entering the married state as expeditiously as decorum permits.

Oh God. Bertie damned well *would* do that, if he'd heard the gossip. And he might well tell Father and Mother why.

To that end, he has presented me with a list detailing a number of young ladies he believes might suit the purpose.

Aubrey shut his eyes. It was almost tempting. His marriage settlement would provide enough income to keep his set at Albany as well as a home for a wife. He and Lucien could still have their Saturday and Wednesday nights. A woman who married him so quickly would be marrying for money and status anyway, not for him.

Rupert would maintain him indefinitely—of course he would—but Aubrey couldn't allow it: not now. Couldn't even tell him that he'd lost all hope of a career, in case it seemed like a hint.

It took a while for the cramping ache in his chest to ease to manageable proportions.

I have not troubled to include his list in this missive, since I am reasonably certain none of the suggested candidates would meet your particular needs, and believe it unlikely you could effectively meet theirs. However, you must resign yourself to the fact that Bertie will never approve of your continuing indefinitely in the bachelor state.

Bertie had never approved of a single thing Aubrey did: he wasn't likely to start now.

After giving the matter some considerable thought, and after discussion with your Mother, I have decided to replace your allowance with the settlement you should have received upon marriage. I only grow older, and I should like to ensure that matters are left as I would choose them to be.

To that end, and since evening is evidently a busy time for you, I invite you to attend me at Letchworth House at eleven o'clock tomorrow morning, remaining afterwards to take luncheon with us.

I trust my letter has provided sufficient incentive for you to clear your calendar in our favour upon this occasion. However, we will, of course, understand if you have a vital engagement.

Your Affectionate

Father

P.S. Do remember to ask Mother about her charity work: she has had some successes recently which I know she will want to celebrate with you.

P.P.S: Please convey your Mother's and my warmest regards to Hernedale.

Aubrey stared at the letter. He read the last line again. *Warmest regards.* He scanned back up the page. There! None of the candidates would meet his *particular needs.* And they sent *warmest regards.* To Rupert.

Dear God.

Was it shock over the gossip, or would they always have responded like this? If he'd told them, years ago, how things stood between Rupert and himself... Not about Henrietta: they'd never countenance infidelity with another man's wife— But Rupert... They might have welcomed Rupert as—as what? He wasn't sure, and now he'd never know.

Economic security and his parents' acceptance were literally in his hands, when he'd expected to battle for the first, and never dreamed the second possible. But he'd been ripped from the lovers who'd shared half his life; was raw and bleeding and shockingly reduced. Each agonised breath leaked, warm and sticky, from eyes and nose.

They left me.

— Chapter Twenty-Five —

SWATHED IN HIS dressing gown, feet up on a footstool in front of the fire, Lucien was re-reading Carpenter's *Sex-Love* when the heel of a palm thumped on his door. Mrs Emmott. He locked the slim book in his desk, then opened the door.

"It's quarter to six, Mr Saxby. I need to be in the kitchen, making your bloody dinner, not answering doors and climbing stairs for you."

He stared at her. "Er. Yes?"

"Swanky bloke in the dining room. Get him out in ten minutes: I got to lay the table."

"Righteo." It had to be Aubrey—no other swanky bloke would visit him—but why?

Mrs Emmott turned away. "Quarter to bloody six. What time d'you call that to drop round?"

Aubrey was standing over the meagre fire Mrs Emmott lit to take the chill off the room before dinner.

Lucien closed the dining room door silently behind him. "Aubrey?"

Aubrey turned, his face twisted.

"Shit! What's wrong?"

"Will—you come home with me?" Aubrey husked. "I know—it's not our night till tomorrow, and I might be upsetting your—"

"Just wait here while I get changed, all right? I can't invite you to my rooms: boarding house rules."

"All right." Aubrey's gaze lingered on Lucien's green silk dressing gown.

"Won't be long."

A knock at the front door. The kitchen door slammed open. "Get that *bloody* door, will you, Mr Saxby, since you're there."

"Right you are, Mrs Emmott," Lucien called. "Back in a sec," he told Aubrey.

Frank the footman stood outside, a pair of valises in each hand.

Buggery and damnation. He didn't have time for this.

"Got a load more stuff for you," Frank said, "but there's a cab right in the way. Won't move, either. Just as well I got Jack and Eric to help." He jerked his chin to indicate another two footmen further down the street, both laden with valises and hat boxes.

"I'll get the hackney driver to move."

Lucien startled. He hadn't realised Aubrey was behind him.

"My fault, anyway." A tired smile, and Aubrey stepped out of the house.

So that was that problem solved. Now to get William's cast-offs upstairs in under ten minutes, and get himself ready to leave with Aubrey in the same time. He took two of the valises from Frank and led the way.

In his living room, he paused. "It'll have to go in here." Not enough space in the bedroom. "Behind the table, thanks."

Frank stacked the valises he was carrying, then took the others from Lucien as Jack and Eric shouldered into the room.

"I'll leave you to organise this, Frank. Got to get changed: I was on my way out when you knocked."

"Righto. When should we collect the empty luggage?"

"Couple of days? I'll need a chance to unpack."

"Thursday?"

Jack and Eric tramped out of the room.

"Thanks."

Lucien changed in his bedroom, and combed his hair. When he came out, the stack was broader and higher, and more was coming in. He shrugged into his overcoat, then flipped open his pocket watch. After ten to six. "How're we doing?"

"Couple more loads," Frank told him.

"Righteo." He slipped the watch back into his waistcoat pocket. "I'll be downstairs with my visitor."

Aubrey was waiting in the dining room, watching the footmen tread up the stairs.

"Sorry to keep you: they're almost done. Didn't expect this today."

"Planning to open a shop?" Aubrey's narrow lips ticked up on one side, but he didn't look amused.

Lucien mustered a laugh. "Just stuff from William. I think he's run mad. God knows where I'm going to put it all."

Aubrey stared at him, wordless. Lucien held his smile in the face of Aubrey's bewildering blankness.

At last, Aubrey wet his lips. "Any special reason for it?"

"Probably just took it into his head I needed it. You all right?" He looked worse than before.

"Quite all right." Aubrey's tone was light.

Buggery.

Frank rapped on the open dining room door in a way he never would in Camberhithe House. "All done, Mr Saxby."

"Thanks." Lucien tipped the footmen, desperate to get Aubrey back to Albany before he cracked. "Give my regards to Mr McHenry and Mrs Spence." He closed the front door behind them. "Got to get my hat and cane and lock my door. Back in a sec."

When he came downstairs, Aubrey was standing in the narrow hallway, and Mrs Emmott was jangling cutlery aggressively on the table.

"Oh, Lord. Sorry. Let's go." He let them into the street and glanced around. "Did you say that was your cab waiting?"

"Over there." They climbed in and closed the door, and the horses started moving. "Your landlady's a bit of a dragon," Aubrey observed.

"She's... busy." Lucien fell in with Aubrey's apparent strategy of keeping himself distracted. "And running a boarding house doesn't pay well, not in this area, anyway. It's hard work, with only her daughter and herself to do everything."

"Didn't see a daughter."

"It's a boarding house for single men, and she's a responsible parent. Her daughter stays in the kitchen and laundry: only works in the body of the house when all the boarders are out."

"Ah."

"Another reason for Mrs Emmott being personally unapproachable, too: some men are pigs."

"An even more unpleasant job than it seems on the surface."

Lucien smiled tightly, thinking of Mrs Emmott carrying breakfast to men's rooms: accepting extra work and personal risk to save the cost of heating the dining room. "That's being in service for you."

Aubrey stretched out a leg and rubbed his calf along Lucien's, then left it pressed against him. Leaning into the corner of the cab, he tipped his head back and his top hat forward, closed his eyes, and swallowed.

Lucien watched him. Should he try to distract him, or did Aubrey need a moment to manage his emotions? He looked fragile enough that even holding his hand might set him off.

"How's the writing going?" he ventured.

"Oh God!"

"Sorry. Bad choice of topic?"

"I have a deadline. An actual—!" Aubrey took a deep breath. "Two weeks. I won't make it."

"Oh." Was that why he was so upset?

Aubrey opened his eyes and leaned forward. "Will you help me?"

Lucien stared at his pale, strained face. "With—*writing*? I don't— I mean, I'm not a fiction writer or editor or anything of that sort. Anyway, your writing's bloody good as it is."

"I'm tangled up in knots with this one and—" Aubrey paused. "No. Fact is, I get tangled up in knots with every story, and it takes me too long to make them publishable. I want to write, and I think I could be a decent author if I could just—if I could just *tell* when a thing's good enough. And how to start something new. I need help."

Lucien watched him. "You mean reassurance?"

"No. *Help*, sweetheart. With planning, and speeding up, and not brooding over every comma, like you said."

"Ah. Well." Lucien took his hand, turned it over, and kissed the inside of his wrist. "That I might be able to help with."

"Thank you. But only if you're not already sick of words by the time you arrive."

That Aubrey could be considerate even amid distress made Lucien's heart turn over. "Grieve said we should find a justification for me visiting you," he murmured. "Might this be one?"

"It's a start." Aubrey smiled tiredly. "Thank you. That's one thing down, anyway, or at least, on the way to being resolved." He leaned his head back again and closed his eyes.

So that hadn't been the main problem. Maybe he should've spun out the writing conversation to keep Aubrey's mind occupied. Too late now.

"Anyway. We were talking about—" Aubrey swallowed, eyes still closed "—about Camberhithe. Don't— Well, don't feel obliged to continue if you'd rather not, but if you don't mind…"

"I don't. But I'm not sure what there is to say."

"Well. How did you meet?"

Ah now, *this* he could do. Lucien settled in to talk about William. He could easily spin it out until they got to Albany. Then he'd find out what the devil was up with his lover.

WHEN LUCIEN WALKED into the drawing room, Aubrey was already at the sideboard, decanter in hand.

"Take a seat." Aubrey nodded towards the sofa, then joined Lucien, handing him a glass of brandy. "Got to tell you something."

"Have you." Recent experience suggested that wasn't an introduction to good news.

Aubrey set his glass carefully on the occasional table. "Look, I don't mean to bore you or embarrass myself, but after the day I've had, I've—" His lips twisted. "Well, let's say I've learned it doesn't pay to keep what you're thinking from a lover, and—and fret over it alone, even if it seems a small thing."

"And... what are you thinking?"

Aubrey met his gaze. "I thought you might become exclusive with another fellow. Let him maintain you. Leave me."

"But—*why*?"

"It was—" Aubrey gestured vaguely. "You know, visiting another chap late into the night. And then—it turned out to be *Camberhithe*, who—you know—wealthy, sickly, no wife, probably lonely. It just seemed—"

"Dear God." Lucien stared at Aubrey. The next moment, his glass thumped down on the table and he was laughing uncontrollably. "*William*? Oh dear *God*!"

"I stopped thinking that quite quickly, when you wouldn't accept anything from me. But then today... I thought that might be his overture. Well, I mean. Why else would a chap send clothes, and so many? Why else would you accept them?"

Lucien reached for Aubrey's hand, still grinning. "He'd certainly look after me, given half a chance, but not for that reason."

"I see that now." Aubrey's hand turned in Lucien's, squeezing his fingers. "It was— Well, it's been a bit of a bad day, frankly: I was predisposed to fear the worst."

"Aubrey. I have a job. A perfectly respectable job."

"Fellow with a job might still prefer to live more comfortably if he could. *I* would."

Lucien paused. "Even if it meant leaving me?"

"No." Aubrey held Lucien's hand to his cheek. "No. I'd take the damned job. Any job."

"Well so would I, you daft nob. Even if independence wasn't more important to me than comfort anyway."

"Even though I'm a nob?"

Lucien kissed Aubrey's warm forehead. "Just because you're you."

Sighing, Aubrey rested his head on Lucien's shoulder. "Must've taken a lot for you to get past that." His tone was uncertain.

"You underestimate your very considerable charms."

Aubrey huffed a laugh, but his body was tense.

"Anyway," Lucien murmured against his temple. "You love me, too. Must've taken a lot to accept that, with your background."

"I do. Be difficult not to, you know. I've never met a kinder, more generous, more honourable fellow, and I can't imagine a better companion."

Lucien's heart swelled till it filled his throat and forced tears into his eyes. He tightened his arm around Aubrey and pressed a long kiss to his forehead. "Dear God," he husked. "What a unique treasure you are, my love."

Aubrey sucked in a long, shuddering breath, and then he was clinging to Lucien and sobbing: painful, gasping, breath-robbing sobs.

"What's the matter?" Lucien held him. "Did something—" He rubbed soothing circles on Aubrey's back. "You obviously didn't visit me to ask about William."

Aubrey's head rocked on Lucien's shoulder. No. "They left me," he croaked.

"What? Who did?"

"Rupert—" Aubrey sucked in another shuddering breath. "Lowdon wrote to him. He's— Oh God, Lucien, he's left me. And—and so has Henrietta. And then I thought you would, too. And—"

"Ah no, love: I'm here. Right here." Lucien dug a hankie out of his pocket and tried to mop Aubrey's face while holding him. Tightly, because tight felt safe, for Aubrey. Anchored.

"They *left* me!"

He wanted to say, 'I'm here: you don't need them.' But with Aubrey weeping, desolate, into his jacket, that clearly wasn't true. Aubrey loved him—more than he could ever have hoped—but he loved the Hernedales too, and he was grieving a terrible loss.

If he could just—*be* the only person Aubrey loved! If it was down to him, Aubrey'd never be this sodding miserable. If he could be everything Aubrey needed, he could—could manage things, so Aubrey stayed happy. He could *make* him happy; keep him happy.

But he couldn't be. He wasn't. Aubrey needed the Hernedales, too. And since he needed them, Lucien desperately wanted them for him. And the sodding nobs had bloody well abandoned him.

Tucking his face into Aubrey's hair, Lucien held him, and rocked him, and tried not to cry with him. Because that wouldn't help at all.

AUBREY TOLD HIM everything. Lucien was certain of that, because he told him some bloody personal things about Hernedale.

"Should you be telling me this?" he asked uncomfortably.

"I don't want you to blame him: it's not his fault. And there's no other way to explain that."

"But I'm sure he'd rather I didn't know. If it didn't trouble him, he wouldn't have reacted this way."

"It shouldn't trouble him!" Aubrey, his head resting on Lucien's belly, started weeping again. "There's nothing *wrong* with him. I'm so sick of stupid rules dictating how we're allowed to love. We're made to feel ashamed if we want sex, and ashamed if we don't. Ashamed if we never marry, and ashamed if we adore the people we marry. Who damned well decides what's right for everybody?"

"I don't know. Society." Lucien stroked Aubrey's hair. "A cobbled-together monster that everyone obeys or hides from because if they don't, they're punished."

"Bloody Lowdon! Trying to make Henrietta ashamed of flirting, and of having a brain. Trying to make Rupert ashamed of loving her and not controlling everything she does. I'm *sick* of it!"

Lucien held him, wordless. He should loathe Hernedale for devastating Aubrey. But even as he seethed over his autocratic high-handedness, he ached for the steadfast fellow who'd stood by Aubrey through scandal when he was barely more than a child, yet considered himself inadequate: a burden to his lovers. On the other hand, he'd like to spit sodding Lowdon on a sabre like the green mamba he was: throat to skull would do nicely.

"As for Eton: I didn't— Most of them came to *me*, you know." Aubrey's voice was thick and nasal. "Nobody got hurt."

"Except you."

Aubrey sighed. "Well."

"That was probably my fault."

"Don't be—"

"The rumour reviving, I mean."

Aubrey stared up at him through puffy red eyes.

"I'm sorry. I told William I was meeting the Hernedales that first Sunday, and he remembered the rumour later. Thought I'd convinced him it was malicious nonsense, but maybe he'd already told someone else. I'm so sorry."

"Well." Aubrey burrowed into him again, shoulders tense. "Long as you're not afraid to be associated with me."

Lucien rubbed the back of Aubrey's neck. "Couldn't possibly do without you."

"Anyway, Henrietta said she'd put a stop to the rumour." Muscles eased under Lucien's fingers. "And I won't need work since I'll have a settlement."

"You were serious about finding work?"

"Mmm."

"Good Lord," Lucien murmured.

Aubrey shook with silent laughter. "I could've done it."

"I know."

"Now I'll start a charity for sick children instead."

Lucien stilled.

"That'll keep me busy."

"Very."

Aubrey's fingers slipped between his shirt buttons. "Tell Ben? His baby should come first."

"I will." His voice was hoarse. "Thank you."

Lucien's shirt grew warm and wet beneath Aubrey's face.

"Rupert—would be the best person to advise me on managing a charity. But it might be too—"

Lucien waited, but Aubrey didn't say anything more.

"Will you talk to him?" Lucien asked at last.

Aubrey sucked in a deep, shuddering breath. "He said he'd come and see me. When he's ready."

"And—you mean to wait for that?"

"What else would I do?"

Damn it. Lucien didn't want to send his vulnerable fellow out to court another rejection, but he couldn't fix his relationships for him. "Well I tell you what, love. When an enemy's convinced your ally to do something that injures you both, what you *don't* do is leave your ally to bleed alone with the enemy's words ringing in his ears. You fix yourself up as best you can, then drag yourself over there on your last remaining limb and slap a bandage on his wound. And then you make your own bloody point."

"He's distressed. He needs time to himself."

"And you left when he asked you to, so he's had that. Seems to me if he has much more time to himself, he'll dig himself into a pit of despair and drag the spoil in on top." He rubbed Aubrey's neck, letting him think it through.

When he didn't answer, Lucien sighed. "Look, it'd be different if this was Hernedale's own idea, but it wasn't. Lowdon meant to make him doubt his worth and his manhood, and because of—well, circumstances Lowdon couldn't have known, he's succeeded. Lowdon meant to make Hernedale act the dictator in his marriage, and he's bloody well succeeded. Hernedale mightn't mean to control his wife, but he's doing it anyway, however good his intentions."

Aubrey sat up, staring. "Oh, God. He is, isn't he?"

"And I can't see Lady Hernedale taking kindly to him coming over all autocratic. Besides, this isn't what any of you signed up for when you made your arrangement."

"No." Aubrey curled up against Lucien and reached for his hand. "It definitely bloody well isn't."

— Chapter Twenty-Six —

TUESDAY, 27TH MARCH 1906

The following morning, Lucien left Aubrey curled up in bed—pale and exhausted, eyes burning red, nose and eyelids swollen and pink—with a promise to come back later. "Around seven, while everyone's busy getting dressed for dinner."

Mind dull and fuzzy with fatigue, burdened with rage that he couldn't just *fix* this for Aubrey, he trudged upstairs to his office. Into a cacophony of agitated voices.

Bloody, sodding hell. What now? He hooked his hat and riding cane on the coat-stand.

"Saxby!" Miss Enfield called.

"Here." He slid off his overcoat, already exhausted by all the excitement.

"We *won*!"

"That's good." He hung up his coat and turned to face a room full of arguing men. And Miss Enfield. "Won what now?"

"Our Downing Street article! With the countess!"

"Yes?"

"Just had a statement from Mrs Drummond. The PM set a date to meet them!"

"An actual date?" He pulled out his chair and dropped into it. "To meet the WSPU? About *suffrage*?"

"19th of May!" Miss Enfield raised her voice over the swelling din in the office. "Over two hundred Members of

Parliament signed that petition you wrote about. Nearly a third of all MPs! From all parties! Most of them because of the Downing Street incident, and because of the way we presented it, and because of your dashed countess!"

"She's not mine." Not Aubrey's either, anymore. He swallowed an aching lump in his throat.

"You know what I mean," she said impatiently. "Your contacts. Your sources. We made a *difference*. And my name's on the by-line! Of an influential political article!"

"Congratulations." He dredged up a smile. "Truly. You worked hard for this."

"And women's suffrage finally has some momentum! Finally!"

"I mean." Lucien rubbed his face, biting back a yawn. "Provided the PM'll listen to ladies."

"But it's the MPs as well! He's agreed to meet a delegation of the petition signatories, as well as representatives of all women's suffrage groups. All of them!"

Lucien's spine straightened. "*What?*" No riots; no injuries. Just a third of MPs changing their minds, partly because of their article. Because Lady Hernedale's statement had enabled them to write their article the way Miss Enfield wanted it written.

It shouldn't have taken that—they shouldn't have needed a nob's support to express their outrage in print—but hadn't he complained that wealthy women weren't walking beside working women; weren't using their influence to gain votes for women? He couldn't have it both ways. It was an imperfect world. But in this imperfect world, some people, at least, were trying to help.

Dragging his weary body to its feet, he bowed to Miss Enfield. Not the measured dip of the head a butler might offer a nob, but a courtly, absurdly old-fashioned bow. "You were right," he said. "Right to angle the report as you did. I'd never have chosen to present it that way, but you were right. You got the result. The palm for this absolutely goes to you."

Miss Enfield's laugh was high with excitement, and a bit unnerved. "Bloody hell, Saxby! You're well on your way to becoming my favourite fellow."

"Just give up, Saxby," Chiddicks sneered from behind them. "There're easier petticoats to lift. Younger and much prettier, too."

All Lucien's hurt and frustration—all his disgust of the bitter, inadequate men who could only feel strong when they were crushing others; who kept others semi-silenced unless some nob spoke for them; who forced others into dark alleys and poisoned their joy with fear; who set police and hard labour upon them; who injured their own lovers and children—swelled to squeeze his heart and throat. And then burst.

He slowly turned to face Chiddicks. "How would you like," he asked, "to be dangled out of this window by your stunted *sodding* bollocks?"

The room silenced. Chiddicks swallowed and straightened his shoulders. "Now just a minute, Saxby!"

"Because I'm *bloody* tempted to oblige, regardless of your sodding opinion."

"Steady on!" Old Tomlinson muttered. "Steady on!"

Lucien turned on him. "I'll steady on when Chiddicks learns some bloody manners! Would you put up with that sort of comment if it was about you? If he'd devalued *your* achievement by suggesting a deserved accolade was no more than lecherous flattery? If he'd said there were easier trousers than *yours* to unbutton—"

"Good God, Saxby!" Old Tomlinson clutched the table.

"—and younger and handsomer, too?"

"You can't use that sort of language to a work colleague!"

"No," Lucien said slowly, "he bloody well shouldn't. Should he?"

A frozen silence, while Old Tomlinson stared at him, and Lucien stared back.

Then the man dropped his gaze. "Chiddicks! Mind your language. There are ladies present." Which missed the point, but

Chiddicks flushed and turned away, which was better than nothing.

It shouldn't have been necessary to point out that women were as entitled to basic respect as men. It shouldn't have needed a man to speak for a woman. But that was how the world was, for now. Unbalanced. Unjust. Those whose words had weight had to speak for those whose words were accounted no more than feathers just because they were poor, or uneducated, or wore petticoats, or loved their own sex; for those whose voices were heard only by the indulgence of the powerful, not by right.

Lucien met Miss Enfield's gaze. "Sorry for spoiling your triumph."

"I'm currently enjoying satisfaction of a rather different kind." She patted his arm. "Thanks, Saxby. It won't last, but I appreciate it. And by the way, do let me know in advance the next time you mean to let rip: I'd hate to miss it."

DESPITE THE ACCEPTANCE in Father's letter, Aubrey was quivering inside by the time he walked into his parents' drawing room. But they greeted him without a hint of consciousness, and without mentioning Rupert or the gossip at all.

Aubrey's man of business was perfectly capable, but Father, of course, wanted to explain the provisions of his settlement in minute detail. After an hour in the dark, wood-panelled study, Aubrey felt a little better informed, and much wealthier, but essentially incompetent. When it came to finance, his mind was brutally uncooperative. Just as well Father was patient.

Lunch should've been pleasant, but he spent it in a fog of anxiety, waiting for someone to mention Rupert. That discussion would always have been nerve-wracking. Today—grieving Rupert's absence and furious at his blind paternalism; over-aware that Mother and Father had heard humiliating gossip about a period he tried to forget—it was unspeakable. *A blubbering catamite.* The words sliced him to the soul.

But Mother was delighted when he asked about her charities and social engagements, and Father enjoyed talking about his clubs and astronomy society, and Rupert didn't come up. Aubrey was relieved, and also, inexplicably, hurt.

Maybe, he thought, walking to Hernedale House afterwards, they'd never meant to raise the subject face-to-face. Maybe the only mention they'd ever make of it would be that single, oblique postscript.

Just days ago, one of his deepest fears had been that his parents would discover his relationship with Rupert and Henrietta. Now... Now he knew how it felt for them to know— about Rupert, at least—and accept him anyway. He wanted that, more than he'd have believed possible even twenty-four hours ago, even if it meant confirming degrading gossip. He wanted to bring Rupert to visit them, not as his friend, but as his lover. He wanted to say to them, "Ask Rupert about his charities".

Having stood for a few hours in clear light, he didn't want to crawl back into the shadows. But that might be what it took for them to tolerate him as he was.

Unless... Maybe they hadn't heard the gossip: maybe Bertie'd done the decent thing, and not enlightened them. Maybe Father'd meant exactly what he'd said in his letter: that he didn't want Aubrey pushed into marriage when he wasn't a marrying kind of chap. Maybe there'd never been any light at all, only hopeful imaginings and self-delusion.

He might never know, he realised, as he trod up the steps to Hernedale House. Impossible to introduce the subject himself, only to explain that Rupert wasn't his lover anymore.

He might introduce Lucien, instead.

But there, imagination balked. There was no chance on God's green earth that his parents would accept Lucien. A Daily Mail Society journalist, raised in service and trained as a valet? They'd never see past that, any more than if Aubrey meant to marry a woman raised to be a lady's maid.

A footman took his outdoor things.

"Hernedale?"

"In his study, Mr Fanshawe," Mannings said. "But he's not to be disturbed."

Well he was damned well going to be.

"Lady Hernedale is in the front drawing room," the butler suggested.

Aubrey paused. He could discuss things with her first. But no: he was just trying to put off the awful moment. Henrietta'd already told him what she wanted. Besides, he shouldn't be alone with her until he'd thrashed this out with Rupert. "Please advise Lady Hernedale that I'm here." She'd know why. "For now, I'll see Hernedale."

"I'm afraid he's not to be disturbed, Mr Fanshawe." Mannings slid in front of him.

"That doesn't apply to me. He'll see me."

While Mannings stood frozen between proper form, which Rupert would certainly prefer, and contradicting a man who'd been Rupert's close friend long before he started to work for him, Aubrey strode around him and down the hallway.

He couldn't linger outside the study door nerving himself up—Mannings might regain his sense at any moment—so he knocked once, then stepped into the room and closed the door.

Rupert looked up from a document, his face tired and strained. Hope and hurt and loss blazed in his eyes when he saw Aubrey, and then they shuttered. "I'm sorry. I can't talk today."

"Can't talk to anybody?" Aubrey gripped the back of the visitor's chair. "Or just—can't talk to me?"

A diffident tap. Aubrey and Rupert stared at one another across the wide desk. The door opened and Mannings glided in.

"Please excuse the intrusion, my lord. Might I offer refreshment? Or perhaps some—" he paused delicately "—other service?"

A pair of burly footmen waited beyond the open door.

"I told Mannings you'd see me." Aubrey held Rupert's gaze. *Will you really have them escort me out?*

Rupert glanced at Mannings beside the door, at the footmen in the hallway, then stared at Aubrey. Blowing out a long breath, he rubbed both hands over his face. "Tea, please, Mannings. And some sort of snack."

Mannings ghosted out, closing the door without a sound.

"Damn it, Aubrey." Rupert propped his elbows on the desk and dropped his head into his hands.

"I'm sorry. I'm sorry, swee—" Aubrey swallowed past the lump in his throat. "Please can we talk?"

Rupert leaned back, his eyes closed. "Pull up a damned pew."

So Aubrey dragged the visitor's chair around and sat staring at him, absorbing every inch of his beloved, familiar face and body. "You look so tired."

"Bad night." Rupert's lips twitched in a parody of a reassuring smile.

"I'm sorry. And I'm so very sorry I didn't realise before that you felt—well, the way you feel."

Rupert opened his eyes. "What way is that?"

Aubrey took a deep breath. "Unmanned. Because if I had, I'd have done more to reassure you."

"Reassurance won't fix me."

Aubrey's fists clenched in his lap. "There's nothing damned well wrong with you! You're *you*—perfectly you—and that's all I ever wanted you to be. All Henrietta ever wanted."

Rupert squeezed his eyes shut and swallowed. "Hettie," he husked, "was *desperate*."

"No, sweetheart! No! She'd never—"

Oh. Oh God. That night. When she'd teased Aubrey for being susceptible, and he'd asked if she was, too, and Henrietta... *Oh my dear*, Henrietta had breathed, *I'm positively desperate*.

"Rupert, *no*. She didn't mean—"

"It was a clear statement of fact."

Rupert had turned from them after she'd said it. He'd been wounded. And they hadn't noticed.

"But why didn't you—?" No. No, he wasn't going to blame Rupert for being hurt. "We didn't know you felt that way. I didn't know. You'd always seemed comfortable with—with your libido. *I'm* comfortable with it."

"Then why did you say what you did about that condom?"

"The—?" Aubrey cast his mind back.

"That my valet would know it couldn't possibly be mine. That nobody'd believe I might have a mistress."

"No. Wait a minute. I didn't mean—" But it was clear now, how it might've sounded to a man who felt inadequate. "Ah, no, sweetheart." Aubrey reached for his hand, but drew back before he touched. "I only meant he'd know you didn't own a case like that. I only meant... you're not away from home often enough for a man who keeps a mistress or regularly visits prostitutes. Not— Oh Lord, Rupert, I'd never have said that. Never!"

Rupert said nothing.

"How—long have you felt this way?" Surely not all the way back to Eton? Aubrey'd found other chaps for quick satisfaction from the start, from before they considered their relationship a relationship.

"It was only an occasional niggle to begin with. But then—" Rupert opened his eyes and reached for the phallic paperweight with a quivering hand. "Six years. Six *years* to seed a child in a healthy woman. D'you know what I was thinking, Aubrey?"

"No," Aubrey whispered, watching his fingers on the talisman.

"I was thinking— That Hettie was twenty-nine: it was getting too late. That I was damned if I'd let Frederick inherit the estate just to—well, as Catullus says, to fuck it away—and leave the rest of the family and my charities destitute. I was thinking, if I failed again this year, that—that I'd ask you and Hettie to consider—" his hand closed over the phallus and his knuckles whitened "—consider making up for my incapacity."

Aubrey did lay his hand over Rupert's, then: how could he not?

"Can you see—what a dreadful thing it would've been? I'd have cheated my family of their inheritance; my name of its lineage. I'd have denied you paternal rights to your own child. I'd have asked Hettie to bear another man's child and never acknowledge him. This— It goes beyond my inadequacies in the bedroom to twist my thinking. And I don't know what else it's twisted."

Aubrey clutched the back of Rupert's hand, the knuckles hard and knobbed under his palm. "Not us, sweetheart. Not you and me. That was never twisted. And not being with Henrietta either."

"Other people wouldn't think that, if they knew."

"I don't damned well care what other people think! They've no way of judging what lies between us except their own prejudices, and even those are only fashions. This amulet." He squeezed Rupert's hand. "Almost any man in England will tell you it's pornographic, even those who know damned well it was designed to protect against vicious envy. I love you and I love Henrietta, and I know you both love me. We've always respected one another. We've never purposely hurt one another. Are you telling me that these—" he jerked his chin at Rupert's paperwork "—*these* marriages, where women and children are frightened and beaten, are more honourable than our relationship? Because I don't damned well believe it."

"No," Rupert murmured. "No, that can't be right."

"We were happy, Rupert. All of us, I think. You *were* happy, weren't you? Except for this problem that's only a problem because other people say it is."

"Hettie wasn't."

"Dear God, Rupert! Let's call her in here and ask, shall we? Because I'm certain she loves and wants you just as you are. She wouldn't choose me over you for the sake of more frequent tupping. She knew when she married you that she wouldn't get that from you, but she chose you anyway. She doesn't need you to be the whole of her life, any more than I do. Any more than you need me to be the whole of your life. We all have other interests and family and friends: people who meet our other needs. We only need you to be *you*."

Rupert's hand turned in Aubrey's, and uncurled, and then their fingers interlaced, the bronze phallus warm between them.

"Me wanting sex with other people from time to time— That has nothing to do with your libido, and everything to do with mine. And if you're suggesting you should've been responsible for my libido, or that you were somehow responsible for what I chose to do with my body, well... honestly, that's patronising. Arrogant, too."

Rupert sucked in a quick breath.

Aubrey squeezed his hand, hoping to lighten the blow. "As for the alternative you think you should've provided: I don't want you forcing yourself to satisfy me. Just thinking about it makes me feel humiliated and selfish and greedy—as though there's something excessive about my libido."

"No! I didn't mean to—"

"I know. You wouldn't. But when— Look, it's none of my business, but can I suggest you ask Henrietta how she feels about it, before you inflict that particular generosity on her?"

Rupert's face tightened. Aubrey followed his gaze to a mosaic mounted on the wall. Priapus weighed his massive phallus in one pan of a scale, balancing it against a huge basket of fresh produce.

Aubrey sighed. "Rupert." He waited till he had his attention. "I don't want you just for sex, wonderful though it is."

"When we have it," Rupert muttered.

"Exactly." Aubrey refused to endorse his needless shame. "When we have it, it's wonderful, but so is almost everything else about our relationship. I want you for *you*: all of you. I don't need a relationship just for sex: I can get that elsewhere relatively easily, as you very well know. I don't want Henrietta and Lucien just for sex, either, or to make up for any lack in you. They couldn't, anyway. In the first place, because you're not lacking, and in the second, because they're simply not you. You're not interchangeable. I mean, you didn't want Henrietta just for sex, did you? Unless—" he glanced from Rupert to Priapus as suspicion gathered "—you only married her to bear you an heir."

"Good God, no!"

"Well thank God for that." Henrietta deserved to be more than a brood-mare to a man she loved.

"I wanted her for herself, and you for yourself. And I do see what you mean." Rupert's hand tightened on his. "But the fact remains: I'm no good for you. Saxby probably isn't, either. We hold you back. You need to marry."

"Actually, I don't." Awkwardly one-handed, Aubrey reached into the inside pocket of his morning coat and pulled out Father's letter and the documents detailing transfer of assets. "And even if I did, it'd be up to me to make that decision, not up to you to drive me into it."

Rupert slid his hand from Aubrey's, put the paperweight down, and read the letter. He paused at the end, staring at the postscript. "Does he mean—"

A discreet tap. Rupert folded Aubrey's papers, and they waited, watching the door.

Mannings brought in the tea tray, followed by a footman carrying a large three tier cake stand holding sandwiches, scones, cakes and biscuits.

Aubrey and Rupert exchanged glances.

"Lady Hernedale thought you'd prefer to have an early afternoon tea here."

Aubrey mentally translated that statement. Henrietta didn't want anything to interrupt their discussion. She hoped Rupert's manners would prevent him asking Aubrey to leave while there was food on his plate. She hoped if Aubrey stayed long enough, he might change Rupert's mind.

Rupert's lips twitched, and so did Aubrey's, and then they were both laughing at Henrietta's absurd optimism. Of course Rupert would ask Aubrey to leave if he became too uncomfortable, and of course Aubrey'd oblige. Or vice versa, in Aubrey's set.

But Aubrey's heart ached too. For the resourceful woman of ideas gagged and robbed of her independence when Lowdon forged a terrible union of Rupert's insecurities and his sense of responsibility. For the enterprising woman deprived of the relationship she'd held out for so steadfastly. For the bold woman reduced to subterfuge, and to supplicant hope that her men would take her wishes into consideration when they decided her future. If Rupert, stricken deaf by Lowdon's venom, couldn't hear her, then it was up to Aubrey to fight for her happiness as well as his own.

"Hope you're hungry," Rupert said as the footman set the cake stand on the desk, "because this looks like a week's worth of afternoon teas."

It looked like a propitiatory offering to semi-oblivious gods: *Remember me.*

Aubrey managed a smile and a light tone. "What we wouldn't have given for a spread like this at school."

Rupert met his gaze with such painful yearning that Aubrey glanced reflexively at the butler and footman. But they'd already turned away, and a moment later, the door closed behind them.

"Rupert," he whispered.

"You should marry anyway." Rupert stared at the sandwiches. "You'll want a family one day. Children."

"Except I don't."

"You might, one day."

"I'll address that 'one day' when I see it. For now, I don't want a wife, and I don't mind if I never have children."

"I—don't understand that," Rupert admitted.

"Because you've always wanted a family."

"Thank God for Hettie." A flicker of a smile crossed Rupert's tired face.

"Thank God for Henrietta," Aubrey echoed. "And thank God for you and Lucien. Fact is, I've never met anyone I wanted to marry apart from you and Henrietta, and—unless things change radically between us—Lucien, too, eventually, if he'd have me."

"I hate to disillusion you, beloved, but you can't marry a fellow."

Aubrey's heart tightened at that 'beloved'. "But—if I could, I would."

Rupert sucked in a deep breath. "That shouldn't hurt." He took Aubrey's hand and brushed a thumb over his knuckles. "It shouldn't hurt, that you have someone instead of me. I should be happy for you."

"But I don't want him instead of you. I want him as well as you. As well as you *and* Henrietta."

"I wish you could." Rupert closed his eyes and held the back of Aubrey's hand to his cheek. "I wish *we* could."

"Rupert. Henrietta's not debauched. She's just forging her own path, like I am, like you were. Whether or not you'd had a higher libido, she'd have done that, because she always has. Don't—*please* don't let Lowdon poison you into thinking love is debauchery."

Rupert sighed. "When I look at her—when I see you—I know that. But when I'm alone, I'm not sure. And maybe that's my rationality asserting itself."

"It's Lowdon's damned words asserting themselves! He's made you doubt yourself, and through that, he's made you doubt Henrietta's judgement."

"My Lady of Lucidity," Rupert murmured.

"What would he know about love? Does his wife look happy to you?"

Rupert's lips tightened. "She looks as though she needs to be several hundred miles from him."

"Then what business does he have telling you how to manage your family? He's tried to control and undermine Henrietta since she was a child. And now he's done it. Through you."

"What?" Rupert dropped his hand.

"You've ended her relationship with me. She didn't want to end it, and nor did I."

"We made this agreement together, and now someone disagrees. So the agreement is ended."

"Rupert, ending the agreement would leave none of us together. Your plan leaves you and Henrietta together, but shuts me out. What if I forbade you and Henrietta to be together?"

"That's different! She's my wife!"

"And I've loved her as long as you have! She and I built a relationship together, just as you and I did. And—and God knows you're entitled to end my relationship with you—I can't force you to want me—but I don't see what moral right you have to end my relationship with Henrietta, when neither of us wants to end it."

"I'm her husband." Rupert leaned back in his chair.

"And that gives you legal rights, yes. But what *moral* right do you have? She said she didn't mind which of us she married, *provided* we could all stay together. It was a condition!"

Rupert ran his thumb along the paperweight.

"D'you think she'd have married you if you'd said then that she couldn't be with me? Or—what if she'd married me, and I forbade your relationship against her will and yours?"

"Damn it," Rupert whispered.

"I understand your concerns, sweetheart. I've been unacceptably careless, and I need to improve. But a problem is... Well, it's to be discussed and resolved between us all, isn't it? No need to destroy the whole relationship unless I refuse to fix the problem."

"It could've betrayed us all."

"But it didn't. I'm not trying to minimise it—it was a stupid, dangerous thing to do—but it didn't, this time. And I'll make sure there's never another time."

"I appreciate that, but—"

"We *all* agreed, Rupert! You can't end that agreement for us all, only for yourself. I don't agree to end it. Henrietta doesn't agree. And I can't leave her, not when she doesn't want me to."

Rupert's face froze. "You'd—go behind my back?"

"No." Aubrey reached for Rupert's hand. "No, sweetheart. Neither of us would. But I'm committed to Henrietta. As long as she wants me, I'll fight for our relationship, even if it means fighting with you."

Rupert's hand lay inert in Aubrey's. He stared at him as though he were a stranger.

"Rupert? You'd never realised Henrietta and I had a relationship that was separate from you? Even though you knew your relationship with her was separate from me, and that your relationship with me was separate from her?"

"Damn it. That sounds— But... no, I suppose not. Only, you met one another through me, so I was the— And then... I just thought I was letting you both down."

"Oh sweetheart." Aubrey kissed Rupert's hand. "I love you. I can't bear to be without you. But I can't bear to be without Henrietta or Lucien, either. Any more than you'd want to be without Henrietta." He steeled his nerve. "Any more than you're enjoying being without me."

Rupert sighed and leaned his forehead against Aubrey's. "Dear God, it's difficult. So difficult." Aubrey squeezed his eyes shut against the familiar warmth; against the softness of Rupert's skin and their mutual anguish. "But it seems the right thing to do. To protect Hettie and the baby from disgrace. To meet her needs myself."

"You can't meet all her needs, Rupert." Aubrey stroked his cheek. "Not because of your libido or hers, but just because no one person can. You can't know what she needs as clearly as she does. Forcing your will on her the way Lowdon does, even if you think it's for her own good... Well, you'll just end up being resented as much as you're loved."

"Oh God." Rupert rolled his forehead against Aubrey's. "I did, didn't I? Told her what to do."

"She turned down dozens of chaps who wanted to control her. She married you trusting you wouldn't."

"God damn it!"

"And—you told me I was disposable, sweetheart. You put Henrietta's interests before mine, without discussion."

"No!" Rupert straightened and grabbed Aubrey's hand. "I was putting her interests before *mine*!"

"*And* before mine. You showed me your marriage was more important to you than our fourteen-year relationship. You decided I was detachable. You'd never have suggested Henrietta take herself off and find somebody else: you'd have tried to fix the problem with her."

"I never meant you to feel disposable: you're *not*. I was just trying to do my duty."

"But you didn't only hurt yourself in doing your duty: you hurt Henrietta and me, too. Those *weren't* her needs. She *didn't* want more from you. You just—decided. For all of us. Without discussion. Based on what bloody Lowdon wrote in a letter that was obviously intended to hurt you in every conceivable way."

Rupert sucked in a deep breath and blew it out slowly.

"This— Sweetheart, this is an unequal situation. You've decided to end Henrietta's and my relationship, but I can't decide to end your relationship with her, and she can't decide to end your relationship with me. You control two of my relationships, and both of Henrietta's, and also both of your own. All the power lies with you."

"I—" Rupert coughed. "I've never thought of it that way."

"Nor had I, till this came up. It was all so easy; it worked so well. I won't say I didn't feel left out at times—"

Rupert stared at him.

"Oh, come on Rupert. You and Henrietta... You live together, and openly share a bed, and I can't have that with either of you. You're socially accepted as lovers, and I'm not."

"But that's always been the case for you and me!"

"And it's always been frustrating. But it hurt more once you and she had one another all the time, and I was still the hidden lover for both of you."

"I can see that, now you say it." Rupert rubbed the backs of Aubrey's fingers. "But that's not— It's just another reason I'm bad for you, isn't it? You'd have to marry to avoid that."

"Well I won't. No point standing in the light with someone I don't love. As for you being bad for me, I'm happier having whatever time I can with you than I could ever be without you."

"But that's—"

"Sweetheart, this is *my* choice to make—to put up with certain difficulties because the whole brings me joy—not yours, to push me into what you think is best for me." He squeezed Rupert's hand, to take some of the sting from his words. "I couldn't have imagined it when we were younger, but I've come to realise that this—you and me and Henrietta and Lucien—is the closest I'll ever have to my ideal family, and I want it, so *bloody* badly. And— I'd really rather you didn't leave me, if you still want me."

"You know I do," Rupert husked.

"And I want my relationship with Henrietta back, if she still wants me, which—well, I'm big-headed enough to think she does. And I want some security. The same security I—well, that I *had*—in my relationship with you. I want to know that if my relationship with Henrietta ends, it'll be because she or I chose to end it, not because you did."

Rupert smiled wryly. "You don't want much, do you?"

"Not much at all." Aubrey's chest ached. "Just the freedom to grow my relationships my own way. The same freedom you have, sweetheart. No more than that. And I'm sure Henrietta wants the same."

"Oh." Rupert cupped Aubrey's hand in both his own, and stared down at it. "Yes. I—think I see. I'll need to think about this. It's a lot to take in."

Aubrey huffed a laugh. "It's been a lot to think through."

"I can imagine. Will you—will you leave this with me? I need to talk to Hettie, and— Actually, no: I need to listen to her. See if we can—" He took a deep breath "—if *I* can repair what I've done to her. And I need to work out how to repair what I've done to you."

"I've already told you what I need, sweetheart."

"I know." His lips twisted. "I should've been taking notes. A couple of ledgers would've sufficed."

"Well, if you forget anything—" Aubrey brushed dark hair back from his temple "—I'd be delighted to remind you."

Rupert managed a grin. "Very good of you."

"Behold in me your relentless remembrancer."

Rupert's grin slipped, and they stared at one another. And then warm, dry lips pressed Aubrey's, drawing a burning prickle to his eyes. Rupert's head turned, and his cool cheek, rough with incipient stubble, nestled against Aubrey's as though he'd never left.

"Oh God, Rupert," Aubrey whispered.

"We'll work it out, beloved. I promise. I've got a lot of thinking to do, but—somehow we'll work out a way that suits us all. Equally, this time. In pairs as well as all together, like you said."

"And we'll tell one another when something bothers us, even if it's embarrassing or seems trivial?" His mouth was close to Rupert's ear, so he murmured it. "Because I don't want to hurt you, sweetheart, but I can't know what hurts if you don't tell me; and you shouldn't have to try to divine my problems, either."

"All right. I'll try, at any rate."

Aubrey slid his hands under Rupert's jacket, and Rupert leaned closer, draping his arms over Aubrey's shoulders.

"Rupert. Henrietta will need to hear this from you. Tell her soon, will you? I know you need to think, but set her mind at rest first."

"Yes, I meant to."

Aubrey pressed a kiss to Rupert's familiar, shallow-stubbled throat. To his lover's throat. His lover, still. His lover always, if he had any say in it. Then he rested his cheek against Rupert's and closed his eyes, and they breathed together.

After a while, Rupert stirred. "Tea's probably cold by now. Don't s'pose you'd care for a scone?"

Aubrey rested his chin on Rupert's shoulder. "Only if I don't have to move to eat it."

Rupert's head turned towards the desk and back again. "Jam is involved. And significant quantities of clotted cream."

"Best not, then."

"Sandwich?"

"Only if you have a burning desire for egg and cress down the back of your collar."

"Now you mention it… But I dare say I can resist the urge." Rupert settled into his arms. "We'll just have to starve together."

"Will we?" Aubrey crushed him closer. "Well. I can think of worse fates, sweetheart."

— Chapter Twenty-Seven —

CONGRATULATIONS WERE in order, but each time Lucien submitted copy, Jameson had been emphatically too busy to speak. Probably torn between delight that his paper had made a real impact—and spectacular sales—and horror that it had promoted women's suffrage. On the other hand, he hadn't taken Lucien to task for the altercation in the office either, though he must've heard about it.

At the end of the day, Lucien hauled himself up the stairs of his boarding house and into his rooms, ready to collapse for an hour and a half before visiting Aubrey. And was confronted by a wall of boxes and valises.

Bloody hell. And Frank would collect the luggage the day after tomorrow.

Sighing, he hung up his outdoor things and began to sort through the stack. William's shoes, collars and gloves wouldn't fit him, so he set them aside to sell. With the proceeds, he could pay for alterations and buy a pair of evening pumps; maybe a new collar and evening gloves, too.

He paused, realising it'd been over a month since Cath altered his evening dress: she could probably do with more money, if not the extra work. Since he couldn't set off for Albany for over an hour anyway, he packed payment and a few clothes into a valise and walked to Great Wild Street, stopping in at a couple of shops along the way.

Cath opened the door to his knock.

"Hullo." He tipped his hat. "Wondered whether you'd be interested in altering more clothes."

She eyed the valise. "Come in."

While Cath closed the door to her rooms, he hung up his outdoor things, then glanced around. Winnie sat on the hearthrug, supporting Jem, and Sam glanced up from drawing on the hearthstone with a charred stick. Lucien smiled and waved at them.

"Ben ain't here, love," Cath confirmed, "but you're welcome to stay."

"If you're sure. Can't stay long anyway."

"Bugger the gossips. They'll say what they want, and I'll tell them to mind their own bloody business. Practically family, ain't you?"

Was he? Did just being a godfather-in-waiting make him practically family? "Would you tell Ben I can't be at club tonight? Got to look after a—a friend."

"Course. Show us these togs, then."

Lucien opened the valise and laid the morning coat, shirt, and trousers on the table.

"Lovely." Cath stroked the dark silk-and-wool blend. "Same alteration as before?"

"Yes. There're more, if you want to alter them all. No rush: you could do one a month, or whatever suits you."

"I like the sound of that: you pay better than the dressmakers and tailors."

"Well." It wasn't much more than he'd have paid a tailor, who'd have passed the job on to skilled workers like Cath for a pittance. "But this work'll run out."

"Yeah, I know. I'll keep doing a few bits for them, and all, so I don't lose the work. Cup of tea?"

"I'll make it, if you like." Lucien took a small packet of tea leaves from his jacket pocket. "Brought some along, so I don't drink you out of house and home."

"Ah, ain't you thoughtful!" Cath beamed benevolently. "Nice and weak for me, love: I don't like tea so strong I have to chew it. Same for the kiddies."

"Speaking of children." Lucien swung the kettle nearer the heart of the fire to boil. "My friend's starting a foundation for sick children. Wants to help Jem."

Winnie stared up at him, her weary triangular face half-hidden in a cloud of dark hair. He smiled back.

"This friend." Cath paused. "Ain't got the initials L.S., has he? It ain't a charity with just the one beneficiary?"

"Well I would, but no. He's a nob who wants to help sick children in general."

"That right?"

"Says he'll pay for whatever medical care Jem needs."

Cath stared at him, then at Winnie and Jem. Then she covered her face with her hands, thin fingers pressing into untidy blonde hair.

Lucien turned away, offering her privacy. He watched Sam draw big-headed figures with no discernible bodies, attenuated stick-like legs, and thin arms bristling with too many fingers. The faces all had tiny, pin-prick eyes and long, uncertain smiles.

Lucien pointed at a circle above their heads. "That the sun, Sam?"

Sam stared at it, and then at him. "It's a *ball*."

"Course it is. I think I might need specs."

Winnie giggled and Lucien grinned at her. "I brought you a ribbon, Winnie, for your pretty brown hair."

"What did you bring me?" Sam asked.

Lucien hadn't thought beyond Winnie having something that was just for her and had never belonged to anyone else. "For you, Sam..." He patted his pockets. "A pencil! And..." He found a few old pages. "Paper!" He unfolded them with a flourish. "A bit used, but still plenty of space for drawing."

By the time he'd made and poured the tea, Cath, eyes and nose pink and puffy, had unpicked the waistband of his new trousers and was starting on the inseams. "Bless you, Luce," she said, as he put the cup beside her. "Bless you."

Flustered, Lucien opened the valise again. "Er, I picked up a tin of digestive biscuits on my way over, to go with the tea. If you and Ben don't like them, maybe the children could...?"

As if by magic, Sam was beside him, staring into his valise.

"Who doesn't like a nice digestive?" Cath wondered. "Bung it on the table, Luce."

Lucien opened the tin, put the coil of red satin ribbon beside it, then went back to the hearth. "Can I hold Jem while I'm here?" Winnie let him take the sleeping baby with every evidence of relief.

"Get a plate, Winnie," Cath said.

Lucien sat at the table with Jem while Cath looped the ribbon around Winnie's head and tied it in a perfect bow, then served four biscuits onto the plate. Winnie and Sam settled on the hearthrug with a cup of tea each and the plate between them.

"Hoy! Where's your bloody manners?" Cath demanded. "Say thanks to Uncle Luce, then."

"Thanks, Uncle Luce," the children chorused.

Lucien grinned into Jem's fluffy hair, inhaling his baby scent. "You're very welcome."

Cath set the suit aside, helped herself to a biscuit, and sipped her tea. "Ah! That's lovely. You're a good man, Lucien Saxby."

Tension arced through him, squeezing his eyes shut. He wasn't a good man. Here he sat, in Cath's home, holding her wheezing baby, buying her approval with a handful of tea-leaves, with soft words and easy courtesies. Knowing he'd fucked her husband in St James' Park, and had every intention of doing it again. Knowing she'd feel disgusted and betrayed if she knew.

It didn't matter that he hadn't bought the tea with deceit in mind, or that he genuinely liked her and her endearing children, or that he loved—*loved*—that she considered him almost-family, or that he wanted to earn that place. The fact was he was here under false pretences.

Aubrey was right. There was no difference—none at all—between fucking someone else's wife and fucking someone else's husband. He should keep his bloody hands off Ben. He didn't lack discipline, for God's sake. He certainly wasn't desperate, not now he had Aubrey. And even if he had been, ethics should triumph over impulse every time.

But if he did that, then— He'd never again touch Ben's hand with tenderness. He'd never again sink into his soft kisses, or hear his breathless moans as they met one another's need and, together, alchemised ache into ecstasy.

And, oh God, today—this horrible, sodding day, after an almost sleepless night of holding Aubrey through grief and loss and abandonment, helpless to make any of it better—today was not the day for this. This pain, this decision, was for another day. It had to be, because today wasn't big enough to hold more pain. And he wasn't strong enough.

Jem's fine fuzz of hair tickled his cheek, reminding him he had a responsibility now; he'd made a commitment. He couldn't just duck out of this family's life to escape the guilt of fucking Ben.

But it was more than fucking, wasn't it? It was the warmth in Ben's eyes when he looked at him, and Lucien's own delight whenever he saw Ben. It was the delicious complicity of sly teasing— *Nearly as good as a nice hard shag, eh Luce?* It was a sense of affinity. It was—*love*.

Not the kind of love he had for Aubrey: the hollow ache of absence, the desperate need to be with him. Ben would never kneel at his feet asking for kisses, and Lucien wouldn't want him to. His love for Ben was affectionate and slow-burning, easily encompassing separation, confident that the casual promise of 'see you' would be honoured. It was completely different, and yet, as Aubrey'd tried to explain, no less meaningful.

He was appallingly, shockingly attached. A hundred minute harpoons of support and sharing, of habit and familiarity, of intimacy and small generosities, had pierced deep into his soul, trailing cords of need and desire and empathy that bound him to

Ben. And, in honour, he'd have to tear every one of them free and become the good man the family needed.

His nose burned and tears prickled behind his eyes. "I— should go." His voice was hoarse.

"Luce," Cath said softly.

He blinked hard, sucked in a deep breath and looked up.

She watched him over the rim of her cup, her gaze knowing. "I'm glad he's got a nice fellow like you."

His breath fled.

"When you work all day long, and all evening, too, and you got children wanting you all the time, sometimes you want a bit of peace. But I also want him happy. And I like to know he's got alternatives, cause then I ain't got to feel responsible. I like a bloke who'll see to himself and not pester me when I ain't interested."

A sense of unreality shrouded Lucien. He couldn't be in Ben's home, holding Ben's baby, discussing fucking Ben with Ben's wife, while Ben's other children sat a few feet away, chewing the digestives he'd brought them.

"You're... not saying that just because—"

"I ain't saying nothing I don't mean," she said, a bit sharply.

"Right. Cath, I'm sorry. I should've asked. Checked." His hands trembled. He held Jem closer, his muscle and bone vibrating with the baby's every breath. "Before—anything. It's not really appropriate to pry into other fellows' business. But even so."

"Well I don't know about the wives of your other blokes, but I was all right, as it happens. Ben told me about you from the start. Must be—what?—three years ago now? Yeah, cause Sam was just crawling."

"He— Really? And—you didn't mind?"

"I ain't losing by it." She laughed at the expression on his face. "He loves me; he'd never hurt me. And he's a good man: never lets nothing get in the way of home and family—nor work, neither, since that's what it takes to keep us all. Why would I grudge him his pleasures? Ain't as though he grudges me mine.

Besides—" she grinned "—I'm sure I don't need to tell you that a happy bloke's nicer to be around than a miserable bugger."

Lucien's head whirled. "And—a happy woman?"

"Ah, you're a lovely bloke, Luce. Don't you worry: he keeps me happy, and all. Has done since we come off the streets together seven years ago."

"You were living on the streets?"

She laughed so hard she almost choked on her digestive. "*Working* them, love. We was both streetwalkers: it's how we met."

Lucien glanced compulsively at the children, chasing crumbs around the plate with their fingers.

"Never mind," Cath said. "We'll tell them it ain't worth it unless you can choose your customers, and be certain they're safe, and all."

Lucien choked on a breath. "That—does seem vital advice."

Cath put her cup down. "Does that bother you, Luce?"

"Well… You and Ben: no. I just—" He cast an anguished glance at the children.

"Yeah. Can't say I don't worry myself. But they'll be grown one day and making their own choices. Least we can do is give them a bit of advice."

Lucien bowed his head to inhale calming baby scent.

"It's a fact you can make better money at it than almost anything else, at least while you're young and pretty. And you can pick and choose, then, and all."

"So—why did you stop?"

"That's an old story, love. I'll tell you it someday. When the kids ain't around, eh? But the end of it is Ben thought we should get off the streets before I met with a long drop at Holloway."

Lucien flinched and Jem stirred. He rubbed the baby's back, trying to soothe him.

"Ah no, it weren't that bad. Though, right enough, it might've got that way. He didn't have to work hard to convince me: he's a charming bugger, when he likes, and good-hearted with it. Who wouldn't love the old sod?"

Jem grunted and sighed. Lucien resettled his head tenderly, and the baby coughed, then drifted back to sleep.

"Tempting to go back, mind, what with Jemmy and all. Make a few shillings now and then." She sighed, watching the baby's quiet face on Lucien's shoulder. "We talked about it; specially when he was really bad."

Jem's soft, wheezing snores and the rattle in his chest that vibrated along Lucien's arm were bad enough. How bad had 'really bad' been?

"But it weren't worth the risk. Couldn't neither of us afford to catch something fatal from some fuckster who took more'n we offered, or be beaten to death by a sod who'd rather not pay, and leave them all behind." Her gaze drifted to Winnie and Sam, who'd given up on the spotless plate and were lying on their sides, rolling a rag ball between them and chanting a counting rhyme in between sips of tea.

"Anyway," Cath said, "best you know where we come from. Give you a chance to think better of getting involved with us before anyone gets too attached."

"Too late," Lucien murmured into Jem's hair. "But it doesn't matter: wouldn't have put me off anyway."

Cath met his gaze. "Still want to be Jemmy's godfather, after all that? Cause I'd rather you wasn't, if you ain't sure."

"Of course I do."

"Then you are."

Lucien inhaled baby-scent, listening to his little godson struggle for breath as he slept.

"We wasn't sure you would." Smiling, Cath reached across the table and squeezed his hand. "Tell you what, love: looking at the pair of us, I reckon our Ben's got bloody good taste."

AT FIVE TO seven, Lucien tapped on his fellow's front door. His only fellow now, apart from Ben. There'd be no others until he was certain they were single or else had their wives' and lovers' agreement. But it wasn't a hardship: he wasn't lonely anymore.

So much for multiple lovers being an aristocratic vice, though: Aubrey'd find his epiphany over Ben hilarious. Well, they could both do with a laugh.

Aubrey opened the door in his dressing gown and slippers, looking pale and tired. Stepping in, Lucien hung up his riding cane and hat while Aubrey closed the door, then turned and held both his hands.

"You all right, love?"

"Yes." Aubrey bent to kiss him.

"You spoke to Hernedale?"

"And my parents. Everything's all right, thank God. Let's get you into a dressing gown, and I'll tell you what happened."

They curled up together on the sofa while Aubrey spoke.

"It's all resolved then?" Lucien said at last.

"More or less. It's just details, now, and... learning how to be with one another again, after the hurt we've all caused."

Lucien kissed his forehead. "I'm glad."

"Oh Lord, sweetheart, I just— I can't tell you how relieved I am."

Relief flooded Lucien, too, flushing twenty-four hours of tension from his body. "Love you," he whispered into Aubrey's hair.

Aubrey huffed a laugh into his collarbone. "You love a daft, clumsy, ridiculous nob."

Lucien lifted him—awkwardly, because Aubrey hadn't been expecting it and was all arms and legs—and settled him on his lap, facing him, Aubrey's knees bracketing his hips. "Just you, my love." Lucien drew his head down and kissed him thoroughly. "Not the whole bloody Greek chorus of grace and genius you think you should embody."

Aubrey's arms rested on his shoulders, and he leaned his forehead against Lucien's.

Lucien closed eyes burning with fatigue and let his world reduce to Aubrey, exhausted and subdued but no longer grieving. To Aubrey, solid and heavy and bony on his lap and in his arms.

To the warmth and pressure of long legs braced along his thighs, and the rush of breath across his face.

"Lucien?" Aubrey murmured.

"Mmm?" Lucien didn't open his eyes.

"I got my settlement today."

"That's good."

"It's a couple of properties, and a portfolio which should return a very generous annuity."

"No need to scrape a living with concert performances, then."

Aubrey laughed weakly. "Think my father might've made a settlement just to avoid the embarrassment if I'd tried."

"See? You always had alternatives."

"Poor Father and Mother. I couldn't have done that to them."

"Because you're a sweetheart."

Aubrey laid his cheek along Lucien's. "Lucien? We know one another a lot better now, don't we?"

"Mmhm."

"So maybe you'd consider— I mean, I'm rolling in lucre now, and you're—"

Lucien held a finger over his lips. "Don't. Please." He replaced his finger with his lips, because it was touching that Aubrey wanted to look after him.

When he ended the kiss, Aubrey took a deep breath. "All right. But—"

Lucien slid a finger across his lips again, but Aubrey pushed his hand aside and sat up on his knees. "Let me *speak*, Lucien. This is important to me."

"Why?" Lucien opened his eyes, his peace ruptured. "Do I embarrass you?" He gestured at his clothes. "You want me to dress better? Not to work?"

"It's not—" Aubrey took a deep breath. "No. Don't be hurt. It's truly not that. It's just— I don't like to think of you struggling, when I have so much."

"I'm not—" Lucien stared up at him. "Why on earth do you keep thinking I'm struggling? I've told you I'm not."

Aubrey stared back. "I—don't know."

"Working for a living isn't 'struggling', it's just normal. You're the odd one, not needing to work. Granted, I can't afford to buy the best, but what I have is adequate, and better than most."

"But what about when we're old? When you're too old to work?"

Lucien's heart stopped, and his breath caught in his throat. "Why? We spoke about loving one another into the future, but— D'you mean for us to be together so long? Till we're too old to work?"

"Why not?" Aubrey argued. "Granted, we might separate some day, but we might just as easily still be happy together in thirty or fifty years' time. I mean, why assume we *won't* be, when there's no certainty either way?"

Breathless and giddy, Lucien cupped Aubrey's head in both hands and drew him closer. Stroking his cheekbones with tender thumbs, he caught his lower lip between his own and tugged, then slid deeper into Aubrey's welcoming mouth. Might he really hold this man for thirty years? Might he still be kissing him in fifty? He surfaced to gaze at high cheekbones; at the delicate skin of Aubrey's closed eyelids; at long, dark lashes lying on his cheek.

"That's all very well," Aubrey continued, as argumentative as before even with his eyes closed and his jaw resting in Lucien's palms, "but the sweetest kisses in the world won't persuade me to let you do without, just to save your damned pride. Wouldn't it hurt you to see me go without?"

Lucien brushed a soft kiss over narrow lips. "All right," he murmured. "You can save me if I really need it."

Aubrey's eyes sprang open. "That's damned gracious of you."

Lucien smiled against his lips. "I'm not very likely to need it, love."

"No?"

"No. I'm—erm—pretty well off, as it happens. Or will be. I'd prefer more control over how I write my copy, but I like my job, so I wouldn't stop working in any case. As for the future: I'm an only child. Provided my parents don't make a catastrophic error—and they're careful people, love—I'll inherit a hotel."

Aubrey knelt up, staring. "Your parents own a hotel?"

"I mean—it's not the Savoy," Lucien explained, "but it's popular with the gentry and foreign visitors, and doing very nicely."

"Then—" Aubrey sat back on Lucien's knees "—why don't you live there, instead of that boarding house?"

Lucien raised an eyebrow. "Why don't you live with your parents?"

Aubrey paused. "No, all right, I see."

"Point is, I'm not exactly desperate. Not at all, in fact. I don't need rescuing."

"Well that's reassuring." Aubrey folded himself back into Lucien's arms. "I worried."

After dinner, they went straight to bed, because the day had felt as long as a week. There, they made slow, tender love by the amber light of banked fires. But Aubrey was so pliant, so sweet and fragile, that Lucien stopped.

"You all right?" he whispered.

"Yes." Aubrey's eyes glittered in the dim light.

"You sure?" Lucien kissed his eyelids, and tasted salt. Damp clung to his lips.

"I'm—emotional. Tired. Relieved beyond words. And I don't—" Aubrey's throat clicked as he swallowed. "I just want to lose myself in you, and not think about a thing beyond you and me and this moment."

And *that*— Oh, that was easy. That was a thing Lucien could do, for his someone. For Aubrey, who was willing to melt at his touch. Who trusted Lucien enough to allow him free rein with his body; to immerse himself without reserve in the sensations he wrought. Who gasped at Lucien's lightest touch, and moaned and quivered under his tender lips and teeth and tongue. Who clung to him, begging in fevered whispers for more, when Lucien pressed inside the close warmth of his body. Who wept as Lucien carried him to the precipice of ecstasy, cast him aloft, then caught and cradled him all the way down.

And when his crisis was over, Lucien held him till he slept, then closed his own burning eyes, ready for oblivion.

Because the morning was nothing to fear. It was only the dawn of another day in his life with Aubrey. Just one of thousands of days to come, threaded, like pearls, on the cord of their shared life. A cord which intertwined with the cord of his life with Ben's family, which intertwined with the cord of Aubrey's life with the Hernedales, to create a beautiful complexity.

A priceless wealth of days, each one layered with love and sealed with the certainty of belonging.

All their tomorrows.

— Author's Note —

Events

All scenes involving the WSPU are closely based on Sylvia Pankhurst's account in *The Suffragette: The History of the Women's Militant Suffrage Movement*, first published in 1911.

The WSPU did promote the idea that wealthy women would act in the interests of poor women, if they had the vote.

While the treatment of the WSPU women at Downing Street did lead to a petition being circulated among MPs, the article written by Lucien and Madeleine is wholly fictional.

The term 'concentration camp' was coined in 1901 to describe camps set up by the British to contain political prisoners. During the Second Boer War (1899-1902), British forces forcibly removed African and Boer civilians to concentration camps. It is estimated that around 25% of inmates died in the Boer camps, and 12% in the African camps. However, since African deaths were under-recorded, the latter figure is questionable.

Popular Culture

Two Naughty Boys was performed at the Gaiety Theatre, opening on 8th January 1906.

Dr Wake's Patient was performed at the Adelphi Theatre from 1905-1906. All dialogue ascribed to it is quoted verbatim from the play.

Ask a Policeman is a music hall song composed in 1889 by E.W. Rogers and A.E. Durandeau. The characters in this novel place a more sinister meaning on the lyrics than the writers intended.

The pubs mentioned in this book still exist. The Lamb and Flag Pub and the Nell Gwynne Tavern are both in Covent Garden, and Ye Olde Cock Tavern is in Fleet Street.

Characters

William's health issues are extrapolated from my own experience of living with misdiagnosed (and therefore untreated) Crohns Disease for several years.

The following characters in this novel were actual historical figures:

Sophia Duleep Singh
Flora Drummond
Annie Kenney
Emmeline Pankhurst
Christabel Pankhurst
Sylvia Pankhurst
Adela Pankhurst
Theresa Billington
Irene Miller
James Keir Hardie, MP
Sir Henry Campbell-Bannerman, Prime Minister
Mr Ponsonby, the Prime Minister's secretary
Vernon Rendall, Editor of the Athenaeum

Gutter Roses

A Radical Proposals Short Story

Jude Lucens

Greenwose Books

Scotland

For everyone who ever believed
it was their fault

— Acknowledgements —

Many thanks to wonderful beta-readers Anne, Liv, and Lotta: your feedback was invaluable.

Many thanks, also, to Lennan for the fabulous cover art and design, and to Shelby for a terrific—and speedy—edit.

And thanks, always, to Chris: brainstormer and world-builder, alpha and omega reader, supportive critic and critical support, without whom I'd never have time or capacity to write.

Any remaining errors, offences and infelicities are, of course, my own. In all likelihood, one of the kind people above suggested they were a bad idea, but I thought I knew better.

— Gutter Roses —

London, August 1898

Gaslight and loud voices spilled from the busy pub into the street, along with the dog-shit stink of cheap tobacco. Cath stood at the corner of the building, far enough from door and windows that the light wouldn't blind her, but near enough that any bloke who come out would notice her. She glanced down and opened another button on her blouse. Not that her tits was small, but there weren't enough there to show a curve above the fabric.

"Size ain't everything," Ben said.

Cath laughed. "That what you tell all your fellows, is it?"

Small and gorgeous, Ben leaned against this wall alongside her almost every night. It'd got so any night he wasn't there seemed a bit flat. He grinned. "Just the ones that need to hear it."

"Cheeky bugger. Maybe *you* need to hear it."

"Nah. Get enough repeat customers that I ain't worried."

Ben's rolled-up shirtsleeves and tight, slightly shabby waistcoat drew attention to his muscular body. White light glaring from the electric lamppost nearby made some bits of him too bright and set other bits in long black shadow. Might've made another fellow look like something from a Punch and Judy, but Ben looked all right. More'n all right. Cath gazed at his warm brown skin and short, tight curls, and lingered over his full lips. "Bet you bloody do."

His mouth tugged up on one side. "You ain't half bad yourself."

She wasn't, but lamplight did no favours for her short, narrow body, and, even in daylight, straight blonde hair and blue eyes didn't exactly stand out around here. There was enough like her that nobody needed to seek her out.

"Hoy. One for you, I reckon."

She followed Ben's gaze to a tall, broad bloke coming their way along Gower Street. Tidy dressed—good clothes, but not swanky—and a bit unsteady on his pins. "If it is, he'll have to be satisfied with my hand." There was a few other people in the street, but he was looking at her direct, and no mistake.

Ben shot her a quick glance. "Ain't that time of month is it? Couple of weeks, yet."

"Eh. Just sore. First-timer earlier: didn't have the heart to make him slow down and then I just wanted it over."

"Silly cow," Ben said indulgently, still watching for customers. He was smiling warmly; not at her, but definitely about her.

"Daft bugger." Her heart squeezed and warmed in a way it probly didn't ought to, for a friend.

"He's coming your way. I'll make myself scarce."

Minutes later, terms agreed, she stood with her back to the wall in a dark, quiet mews, trying to breathe shallow cause the bloke's breath had enough alcohol in that she couldn't smell the horse shit wedged in the crevices between the cobbles.

"Ain't you got a room?" he boomed.

She winced. "Too far away." It wasn't, but if he thought she was bringing him home, he had another think coming. "Let's be quiet, eh? Don't want to wake up the grooms and what-not."

The bloke shoved a sweaty hand down her chemise and squeezed her tit. She gritted her teeth. Weren't entirely his fault: a warm evening and a bellyful of spirits would heat any fellow. His other hand tugged at her skirts. That bloody well *was* his fault.

She held them down. "Now we talked about this, didn't we, eh? Just my hand. If that ain't what you're after, you'll have to find someone else."

"But—" He pulled his sticky hand out of her chemise so hard it yanked her tit, and she gasped. Leaning on her, he pressed his face into her neck, pricking her throat with stubble. Be a bloody rash there later. "It's you I want."

"That's nice. You can have my hand: you'll like that."

His weight was crushing her into the wall.

"Stand up a mo," she said. "Let me get my breath."

He leaned harder, freeing up both hands to lift her skirts.

"Now what did I say, eh?" Cath said, breathless. "That ain't my hand, is it?"

"M'wife died."

Oh buggery.

A warm, wet, slightly slimy patch on her neck said he wasn't lying.

"You—you 'mind me of her." His voice rose to a honk.

"Sssh. Sssh." She eyed the mews windows.

"I ain't never gonna see her no more. An I just—" He gasped. "All I want—"

Buggery. Shit. Dammit. Cath burrowed a hand awkwardly through the slit in the side of her skirt to her petticoat pocket, and felt about for the small round tin. "All right then, but you'll have to be quick. Here's a condom."

"I never use them dirty things." His hand slid up into her split drawers.

Cath clamped her legs together. "It's clean, pet. Washed it myself. Tell you what: you step back and I'll put it on you. Let's have some fun with it, eh?"

"Give us a kiss."

"When you got this on, eh?"

"Don't need it."

"Yeah you do, cause I never do it without."

The weight of his body eased, and she took a deep breath. Next thing she knew, she was on her back on the cobbles, all the air knocked out of her, her back and head hurting like the dickens.

He flung her skirts up and forced her thighs apart with his knee.

Shit. Shit! She could hardly see the fuckster past the white stars spinning in front of her eyes. "All right now. Let me just…" She flicked the condom tin open one-handed, and he smacked it away.

"Don't bloody listen, do you?" The tin rang on the cobbles, far out of reach. Condom had probly bounced out of it, anyway. "Told you I don't use them fucking things."

"Look. Stop. Just wait a—" She struggled to sit.

"Selfish bitch." He slapped her face so hard it wrenched her neck, then fell on her, trapping her with his bulk. "Can't just let a grieving fellow have what he needs. Got to bloody spoil it. I *said* give us a kiss." He latched his open mouth to her lips. She clamped them shut, panting through her nose. His tongue, thick and wet and drooling, pressed hard against her. Cobbles dug into her back and her head throbbed and she couldn't bloody *breathe* with him on top of her; with his mouth so tight over hers.

He cocked his hips and reached underneath, fumbling with his trousers, his knuckles hard against her groin.

Cath groped over the cobbles for a weapon. Bit of harness, maybe. Even a horse-shoe nail. But the stableboys had made a bloody good job of sweeping the road clean. A cobblestone rocked under her hand, and she dug at it, gasping as fingernails split.

His cock shoved at her groin, thick and demanding, half-soft with booze. Swearing, he reached underneath again to brace it.

Cath forced her hurting fingers under the cobblestone. She wrenched it free at last, and thumped him over the head as hard as she could. But it weren't very hard, what with the angle being so awkward.

"You fucking *bitch*!" He reared back, mouth all agape with astonished hurt. Yeah. Bet his wife never spanked him over the bloody nob with a rock.

"Now look," she said, reasonable as she could. "Just get off—"

He drew back a meaty fist.

Panicking, she smashed the cobblestone right in his face, two-handed. Right in his nose and open mouth. He fell on her, solid, not moving, crushing her hands over the cobblestone between them.

Cath squeezed her eyes shut and cried with relief, as his weight and her own sobbing breaths ground the cobblestone into her ribs; as he bled, warm and wet, on her face. But she couldn't breathe right, and the road pressed hard lumps into her back and head. She struggled to free her hands, scraping them on the stone; gasping and whimpering like a kiddie when half-torn nails caught in cloth and ripped further.

What if he woke up?

Hands free, she shoved and heaved at him. God, but he was heavy. Heavy and floppy and— whenever she lifted one bit of him, another bit sagged, holding her down. She wedged her heel between cobbles and tried to roll, to take him with her, but he didn't budge.

God. Shit! What if he never bloody woke up? What if bobby peeler found her under his corpse with murderess written all over her in his blood?

She shoved and kicked and tried to roll, panting, muscles burning, light-headed with panic.

"Cath?" The voice was muted. "You still in there?"

"Ben! Help!"

Quiet footsteps across the cobbles, then a pause. "Bloody *hell*!"

It took a few tries, but between them, they rolled the bloke off her and onto his back.

Cath shoved the cobblestone off her chest and sat up, shaking. She stared at the bloke: his face black with blood in the dim light, nose out of shape, broken teeth gleaming in his gaping mouth. "Shit," she whispered.

"Yeah." Ben swallowed hard, then stood up. "I take it he earned that?"

"He— tried to rape me."

"Right. Fair enough. Up you get, love." She took his hands and he heaved her to her feet.

"Is he—"

"Nah. And he can breathe through his mouth. Time to go." He put an arm round her, which was just as well cause her legs wobbled like she'd had a few drinks too many.

"His wife died," she whispered past the thickness in her throat.

"Yeah? Lucky he didn't bloody follow her, ain't he?"

"He was grieving."

"No fucking excuse to make someone else grieve, is it? Don't you go feeling guilty over him, Cath."

"Yeah." She took a deep breath. "Yeah, all right. Should we take his purse? Make it look like he was robbed while he was taking a piss?"

"Some other bugger can chance that. Let's get out of this."

They walked through dark streets, staying back from other pedestrians. When they come to lamp-lit roads, they watched from the shadows till no one was about, then slipped over, quick as eels, to the safe dark of another unlit street or passage. They stopped at last, at the end of a murky alley thick with the warm, sweet stink of mouldering rubbish.

Ben glanced around the narrow, deserted space. "Think you can keep out of mischief while I get you a clean blouse?"

"Cheeky bugger," she managed shakily.

He snorted and sloped off.

Cath leaned against a soot-blackened wall, as far out of sight as she could, and not just to hide the blood on her, neither. Her head and back hurt, and her cheek was hot and sore, and her whole body shook. She swallowed, trying not to throw up.

Felt like she waited there a long time. A long, cold, terrifying time, even though the night was warm and no one else come into the alley. But Ben come back at last, with a wet cloth and a clean blouse. "Borrowed 'em from Mary." Which meant her sister knew about this. Cath weren't looking forward to that conversation.

He wiped her face and neck and hands and hair with the cloth—"Ain't perfect, but it'll do till you get home"—then unpinned her hair and twisted it up again, "to hide the bloody bits." Finally, he unbuttoned her blouse, replaced it with Mary's, and buttoned it up to the throat—"That'll cover the blood on your chemise and stays"—and arranged her embroidered belt neatly over it.

"Shit!" Her heart cramped painfully. "I left a condom tin in the mews!"

Ben straightened and stared at her. "Anything to show it's yours? Best not go back unless we have to."

She shook her throbbing head. "Cheap tin; everyone's got one."

"Then it can stay there. And Father Thames better have this blouse."

Cath sighed. "It's a nice one, too."

"Not nice enough to bloody swing for. Back in a mo." Ben rolled the blouse into a ball and took it away.

"Buggery." Cath wrapped her arms around herself, tucking her stinging fingers into her armpits. Her body'd stopped shaking, but something cold was stuck in her chest, making her quiver deep inside. "*Buggery*." Her face twisted when she didn't mean it to, and the next thing she knew, she was crying again. She yanked a hankie from her pocket and mopped her face and blew her nose, but the tears kept coming, and by the time Ben got back, she was sobbing.

"Ah, c'mere." He held her gently. "Fucking fuckster. Hope he gets his fucking throat slit or chokes on his own fucking teeth."

His words and his warm body and the comfort of his arms made her cry all the harder. He stroked her hair and let her lean on him, though his own body shivered now and then.

"Sorry. Sorry. I'm a bloody watering can tonight."

"I'd cry too, if I'd been stuck under a rapist thinking I'd swing on his account."

She blew her nose then rested her head on his collarbone. "Thanks, Ben. For everything."

"Yeah, well. Thought you'd been gone a bit long for just giving a fellow a hand."

Something about Ben—about being close to Ben—was thawing the cold lump in her chest, easing the quiver inside.

Laughter took her, sudden and surprising.

"What now?"

"Just... I'm such a bloody fool. Bloke collapses on me, and there I bloody lay like a Sunday morning, thinking, 'Oh, that's all right then. I'll just have a bit of a lie-down and get my breath before I shove him off.' You'd think I'd have the sense to knock him off me in the first place."

"Ain't exactly your precision weapon, ain't a cobblestone. You want to carry a knife in your drawers."

"Bugger me!" Cath straightened. "I've got a pen knife in my bloody garter! Didn't even think of it. Silly cow."

"Well you ain't a naturally violent person, and it's hard to think straight when you're took by surprise. Anyway, probly just as well: you'd have done for him with a knife. This way, he's just got a nice, permanent reminder to mind his bloody manners."

"If he survives the night."

"Ain't your fault if he don't. He made his choices and took his chances." Ben leaned against the wall, drawing her with him.

She sucked in a shuddering breath and sighed. "S'pose I ain't working round Gower Street no more."

"Me neither, since he saw me with you."

"Ah shit." She burrowed closer. "I'm sorry, love."

"Rather that than he got what he wanted."

Seemed like she'd caused a lot of trouble, though, for herself and Ben, too. Maybe she should've just let the bloke have his way: at least she wouldn't be worrying about bobby peeler coming for her. As it was, if he lived, he could point the finger, and if he died, there was enough people saw her with Ben, and then saw her go into the mews with the sod, that—

"Hoy. Stop feeling bad about it. Fuckster got what was coming to him. Ain't your fault he's a bloody pig: that's on him."

"Maybe. But... what now?"

Ben sighed. "Been thinking. What d'you reckon to coming off the streets?"

She leaned back to stare at him.

He shrugged. "I'm going to, at any rate. I stand out a lot more'n you, and no one who saw us tonight ain't going to believe I wasn't an accomplice, at least. I keep working the streets, and it's only a matter of time before the blokes in blue catch up with me."

"Shit! I never thought of that."

"Ain't your fault, is it? But I need to be somewhere they ain't looking for me."

"But—" How would he live? "Any other job, you ain't going to make as much."

"Yeah, well, ain't got no choice." He met her gaze, and his face softened. "Hoy. Ain't impossible, you know: most people do it."

Most people struggled to keep a roof over their bloody heads. Streetwalking paid better than anything else she could do, and she was her own boss, besides. Anyway, she'd probly be all right: women that looked like her was ten a penny. Course there was people who could identify her, but who'd risk being known as a squeaker? She'd just move her pitch across the city; move boarding house, too. She could help Ben out with a bit of cash now and then, while he got on his feet.

"Besides," Ben added, "I've had a couple of close calls myself, with customers like that. Seeing you stuck under him like a herring under a whale... Well, it ain't a position I ever want to be in. Ain't a sight I ever want to see again, neither."

Buggery.

Next fuckster might kill her. Or she might kill him, and swing for it.

"Well I ain't taking factory work," she told him. "It's bloody dangerous. Reckon I'd live longer on the streets, even with Mr Stoved-Nose and bobby peeler after me."

"You're good at fancy sewing." He tapped her embroidered belt.

"Yeah, but Mary works all the hours God sends and still struggles to make ends meet." She rested her aching head on him.

If some fuckster raped her without a condom, she might end up with— But she'd barely survive on sewing, and once her eyes started to fail, then—

"You know," Ben murmured, "I reckon you and me could make a go of it, if you like."

"What?" She stared at him.

He glanced away. "Might be all right, with two wages coming in, and sharing expenses."

"I ain't sending *you* into no bloody factory neither."

"Nah. Got a cousin works on the docks: he'll get me in there. Won't bring in as much as streetwalking, but between that and your sewing, we'd manage."

She stared at him, trying to see his expression in the dim light. "You reckon?" She'd never thought about that before; not with Ben. But she saw it now. A shared room. A warm fire. Maybe a kiddie one day. But mostly, she saw Ben. Working alongside Ben. Eating with Ben. Holding Ben. Every night. Every day.

"Yeah. If you like." He met her gaze. "Best if we both stay off the streets for a couple of years. After that... well, we could go back if we want—other side of the river, maybe. Or maybe keep on with the other jobs, and only go out of a night when we get a bit short."

"Or if you want a bloke, or a bit of a change." She nudged him gently.

"Or if you want a bird, or a change. S'different when you ain't asking to be paid. Safer."

Cath quieted to have a bit of a think, and Ben didn't seem to mind: just held her, not too tight, and waited.

Fact was, she didn't fancy going out again tonight. Or tomorrow. There'd been pushy blokes before, of course—most of them was at least a bit pushy—but she'd always been able to talk them round or get away. The thought of facing another bloke like that bugger tonight was—

"You really fancy me?" she said. "This ain't just—"

"Yeah, I fancy you, Cath, if you want me. More'n that, I like you." He pressed his cheek lightly to hers. "Besides, it'd be safer all round, cause the next fuckster tries anything like that with you, I'm going to rip his fucking head off and shove it up his arse, and that'll definitely annoy the blokes in blue."

Cath snorted. "Go in easier if you let me stave his nose in first."

"See? We fit perfect together."

"You ever need any noses broken, just let me know." She leaned into him, and he held her loosely. It was nice: felt warm and safe, and his body was a comfort along hers.

"Cath. You ain't got to decide now. And it's all right if you don't want to pair up. We can carry on as friends; help each other out."

"Hoy!" She poked him in the ribs. "You don't get away that easy."

"You sure?"

"Yeah." She rubbed the bit she'd poked. "I want you, too, Ben. And you're a lovely bloke; can't help but like you."

"Then it's settled." Lips and warm breath brushed her hair.

"Yeah."

And, just like that, she weren't alone no more. Which was a daft thing to think, because she was never bloody alone. There was Mary, and her friends, and it was hard to get any bloody peace from the other women in her boarding house. She'd never felt lonely, that she could think of. But there it was: it felt like she weren't alone no more.

Cath snuggled closer. The quiver inside was almost gone, and what was left come out as another laugh.

"What now?" Ben stroked her hair.

"Just thinking." She couldn't stop laughing. "Bloke was— was loud enough to wake the dead. What if—someone come out and found me under him? What was I going to say? 'Scuse me, kind sir, can you just roll this bloody ox off me? Blood? Well, I don't know about that, sir. I was just—just laying here, minding my business, as you might say, when he fell on me. Cobblestone? What cobblestone's that, then? Oh! Oh, you mean this cobblestone in my hands that exactly matches the dent in his phiz?'" She clung to Ben, laughing, tears pouring down her face. "'Nah. Got no bloody idea how that could've got there.'"

God, but it felt good to laugh. Good to hold Ben while she laughed, while he held her back.

Ben was laughing too. "You're bloody mad, you are."

"Yeah? Too bad for you: you're stuck with me now."

"Ain't a hardship."

Cath tightened her arms around him, holding her stinging, burning fingertips clear of his clothes, tucking her face into his neck.

After while, he said, "Weren't bloody funny, you know."

"Got to laugh, though, ain't you? Else you'd spend your life leaking into hankies."

"You ain't wrong."

They leaned together companionably in the warm, quiet night.

"Hoy," Ben murmured.

Cath looked up.

"We'll make sure we get some proper laughs in, too, eh?"

"Yeah." She rested her aching head on his shoulder. "That sounds all right, that does."

— About the Author —

Jude is a bi, demi, polyamorous, pagan woman of colour, is a carer, and has been chronically ill for most of her life. She writes historical romances about marginalised people affiliating and building family in the face of restrictive, often punitive, social norms.

For several years, she was a 1st Century Roman and Early Medieval re-enactor. Her primary focus was combat and target archery, and her secondary, living history and craft demonstrations—mostly fletching and ring-mail making—as well as explaining period clothing, weaponry, armour and basic combat techniques. She has hung up her bow and cedarwood arrows, and now makes silver and bronze jewellery instead.

Find Jude on Facebook, on Twitter @JudeLucens, and on Goodreads.

http://judelucens.com/

CPSIA information can be obtained
at www.ICGtesting.com
Printed in the USA
LVHW090032130319
610461LV00002B/221/P